RALPH;

OR,

The Boys of Merrytown Abbey.

COMPLETE.

BEAUTIFULLY ILLUSTRATED.

LONDON:
HARKAWAY HOUSE, 6, WEST HARDING STREET, FETTER LANE,
FLEET STREET, E.C., AND ALL BOOKSELLERS.

RALPH;
Or, the Boys of Merrytown Abbey.

"RALPH, WITH FLASHING EYES AND EVERY MUSCLE OF HIS FACE QUIVERING, STOOD OVER HIM."—(See page 6.)

RALPH;

OR THE BOYS OF MERRYTOWN ABBEY.

CHAPTER I.

IN WHICH HARMONY IS TURNED TO DISCORD.

"WHAT'S the new fellow's name, Harold?"

As Charlie Chadwick, a bright-eyed, open-faced, well-knit lad about fourteen years of age, put this question, he tilted his straw hat on to the back of his head, and glanced at his chum, Harold Lakeman.

"Ralph Mornington," replied Harold. "Nice name, is it not?"

"'What's in a name?'" quoted Charlie. "Do you know anything about him?"

"Positively nothing, beyond that his father is a fire-eating general somewhere in India, and as rich as the Bank of England."

"That's something, at all events," said Charlie. "I wonder where he is hiding himself? It looks bad for a new fellow to skulk."

"I don't fancy that you will find Ralph Mornington one of the skulking sort," Harold Lakeman observed. "Mr. Muffler has him in tow, and is showing him over the Abbey. You had to pass through that ordeal once, Charlie."

"I had, and the impression has never left me. It may be a fine thing to live in a building five hundred years old, but——"

"You wish it were not quite so full of strange noises?"

"And ghosts," Charlie added.

At this moment the boys stood on one side to make room for Mr. Thaddeus Stormaway, B.A., the head-master, to pass.

"By the way, Chadwick," he said, halting and turning back, "I believe there is a spare bed in your dormitory?"

"Yes, sir."

"Thank you."

The head-master went his way, and the boys remained silent until he was out of hearing.

"Harold," said Charlie, "we have captured the new fellow. Ralph Mornington is ours."

"May he turn out to be as good as he looks," Harold rejoined "Here he comes; and alone, too."

"And looking as much at home as if he had been here six months, instead of as many hours."

Ralph Mornington, the boy just imported into Merrytown Abbey, approached, his finely-shaped head erect, his eyes sparkling with anticipation, his lips wreathed with a smile.

There was something about this lad, over whose dark curly head fifteen summers had passed, that won their hearts.

A handsome face, a well-proportioned figure, and a jaunty yet not offensive air are pleasant features in a boy; but Ralph Mornington possessed another.

He had magnificent eyes, which laughed and danced when he felt merry, glittered when he was displeased, and melted when he had occasion for sadness.

Ralph suddenly altered his course, and turned to the left, when Charlie Chadwick's voice brought him to a standstill.

"Did you call me?" Ralph demanded, pleasantly.

"Yes; don't go that way, or you'll find yourself in the kitchens. The cook is a perfect virago, and she would just as soon hit you over the head with a frying-pan as look at you. She threw a rolling-pin, not long ago, at Tommy Toddler, and spoilt his appetite for a week.

Ralph Mornington threw his head back and laughed.

"You are, of course, aware that I am a stranger here," he said. "A gentleman named Muffler escorted me round this quaint old house, and when dismissing me, told me to find Charles Chadwick."

"I am he, and very much at your service."

The two boys shook hands, as did Harold Lakeman, with the new boy, and all three were soon chatting affably.

"I am awfully glad you are to sleep in our dormitory," Charlie said. "There is generally plenty of fun going on. Oh, but I say, I forgot to ask you one thing—are you afraid of ghosts?"

"You have asked me a puzzler," Ralph returned. "I have no reason to be afraid of ghosts, because they have never troubled me. But seriously—surely you don't believe in such things?"

"How can I help it," rejoined Charlie, as he glanced up at the old ivy-covered walls, "when we are roused from our sleep by such sounds as mortal never made? Then there are the mysterious footsteps, and——"

"Don't fill our new chum with horrors," Harold interposed. "There goes the bell. Stick to us, Mornington, for we sit where we like at tea-time, and there is generally a scrimmage to get next to a new boy."

"I will take the hint," Ralph replied. "I begin to feel at home already, and judging by the general introduction I had in the school-room, I think I shall like all of you."

"With a few exceptions," observed Charlie. "We muster just over sixty, but there are two or three fellows here who would be better away. I will point them out to you when I get a chance."

This conversation brought the three boys to an old-fashioned door, with a broad passage beyond.

Just outside a spacious apartment, which in days of old might have served as a refectory, stood a page-boy tugging vigorously at a bell-rope.

This youthful retainer, clad in a mulberry-coloured jacket and continuations to match, was the oddest-looking boy that Ralph Mornington had ever seen.

His straw-coloured hair stood half upright upon his dumpling-shaped head; his right eye squinted to the left, while his left eye veered round to the right, and his limbs hung so loosely upon his body that he might have borrowed them in a hurry and failed to return them.

"Hallo!" cried the mulberry-hued bell-ringer. "Here's a new wictim. My name's Timothy Slowbob; what's yours?"

Ralph Mornington scarcely knew whether to laugh or to feel angry as he gazed at the strange specimen of human nature; but a moment's reflection told him how wrong it would be to snub the lad, whose lines might not be cast in pleasant places.

He answered the question frankly, and then Timothy Slowbob winked in the most appalling fashion.

"There's no pride about you," he said, "and I'll take care that you have some of the best pieces of bread-and-butter, and that your cup is full. Mrs. Jumble, the housekeeper, is a reg'lar nipper, she is."

"Come away," whispered Charlie, tapping Ralph on the shoulder. "Timothy will bore you to death if you give him half a chance."

"I never saw such a peculiar boy," Ralph returned, smiling. "Where, in the name of wonder, did Mr. Stormaway discover him?"

"He is a waif and a stray from the parish," Charlie replied, "and we would rather part with all our pocket-money than lose him. Timothy is a novel character, as you will soon find out."

The boys were now trooping into the hall, and Ralph became the cynosure of some sixty pairs of eyes.

He bore the ordeal bravely, but felt relieved when Mrs. Jumble, a very stout lady, sailed into the room and presided over the tea-urns.

A limp-kneed, elderly man, rejoicing in the name of Matthew Stickers, and Timothy Slowbob served at table, and it needed no accustomed eye to perceive that the two were at daggers drawn.

Whenever Timothy Slowbob got the chance he ran against Stickers, who lost no opportunity of retaliating with sly pinches and digs with his knuckles in the region of the page-boy's ribs.

Frequent were the skirmishes as the frugal fare was passed round, but Mrs. Jumble paid no heed whatever.

She was used to muffled squeals from Slowbob and smothered groans from

Stickers, and, hating them both as she did, perhaps she secretly rejoiced to see them torture each other.

Suddenly, however, she glared at the page-boy and became rigid with indignation.

"Slowbob," she said in an awful voice, "how is it that you have lost three buttons from your jacket?"

"What, only three, marm?" Timothy rejoined, complacently. "It ain't my fault if the tailor only blows 'em on. And, as for that, marm, if them buttons was stitched on with hawsers they wouldn't hang on to sich cloth as I'm put into."

"Hear him!" gasped Matthew Stickers; "only hear him. Oh, what a dreadful boy he is!"

"I will report your conduct to Mr. Stormaway," said Mrs. Jumble in a voice tremulous with suppressed rage.

"Let me see," observed Timothy Slowbob with the air of a philosopher. "This is Thursday. On Monday there was two reports, on Tuesday there was three, and yesterday there was——"

"Leave the room!" cried Mrs. Jumble, starting to her feet. "Stickers, I command you to turn that audacious boy out."

"He turn me out? What, him?" said Slowbob, contemptuously. "Stickers knows a better game than that. I'm a going, marm. Don't you trouble to fly into a passion about me; it destroys your good-looking face, marm."

And out went Timothy Slowbob, winking demoniacally at all such boys as were looking at him.

"Mr. Stormaway will dismiss him for this, I suppose?" Ralph whispered.

Charlie Chadwick shook his head.

"No," he replied; "Timothy is bound for seven years. He is a kind of a fixture, and if the house ever changes hands, it is my belief that the new occupier will have to take him with it."

"How Mr. Stormaway must suffer!"

"He does."

Those two words spoke volumes.

Ralph had no time to ask any more questions, for the meal had come to an end, and Mrs. Jumble sounded a table-bell, which was a signal for the boys to rise.

An hour later Ralph was put through his facings by Mr. Stormaway, and, to the delight of Chadwick and Lakeman, he was appointed a place in their own form.

Then the evening lessons were conned, the ushers hovering about meanwhile.

When they withdrew, the boys were left to themselves for half-an-hour, and they crowded round Ralph, putting a hundred questions to him, all of which he answered, and was forthwith rated a brick.

"I say, Chadwick," cried a big fellow, pushing his way to the front, "have you told Mornington that all new boys must show what they are capable of doing?"

"No, I have not, Jack Walbut," Charlie replied. "Mornington is tired out after his long journey."

"Oh, bosh!" said Walbut, running his fingers through his long, straight hair, and grinning maliciously. "We can't make an exception of our rule to please him. I suppose he can sing, recite, dance, or something?"

"Really," Ralph said, "I am not at all inclined to attempt any of those accomplishments."

"Then I may as well tell you the penalty for refusing," Walbut returned. "I, as a senior boy, sentence you to eat three spoonfuls of dry mustard. I brought the stuff with me in case you should be obstinate."

"Indeed," Ralph replied, "I shall certainly not sup on the delicacy so kindly provided by you."

Walbut clenched his hands and swaggered up to Mornington.

"Oh, you won't, eh?" he said. "Well, do you know what you will have to do?"

"No," answered Ralph.

"You'll have to fight me," said the bully.

"Again I refuse," Ralph responded. "I promised my father that I would never fight except when my honour was impeached, or when really compelled to do so under force of circumstances."

"We don't want to hear what you promised your father," Walbut sneered. "It strikes me that you haven't left your mother's apron-strings long."

"My mother is dead," Ralph said sadly; and he brushed his hand across his eyes.

"He is going to cry," exclaimed Walbut with a brutal laugh. "Ralph Mornington, I dub you a milksop and a coward."

The words were scarcely out of his mouth when he went down with a thud upon the floor, and Ralph, with flashing eyes and every muscle of his face quivering, stood over him.

"I am sorry for this," Ralph said a moment later amid dead silence, "but you brought it on yourself. Let me help you to your feet. I have shown you that I am no coward ; and as you will naturally require satisfaction for the blow, which I wish had not been quite so hard a one, I will fight you when and where may suit your convenience."

"Bravo !" cried several of the boys.

Walbut pushed Ralph's hand away, and as he staggered to his feet a ray of light fell upon his face and revealed an ugly bruise on his cheek.

"Ralph Mornington," the bully hissed, "you shall learn that I have other ways of fighting than with my fists. From this moment we are enemies. I know not how or when, but you shall bitterly rue this night. Mark it down in your memory, for if I live I will give you good cause to beware of me."

"Who is the coward now ?" said Ralph, appealing to the boys. "Enemies, indeed ! Pshaw ! It is not in my nature to be friendly with one who throws out dark, revengeful hints, but I will be on my guard and——"

A warning cry from a watchful youth sent the boys scampering to their seats.

A moment later the door opened, and the head-master, followed by the ushers, entered the room to take their leave of the pupils for the night.

CHAPTER II.

THE GHOST WALKS.

THE dormitory into which Chadwick and Lakeman escorted the lad who is to be the hero of this story, contained six beds, but there was quite sufficient room for twice as many.

It was double-lighted, the deeply-recessed windows looking north and south.

The ceiling was lofty, and the walls were panelled in oak and quaintly carved.

"There is the future home of your dreams," Chadwick said, pointing to a bed near the door, " and I hope they will be pleasant ones. Don't begin by allowing Walbut to trouble your slumbers. He is a rank bully, and deserved what he got."

"I had almost forgotten him," Ralph replied as he threw off his jacket. " Let him go his way, and I will go mine. What a splendid room this is ! I can fancy cowled monks crossing this floor, and knights who have sought the hospitality of the Abbey divesting themselves of their armour and falling to rest as calmly as children after roaming."

"Why, you are dreaming already, Ralph," Harold Lakeman chimed in. " Wait until you have been here a few days. If you are of a romantic turn of mind, you will see enough to make you believe that you are living in the fifteenth century."

"I wish those who did live then, or at any time, would leave us alone at night," said Charlie Chadwick. " If I were a ghost, I would choose for an abode some more pleasant place than this crumbling old Abbey."

"It seems to me that you have ghosts on the brain," Ralph remarked, laughing. " When I see one I shall believe, and not before."

"You will not have to wait long, I fancy," Charlie returned as he rolled himself into bed. " Make haste and follow my example, or Stickers will take away the candles and leave you in the dark. Good-night."

Three other boys, named Dick Heron, Harry Burleigh, and Tommy Toddler, occupied the dormitory, and these three youths exchanged glances as Ralph prepared to court the drowsy god.

"There is something wrong with my bed," said Ralph. " Oh, I see, some kind friend has doubled the sheets."

"That's Tommy Toddler, I'll be bound," Chadwick cried.

"Oh, of course," said Tommy with an injured air. " Fasten the blame upon my shoulders. Pitch into me ; I can bear it."

"If I could reach my boots I would make a target of you," Charlie rejoined. " However, I will reserve the punishment for the morning. A dose of wet towel will do you good."

Tommy Toddler muttered something under his breath as he bounced into bed.

He was no sooner in than out, and sat upon the floor rubbing his ribs.

"Who's been putting chunks of knotty wood under my sheet, I should like to know?" gasped the sufferer. "Look here, Heron."

"Don't blame the wrong party," Harold Lakeman sang out; "Heron has quite enough sins to answer for as it is."

"Then it was you!" spluttered the indignant Tommy.

"Of course it was, dear boy," Harold replied calmly. "I made certain that you would play Mornington some stale trick, so I tried to think of something new."

"All right," Tommy grumbled; "I'll be even with you. A good thing keeps well, and I will bide my time."

Bump, bump, went the pieces of wood upon the floor, and Tommy Toddler was still rubbing his ribs when Matthew Stickers opened the door cautiously, and thrust in his head and shoulders.

"Who's that out o' bed?" he demanded.

"Mind your own business," Toddler retorted. "I gave you three-pence last week for not splitting on me when I broke a window, so you can shut up."

"Good," said Stickers as he took up the candles and blew out one. "Master Toddler, you are not only larkin' when you orter be fast asleep, but you acuses me of taking a bribe."

"You know you asked me for the money," Toddler returned. "You said you were short of tobacco. I'd have seen you at Jericho first before parting with a farthing, only I had been flogged once the same day, and felt like a red-hot jelly."

"If I had a bit o' pencil about me, I'd make a note o' your words, and make you prove 'em before a judge and jury," Stickers said.

This terrific threat failed to have the desired effect upon Tommy Toddler.

"You are an impostor, and levy blackmail whenever you get the chance," he cried. "Every boy in the Abbey knows it, and if it didn't look like peaching, I'd report you to Mr. Stormaway."

Matthew Stickers trembled in spite of himself.

As he turned round to make some remark the second candle went out in the most mysterious way, and something soft and wet dabbed him heavily in the face.

"Oh, lor'!" he yelled, dropping both candlesticks with a crash; "what's that?"

"Only a sponge that was happily within my reach," said Charlie Chadwick. "Clear out of the room, and think yourself lucky to get off so easy."

Stickers was too wise to stay and argue out the point.

He groped his way to the door and departed hastily, his movements being accelerated by one of the pieces of wood which Tommy Toddler hurled wildly after the fugitive.

"When I was a young 'un," Stickers growled, when safe in the corridor, "boys was boys; but now they are more like ravenhouse wolves. Stickers, you are a long-suffering man. The airly martyrs in the Rummum areas led lives o' peace compared to yours. Ah," he added with a sigh, "when will it all end? Slowbob baits me like a bull, and the boys draws me like a badger."

Moaning, grumbling, and complaining, the man-of-all-work went his rounds, and darkness and slumber soon reigned within the walls of Merrytown Abbey.

It did not take Ralph Mornington long to sink into a state of repose.

Excitement and fatigue had done their work, and no sooner did he close his eyes than he was asleep.

Suddenly he was roused by the touch of a deathly-cold hand, and startled into wakefulness, he raised himself upon his elbow, and tried to peer through the gloom.

The blinds being of a dark green colour, plunged the room into pitchy darkness, and Ralph could see nothing whatever.

"Another joke, no doubt," he murmured; "I wish those fellows would leave me in peace for a few hours. To-morrow night they may do what they like, and I will be ready for them, but now——"

The thread of his thoughts was broken as something like a long trailing garment swept audibly past the foot of his bed.

"I see that I must be on the alert," Ralph mused as he grasped his not over soft pillow. "I'll floor the first fellow who attempts to play me a trick."

Again the strange rustling sound came to his ears, and in spite of himself our hero began to feel a little nervous.

"How foolish I am!" he said. "This comes of listening to Charlie Chadwick's ghost-stories."

"Who is prowling about there?" he added, raising his voice. "You had best leave me alone, or you will find that I am in no mood to be trifled with."

Ralph listened, and heard a deep-drawn sigh, followed by the words, uttered in a low, sepulchral tone:

"The love of gold brings its own curse. Oh! why am I doomed to wander thus in the dead of the night without peace or hope?"

Our hero felt his blood run cold, and before he could recover his self-control sufficiently to decide upon any definite course of action, he saw a shapeless form, darker than the prevailing darkness, flit past him.

He struck at it, but his hand encountered nothing but thin air; and then, with his heart thumping against his side, and a strange ringing in his ears, he leaped out of bed.

"Chadwick — Lakeman — all of you!" he cried. "Wake up! Wake up!"

"Hallo! what's the matter?" demanded Charlie, as he sat bolt upright. "Oh, you have spoilt such a lovely dream. I thought I was living in a place where a fellow could get unlimited tarts without paying for them."

These words set Ralph thinking, and he determined that he would not be caught napping.

"Come," said he, "have done with this tomfoolery."

"What tomfoolery?"

"Why, one of you has been playing the ghost, and groaning out something about the love of gold bringing its own curse."

This statement was followed by a soft thud, proclaiming that Charlie had assumed a horizontal attitude with startling suddenness.

"What?" he gasped. "Did—did your hear those words?"

"As plainly as I have just given them utterance."

"Then you are doomed!" Charlie almost shrieked. "You've seen and heard the spectre-monk of the Abbey. People say that he never appears unless something dreadful is going to—— Good gracious! what's that?"

"It's only I," Tommy Toddler replied. "I've fallen out of bed and on to these confounded chunks of wood again."

Tommy spluttered out this explanation as he scrambled to his feet and scudded towards the door.

"Where are you going?" Harry Lakeman bellowed. "Do you want to alarm the whole house?"

"That's just what I am going to do," Tommy Toddler shouted back. "I am not going to stay in a place where spectre-monks wander about. Help! Murder! Ghosts! Help! Help!"

"Come back, you miserable little coward!" Ralph exclaimed, making a grab at Tommy and missing him.

The warning came too late.

Timothy Slowbob, who slept in a room just large enough for himself and the rope communicating with the alarm-bell, skipped nimbly to his feet, and sent forth such a peal that it startled every human being within the Abbey.

Mr. Stormaway kept a shaded lamp in his room in case that his immediate presence might be required at any moment, and, raising it aloft, he, without a moment's hesitation, rushed upstairs.

Tommy Toddler's voice—for the horrified youth shouted again and again—guided him.

"All right!" Mr. Stormaway cried with all the strength of his lungs. "Don't be afraid; I am coming!"

And so was somebody else.

During the previous winter, Merrytown had proved a profitable hunting-ground for burglars, and in a weak moment Mr. Stormaway had purchased an old-fashioned bell-mouthed blunderbuss, and entrusted it, with a liberal supply of ammunition, to Matthew Stickers."

For months this fearful weapon had rested, loaded up to the muzzle, in the man-of-all-work's sleeping apartment, but at last it was to play an important part.

Stickers, more than half asleep, hurled himself out of bed, fell over a chair, bumped his head against the chest-of-drawers, and rolled into the corner in which the blunderbuss reclined.

He seized it, dashed valiantly out of the room, and went down the stairs three at a time until he came to a landing.

Here he paused, and, looking over the balustrade, saw something green and misty flitting about.

Stickers took it for the light from a burglar's dark lantern, and, bringing the blunderbuss to his shoulder, pulled the trigger.

Bang !

The report was terrific, and so was the concussion.

The green and misty light went out, amid a smashing of glass and a sharp cry of horror.

Bowled over by the recoil, Matthew Stickers lay upon his back, his thin legs, like pipe-stems of an abnormal mould, darting about hither and thither in the most extraordinary style.

"I've hit him, and that's a comfort !" Stickers cried joyfully.

"Hit him, you idiot !" replied a voice from below ; "it's a miracle that the slugs struck the lamp without hitting me."

Stickers heard these words like a man in a dream.

"Fetch another light !" Mr. Stormaway cried. "There's nothing the matter. Stop the bell, Slowbob ! Peace, Toddler, peace ! What has frightened you ?"

"It's a mercy I didn't blow him to sassidge-meat ; but I s'pose I shall be blamed for doin' of my dooty," Stickers muttered as he shuffled back to fetch a candle. "Oh, here's a rumpus ! Won't there be some thwackings goin' on !"

By the time that Stickers brought a light upon the scene, the corridor was crowded with half-dressed boys and ushers, while from a distant region came shrill, female voices demanding their wages forthwith that they might get out of the "'orrible place."

"Go to your rooms, all of you," said Mr. Stormaway. "Now, Toddler, when you can keep your teeth from chattering, explain the cause of your alarm."

"I think, sir, that the explanation ought to come from me," said Ralph Mornington, stepping forward.

"Very well," Mr. Stormaway returned. "At all events, you are cool and collected. Proceed."

Briefly and calmly Ralph narrated what he had seen, and Mr. Stormaway listened with an attentive expression on his face.

"You must have been dreaming," he said when Ralph had finished.

"I thought so myself at first, sir," our hero rejoined, "but I soon had good reason to assure myself that I was awake."

"Then," said Mr. Stormaway as a light dawned upon him, "this was a foolish trick to frighten you. Go to your bed. I will make it my duty to investigate this affair to-morrow. And now," he added, turning to Matthew Stickers, "a word with you."

"Don't be too 'ard on a man who thought he was doin' his dooty," Stickers mumbled. "You would have praised me if I had hit a burglar."

There was force in the man-of-all-work's argument, and Mr. Stormaway, having recovered from his fright, could not find it in his heart to blame Stickers too severely.

"I had a very narrow escape of my life," he said ; "and am truly thankful that your rash conduct has not brought serious injury upon me. Give me the blunderbuss ; I will take care of it for the future."

As Matthew Stickers relinquished the somewhat ponderous weapon, a loud scream rang through the corridor.

"What new horror is in store for us ?" cried Mr. Stormaway, aghast.

The new horror was Mrs. Jumble, who, clad in a dressing-gown, bore suddenly down upon the head-master, and threw her arms round his neck.

"Oh, protect me—protect me !" she shrieked. "Ah, this is too much !"

"It is a great deal too much, madame !" gasped Mr. Stormaway, as he staggered under the lady's weight. "Pray calm yourself. Don't you see you are putting me in a very absurd and ridiculous position ?"

"I am limp—I am going to faint !" Mrs. Jumble groaned. "Oh—oh !"

"Slowbob," said Matthew Stickers, "just run downstairs and fetch a pail o' water."

Mrs. Jumble postponed the fainting fit, and glared at Stickers as if she could have eaten him.

"I am better now," she said faintly, and with much dignity.

As she spoke she released Mr. Stormaway, who forthwith stepped backwards, and kept at a respectful distance.

"Mrs. Jumble," he said, "I fear you have allowed this commotion to get the better of your reason."

"No—no !" the housekeeper moaned.

She staggered towards Stickers, who dodged adroitly out of the way.

"It ain't a bit o' use tumblin' against me," Stickers observed; "I can't hold you up."

"You brute—you wretch!" sobbed Mrs. Jumble. "How dare you address me in that style? Oh! Mr. Stormaway, this is a place of horrors. I saw it with my own eyes."

"Saw what?"

"The ghost. It passed me as I left my room to ascertain what all the noise meant. More dead than alive, I watched it as it glided towards the west wing; and then it seemed to fade away and dwindle into nothing."

Mr. Stormaway looked wretchedly perplexed.

He rubbed his chin, rasped the tip of his nose, and made hay of his hair.

"I confess that I am bewildered to a certain extent," he said, "but I am still of the same opinion. This is nothing but a silly practical joke, and the offender must be discovered and punished."

"Think o' the 'orrible noises we have heard, sir," Stickers observed. "The groans, the runnin' up and down stairs, the sounds like wind when no wind was blowin' and——"

"That will do," Mr. Stormaway interposed hastily. "May I ask as a favour that you will speak when you are spoken to?"

"Not another word will you get from me," Stickers retorted rather defiantly. "If a man 'as to earn his livin' as a servant, that's no reason why he should be—— Oh!"

Matthew Stickers skipped into the air.

"What now?" cried the head-master, wildly.

"That there Slowbob stuck somethin' sharp into the calf of my leg," Stickers yelled. "Why is he allowed to draw me like a badger? One o' these days I shall take the law into my own hands, and then there'll be a sensation in the newspapers."

"Slowbob," said Mr. Stormaway, "come here."

The sportive Timothy advanced, keeping a wary eye upon his irate patron.

Mr. Stormaway aimed an open-handed blow at the page-boy's head.

Quick as lightning, Slowbob ducked his cranium, and Mr. Stormaway's knuckles came into contact with the wall.

The head-master thought it time to put an end to the scene.

Having soothed his knuckles by rubbing them gently, and bottling up his wrath, he uttered a few impressive words, assuring his hearers that within a few hours the ghost should be laid, and then marched off to his room.

CHAPTER III.

AN ENCOUNTER WITH P.C. WORRYBOY.

As may be imagined, repose was at a premium that night, and when morning dawned, and light gave courage to all, but few were inclined to leave their beds.

Even Mr. Stormaway looked pale and anxious.

Mr. Muffler had suddenly acquired a propensity for looking over his shoulder, and Mrs. Jumble remained within the sacred precincts of her room.

Two foreign gentlemen, M. Alphonse Carleon, the French master, and Herr Fritz Halfamann, slept out of the house, but took their meals at the Abbey.

When they heard what had happened, the Frenchman shrugged his shoulders, while the German gave himself a kind of roll, and knitted his bushy brows.

"It is de poys—de leedle poys—dat do de meeschief," he observed. "Ah, no poy but an English poy would think of browling about de house mit nearly nodings on. My frient Carleon, you know vat de poys are."

The Frenchman remained silent, but by the way he displayed his white and gleaming teeth, it was quite evident that he had not much affection for the "poys."

The clock was just on the stroke of eight—the usual breakfast-hour—and Matthew Stickers emerged from the pantry with a tremendous pile of plates. He had not taken many paces when a low, sepulchral voice cried:

"Old sinner, turn from your wicked ways!"

Matthew Stickers trembled until the plates rattled again.

To turn round with such a heavy load was not an easy task; but the man-of-all-work contrived to do so, and saw—nothing.

"Strikes me," muttered Stickers, "that I'm goin' wrong; and no wonder. This 'ere place will soon be wisited by the loonacy commissioners. I expect we shall all go wrong in the head."

"Ha, ha! you're going mad!" laughed a voice in his ear.

Round again went Matthew Stickers, but there was nobody in sight.

The pantry-door was wide open, and the man-of-all-work could see under and above every shelf and into all the corners.

"Well," he gasped, standing with his legs wide apart, "this beats what happened last night. Do ghostesses walk in the daytime?"

"They do. Beware—tremble!"

With a jerk, Matthew Stickers sent the plates flying into the air, and almost before they came to the floor with a crash and a smash, he, without turning his head, fled wildly in the direction of the dining-room.

The first person that Stickers came into contact with was Herr Fritz Halfamann.

The German tutor was short, round, and bullet-headed, and he went over as neatly as if some magical power had suddenly converted him into a nine-pin.

Stickers then cannoned against a corner of the table, upset a huge tea-urn, and finally shot into the fireplace.

"Murder!" he yelled with his eyes closed. "Murder! Take it away! Don't let it follow me!"

Ralph and Charlie Chadwick hastened to his assistance, and succeeded in placing him full-length on the hearth-rug.

"Dot man haf got a stroke of de madness," spluttered the German tutor. "M. Carleon, strike him on de head mit de poker. He vill bite all of us, and den ve——"

"I ain't mad, you German poloney!" Stickers cried as he started to his feet and laid violent hands on the fire-poker. "The fust man as attempts to do me an injury will get such a dig in the ribs as will let daylight through him."

M. Carleon, who had valiantly possessed himself of a large poker, now lowered it towards the floor, but stood ready to defend himself in the event of any fresh symptoms of insanity displaying themselves on the part of Stickers.

"Ah," observed the latter, "you Frenchies can fence, I've heard, but I can hit, and hit hard, too! I've an Englishman's fist and can use it!"

At that moment Slowbob, with his hands deeply embedded in his pockets, presented himself.

"I think there's something broke. I heard a light smash," he said.

A thought flashed into Matthew Sticker's brain as he turned his frightened eyes upon the irrepressible page-boy.

"Somethin' broke!" he repeated in a tone hoarse with emotion. "Imp in a mulberry soot of clothes, how long was it since you was near the pantry?"

"How long?" Slowbob returned. "Let me think. How long?"

He put on a thoughtful look, and whistled softly.

This so exasperated the man-of-all-work that, poker in hand, he danced up to Slowbob, who stood his ground and moved not a muscle.

"I b'lieve," Stickers said, "that you was behind me—that it was you who spoke, and caused me to chuck the plates up."

"Do you, indeed?" Timothy responded with so comic a grin that the boys went into fits of laughter. "Stickers, I'm not one to talk about a man's piccadillys."

"Peccadillos," corrected somebody.

"It's all the same to Stickers," Slowbob said calmly. "Well, I'm not one to mention a man's weaknesses, but it strikes me, Matthew, that you've been flirting with the beer-barrel rather too early."

The poker slipped from the man-of-all-work's grasp.

Speech and strength left him, and before either returned, Mr. Thaddeus Stormaway strode into the room.

After a series of skirmishes, accompanied by sundry boxes on the ears, he succeeded in chasing Slowbob out of the room, and then stared hard at Stickers.

"Are you mad?" the head-master demanded.

"Dat's vot I say," Halfamann chimed in. "Is the man mad? Slowbob says that he haf peen flirting in the peer-parrel."

"Slowbob is a—a perwerter of the truth," Stickers cried. "Oh, Mr. Stormaway, as I was leavin' the pantry, woices—awful woices spoke to me ! ”

“ Voices, indeed ! ” said Mr. Stormaway, contemptuously. “ Don’t talk such nonsense to me. How dare you wreck my property, and then find an idle excuse for so doing ? Leave the room ! ”

“ What for ? ”

“ Because you are not in a fit condition to remain in it,” the head-master replied sternly.

Matthew Stickers reeled as if he had been shot.

“ This is ’ard—wery ’ard on a man as hasn’t had so much as a cup of corfee,” he muttered as he tottered towards the door. “ I s’pose I must bear it, though. Slowbob, you and I will tot up accounts afore this ere day is over.”

For some moments after the man-of-all-work had departed, Mr. Stormaway maintained silence.

“ It seems to me,” said he at last, “ that this establishment is losing its name for good order, and is degenerating into a bear-garden. Now that I am here, I wish to refer to last night’s occurrence. If the guilty party will confess to having played so silly a joke, I will forgive him freely ; but I will show him no mercy if I find him out by my own exertions.”

All the boys did was to sit still and look at each other.

“ Very well,” Mr. Stormaway resumed. “ Not another word will I say about the matter until I am able to point out the foolish lad who has caused all this commotion. Believe me, I will be watchful.”

So saying, the master stalked out of the room.

“ Vot sal ve do for ze blates ? ” observed Halfamann. “ Ze poys cannot feed off ze poards like ze leedle dogs.”

There was a roar of laughter at this, and while the sound yet filled the room, two maid-servants entered and soon put matters right in a crockery-ware sense.

The proceedings that morning at the Abbey were, to say the least, rather peculiar. The boys discussed the ghost whenever they got the chance, and, as a matter of course, forgot their lessons.

Many a youth smarted under the head-master’s cane, but at last, to the relief of all, the hands of the clock pointed to the hour of twelve, and the school was dismissed.

Two days passed away, and nothing worth recording happened, save that Jack Walbut watched Ralph Mornington narrowly, but gave him a wide berth, and our hero seemed scarcely to notice him.

“ This is the first Saturday in the month,” Charlie Chadwick said, “ and we are allowed to go out of bounds to purchase anything we may require.”

“ How jolly ! ” Ralph returned ; “ I have been longing to buy a few things. I suppose there are plenty of shops in Merrytown ? ”

“ Any number of them,” observed Lakeman. “ There’s Puffy the confectioner, for instance. It makes a fellow’s mouth water to look at the windows of his shop.”

“ Then come along,” said Ralph, “ I have plenty of money, and more to come whenever I like to apply to my father’s solicitor.”

“ Your father must be awfully kind to you,” Charlie remarked.

“ He is,” Ralph replied. “ He made me promise that I would never get into debt. I am to have everything in reason, but to avoid extravagance.”

As the boys reached the school-gates, which were thrown open for the occasion, Matthew Stickers emerged from an out-house.

“ There’ll be mischief to-day,” he muttered, shaking his head. “ I see future trouble in that new boy’s heye.”

Something came hurtling through the air, and struck the man-of-all-work on his face, something else followed and struck him on his bald head.

“ Slowbob,” he gasped, “ do that again if you dare, and I’ll—I’ll have every button off your jacket.”

The youth alluded to was at that moment engaged in gazing complacently at the sky.

“ Say it’s me,” Slowbob retorted. “ Go on ! What next will you accuse an innocent boy like me of ? ”

Stickers made a short run at his tormentor, and coming full butt against Slowbob, who doubled himself up suddenly, shot over him like a rocket.

When Matthew picked himself up, which he did very slowly, the page-boy had vanished.

“ I’ve laid in a stock of gravel-rash, enough to last me a twelvemonth,” Stickers groaned as he felt his nose tenderly. “ What’s the world coming to ? There ought to be a Hact of Parleyment to put down boys. A few of ’em wouldn’t be missed, anyhow.”

Ralph and his chums went their way laughing, and a few minutes' sharp walking brought them to Merrytown.

The "town" might have been dispensed with, as the place was nothing more than a long, straggling village, with an aggravating pump at one end and a corpulent policeman at the other.

"I see that Worryboy is at his usual post," said Charlie Chadwick.

"Yes," Lakeman returned. "Keep a wary eye on him, old fellow. He owes you a grudge, remember."

"The spiteful beast!" Charlie rejoined. "I only asked him how many times round his waist went to a mile, and he threatened to run me in."

At that moment Police-constable Worryboy sniffed the air suspiciously and cast a glance from a pair of lack-lustre eyes at the boys.

To avoid a collision, they passed to the other side of the street, but Worryboy was not to be denied.

With lofty and sounding steps, only acquired by long official practice, he approached, note-book in hand.

"See here!" he said, extending a fat fore-finger towards Charlie, "don't come any of your tricks to-day, or you'll find me down on you."

"Oh, spare me," Charlie replied; "I have no desire to be crushed. Remember you are fat."

Worryboy blew himself out to a tremendous size, and wrote something in his note-book.

"Noble officer, do you want a knife to sharpen your pencil?" Charlie demanded, laughing.

"You don't want anything to sharpen you," said a butcher. "Now, then, get along with you. I don't pay rates and taxes to have my doorway blocked by a parcel of boys."

"Certainly not," commented Worryboy. "Move on! I can't think why Mr. Stormaway lets you out at all."

"Make a note of it," said Charlie Chadwick. "Come along, boys! The aroma from that shop is not one of roses, and it throws me into a perspiration to look at Worryboy."

"It's a mercy he doesn't melt in that uniform," Ralph observed, quietly.

"He never takes it off," Lakeman chimed in. "If he did it would take a four-horse power steam-engine to get it on again."

P. C. Worryboy had been gradually getting purple in the face, and now he fairly boiled over.

With a roar that would have smitten a bull with envy, he charged at the boys.

Ralph happened to be nearest, but he was ready for the enraged constable, and catching him by the belt, he waltzed round and round with him until Worryboy became so giddy, that he scarcely knew whether he stood on his heels or his head.

Suddenly Ralph relaxed his hold of the belt.

The effect of this manœuvre was decisive and alarming.

Worryboy, plunging into the shop, grabbed at the butcher.

Over the block they went, rolling into the little back-parlour, where, after a considerable amount of struggling and pummelling, they managed to scramble to their feet.

"If this ain't a locking-up case, I should like to know what is," Worryboy bellowed. "Where are they?"

"Gone!" the butcher roared. "Oh, the back of my head! I did the post-man's knock with it on the floor. Just feel these bumps."

"Never mind," said Worryboy; "we'll be revenged for this. I'll call you as a witness, and——"

"It seems to me," the butcher interposed, "that if you had left the boys alone, this wouldn't have happened. I shall take no more trouble about the matter, but wait my chance."

"Think of the law," Worryboy urged. "You mustn't take the law into your own hands, remember."

"Bother the law!" the butcher retorted. "I've been turned upside down, and chucked about like a shuttlecock all through your interference. I've spoken my mind to you now, so clear out. You shut half the light out of my shop."

Worryboy could scarcely believe his ears.

As a rule he was respected by the adults of Merrytown, and feared by the juveniles.

But now he was told to clear out.

It was monstrous, and a thing to be put down with a strong hand.

"Chopps," said P.C. Worryboy in an impressive tone of voice, "you will live to rue this hour. As soon as I can see straight, I have a number of things to put down in my pocket-book, and I shan't forget to make a note of your conduct."

Mr. Chopps seized the instrument

with which he dealt confusion and death to the bluebottle tribe, and clutched it viciously.

"Will you go, you big bluebottle ?" he yelled. "Once—twice—thrice——"

Before the last word was fairly out of Chopps' mouth, Worryboy stood in the middle of the street.

"The boys first and Chopps afterwards," he muttered. I've had chops and boy sauce. Ha ! ha ! and soon I'll have revenge."

CHAPTER IV.

AN EXCITING EVENT—HONOUR TO THE BRAVE.

THE boys, after parting hurriedly with P.C. Worryboy, hied towards the shop of Mr. Puffy, confectioner.

The proud proprietor of this establishment, a pale and rather flabby man, stood behind the counter when his customers entered.

Mr. Puffy at once cleared the board and prepared for business, while an obliging young lady pointed to three spindle-legged stools.

"Thank you very much," said Ralph. "We may as well be seated. Now, boys, peg away ; have what you like, and don't be afraid. What do you say to a pigeon-pie to start with, Charlie ?"

"He looks just the sort of boy to eat a pigeon-pie," Mr. Puffy observed, smiling.

The obliging young lady giggled, and blushed archly when she saw that Ralph was looking at her.

Charlie and Lakeman needed no second bidding.

They did peg away, Ralph doing his share manfully.

Then came the reckoning, which Mr. Puffy performed with a serious air.

"Two pigeon-pies, four shillings; nine Coventrys, five-and-six ; six Baths, six-and-six ; six custards, seven-and-six ; three bottles of lemonade, eight-and-six, if you please, sir."

"Can you oblige me with change for a five-pound note ? " Ralph asked, quietly.

Mr. Puffy took a step backwards and stared hard at the lad.

He had been in business a good many years, but this was the first time that such a question had been put to him by a boy.

"Ye—es, sir," he stammered. "Certainly, sir. Made it yourself, sir, I suppose ? " he added, with a feeble attempt at a joke.

Ralph made no reply, and Mr. Puffy, having looked at the watermark of the note, counted out the change with a trembling hand.

"Four eleven six. Very much obliged, sir."

"We may as well make it even money," Ralph remarked. "Put eighteen penny open tarts into a bag."

"You shall have twenty for the money," Mr. Puffy returned, magnanimously. "Proud to receive your patronage, sir—indeed I am."

The tarts were packed in a neat, white bag and handed over to Charlie, who volunteered to take charge of them.

"Don't hold the bag tightly," was Mr. Puffy's warning. "Open tarts, if not carefully carried, have a tendency to run."

"You may leave it to me," Charlie responded.

At that moment he happened to look towards the window, and saw two very large noses flattened against it.

One of the nasal organs belonged to P.C. Worryboy, and the other was possessed by Salem Cockey, the beadle of Merrytown parish.

"Ralph ! Lakeman !" Charlie whispered. "See there ! We are trapped ! What is to be done ?"

"I vote that we walk out quietly," said Ralph. "If the constable or the gentleman in the cocked hat forces us into a row, we must put up with it. I am game for anything."

"So am I," Lakeman returned, as he pulled his hat well over his eyes. "You shall lead us, Ralph. Stick to those tarts, Charlie !"

Chadwick nodded.

If a scrimmage took place the tarts would surely stick to him.

Ralph was first out of the shop, Lakeman next, and Charlie, balancing the bag with his chin, brought up the rear.

"Here they are," cried Worryboy, joyfully ; "and now I'll let 'em have it."

"Do," said Salem Cockey, rubbing his hands. "They are the torments of the place. I'll stand by you, old friend."

Ralph drew himself up to his full height, and looked the constable straight in the face.

"You will do well to allow us to pass along in peace," he said. "Your name is a peculiar one, but I have yet to know that it is consistent with your duty as a policeman to pester the public."

"He's a new boy at the Abbey," Salem Cockey said. "Let him go."

"Not me," replied Worryboy. "He's the one who sent me flying on the top of Chopps. I've made a note of it. Now, my lads, it's no use running away, so—— Oh !"

He had advanced to take hold of Ralph, but found out to his cost that he had made a mistake.

Ralph tripped him neatly up, and sent him sprawling on the pavement.

"To the rescoo, Cockey !" he shrieked. "If you're a man, knock 'em down and pick me up."

But Salem Cockey failed to do his part as a friend, and hastened nimbly to the other side of the street.

"Now," said Ralph, whose blood was fairly up, "what do you mean by your conduct ? "

Worryboy raised his hands and the soles of his boots simultaneously.

"It ain't fair to hit a man when he's down," he mumbled. "It's against the law to hit a policeman at all. It means forty shillings or a month 'ard."

"You are a miserable coward at the best," Ralph said, contemptuously. "You are a brow-beating bully, and a little taking down will do you good."

"I will give him a tart," Charlie suggested; "it may sweeten his temper."

Chadwick fished one of the luxuries from the bag, and with unerring aim, fastened it upon Worryboy's nose.

"Let him have the lot !" Lakeman cried.

No sooner said than done.

The tarts were carefully bestowed about Worryboy's face, who kicked, and roared, and spluttered under the ordeal.

"Help !" Salem Cockey shrieked. "Help ! They're a murderin' of him !"

Windows flew up, doors opened, and all sorts of people came running out.

Some took the constable's part, others sided with the boys, and an all-round fight seemed imminent, when an alarming cry arose:

"Runaway horse ! Runaway horse ! Stand clear there, for your lives !"

This was no false alarm.

A horse attached to a dog-cart came dashing at full gallop down the street.

The reins were trailing on the ground, while the sole occupant of the vehicle, a pretty young lady, sat pallid and motionless with terror.

"Stop the horse, Worryboy !" somebody shrieked.

"How can I stop anything with my eyes bunged up with jam ?" the constable howled back.

Nearer and nearer came the runaway horse.

It seemed as if nothing could save the dog-cart from being smashed to pieces, and the young lady killed.

A few men made futile attempts to stop the infuriated brute, but the majority gave it as wide a birth as possible; but rescue was at hand.

The lithe figure of Ralph Mornington sprang like an arrow from the bow at the horse's head.

He succeeded in grasping the bridle, otherwise that leap would have been his last.

Checked in its mad career, the horse reared and plunged frantically, but Ralph held on.

Now his feet were grating and clattering on the ground in unison with the horse's hoofs, now he was tossed wildly into the air; but never for a moment did he relax his hold.

The horse had found its master, and succumbed.

Then how brave were the beholders !

Four men rushed to lift the almost unconcious young lady from the dog-cart, half-a-dozen held on to the wheels, and an individual, who might have been Worryboy's twin brother in regard to fat, threw his arms round Ralph's waist, and implored him to take care of himself.

"Get away," said our hero, "you are smothering me ! "

A hush fell upon the crowd as a tall, aristocratic-looking gentleman appeared.

He was out of breath, and his face was whiter than the starched summer waistcoat he wore.

"Good Heaven, what an escape, Ethel !" he exclaimed. "Who stopped the wretched horse that might have robbed me of my only child ?"

The girl could only point to Ralph, who was modestly standing by.

"How can I repay you, my brave boy?" said the gentleman. "Give me your hand. Ah, it is a sound, honest one!"

"I am more fully paid by being conscious that I have been of some little service to your daughter," Ralph replied. "Please do not say anything now about so trivial a matter."

The gentleman took a Russia-leather case from his pocket, and Ralph, thinking that money was about to be offered him, shrank back.

"You mistake my motive," the handsome stranger said, smiling. "I know better than to insult so noble a lad with a paltry gift. Here is my card; and now tell me where I can find you."

Ralph told him as he glanced at the card.

To his astonishment he saw that he was speaking to Lord Henry Auburton.

"I have some little influence, and may be useful to you after you have left school," his lordship said. "Mornington! Are you one of the Berkshire Morningtons?"

"Yes, my lord."

"I know your family well. Dear me, this is but a small world, after all. Your father and I were old school-fellows."

"I am delighted to hear that," Ralph observed with sparkling eyes.

"Ethel," said his lordship, "shake hands with our brave young friend. You shall express your thanks to him on some more suitable opportunity."

The girl put out a daintily-gloved hand, and her beautiful eyes spoke more eloquently than words.

Lord Henry Auburton was about to lead his daughter away, when Worryboy stepped to the front.

"Bless me!" cried his lordship, starting; "what is this?"

"You may well ask what it is," Worryboy rejoined. "I'm a goin' in this 'ere state, and show Mr. Stormaway the style in which his pupils treat the law."

"I should advise you to treat your countenance to a little soap-and-water," his lordship remarked, "or you will find the flies rather troublesome."

Laughing heartily, and nodding pleasantly to Ralph, Lord Auburton turned into the nearest hotel, in order that Ethel might rest after her terrible fright.

"Hurrah for Ralph Mornington!" shouted Charlie Chadwick. "Up with him, shoulder high. We'll take him back in triumph to the Abbey."

The spectators entered into the spirit of the notion.

Half-a-dozen men hoisted Ralph into the air, and with Charlie and Lakeman in advance, singing "See the Conquering Hero Comes," a procession was formed.

"Really," said Ralph, laughing in spite of himself, "this is too ridiculous. Please let me walk?"

But nobody would hear of such a thing.

"We'll call him Brave Ralph," shouted Charlie Chadwick.

"Rollicking Ralph sounds better," Lakeman said. "He has proved himself ready for a lark, as well as a hero. Three cheers for Rollicking Ralph!"

They were given heartily just as the Abbey gates came in view.

"Let 'em holler," muttered Worryboy to Salem Cockey, who brought up the rear. "They'll be hollerin' to a different tune after I have seen Mr. Stormaway. If my fingers wasn't so sticky I'd make a note. Jigger them bluebottles; they're enough to eat a fellow's nose off."

"It's the jam," Salem Cockey said. "If it gets hard you'll have to bile that head o' yours, and I know what the boys will call it."

"What?"

"A calf's head."

CHAPTER V.

A DOWNFALL OF RADISHES—THE BULLY AND HIS TOADY—MISCHIEF AFLOAT.

WHEN the procession reached the Abbeygate, Matthew Stickers was gazing viciously about him.

It seemed to rain turnip-radishes.

Some smote him on the top of the head, others caught him on the tip of the nose, making him blink and sneeze; and every now and then one of a larger growth tingled his ears playfully.

"A PROCESSION OF YOUTHFUL CULPRITS WAS AT RALPH'S HEELS."—(See page 73.)

"Where do they come from?" Stickers gasped. "I never heerd o' sich a thing. There'll be a deluge o' wegetable marrers next, with a few pumpkins chucked in. Hearts alive, that was a hot 'un!"

The "hot 'un," so beautifully expressed by Matthew Stickers, was the largest of the radish kind with which he had been so mysteriously assailed.

It came flying sportively through the air, and catching the man-of-all-work on the chin, completely staggered him.

"I've read o' showers o' frogs and sich like," he said; "but this—there's another whopper!—beats everything."

Matthews Stickers looked everywhere but in the right place.

Had his attention been called to a clump of laurels he would have discovered Timothy Slowbob who, with an ample stock of ammunition, was thoroughly enjoying himself.

The page-boy's odd eyes gleamed with mischief, and every time he succeeded in making good his aim his cheeks distended with suppressed laughter.

In all probability Stickers would have caught Slowbob red-handed at his urchin sport, but a furore at the gate startled him.

"It's a riot!" he exclaimed, as he caught sight of the people. "'Ere's a go. They've got that new boy, and they mean to lynch him in the Habbey grounds."

At this moment, Slowbob, unperceived by the man-of-all-work, left his retreat and ran towards the gates.

Stickers followed him, and in a few moments the true state of things was explained.

"He stopped a horse and saved Lord Auburton's daughter from being killed!" Charlie cried, excitedly. "Ralph is the finest fellow in the playground!"

The page-boy proved more than equal to the occasion.

Diving deftly through the crowd he closed the gates, and captured one of Worryboy's legs.

"Marcy!" roared the fat constable. "Don't you see what you've done?"

"Can't be helped," Slowbob replied, calmly; "you ought to think yourself lucky it ain't your nose. When Mr. Stormaway tells me to open the gates I'll do it, and not before. Ha! ha! who's been painting your face?"

"I'll paint you!" Worryboy yelled. "Mis—ter—Storm—oh, lor!—away!"

The noise brought the head-master quickly to the spot, and the constable being released, proceeded to hop about like a wounded sparrow.

"This 'ere's a case for crutches," he moaned. "See how my left leg jiggles. It's broken."

Mr. Stormaway turned right and left in his bewilderment.

The story of Ralph's heroism was poured into one ear; Worryboy shrieked out his woes into the other; and Stickers tried to get a word in here and there.

At length the head-master grasped a few of the facts.

"Go away," he said to the constable. "I am afraid I shall have to complain of your conduct. This is not the first time you have interfered with my pupils."

"I interfere with 'em?" Worryboy shrieked. "Are you near sighted? Can't you see that I'm a walkin' mass o' raspberry jam?"

Mr. Stormaway turned a deaf ear to the constable, and then proceeded to dismiss the people, and having done so, he spoke a few kind words to Ralph.

"You have done well," he said, and then glancing at Charlie Chadwick: "I am afraid that I shall have to put a stop to these pranks in Merrytown."

"Yes, sir," Charlie rejoined, demurely. "Worryboy ought to be ashamed of himself."

Mr. Stormaway passed his hand before his mouth to hide a smile, and turned away.

"Beg pardin', sir," said Matthew Stickers, skipping after him, "if you won't take it as a liberty, I should like to ask a question."

"Well, what is it?"

"It's rather a skyentific one," the the man-of-all-work continued. "Did you ever hear o' radishes comin' from the clouds?"

"What?" cried Mr. Stormaway.

"It's been pelting hard with radishes," Stickers declared; "red and white turnip ones, sich as are sold at four bunches a penny, and I want ter know what it means."

Amazed and aghast at such a statement, Mr. Stormaway could do nothing but stare at his man-servant.

"Stickers," he said at length, "your conduct has been so idiotic of late that I am afraid I shall have to discharge you. Raining radishes ? Pooh, pooh! You are light-headed! Keep away from The Swan and Bottle, and you will soon clear your brain of such idle fancies."

"I haven't been near the Bon and Swattle—I mean the Swab and Wattle," returned Stickers, getting mixed as he spoke, "for more than a week. P'raps, sir, you think I've the delilerum trimmings coming on. Look 'ere, sir, the wery ground is speckled with radishes."

This was indeed the case, and Mr. Stormaway burst out laughing.

"A thoughtless joke on the part of one of the boys, no doubt," he observed.

"There wasn't even the shadow of a boy in the playground," Stickers declared.

"Where was Slowbob ?"

"I never thought of him," the man-of-all-work rejoined. "I'll just run my heye over the kitchen garden, and if I find——"

"Go about your work," said Mr. Stormaway, interrupting him. "That unfortunate boy is a perfect plague, and you are old enough to know better than to take notice of his idle pranks."

The head-master went his way, leaving Stickers grumbling and growling as usual.

Worryboy still hovered about the school-gates, but finding that nobody paid any attention to him, he repaired to a neighbouring pond, and made himself a little more presentable.

"I'll bide my time," he said. "There'll be another day to-morrow. Salem Cockey, hear my wow. I don't think I'm a hard-hearted man, but if I can lure a boy—I don't care how small he may be—into my house, I'll—I'll pickle him like pork."

The news of Ralph Mornington's adventure spread like wild-fire.

As the boys returned they crowded round our hero, and cheered him to the echo.

Jack Walbut alone stood apart, biting his nails and sneering.

"I don't see anything to make such a fuss about," he observed to one of his toadies named Lemon Sleath.

"Neither do I. You would have done the same, I am sure."

"Of course I would," Walbut said. "So they have nicknamed him Brave Rolliking Ralph. He is the darling of the hour, and the hero of the school. Wait a bit. I think I can see my way to make a sudden change in the affairs. Sleath, come with me."

"Do you want me to fag for you ?" the toady whined.

"No. I have something particular to say. Go to the drawing-class-room, and I will follow you. Sleath, I take it that you don't like the new boy ? "

"I hate him !'

"Why ? "

"Because you hate him ! "

"Bravo !" said Jack Walbut, grinning. "Work with me, and we'll turn the tables on him. Hush! Run away! That low workhouse cad, Slowbob, is watching us."

CHAPTER VI.

THE FRENCH MASTER RECEIVES A MYSTERIOUS LETTER—THE MEETING AT THE MISER'S MILL.

NIGHT was closing in as Alphonse Carleon, the French tutor, passed along the High-street of Merrytown.

The sky was filled with heavy clouds, promising thunder.

Carleon lodged in a strange old house standing back from the road.

An old, rusty, creaking gate opened into a garden full of weeds and rank grass, and up the uneven path went M. Carleon until he stood within the shadow of a gloomy porch.

As he touched the handle of the door a vivid flash of lightning parted the clouds, and the Frenchman saw a man standing so near him that he started violently and ejaculated something in his own language.

"It's all right, guv'nor," said the man, "I've been waiting to give you this."

He put an envelope into Carleon's hand, and disappeared swiftly, the rolling thunder following him in his flight.

"Strange ! " murmured the Frenchman. "What can this mean ? Surely nobody has found me out here ? No, no ! That is not possible. Years have passed away, and time has wiped out everything."

Nevertheless beads of perspiration stood on his brow, and he shuddered as he made his way into a room on the left-hand side of the hall.

Another flash of lightning showed him the reflection of his face in the mirror.

It was a face white and livid, with a pair of dilated, frightened eyes, and a moustache that bristled as the muscles near to it quivered with excitement.

Alphonse Carleon pulled down the blind and drew the thick heavy curtains to shut out the glare of the lightning, and turned up the lamp.

"Now to read," he said, as he tore the envelope open. "Hah! What is this?"

"'*A friend desires to see you to-night. Come to the Miser's Mill at twelve o'clock. Fail not, or you will compel me to send to the Abbey.*'"

This mystifying communication bore no signature.

Carleon read the lines again and again.

"I must go—I will go," he said, bringing his clenched hand down upon the table. "*Quel malheur!* what horror is in store for me? I have never seen this writing before. It is that of an Englishman, so why should I trouble my mind with vague fears?"

The storm was now raging in the height of its fury.

Flash after flash illumined the atmosphere, and peal after peal shook the old house to its very foundation.

The wind roared and howled in chorus, and it seemed as if all the elements were at war.

Now and then a dull thud or rending crash told that some tree or stack of chimneys had succumbed to the awful conflict, but the Frenchman was deaf to all save the words of the unsigned letter.

They rang in his ears, and he found himself repeating the last sentence, "'*You will compel me to send to the Abbey.*'"

There was a threat in these words. What did it mean?

Alphonse Carleon tried to steady his nerves by drinking a little brandy, but the spirit set his brain on fire, and as the hour of midnight drew near, his throbbing heart felt as heavy as lead.

At last it was time to go, and throwing a cloak over his shoulders, he emerged into the open air.

Rain fell heavily, and the thunder growled low down in the sky, but the worst of the storm was over.

The Miser's Mill crossed the river about a mile from Merrytown.

It was a tumble-down, ruinous place, and had never been occupied or worked since the death of Caleb Carker, a wretched old man, who lived and died in the chamber above the water-wheel.

The Miser's Mill, as it was known, had a very bad reputation.

The country folk declared it to be haunted, and few had sufficient courage to pass it after nightfall.

There were men bold enough to state that they had seen the ghost of Caleb Carker creeping, lantern in hand, across the bridge connecting the mill with the river-bank, and Jeremiah Sinkins, the parish clerk, alarmed his listeners one night by declaring that flowers planted on the miser's grave refused to grow, but faded and died within an hour.

Alphonse Carleon had heard all these rumours, and laughed them to scorn; but there was no smile on his lips as he stood before the Miser's Mill half-an-hour after midnight.

It was so pitch dark now, that even an occasional flash of lightning would have been a relief.

The Frenchman was wondering whether he had not been made the victim of a hoax after all, when a voice spoke to him.

"Cross the bridge," it said, "and keep straight on. I have left the door open for you. We will have a light presently."

Carleon had brought a revolver with him, and diving his hand into his coat-pocket, he grasped the weapon.

To pass over the bridge and through an open door was the work of a few moments.

"Am I in the presence of the writer of a letter brought to me?" asked the Frenchman.

"Yes," was the reply. "You may talk to me in your own language. I speak French like a native."

"Who are you?"

"Close the door, and you shall see."

Alphonse Carleon, still clutching the revolver, did as he was requested.

Instantly the dark slide of a lantern was withdrawn, and a disc of light fell upon the Frenchman.

"Don't move," said the voice. "I have candles with me, and will light them. The trap door has rotted away and fallen into the stream. Ugh! I had a narrow escape of pitching head-long through it."

The French tutor made no reply.

Every nerve in his body was tingling, and each moment seemed an age to him.

But he was not kept long in suspense.

Two wax candles were lighted, and then he saw the man who had sought an interview with him.

He was about five-and-twenty, but so unkempt was his hair, and so travel-stained were his sharp features, that one might have been excused for adding a score more years to his age.

His attire was almost in rags, but he had withal a graceful bearing, pro-claiming that he had seen better days.

"You have forgotten me," he said, stroking his tangled, straw-coloured moustache. "Well, four years of hard knocking about the world make a difference. I suppose you do not find much use for the billiard-cue or the dice-box in this humdrum place."

Alphonse Carleon started, and his face seemed to grow luminous as he backed towards the door.

"Alfred Richling," he said, hoarsely; "I—I thought you were dead."

"My good fellow," observed the other, "Alfred Richling had but a short existence, and an advertisement in the *Times* killed him; but his second self lives in me."

"You assumed the name, then?"

"Yes; I am Richard Mornington, and cousin to the lad who has just arrived at the Abbey."

The Frenchman took a long breath, and his white teeth gleamed in the candle-light.

"You have sent for me," he said, scarcely above a whisper, "and I am here. Well?"

"Yes; I wan't a little chat with you," Richard Mornington returned. "I cannot ask you to sit down, but I can ask you to help me to empty this flask. I spent my last shilling in the purchase of it."

"You want money?" Carleon said. "I am a poor man, but much happier than in the days——"

"When you were a professional blackleg and sharper," Richard Morn-ington interposed, complacently. "They must miss you at Monte Carlo; still there are plenty of blacklegs left to do the work."

"Hush—hush!"

"Oh, we can speak out here without fear. To return to your own remark. I want money, but not much. A sovereign will serve me for the present."

Alphonse Carleon looked immensely relieved as he parted with the coin.

"You will not trouble me—you will not ruin me by raking up the past?" he said, almost imploringly.

"Ruin you!" responded Richard Mornington, laughing. "Faith, you did not scruple to empty my pockets; but I will return good for evil, and fill yours, if you will join me in a little enterprise."

"I don't know," Carleon replied, shaking his head. "Here at least I live a quiet life, and am only unhappy when I dream of what I once was."

Richard Mornington stamped his foot, and a dangerous expression stole over his face.

"Listen to me," he cried. "Four years ago, when my father died a penniless man, and my uncle, the general, started me in life with a thou-sand pounds, I fell into your hands. What became of this money?"

"I confess that I had most of it," Alphonse Carleon stammered; "but it brought its own reward—disgrace."

"You can moralise now that you are a drudge," Richard Mornington retorted; "but I should not like to offer you another golden pigeon to pluck."

The Frenchman shrugged his shoulders.

"I have nothing to say," he re-marked; "but what is the use of talking when the evil is done?"

"Again, listen," said the other, striding forward and tapping him on the chest. "When General Morning-ton dies, his son Ralph inherits his estates and fortune. If Ralph Morn-ington should die before he reaches the age of manhood everything comes to me."

"You want me to commit murder?" Carleon cried in horror.

"The words are yours, not mine," Richard Mornington replied. "Fool! Do you think that I require you to shoot, stab, or poison him? Are there no other means? Ralph is the very soul of honour, and were he to be disgraced——"

"I think I understand you now," muttered the Frenchman.

"He would die of a broken heart," Richard Mornington continued. "The general is in India, and will remain there for some years. He thinks that I am in Australia, but he must wonder why I never write to him. Ah, if he only knew where his thousand pounds went."

"I think I understand you now," repeated Alphonse Carleon slowly.

"I am glad you do," Richard Mornington observed, meaningly; "it would be a most unpleasant state of affairs if any misunderstanding arose between us."

"What would you have me do?"

"Use your wits. They used to be sharp enough, but they may have grown a little rusty."

"You are in no hurry, then?" the Frenchman said.

"Not violently so," Richard Mornington replied. "I am down on my luck at present, but I have a few friends who supply me with small sums of money, and if I live they shall have reason to think well of me."

"You must give me time," Carleon resumed. "I cannot think to-night; my brain is in a whirl. Everything is indistinct and unreal, save that I know I am in your power."

"Just so," was the cool reply. "Enough! Good-night. Remember that our interests are mutual. I think I see you again as I saw you once—clad in fine clothes, and with plenty of money in your pockets. Hey, then, for the gaming-table with the merry ivory balls spinning round and making music!"

"Where can I find you?" Carleon demanded.

"Here until further notice. I have fished out the story of this ghostly old place, and I don't think I shall be disturbed."

The Frenchman departed without giving utterance to another word, and no sooner had his footsteps ceased to sound on the old wooden bridge than Richard Mornington stepped to the window, or rather the casement, for it was innocent of glass, and drew aside a piece of sacking.

"Jem Muzzler," he said.

"Right you are," growled a voice from the darkness.

And a beetle-browed, broad-shouldered ruffian, swarthy and repulsive in every feature, climbed over the sill and stepped into the room.

"You listened, of course?" said Richard Mornington.

"I didn't stop my ears with my fingers," Jem Muzzler replied, as he dropped a pistol into his jacket-pocket. "I was on the alert and ready to wing him if he gave any trouble."

"You are a treasure, Jem," the young man laughed. "What do you think of my foreign friend?"

"I think you can mould him like wax and twist him round your finger as easily as I twist this ring," Muzzler answered. "I watched him closely. He is a coward at heart, but he might prove dangerous if driven into a corner."

"Your opinion of him is the same as mine. He shall play the game, and I will take the stakes if he wins. If he loses—— Bah! he must go to the wall. Now for a little rest."

Jem Muzzler blew out the candles, remarking as he did so:

"If anybody saw the light through a chink it will be all over the place that Caleb Carker's ghost is walking again. This is a fine crib. I wonder whether the old hunks stowed any money away here? Now just one word."

"Well, what is it?"

"If your cousin were to meet you, would he know you?"

"No; I was about his own age when we saw each other last, and he was quite a little fellow then."

"That's lucky. Let me put this bit of sackcloth under your head; you'll sleep all the better for it."

And so Richard Mornington, a gentleman by birth and education, slept in the same cheerless apartment with Jem Muzzler, half poacher, half gipsy, and an outcast of society.

CHAPTER VII.

THE MYSTERY INCREASES—RALPH CATCHES LEMON SLEATH IN HIS ROOM —STRANGE CONDUCT ON THE PART OF JACK WALBUT.

THE first post in the morning brought Mr. Stormaway a letter.

The envelope was blue, and creased and crumpled all out of shape.

It was neatly sealed with a piece of soap, bearing the impression of a farthing.

The head-master of Merrytown Abbey felt very much inclined to open this missive with the tongs, or to pitch it unread into the wastepaper basket.

Slowbob happened to come into the room with a cup of cocoa, and Mr. Stormaway improvised the youth's services.

"Open that envelope and hand its contents to me," Mr. Stormaway said. "Don't leave the room just yet. I shall have a few words to say to you presently."

"He's got them radishes on his mind," Slowbob thought as he dropped into a submissive attitude. "Now for a wigging. Cheer up, Timothy, and never let your sperrits go down."

"What are you muttering?" the head-master demanded.

"I was thinking aloud, sir."

"Then think in silence."

"Yes, sir."

It was lucky for Timothy Slowbob that Mr. Stormaway did not observe the exasperating expression on his face as he uttered this dutiful reply.

The head-master took the letter in his hand, and proceeded to unravel its mysteries.

It ran thus :

"HONERED SUR,—This cums hopping you air wel, as don't leeve me at prisint. I puts it to you, sur, that a man as hav' been made a wictim of carn't help his feelin's when riting. Now, honered sur, I don't want to bring disgrease upon any of yure poopils, but I carn't stand havin' tarts heaved at me reckless-like, and I hops you will see that a smawl remoonerat-shon will be given to yure humble sarvent. I'm willin' to forgiv' bein' caught by the leg, wich is paneful.— Anxiousshly waitin' yure reply, I am yures dootifully,
PETER WORRYBOY, P.C."

"This is a base attempt to extort money," said Mr. Stormaway to himself. "I will keep this unique effusion. Remuneration, indeed !"

Here he raised his eyes, and caught sight of the page-boy.

Timothy seemed to be earnestly engaged in examining the beauties of the carved oak ceiling, and became rigid and, as it were, mesmerised under the head-master's gaze.

"Slowbob," began Mr. Stormaway, "I am afraid it will be my painful duty to return you to the parish authorities."

"They wouldn't have me for ever so much," Timothy confessed, candidly. "Salem Cockey said as how the Board of Guardians felt as if cartloads had been taken off their minds when they got rid o' me."

"How dare you address me in that fashion ?" Mr. Stormaway thundered.

"It's them radishes—I know it is," Slowbob pondered. "I'll find somethin' harder for Stickers next time."

"It's my eddication that's at fault," he said, after a pause. "Please sir, if you'll tell me what I am to say, I'll try and repeat it."

Mr. Stormaway twisted himself round in his chair.

"It is useless talking to you !" he cried. "I must try other measures. Leave the room !"

"Yes, sir. Oh, dear me, sir; I had almost forgotten it !"

"Forgotten what ?"

"You are wanted downstairs, sir," Slowbob replied. "There's been fearful goin's on during the night, it seems. The masters are talking all at once, and——"

Mr. Stormaway waited to hear no more.

Pushing Timothy Slowbob on one side, he ran swiftly down the stairs and entered the breakfast-room.

The masters were all there, and the boys stood about in groups.

"Sir," said Mr. Clinton Muffler, advancing to meet his principal, "a most extraordinary thing has happened. The schoolroom was entered last night, and everything upset."

Mr. Stormaway's brow grew as dark as a bank of stormy clouds at sunset.

"Go on," he said. "Let me hear the worst !"

"The maps were removed from the walls and cast down, the ink-stands emptied, your desk was chalked all over with mystic characters, and——"

"Und," chimed in Fritz Halfamann, "more zen half ze poys' pooks vas put up ze shimney. Ach, it is ze most vonderful affaire!"

"It is a most disgraceful affair!" Mr. Stormaway said in a voice thick with anger. "Have you told me all, Mr. Muffler?"

"Not quite, sir," the usher replied, rather nervously. "I regret to say that Stickers cannot rise from his bed."

"Is he ill?"

"No, sir."

"Then what is the matter with him?"

"It is impossible for him to leave his room because he has no clothes to put on," Mr. Muffler replied.

"What!" exclaimed Mr. Stormaway. "No clothes?"

"It is a painful fact, sir. Even his stockings have been purloined."

Mr. Stormaway turned almost as pale as Alphonse Carleon, who was standing near, moody and silent, and apparently thinking of quite another subject than the one under discussion.

"This is really too bad!" the headmaster said.

"Dat's vot I say," the irrepressible German cried. "It's too pad. Mine gootness, vot a ting it vould pe to see zee poys running about mid noddings on! Mine fader vunce lost his preeches; they vas stolen py a man ven he vas pathing——"

"Please reserve your anecdotes, Herr Halfamann," Mr. Stormaway interrupted, testily. "This is no joking matter."

"A choke!" cried the German, elevating his hands. "It is a pad choke for Mistare Stickers. He vill haf to go to ped mit his clothes on when he gets some more, and nevare take zem off."

Mr. Stormaway's mind reverted to Timothy Slowbob.

"No," he mused; "I don't think that even the urchin would dare to play such tricks. The matter must rest for the present," he said, aloud. "Mr. Muffler, you will take my place this morning in the schoolroom. I am going out to consult a friend about this affair."

"What are your commands, sir, with regard to Stickers?"

"I will furnish him with an old suit of clothes of mine, and he must go about his duties as usual."

"*Ach!*" said the little Teuton, as the door closed; "Mr. Stormaway is in a pad temper. Vell, vat vas I saying apout my fader's preeches. They vas lovely ones, prand new, und my fader ven he sees zee man valk off with zem under his arm, wrapped himself in a sheet, and gives zee chase."

"I hope he caught the thief," observed Mr. Muffler, vaguely.

"Ah yees, he caught zee t'ief; und ze t'ief und mine fader haf vun struggle. The t'ief bulls vun vay, and my fader he bulls de oder, and zee pootiful preeches come in two barts——"

"Dear me!" ejaculated Mr. Muffler. "Where were the police?"

"There vas no bolice vere mine father vas pathing," Halfamann replied. "Vell, mine fader fall on him pack mit vun leg of his preeches, und zee t'ief fell town vat you call zee area of a house, mit ze oder leg, and proke his neck."

"A very sad end, indeed," remarked Mr. Muffler, solemnly. "It teaches that honesty is always the best policy."

"Dot's mine obinion," said Halfamann. "If dot barty had not stolen mine fader's preeches he would not have proken his neck. Vot does M. Carleon say?"

"Eh, what?" exclaimed the Frenchman, starting. "Pardon, I was not listening."

"Mine gootness!" Halfamann rejoined; "vat is zee matter mit mine frient? You have zee colour of a dead poy!"

"I am not very well," Carleon replied, averting his ghastly face; "it is nothing—it will soon pass away."

The boys were hungry, and murmuring for their breakfasts, but the appearance of Matthew Stickers put an end to their impatience.

A roar of laughter greeted the man-of-all-work.

The suit of clothes lent him by Mr. Stormaway hung loosely about him everywhere, and as Stickers was fully aware of the figure he was cutting, it only added to his wrath.

"Larf away!" he said. "Prig a man's clothes in the middle of the night and then make fun of him. I'd like to have the dealin' with some of you. Ah, here he is—here's the villain!"

This was Timothy Slowbob, bearing two huge platters filled with slices of bread-and-butter.

The page-boy was radiant with delight, and his peculiar eyes roved about in laughter to such a terrific extent that the spectators feared they would fly out of his head.

"Ain't he a scarecrow?" said Slowbob. "Oh, my, hang him on a tree to frighten birds away. A good high wind would make him look like a balloon!"

Matthew Stickers faced about, and a storm was imminent, when the loud voice of Mrs. Jumble was heard.

"Stickers — Slowbob, to your places!"

It was evident from her tone and manner that the housekeeper did not intend to put up with any nonsense, and the mortal enemies, Stickers and Slowbob, contented themselves with sidelong glances of defiance, and sly kicks when duty called them close to each other.

Mrs. Jumble poured herself out a cup of tea and raised it to her lips.

"Put it down, marm; it's too hot," said a voice.

The housekeeper turned her head and glared at Stickers, who, with his back towards her, was attending to something on the sideboard.

"Mind your own business!" said Mrs. Jumble, sharply.

"I assure you I spoke nivir a word," Stickers returned, meekly.

"You did, I heard you quite plainly," said the lady. "Do not do it again, and above all, do not contradict me when I make an assertion."

"All right, have it your own way; but if I spoke may I be stewed in a saucepan," Stickers muttered.

Mrs. Jumble once more took up the cup of tea and sipped it daintily.

"She knows how to milk and sugar it for herself, don't she?"

This time the voice seemed to proceed from Slowbob.

The housekeeper rose from the table, and sailing down upon the page-boy, boxed his ears soundly.

Slowbob, howling dismally, staggered this way and that way.

He thought Mrs. Jumble had parted with her senses, and as soon as he recovered himself sufficiently to know what he was about, he ran behind Mr. Muffler and implored his protection.

"Oh, sir," he said, "I've done nothing."

"Done nothing!" repeated Mrs. Jumble. "Do you call your impertinence nothing?"

Slowbob had so many sins to answer for, that he came to the conclusion that the housekeeper had raked up some old grudge.

"Well, mum," he said, rubbing his ears hard, "I didn't go for to think that you would set upon me this morning."

"If I hear another word from you I will hand you over to Mr. Stormaway."

"What's come over her?" thought Slowbob, as the housekeeper returned to her place at the head of the table. "They say she's in love with Mr. Stormaway. Perhaps she propoposed to him, and—no, that can't be it. Never mind, I'll be even with her for this."

"I say, Ralph," said Charlie Chadwick, "you heard those voices, I suppose?"

"Most certainly I did."

"It is very strange," Charlie returned; "I am almost sure that neither Stickers nor Slowbob uttered a word."

"Who did, then?"

"That's the mystery."

"Oh, it must have been one or the other of them," said Ralph. "What is the use of bothering one's head over so trivial a matter?"

Charlie looked puzzled, but before he could make any further remarks, the meal came to an end, and the signal was given for the boys to leave the table.

Mrs. Jumble was marching in a stately fashion out of the room, when she came to as dead a stop as if she had run against the wall.

"Fat and ill-tempered!" were the words that had come to her offended ears.

She flung herself round, and almost knocked Mr. Clinton Muffler down.

"Sir!" she cried, bridling up, and turning very red in the face. "Sir!"

"Madame," said the usher, rubbing his hands softly and bowing politely; "can I be of any service to you?"

"Service to me!" Mrs. Jumble almost shrieked. "How dare you insult me?"

Mr. Muffler gazed in speechless bewilderment at the irate lady.

"You must pardon me," he said, after a pause, "but I have not the slightest notion of what you are alluding to."

"Did you not address me in—in a most insolent and unmanly style?"

"I did not," the usher replied, also turning red. "It puzzles me that such a thing could have entered your head."

"And yet the voice was yours—unmistakably yours," said Mrs. Jumble.

"What did you fancy I said?"

This was a question the houskeeper declined to answer, and after flashing an angry glance at everybody, she bounced out of the room.

"Dat goot laty vos not vell," Herr Halfamann observed. "She must take zee physic. Ach! mine grand-moder——"

Mr. Muffler, disinclined to listen to any anecdotes, hurried away, very much perplexed and put out.

"Insolent and unmanly!" he muttered as he reached the schoolroom. "Dear me! Mrs. Jumbles is a good creature, and there was a time—well, well, my income is not sufficient to allow me to dream of such happiness. I fear this ghostly old place is affecting more minds than one."

Everything had been put straight in the temple of knowledge, and the boys took their places as if nothing had happened.

Mr. Stormaway was absent from the schoolroom nearly all the morning.

On his return he called Mr. Muffler to his side, and uttered a few words in so low a tone that they were lost on everybody but the usher.

Mr. Muffler nodded his head gravely, and it being then time to release the boys, he dismissed them.

"There's something in the wind," said Charlie Chadwick to our hero, as they reached the playground.

"What makes you think so?"

"That confab between Mr. Stormaway and Muffler was short, but it means mischief," Charlie prophesied.

"I fancy that the rooms will be searched to see if any fellow has a disguise to play the ghost with," Lakeman said.

"More than likely," Chadwick assented.

"In that case," said Ralph, "I had better run upstairs and clear my trunks of a few things I wish to keep to myself. There is a packet of family letters, and I don't want anybody to read them."

Ralph left his two chums, and in a few minutes had reached the dormitory.

The letters alluded to, our hero had intended to forward to his father's solicitors; but in the hurry of parting with the general, and the excitement of going to a new school, he had forgotten to do so.

Ralph was too honest himself to think of locking even the trunk in which the packet of documents lay, under a heap of miscellaneous articles, for the thought had never entered his head that his belongings would be overhauled.

As he knelt upon the floor and began to fish about, tossing books, garments, and what not hither and thither, he thought he heard a scraping sound proceeding from under one of the beds.

"A rat," he said. "This must be seen to."

The next instant his face flushed with anger.

His eyes had caught sight of the rat—a very large and strangely-formed one.

It was Lemon Sleath.

"Come out!" said Ralph. "What is the meaning of this?"

"Nothing," Sleath whined, as he crawled out on his hands and knees. "I assure you, Mornington, that I was doing no harm."

"I want a proper reply to my question," our hero returned, sternly. "This is not your room, and you have not the slightest right to be in it."

As he spoke he caught the sneak by the collar and dragged him to his feet.

"Oh, don't — don't!" Sleath shrieked. "Please don't tell anybody that you found me here. I'll tell the truth—indeed I will."

He would have grovelled on his knees, but Ralph held him up.

"Well, out with it," said our hero; "and mind you do tell the truth. Wait a minute. Think before you speak."

"I—I was hiding out of Walbut's way," Sleath stammered.

"You are his toady, I hear."

"He makes me fag for him, and uses me cruelly at times."

"Well, I understand that," said Ralph in a kinder tone of voice. "Clear out, and never let me catch you here again, or you will not get off without a tanning."

"Thank you, Mornington," Sleath responded. "You are a kind fellow. I shall always think of this gratitude, and——"

"Get along with you," our hero interposed, snapping his fingers.

Glad enough to get away, Lemon Sleath went scudding downstairs, and Ralph, having possessed himself of the letters, followed.

On reaching the playground he ran up against Jack Walbut.

"Don't apologise. It was my fault," said the bully, mildly. "Have you seen that little beggar Sleath?"

"I saw him some little time ago," was Ralph's cautious reply.

"I wish I could fall across him," Walbut said. "He is skulking somewhere, and I'll teach him that it will not do for me."

With an ill-concealed look of disgust upon his face, Ralph turned away and walked towards his chums.

Jack Walbut called him back.

"Look here, Mornington," he said, twisting his fingers together, "I have something to say to you, but don't exactly know how to say it."

"Take your own time. I am in no hurry."

"Well," Walbut blurted out, "I am sorry that I insulted you—sorry for what I said. The words came from my lips in the heat of passion, but not from my heart."

"I am glad to hear that, at all events," Ralph said.

"I want you to forgive me," Walbut continued. "Will you take my hand?"

"Willingly," Ralph replied. "I did not come here to growl and snarl, or to be growled and snarled at. There," as they shook hands, "all is forgotten and forgiven."

"You have a noble heart," Walbut said. "You knocked me down, and I deserved it. I don't care if the whole school knows what I have said."

"Your confession will never be mentioned by me, at all events," Ralph returned. "Just one word before we part. Be a little kinder to Lemon Sleath."

"I will."

No sooner had Ralph turned his back than Jack Walbut leered, and thrust his tongue into his cheek.

Then his face grew dark and lowering, and crunching the gravel under his heels, he thrust his hands into his jacket-pockets, and slouched into the Abbey.

"Well," said Charlie Chadwick as our hero drew near, "wonders will never cease. Is it possible that you buried the war-hatchet with Walbut?"

"It was his own suggestion," Ralph replied. "What else could I do? He led up to it by asking me whether I had seen Lemon Sleath lately."

Charlie Chadwick rubbed his chin thoughtfully, and Lakeman whistled softly.

"Take my advice and keep your wits about you," Charlie said. "Walbut has an unforgiving nature."

"We had a quarrel," Ralph observed; "it has ended by his offering his hand, and so, please let it rest."

CHAPTER VIII.

THE BLUEBOTTLES BUZZ A LITTLE TOO LOUDLY—BENJAMIN TITE MEETS HIS MATCH.

THE field used for recreation by Mr. Stormaway's pupils lay in a hollow overlooked by the grim old Abbey.

It was as well kept as it was well patronised, and peace and contentment would have made the greensward their home had it not been for the boys of a foundation-school.

The proper name for it was the Jodson's Will, and the boys were known as the Bluebottles, or the Scarlet-runners.

These peculiar nicknames owed their origin to the extraordinary style in which these youths, receiving education for nothing, and sound thrashings when they deserved them, were dressed.

They were garbed in jackets, waistcoats, and inexpressibles of bright blue, studded with startling brass buttons, caps of bright red, tipped with glaring yellow knots of wool.

Each Bluebottle wore upon his breast a pewter escutcheon, and thus it may be said that every boy had his dinner-plate always with him.

The Bluebottles took a delight in hanging about the cricket-field, and shouting out challenges to the Abbey boys, knowing full well that they could not pick up the gauntlet.

To do so would have incurred all the penalties attached to leaving bounds.

A fence to keep the school boys away was elegantly ornamented with tenter-hooks; but they vanished one by one, and when Ralph and his chums reached the field, a dozen of seemingly red-capped decapitated heads were visible.

"Look at 'em," cried one facetious Bluebottle. "They can't get out. They're like monkeys in a cage."

"Stormaway daren't let 'em out too often," observed another. "He is afraid we should lick 'em. Yah! why don't you fight us?"

"'Cause they are afraid," added a third. "Ben Tite would fight the three there, and make no more fuss about it than eating his dinner."

"How long do you intend to put up with this state of things?" said Ralph. "Out of bounds, indeed! Come along, let us clear that lot off, at any rate."

A stack of bean-poles happened to be standing in a corner, placed there by the gardener, and seizing one each, our hero and his chums charged as did their ancestors in the days of Crecy and Agincourt.

Down went the Bluebottles in such a violent hurry that they rolled in a heap on the ground.

"That has settled their hash for a time at all events," said our hero, laughing. "Now then Charlie, bowl away."

But single or double wicket was out of the question.

The Bluebottles, enraged at being dislodged is so summary a manner, first began to hoot and yell, and then to hurl whatever came handy over the fence.

No notice was taken of this procedure, as the missiles flew wide, but at last matters took a more serious turn.

A crunching and rending sound proclaimed that the Bluebottles, driven to frenzy, were endeavouring to tear the fence down.

By this time there were fully a score of the Abbeyites in the field, and they soon congregated in a group.

"There'll be a nice bother about this," Charlie said.

"There will," our hero observed meaningly.

The boys were near the fence now.

Presently a board gave way, and a red-capped head appeared.

Ralph shot out his fist, and the head vanished with marvellous swiftness, and a howl of anguish rent the air.

"I rather fancy that that gentleman has discovered the folly of being inquisitive," Ralph observed, quietly. "Any more wishing for a similar dose? A large stock is kept constantly on hand, and all orders are promptly executed."

A roar of angry voices replied, and another portion of the fence gave way.

"We must put a stop to this," our hero cried. "Follow me, those who are willing!"

Actuated by one impulse, the boys followed Ralph Mornington, and in less than a minute the Abbeyites and Bluebottles stood face to face.

The latter outnumbered the former, having been reinforced by straggling contingents, but no sudden charge was made.

In point of fact, the Bluebottles felt cowed at the determined front their foes maintained, and they hung back, trying to look ferocious and ready for anything, but failed so dismally in the attempt that Ralph burst out laughing.

"A pretty crew you are," he said, "to behave like street-roughs and smash other people's property! Where is your biggest boy? If you have a leader, and he is present, let him show himself."

"Ben Tite—Ben Tite!" cried a dozen voices."

A lanky, loose-jointed youth, with sprawling hands and feet, and towering head and shoulders above our hero, stepped forward with a swagger.

"I'm the captain of Jodson's Will School," he said.

"Are you?" Ralph replied. "Then, Mr. Benjamin Tite, you and I will balance up accounts, unless you like to apologise for what these cads have done."

"Cads!" Ben Tite muttered.

"Certainly," Ralph returned. "Perhaps you are a little hard of hearing, and would like me to repeat my words."

"I heard you plainly enough," said Ben Tite. "Do you want to fight?"

"No, we wish to keep quiet; but if you wish to fight, I have not the slightest objection in the world," our hero replied, quietly.

The leader of the Bluebottles threw off his jacket and cap, and moistened his hands as if he had thoroughly made up his mind for business.

"I expect this will end in an inquest," he remarked, grinning.

"I hope not," Ralph retorted, "for I have no wish to attend as a witness."

Benjamin Tite's long face grew still longer.

He found that he had a plucky lad to deal with, whatever might be the end of the fight.

"You had better get back to your own grounds," he said, as Ralph removed his collar, and tossed his cap to Charlie. "We can meet one Saturday when you are let out."

"There is no time like the present," Ralph responded. "Surely you don't want me to call you a coward to your teeth."

"Oh, I'm not afraid of you, don't think it," said Ben Tite, shuffling his feet uneasily. "I was thinking that we might be disturbed—that's all."

"We had better risk that," Ralph observed.

A ring was formed, and friends and foes, on tiptoe of expectation, mingled freely together.

"Boys of Merrytown Abbey," said Ralph, who was as cool as a cucumber, "I am not in the habit of boasting, but if I do not thrash this big bully, never put any faith in my word again."

This speech, which was received with cheers from the Abbeyites and groans from the Bluebottles, had a marked effect on Benjamin Tite.

He retreated a few steps, and looked at his jacket as if meditating seriously on the policy of putting it on again.

But escape was impossible, and having realised the painful fact, Benjamin Tite filled his lungs with air, set his teeth, and stood ready for the fight.

"You must practise to improve your guard," Ralph said smilingly, as he advanced with his arms at his side. "This will be but a short turn-about, and that is something to be thankful for."

"Take care of yourself, and don't give me so much of your cheek," gasped Tite.

"Time!" cried Charley Chadwick.

No sooner was the word uttered, than Ben Tite, thinking to catch our hero napping, lunged out his left, and then his right.

Parrying both blows neatly, Ralph caught the captain of the Bluebottles a stinger between the eyes, and then closing, threw him heavily.

Benjamin Tite collapsed and went down like a house of cards, and seemed to be in no hurry to get up again.

The Abbeyites went into ecstasies of delight, while the Bluebottles, scowling, shouted out all kinds of advice to their fallen leader.

Looking dazed, and blinking hard, Benjamin Tite again faced his plucky antagonist, but the fight was really at an end.

Dodging a couple of mill-sail attempts to get at his head, Ralph paid a great attention to the upper part of Ben Tite's waistcoat, and the wearer doubling up suddenly like an old fashioned parasol, sat down and opened his mouth to the full extent of its very considerable limits.

"He has had enough!" cried Charlie Chadwick. "Three cheers for Ralph!"

"Don't make so much noise, please, or you will bring Mr. Stormaway down upon us," our hero said. "Lakeman, help me on with my jacket."

Only too willing to render any assistance to so great a champion, Lakeman hastened to comply, and just as Ralph was slipping his arms into his sleeves, Benjamin Tite started to his feet, and struck him a blow upon the cheek.

The coward then rushed away at the top of his speed, with the rest of the Bluebottles trailing at his heels.

For a moment the boys of Merrytown Abbey were so taken aback that they did nothing but stare after the fugitives.

"The mean, contemptible scoundrel!" exclaimed Charlie. "Ralph, I hope you are not hurt?"

"The blow was that of a coward—nervously delivered. We have not done with the Bluebottles yet."

"Hear, hear!" Charlie shouted. "Down with the Bluebottles! Down with the Scarlet-runners!"

The cry was taken up vociferously, and the chase commenced at once.

CHAPTER IX.

MERRYTOWN IN AN UPROAR—A GREAT FALL IN HAM AND EGGS.

THE Bluebottles had a good start.

Fear lent wings to their heels; but on the other hand, rage gave the boys of Merrytown Abbey additional speed.

On went pursuers and pursued in the direction of Merrytown itself.

Surely such a holloaing and roaring had never been heard in the quaint old place before!

Nervous ladies darted into front gardens and crushed down plants by the dozen, and male pedestrians stood gaping, amazed, and at a loss to make out what was the matter.

A choleric old gentleman, adorned in a spotless white waistcoat and shirt-front upon which an ordinary-sized boy might have slept in safety, struck out with a malacca cane at the first contingent of the Bluebottles, and brought several of them to grief.

The Scarlet-runners were runners indeed!

The boys of the Abbey overhauled them perceptibly, and, out of breath, Ben Tite's henchmen rushed into every place that afforded even a temporary refuge.

It is only natural that bluebottles should take to grocers' and butchers' shops, and thus it was that Mr. Chopps and Mr. Sandiland discovered their establishment suddenly invaded by scarlet-capped, red-faced, blue-jacketed, and out-of-breath boys. Mr. Chopps hurled a heap of marrow-bones at his unwelcome guests; while Mr. Sandiland, after overturning a canister of tea—fine young birch-broom Hyson—seized the instrument with which it was his custom to pat butter, and did dreadful execution with it.

Many a youth was the greasier for the manful way in which the irate grocer wielded the patter.

Driven out from both places, they fell into the hands of the Abbeyites.

Short and sharp was the conflict.

The Bluebottles cried for quarter, and it was generously accorded them.

But where was the cause of all this uproar? Where was the worst of cowards, Benjamin Tite?

He was nowhere to be seen, nor had any boy caught sight of him from the moment that the crowd turned into the high-street.

"Where's the perlice?" squeaked a lady of vast proportions. "Hoh! What a start these himps did give me, to be sure. I was just a sayin' good-day to Mrs. Robinson when they come bu'sting round the corner. Hoh!"

"You may whistle for Worryboy when he's wanted," observed a cobbler, who had left his work. "What's the matter?"

Nobody knew exactly, for Ralph and his followers turned a deaf ear to all questions.

"I will find that low fellow Tite before I go back to the Abbey," our hero said. "It is impossible that he can be far away."

"Ben Tite's run away with something from the Abbey," observed a woolly-headed youthful native. "He was always a bad 'un."

"He has done nothing of the sort," Ralph said, "but if you can tell me where he is hiding I will give you half-a-crown."

"I see a boy something like him run into that 'ere back-garden," cried another native.

"Are you sure?" demanded Ralph.

Before he could get a reply, Herr Fritz Halfamann appeared on the scene.

"Oh, mine poys—mine poys, vat is dis?" he exclaimed. "Go pack to zee Abbey at vance, unless you vish Mistare Stormaway to tear his hair mit rage. Gootness gracious! zee poys are mat—everypody is mat!"

Ralph explained the state of affairs to the German, but not comprehending he only shook his head and looked bewildered.

"Vat," he cried, "all you poys after von pluepottle?"

"The bluebottle is a cowardly lubber, who struck Ralph Mornington when he was off his guard," Charlie Chadwick said.

"A poy a pluepottle," returned Halfamann. "It is not bossible. Go pack to zee Abbey, or Mr. Stormaway, vill use zee pirch all zee rest of zee day."

"Here he is," shouted Lakeman. "After him, lads."

Benjamin Tite, who had taken refuge behind a low wall in an

adjoining garden, took advantage of Herr Halfamann's presence, and coming suddenly to light, bolted across the main thoroughfare, and turned into a by-way.

He ran wildly with his head down, and furnished with a new stock of breath, hoped to make good his escape.

Ralph dashed after him.

"Don't hamper me, lads," he cried, turning his head. "This is my affair. I'll bring him back to you when I have finished with him. Stay where you are."

At the corner of the far end of the thoroughfare was a provision-store, and it so happened that P.C. Worryboy was holding an animated argument with the proprietor.

"You're right, Mr. Gammon," he was saying. "I orter have more help. I can't be everywhere at once. Was there ever sich a place for boys!"

Little more was said either by Worryboy or Mr. Gammon for an all-sufficient reason.

Still running with his head down, and only conscious that Ralph was overtaking him, Benjamin Tite drew nearer to the constable, who, not having eyes in the back of his head, was in blissful ignorance of the lanky youth's approach.

"Look out!" shrieked Mr. Gammon.

The warning came too late.

Ben Tite's head took P.C. Worryboy in the small of the back, and cannoning off him, the fugitive continued his flight.

Now when a man is smitten unawares, he invariably grabs at the first object that comes within reach, and Worryboy proved no exception to the rule.

The first thing that attracted the attention of his right hand was Mr. Gammon's button-shaped nose, and for the left, he choose to fasten upon a shelf just above his head.

But neither shelf nor Mr. Gammon's nose was equal to the occasion.

The shelf came down with a crash, as did also Mr. Gammon's nasal organ, bringing its owner with it.

Worryboy, Mr. Gammon, shelf, a whole pile of hams, a dozen of fowls, a selection of pickled tongues, several cheeses, and a quantity of butter came down with a rush and a roar into two huge chests of eggs. They were cheap ones—sixteen a shilling—but, according to a shown ticket, warranted fresh.

After a storm comes a calm, and after that mighty smash there was silence.

Worryboy lay at full length, two prime York hams reposing on his breast, and a broken egg in each eye, while Mr. Gammon, half-concealed with butter, cheeses, and pickled tongues, looked as if he had been the victim of an earthquake.

At last the soles of Worryboy's boots began to quiver.

"Wot's run over us?" he asked, feebly.

Mr. Gammon made no reply.

"Was it a runaway locomotive, or a helephant?" demanded Worryboy.

Still Mr. Gammon was silent.

"I know," Worryboy mused. "It was a gas 'xplosion, and the shop-front is blowed hout."

Then the universal provider spoke up.

"The shop-front is not blown out," he said, "but there's nothing left in it. Oh, Worryboy, this is an evil day for me. It was a boy who caused it all."

"A boy!" roared the constable, scrambling to his feet. "Wait till I clear my heyes, and I'll run him in."

"He is not here to be run in," Mr. Gammon said, sadly, as he also rose. "I saw nothing but his shoulders and the top of a flat red cap."

"A Jodson's Willer!" Worryboy gasped. "Hallo! Wat's this 'orrible smell? A drain's bu'st, surely."

"I am very much afraid," returned Mr. Gammon, as he gazed at the hopelessly wrecked cases, "that the firm who supplies me with eggs wholesale must have made a mistake."

"There's no mistake about it," Worryboy retorted as he turned very pale. "This is too hawful for mortial man to bear."

"I'll fetch you a drop of brandy presently," said Mr. Gammon. "Dear, dear! How I shall put the place straight I cannot tell. And the loss, too! I shall be a couple of pounds out of pocket."

"If," mumbled Worryboy, who was now holding his handkerchief firmly over his nose, " if you deloodes the British public into buyin' them heggs, you orter be prosecuted as the law directs. They're bad raw; wot must they be b'iled?"

"Say no more," said Mr. Gammon. "Walk into my back-parlour, and I will put this matter right. We will talk it over. Worryboy."

"THE OLD LADY GAVE THE MAN OF PORK A STAGGERER."—(See page 84.)

"I see 'em runnin' like mad through the broken fence," Stickers chimed in.

"Let your betters speak," said Slowbob, treading gently upon the man-of-all-work's favourite corn.

Uttering a howl or agony, Stickers aimed a blow at the page-boy.

It missed Slowbob, and took effect upon that portion of Mr. Muffler's anatomy where it is usual to tie apron-strings."

"Oh, this is very painful—extremely painful!" groaned Mr. Muffler. "Mr. Stormaway, pray excuse me. I—I will retire."

In the excess of his wrath the head-master pounced upon Matthew Stickers, and bumped his head against the gate-post.

"That's the way to do it! Let him have it!" said Slowbob. "Serve him right! He's always hitting the wrong party."

The irrepressible youth would have come in for his share of punishment, but he fled to a more peaceful clime, and standing afar off, performed a number of gestures expressive of joy at the downfall of Stickers.

Mr. Stormaway then demanded an explanation, which was volunteered by everybody at once.

"I cannot listen to such a clamour," said the head-master, stopping his ears. "One at a time, please. Mornington, I will hear you first."

Ralph unfolded the story from beginning to end.

"We did not expect to find you here, sir," he said in conclusion. "But we should have informed you why we left the grounds."

"What were you going to do with him?" asked Mr. Stormaway, pointing to Benjamin Tite.

"Give him a fair trial, sir."

"And if you had found him guilty, what would have been the sentence?"

"That, sir, would have been decided by the votes of my schoolfellows."

"A pretty state of thing this!" said Mr. Stormaway, smiling in spite of himself. "Let the boy go. I am aware of the annoyance given by the pupils of Jodson's Will School, and I will make it my business to write to Mr. Pudney, the master."

"Don't do that, sir, if you please," came frankly from our hero. "We would much rather fight our own battles."

"Nonsense!" Mr. Stormaway replied. "Go into the Abbey, all of you.

Stickers, stand upright, and don't look as if you were moonstruck."

"Sir," said Stickers, humbly, "a man with bumps as big as heggs on the back of his head may be excoosed for bein' a little lop-sided."

Mr. Stormaway made no reply to this remark, but turned his attention to Benjamin Tite.

"Go away," said the head-master, "and never let me catch you near my premises again. I grant that my pupils were not justified in taking the law into their own hands, yet you may think yourself lucky to get off so easy."

Scowling and muttering, the captain of the Bluebottles limped away, but not before he had cast a malicious glance from his furtive eyes at our hero.

Mr. Stormaway said no more, but as he returned to the Abbey his lips were wreathed with smiles, and it was evident that he was more pleased than offended at what had happened.

As the shadows of twilight were deepening into night, Mr. Muffler received a message from the head-master to see him in his study.

The usher at once obeyed, and was surprised to find a stranger sitting opposite Mr. Stormaway.

"Mr. Muffler," said the head-master, "allow me to introduce you to Mr. James Swately."

The usher bowed until the tip of his nose grazed the table.

"Mr. Swately," continued Mr. Stormaway, "is an old and valued friend of mine. He takes a great interest in mysterious matters such as are puzzling us just now, and he has kindly consented to share a watch with you to-night."

Mr. Muffler turned very pale, and stammered out something to the effect that he was proud and delighted.

"I knew you would be," the head-master said. "You are a man of nerve and courage, and I have no doubt but that the delinquent will be soon brought to light."

"I—I am sure I will do my very best," the usher gasped.

Mr. James Swately was a tall man, with a thin body, and a very large head full of bumps, suggesting the idea that its owner was in constant collision with door-posts and sharp angles.

He had full eyes, seemingly incapable of moving, and he kept them fixed upon the usher until that unhappy man felt himself growing cold with clammy perspiration.

Mr. Swately had acquired the unpleasant habit of speaking through his long nose, which he made great use of.

When he blew it he produced a sound equal to the trumpet stop of an organ, most startling in its effect to people of nervous disposition.

Mr. Swately also took snuff, which made him sneeze prodigiously.

"Yes, sir," said he, still glaring at Mr. Muffler, "you and I will lay this ghost and silence these strange voices. I am not a superstitious man, but at the same time I do not discredit all theories of the supernatural. Do you?"

"Really I do not know how to reply to your question," Mr. Muffler rejoined, twisting himself about uneasily. "In what part of the building are we to keep our watch?"

"Here," said Mr. Stormaway. "There are two doors, and you will keep them open so you may see if anything ghostly passes on either side."

"I shall be more dead than alive by the morning!" Mr. Muffler thought.

"As soon as the boys are in bed you will join Mr. Swately," the headmaster continued.

"Yes, sir."

"One word of caution before you go. You will not, of course, mention this to anybody?"

"Certainly not, sir," Mr. Muffler replied.

Glad to get rid of Mr. Swately and his eyes, he vanished from the room as quickly as possible.

"It's a dreadful thing to think that I must be in such a man's company all night," he groaned.

The boys had just finished their night lessons as the usher appeared.

"You've got a big fat spider on your neck," said a voice in Mr. Muffler's ear.

The usher started, slapped himself violently on the nape of his neck, and then gazed upon the floor with the view of putting an end to the obnoxious insect.

"It's on the top of your head now," cried the voice.

Bang came the palm of Mr. Muffler's hand upon his cranium.

"It's run down your waistcoat, and slipped into the right-hand pocket."

Mr. Muffler, now behaving like a madman, emptied the pocket, but the spider was not visible.

"Mine frient," said Herr Halfamann, who was preparing to leave the Abbey, "haf you got zee jomps of Saint Vitus?"

"No," Mr. Muffler almost screamed; "there is a spider running about me."

"It isn't a spider after all," said the voice; "it's a mouse—cut off its tail with a carving-knife."

This was going too far.

Mr. Muffler's face burned with anger.

"Who has dared to trifle with me?" he demanded.

There was not a boy near him, nor had anyone heard Mr. Muffler addressed.

"Bless me!" exclaimed the usher, "this place teems with mysteries. I begin to fear that I am going to be unwell."

"Goot nicht," said the German. "Vell, it is vonderful, put I vill not haf mine nerves obset apout zee matter."

"Stop!" cried a voice after him; "your coat-tails are on fire."

Herr Halfamann flung off the garment, and began dancing upon it frantically.

"What is the matter?" Mr. Muffler almost shrieked.

"Mine coat vos on fire—it vas mine pest coat."

"I see no fire—not even smoke," the usher said. "My dear sir, you are labouring under a delusion."

"Then why did one of zee poys tell me dat mine coat vos on fire? Ach! zeeze chokes are very pad."

So saying the German tutor resumed the garment, and departed in high dudgeon.

"These are very strange occurrences," Ralph said.

"Strange!" Charlie Chadwick echoed; "they are enough to scare the senses out of a fellow. We might believe that the ghost was the result of a joke, but who can explain these mysterious voices?"

"It is the ghost that speaks, of course," observed Tommy Toddler.

"Bah! That is too idle a notion to entertain for a moment," Ralph returned. "Well, I dare say everything will be explained one day."

"I begin to doubt it," said Harold Lakeman.

At that moment the bell announced that bedtime had come.

Stickers turned down the lamps suspended over the masters' desks, and was in the act of doing likewise to those giving light to the pupils, when a voice addressed him.

"Stickers," it said, "your end is drawing near. Remember your poor mother, the washerwoman."

Matthew Stickers skipped into the air.

Recovering his self-control, he made a dash for the open door.

A long, gloomy, dark passage, through which the wind was moaning and groaning as if it had lost its way, met his frightened gaze.

"Hif it's you, Slowbob," Stickers said, with a hopeful yet feeble smile, "hown up to it. Come, be a good lad for once, and say it's you."

But Slowbob did not own up to it, for the very good reason that he was eating his supper in the kitchen.

"This beats heverythink," Stickers stuttered. "Ghost a-walking, woices in the hair; the place turned hupside down in a single night. When will it all hend?"

He had scarcely sufficient courage left to turn out the last lamp, but he did it finally, and then fled as if for his life.

CHAPTER XI.

HOW THE WATCH WAS KEPT, AND WHAT HAPPENED.

PRECISELY at ten o'clock Mr. Muffler knocked at the head-master's study door.

On entering the room he found that the lamp was turned down, lending a most goblin-like expression to Mr. Swately's face.

"Mr. Stormaway has retired for the night, I presume?" said Mr. Muffler.

"He has," replied his companion, rubbing his hands. "In half-an-hour we will commence our watch in earnest. Mr. Stormaway informs me that all will be in bed by that time."

"Yes."

Mr. Swately rubbed his hands again, and then took a pinch of snuff.

"Oo—ah—aschew! Whoop—ee—ee!"

The very rafters rang with the echoes of that sneeze, and Mr. Muffler slipped behind a high-backed chair.

"My dear sir," he said, "you will rouse the house."

"Do you think so?"

"I do," Mr. Muffler replied; "and if you will take my advice, you will put your snuff-box away."

"I really could not think of doing that," said Mr. Swately. "I suppose you would have no objection to my sneezing out of the window now and then?"

"If you do," responded Mr. Muffler in an exasperated tone of voice, "you will startle Merrytown, and perhaps bring the fire-engine here."

"I will endeavour to moderate the pinches. Ah!—Ooo!"

"Don't—pray don't!" Mr. Muffler cried appealingly; "the ceiling is a very old one, and I am afraid you will bring it down."

"I will be ruled by you, and take no more snuff to-night," said Mr. Swately; "and to prove that I am in earnest I surrender the box to your keeping."

Mr. Muffler replenished the fire, and sitting down in an easy chair, took up the first book that came to hand.

The choice was an unlucky one, the work being "The Night Side of Nature," and Mr. Muffler dropped it as if the covers had turned red-hot in his grasp.

"That book belongs to me," Mr. Swately said, smiling. "Turn to page two-hundred-and-forty-eight, and you'll find a lovely story about a ghost —— What's that?"

The soles of Mr. Muffler's feet rose slowly as if they were desirous of attaching themselves to the ceiling.

"What did you hear?" he demanded, speaking scarcely above a whisper.

"Hark! I thought I heard a tapping on the wall nearest to you."

"No; dear me, no," said Mr. Muffler.

"Then I was mistaken. What were we discussing? Oh, I know. If you will turn to page two-hundred-and-forty-eight of that most delightful book I brought with me, you will find——"

"Really, sir," interposed Mr. Muffler, "in a few minutes it will be our duty to open the doors, and I do not think that conversing about ghosts will——"

"Listen — there is that tapping again," ejaculated Mr. Swately. "It seems to be under the floor now."

"I heard nothing."

"Well, well, you may be right," said Mr. Swately. "Two nights ago I was troubled with the death-watch, and the ticking sound may have kept its hold on my senses."

"Of all the morbid-minded men I have ever met this is the worst," Mr. Muffler gasped under his breath. "My hair will be as white as driven snow by daylight."

The gong of the clock struck the half-hour.

Mr. Swately rose and threw open the doors.

"Now for the ghost!" said he.

His form cast an appalling shadow on the wall.

The lamp was now turned down to a mere glimmer, and both the watchers maintained strict silence.

As the time went, something heavy and pall-like seemed to have settled upon the Abbey, and enveloped it with a nameless dread.

Mr. Swately sat with his elbows resting on the table, and his face, the lower part covered with his hands, seemed to be all eyes.

The night wind soughed through the trees outside, and screeched up and down the dim old corridors; but at eleven o'clock there was nothing to denote that the ghost was walking.

All at once Mr. Muffler heard so hideous a sound that his hair stiffened on his head.

"Gur—gur—gurg—gurgle!"

Mr. Swately was asleep with his eyes wide open, and snoring like twenty men after supping on pork-chops and pickles.

"Wake up, sir—wake up!" cried Mr. Muffler, who was almost beside himself.

"Gur—gur—gug—gug—guggle!"

"This is too awful!" said Mr. Muffler. "I must wake him, even if I have to use the poker. Mr. Swately —sir! Do you hear? Wake up, sir! You are choking! Your eyes are standing out of your head like—like bell-handles!"

"Matilda," murmured Mr. Swately, "it is wrong to throw the crockeryware about. Curb your temper, my dear. Think of the happy hours of the long past when we sat side by side and watched the sun go down."

"He is dreaming about his wife," the usher said, as he shook the sleeper by the shoulder. "Mr. Swately—sir! Ah—h—h!"

At that moment the lamp went out, and by the flickering light of the fire Mr. Muffler saw a tall figure, clothed in white, stalk into the room.

Mr. Muffler's nerves deserted him now.

He did not fly, he did not shout for help, and, least of all, he did not make a dash at the ghost.

There was a tall cupboard in the study, and Mr. Muffler paid a sudden visit to its interior, and took the precaution to lock himself on the inside.

The keyhole was a large one, and by removing the key the usher had a pretty clear view of as much of the room as was faintly illuminated by the fire.

Running the risk of severe colds and bloodshot eyes he peered in the direction of Mr. Swately.

There he sat, snoring away as if he got his living by it, his eyes fixed and wide open, and his long legs stuck out on each side of the chair.

"He is a fearful creature," Mr. Muffler murmured. "But oh, the other—I saw it with my own eyes."

Fit to faint, the usher sat down on a box.

The lid was thin and it gave way with a crash; but still Mr. Swately slept and snored on.

Mr. Muffler, after extricating himself and mopping his face with his handkerehief, took another peep through the keyhole.

His eye became riveted to the aperture.

Behind Mr. Swately towered the ghost of Merrytown Abbey.

Completely shrouded in flowing garments, with not a vestige of its face to be seen, it stood motionless, as if it had suddenly risen from the floor.

Not even its hands were visible.

The arms were down, and the figure had the appearance of a veiled statue.

Mr. Muffler had not the slighest idea how to act, and the last thing he thought of was leaving the cupboard.

Should he shout, kick at the cupboard, or what?

If Mr. Swately woke up suddenly and found himself in the presence of the spectre, it was only natural to presume that he would either fall in a fit or go mad.

Mr. Muffler became fascinated at the sight that met his eyes—or rather one eye.

There stood the ghost, and there sat Mr. James Swately, sweetly dreaming of Matilda and avalanches of crockery-ware.

Presently matters took a turn.

A long thin hand appeared from the folds of those grave-like garments, and wandered round the top of Swately's head.

Though more than half dead with fright, and the very marrow of his bones freezing, Mr. Muffler laughed idiotically.

Another long thin hand appeared, and then the spectre's eight fingers and two thumbs proceeded to examine Mr. Swately's bumps.

"Let my hair alone, Matilda," he murmured with child-like innocence. "It was hard that I had to cut off my whiskers because you pulled them, and now——"

He awoke with a start and yawned heavily.

"So you have put the light out," he said. "Well, perhaps the precaution was a wise one. Now I dare say that you will say that I have been asleep, Mr. Muffler."

Mr. Muffler said nothing.

Speech had failed him, and he could do nothing but keep his eye at the keyhole and continue to glare at the ghost and the man at the table.

As Swately rose to his feet he happened to take a sidelong glance at the floor, and caught sight of the ghostly robe.

"What's this?" said Mr. Swately.

He followed the garment up with his eyes.

Suddenly he dropped on his knees with a bang and rolled under the table, taking with him the cloth, in which he rolled himself with great promptitude.

Mr. Muffler neither spoke nor moved.

In point of fact he was only just conscious.

The floor seemed to be sinking under his feet, and he knew that unless something happened to remove the strain from his nerves he must faint.

The cause of these dreadful feelings came to the rescue.

The ghost, after wandering a few times round the room—Mr. Muffler thought it was coming through the cupboard once —- stalked majestically out of the door and up the staircase leading to the head-master's sleeping apartment.

Not a word had fallen from Mr. Swately's lips, but spasmodic jerkings of his knees and elbows told to some extent what his sufferings were.

The ghost did not return, and Mr. Muffler at last mustered up courage to creep out of the cupboard.

The first thing to do was to close the doors.

This he did with commendable alacrity, and then relighted the lamp, and turned it up to its fullest extent.

"Mr. Swately," he said, trying to speak calmly.

"It knows me," groaned the man in the tablecloth. "I'm doomed. Farewell, Matilda, my own."

"Mr. Swately," repeated Mr. Muffler in a louder key, "get up, sir. We are alone. The—the ghost has departed."

"I don't believe it," Swately said. "You are the ghost and want to frighten me to death. Go away. I won't look at you."

"It is I—Mr. Muffler. Oh, sir, we have had a narrow escape !"

"Eh—what ?" cried Swately, jumping up. "How do you do, sir ? Shake hands, please. I never was so glad to see anybody in my life. Did—did you see it ?"

"I did," Mr. Muffler replied, solemnly.

"Where were you all the time ?"

"Mr. Swately," said the usher, "silence is golden at times, and we must be silent on our conduct in this matter. You crept under the table, and I hid in the cupboard."

"Agreed," returned the other. "But what are we to say ? We cannot declare that we have seen nothing."

"No ; I have an idea which I think will get us out of the difficulty."

"What is that ?"

"We will go up to Mr. Stormaway's room and tell him that a figure has glided up the staircase."

"Done ! That is a splendid notion," said Mr. Swately.

A moment later his face fell.

"Don't—don't you think it wo—wo—would be better if you went alone ?" he stammered. "I will stand at the door and keep guard with the poker."

"Certainly not ; I refuse to go alone," said Mr. Muffler. "You are the biggest—take the lamp and go first. What if I decline to go at all, and acquaint Mr. Stormaway with the facts ?"

"I go first—I !" cried Mr. Swately. "Pooh—pooh ! No, sir."

Mr. Muffler uttered a groan as he snatched up the lamp.

"Come along, I am callous now. Ha, ha ! I am myself again. If the ghost appears a second time I will hurl the lamp at its head."

Poor Muffler spoke very boldly, but his pallid face and quivering lips betrayed that his stock of pluck was extremely small.

"I—I don't mind following you," Swately said, "but pray be careful with that lamp. It may explode—there, you are holding it all on one side now."

"Better to be blown up than lead a haunted life," Muffler gasped. "Tread lightly. Hush—hush ! What is that ? Hush !"

"I wish that you would not have so much of your hushing. It makes me think that the ghost is coming again."

Up the stairs they went until they reached the head-master's room.

Mr. Muffler applied his knuckles softly to the door.

There was no response.

Mr. Swately, who fancied he heard something moving below, flattened himself against the wall like a "grand-father's clock."

"Dear me," said Mr. Muffler, as he knocked again, "I always thought that Mr. Stormaway was a light sleeper."

"Knock louder, then."

Mr. Muffler did so, and a heavy thud proclaimed that the head-master had jumped out of bed.

In a moment he opened the door, and as he caught sight of the usher's face he guessed the truth.

"You have seen something," he said.

"Yes, sir, we have."

"Where is Mr. Swately ?"

"Here I am," said that gentleman. "Oh, Mr. Stormaway—Mr. Stormaway !"

"Be calm. Come in, both of you, and tell me what has happened."

The head-master slipped on a dressing-gown, and gazed at the trembling pair.

"We have seen the gho—gho—ghost," Mr. Muffler said, sputtering out the words.

"Ah !"

"It went along the left-hand passage and up the stairs. It must have passed this very room."

"What !" cried the head-master, running his fingers through his hair.

"Don't tell me that you did not follow it up !"

"Let me explain," cried Mr. Swately, wildly. "It came upon us so suddenly that we were spell-bound. It held us speechless and motionless. Would you—would you mind letting me out of the front door as quickly as possible ?"

"This is in all truth a terrible state of things," the head-master said. "Mr. Muffler, you saw the figure plainly, I presume ?"

"I did, sir."

"What was its height ?"

"About seven feet, as nearly as I can guess."

"Its face—what of its face ?"

"That I could not see, sir," the usher replied. "Its entire form was covered in a shroud-like garment."

"Fearful !" gasped the head-master. "Did it speak ?"

"It said nothing, sir ; it only stood behind Mr. Swately, and felt the bumps of his head."

"How do you know that when you were doubled up in the cupboard," demanded Mr. Swately indignantly.

"At all events, I did not creep under the table and roll myself up in the cloth," Mr. Muffler retorted.

The cat was out of the bag now, and Mr. Stormaway burst into a roar of laughter.

"Upon my word, this is too ridiculous," he said. "So this is the way you two strong-nerved men keep watch. Ha, ha, ha !"

"I can see nothing to laugh at," Mr. Swately observed. "Sir, you insult me. I will not remain under your roof another minute. Let me out, or ring for your servant and order him to do so."

"Pardon me," Mr. Stormaway replied. "You came for the night, and I will show you into a spare bedroom. You cannot leave until the morning."

"Why not ?"

"Please yourself, then," said the head-master. "The night is pitch dark, and it is raining hard. Perhaps you think that a walk along the dark country roads will do you good."

Mr. Swately thought the matter over, and came to the conclusion that he had better stay.

"I see," said the head-master, casting a glance at Mr. Muffler, "that I must take this matter into my own hands. Had the ghost appeared to me, I would have seen what it was made of."

"You say so now," remarked Swately, "but wait until you do see it. Ugh! there is nothing so horrible in 'The Night Side of Nature.'"

"A trick, sir—an idle joke," said Mr. Stormaway. "Good-night, gentlemen. Ha, ha, ha! One in the cupboard, and the other under the table! Ha, ha, ha!"

"Your mirth is highly unbecoming," said Mr. Swately; "and it is my painful duty to tell you so."

"Don't lose your temper," the head-master rejoined. "I can — ha, ha, ha! picture the scene. Mr. Muffler, I beg of you as a resident here, not to say a word about the cupboard."

"I will not, sir," the usher replied emphatically; "but allow me to say——"

"Oh, pray do not make any excuses. Show Mr. Swately to a spare chamber, where there is room for him to creep under the bed if the ghost should come again, and go to bed yourself as quickly as possible."

Mr. Muffler put on a meek air of injured dignity, but he said nothing more, and hurried his partner in the ghost-hunting business out of the room as quickly as possible.

"Is your room a double-bedded one?" Mr. Swately whispered when they reached the landing.

"No; why do you ask?"

"Because," responded Mr. Swately, "I thought you would be glad of company until the morning."

Mr. Muffler smiled. The remark meant one for himself and two for Mr. Swately, who was in such a state of abject terror that for once his eyes roved to and fro.

"This is your room," said Mr. Muffler, pushing open a door. "Good-night."

"Go — go — good-night!" Mr. Swately gasped; "which is your room?"

"The next one."

"If you feel timid you will tap at the wall, won't you?" said Mr. Swately appealingly.

The usher promised he would comply, and silence reigned again.

Mr. Stormaway had given vent to his mirth in the presence of his assistant and friend, but when he was alone his face assumed a serious and thoughtful expression.

"It is strange," he mused, "that I should dream of seeing this same figure. It seemed to me that it came to my bedside and beckoned me to follow it to a place where a vast treasure was hidden. Truly this is a strange old place, and full of strange occurrences."

He went to bed again and slept so soundly that when he awoke, the bright rays of the sun were streaming through the windows.

Mr. Swately had taken his departure two hours previous, and left a short note to the effect that Mr. Stormaway might solve the mystery of the Abbey ghost himself.

CHAPTER XII.

A LITTLE ENTERTAINMENT.

EARLY in the day a melancholy-looking man, calling himself Signor Glorina, called upon Mr. Stormaway, and begged his patronage at an entertainment, including conjuring and mesmerism, which was to be given in the evening at Merrytown Public Hall.

The head-master of the Abbey was a good-natured man, and took tickets at half-price for the boys and masters.

The ushers looked delighted, and thanked Mr. Stormaway, and the boys cheered him.

Stickers and Slowbob were included in the invitation, but Mr. Stormaway deemed it wise to keep them separate, and commanded the former to find a place in the body of the hall, and the latter to locate himself in the gallery.

Masters and boys sallied forth precisely at half-past seven, Mr. Stormaway complacent and dignified, Herr Halfamann beaming with smiles, Alphonse Carleon moody, Mr. Muffler a trifle limp, and the boys jubilant.

Matthew Stickers and Timothy Slowbob brought up the rear at a respectful distance.

Several skirmishes took place between this pair of worthies on the way to the Public Hall, and during the most serious one Stickers fell down three steps into a greengrocer's shop, and destroyed the symmetry of a pyramid of potatoes, a work of art on which the proprieter had spent a considerable amount of time.

The greengrocer was a hot-headed man, and when Stickers emerged from the establishment he wore a ruffled appearance.

His coat-tails required rearranging, and he had also lost half his collar.

"This 'ere's a plot on the part o' Mr. Stormaway to bring trouble upon me," he said, savagely. "Why should I be doomed to walk side by side with a squintin' wampire boy?"

"Come along, old man, or we shall be too late," Slowbob cried, cheerfully. "Did you think you were turning a corner of the street when you fell into that shop? Bring your spectacles next time, or you'll be knocking down a wall."

"You graceless willin'!" Stickers cried. "Come a little nearer. Only let me get hold of you!"

"We are out for enjoyment," Slowbob returned; "and I am astonished at you. I suppose you'll say I pushed you down the steps."

"You did—you know you did!" Stickers said, making a grab at the page-boy. "Come within reach o' me, and I'll make you see cartloads o' stars!"

"I will not contradict you," Slowbob replied. "I pity you, and I'll bear with you. You will know better when you get older."

This conversation brought them to their destination, and Slowbob lost no time in climbing the gallery stairs.

Seats had been reserved for the masters and boys, and Stickers was escorted to a corner-seat exactly behind an iron column, where he could get no glimpse of the stage without painfully craning his neck.

At eight o'clock a bell rung, and a young lady, in a cloud of cheap muslin, curtseying gracefully, sat down and proceeded to torture and drag out dismal groans from a venerable and long-suffering piano.

Then she began to sing.

When the song was finished, a man engaged, but forming one of the audience, threw a bunch of artificial flowers at the warbler.

Some little sensation was caused by the bouquet hitting the young lady in the face, making her blink and sneeze; but silence reigned when Signor Glorina appeared.

"Ladies and gentlemen," he said, "the first part of this entertainment will consist of a series of tricks, showing that the quickness of the hand deceives the eye."

"All my eye," said a voice close to Stickers.

"The gentleman with the bald head is inclined to be facetious," observed Signor Glorina.

"I'll take my appledavit that I never opened my lips!" Stickers avowed.

"You did!"

"I say I didn't!"

"Silence!" cried Mr. Stormaway.

Signor Glorina having received the money in advance could afford to be bold.

"If that man is your servant," he said, turning to the head-master, "tell him to behave himself, or I'll have him put out!"

"Well, this beats the Seven Wonders of the World!" the unhappy Stickers cried. "Here I've been tryin' to look through three foot of hiron, and nearly chokin' myself to see wot was goin' on, and now——"

At that moment old Stickers brought both his hands to the top of his head, and uttered so terrific a yell that the audience rose to a man.

"Stickers, how dare you? What is the matter with you now?" cried Mr. Stormaway.

"It were a big hard honion from the gallery!" Stickers responded, as he fished up the offending vegetable from the floor; "and if one on the nob from it wouldn't make a man holler out, I should like to know what would."

Mr. Stormaway raised his eyes and gazed in the direction of Slowbob.

That mulberry-clad youth was sitting in the front row, and looking as if butter would not melt in his mouth.

"Is my grand entertainment to go on, or is it not?" demanded Signor Glorina.

"Go on!" shouted the boys.

The rest of the audience took up the cry.

"Let that man have a seat in the front row, so that I can have my eye on him," said the professor, pointing to Stickers.

The man-of-all-work was hustled into the place accorded to him, and sat looking for all the world as if he were waiting for a dentist to draw his teeth.

Something like order was now restored, and Signor Glorina performed a few well-worn tricks.

"Behold !" he said, waving a silken scarf in the air. "You see nothing here, and I have nothing in my hands. From this scarf I will produce two bowls filled with water, and live gold-fish."

"I know how dot is done," said a well-known voice. "Zee powls are under him armbits. Zey are fitted mit india-rupper caps, und he vill slip zem into zee scarf."

"Hush, Herr Halfamann—hush !" whispered Mr. Stormaway.

The German tutor looked up with an expression of astonishment.

"Vat zee madder, sir ?" he said.

"Do not interrupt that man, I beg of you."

"Interrubt him !" Halfamann rejoined. "I do not understand. Not von vord bassed my lips—dat I do declare."

"It seems to me," said Signor Glorina, turning very red in the face, " that this is an organised affair. I did not come to Merrytown to be insulted, but to instruct and amuse."

Mr. Stormaway groaned in his agony.

Again oil fell upon the waters of Signor Glorina's wrath, for P.C. Worryboy entered the hall, and the professor felt a little more reassured.

He went on with the trick, and at the conclusion of the first part of the entertainment received a fair amount of applause.

Police-constable Worryboy took up his station just under the gallery, and leaning gracefully against one of the columns, had a bird's-eye view of the body of the hall and the stage.

During an interval of ten minutes the boys winked at him, and he glared back at them, but presently he found something else to attract his attention.

"Pit-pat," went something on his helmet, and bounded off.

Worryboy took off his helmet, but replaced it immediately as something hard and round tapped him on the head.

"Be quiet, you boys in the gallery !" he roared. "What now ?"

This time something glanced off the bridge of his nose, and cannoned off on to the hat of a farmer.

"It's bits of plaster," said Worryboy. "I must report this. A pretty thing it would be if—— It ain't plaster—it's picklin' onions, as I'm a sinner !"

"Yes," cried Stickers, who overheard the remark ; "I had one just now—a whopper. It was radishes t'other day."

Mr. Stormaway hurried from the midst of his pupils, and slipped up the gallery-stairs, and standing bolt upright in the shadow of the wall, kept watch upon Slowbob.

But he could not detect anything in that youth's demeanour suggestive of mischief.

"No," the head-master mused ; "I am mistaken. There are scores of other boys here, and it would be unfair on my part to put the blame on Slowbob's shoulders."

The bell rang again, and once more the muslin-clad damsel punished the poor old piano severely.

Meanwhile, Signor Glorina had changed his magician's attire for a suit of black.

"He looks like a black-beetle out for a walk," somebody said, just as Mr. Stormaway returned to his pupils.

"If the gentleman who made that remark will step on the platform, I will make him fancy that he is a black-beetle," the professor retorted. "Ladies and gentlemen, mesmerism is a fact, and I am a mesmerist. I do not stand here to make a speech ; but to prove what I say is truth, I invite any twelve of the audience to step up here and learn for themselves the power I hold over the human mind."

There was a rush for the platform, the signor's confederates, of course, being chosen first, and most of the remainder were dismissed to their seats.

"Hold hard, I'm a comin' !" shouted a voice from the gallery.

"It is Slowbob, by all that is horrible !" Mr. Stormaway groaned.

And Slowbob it was.

Deaf to the head-master's voice, the page-boy mounted the platform, and squinted so awfully at Signor Glorina that he took a step backwards.

"What do you want ?" he demanded.

"I want to be mesmersized," Slowbob returned, coolly.

"Mesmerise you !" Glorina exclaimed. "It's impossible to mesmerise a boy with a pair of eyes like yours."

"What's the matter with my eyes ?" demanded Slowbob, indignantly.

"Everything is the matter with them ; they are mounted on swivels."

"Ho, ho, ho !" sniggered Stickers, "His heyes mounted on swivels ! Good ! Bravo ! I'm beginning to enjoy myself."

"I came here to be mesmersized," said Slowbob with great deliberation, "and mesmersized I'll be, if you can do it. Send me to sleep right off at once."

"Go down—go to your seat," Glorina thundered.

"Oh, the bullying dodge won't do for me!" Slowbob rejoined. "Fire away with your mesmersizing. Stickers, old man, come up and have a go in at this."

"Dick," said the signor.

A tight-legged, vicious-looking man answered the call.

"Remove that nondescript in buttons from the platform," commanded Glorina.

"Remove me!" cried Slowbob, striking a pugilistic attitude. "I should like to see him do it. Six like him might. Come on, and I'll mesmersize you with these fists!"

Dick dodged carefully around Slowbob, waiting for an opportunity to rush in, but Mr. Stormaway interfered, and carried his page-boy bodily and kicking frantically from the platform.

"I'll—I'll thrash you until you are sore for a month!" the head-master said.

"Pitch into a poor boy who has done nothing!" Slowbob wailed. "That man can't mesmersize. He's an impostor."

Timothy Slowbob had hit the right nail on the head.

Glorina was an impostor of the rankest description, and in the end only his confederates were operated on.

They went through the usual tomfoolery of pretending to run errands; howled with imaginary pain, and many other things too absurd to record; but the sight pleased the simple-minded people of Merrytown and they voted Signor Glorina a wonder.

At last the entertainment came to an end, much to Mr. Stormaway's relief. He was almost the last out, and was descending the steps leading to the street when he felt a tap on the shoulder.

Turning he found himself confronted by Signor Glorina.

"Do you desire to speak to me?" the head-master demanded.

"Yes, just a word. I should like to have that boy with the swivel eyes if you are inclined to part with him," Glorina remarked.

"He is bound to me for seven years," Mr. Stormaway replied with a groan.

"What a pity!" said the professor. "He would make the fortune of any man in my line. Good-night, sir; I shall never come to Merrytown again while that boy is in your service."

CHAPTER XIII.

A SUPPER PARTY—THE MEETING IN THE STREET.

MRS. JUMBLE and the maid-servants had occupied a sitting-room during the temporary absence of Mr. Stormaway and his pupils, and they hailed their return with manifest delight.

Nothing had been seen, but the furniture had creaked in an ominous style, and more than once a hollow sound, like the thud of a wooden mallet, had been heard from the direction of the cellars.

The boys were hurried off to bed as soon as possible, but Slowbob was told to wait at table, as Mr. Stormaway could not in all conscience send the foreign masters to their lodgings without offering them supper.

Mrs. Jumble remained.

"So," she said, glaring viciously at the page-boy, "Mr. Stormaway tells me that your behaviour has been bad again. What do you think will become of you if you go on like this?"

"I'm dubleous on the subject," Slowbob replied; "but lor, mum! just sit down."

Here the impish youth waved his hands before the housekeeper's eyes.

"What is the meaning of that?" she cried with a little scream.

"That's the way Signer Glowormo mesmersized the fellers on the stage," said Slowbob; "and I was trying to see whether it would have any effect on you."

"Go about your work," the housekeeper commanded.

"All right, mum," said Slowbob, dodging round the table. "I'm sorry to offend you. Ha, ha, ha! I'll mesmersize you yet."

"The boy is going mad," Mrs. Jumble said.

"No, I aint, mum," Slowbob replied. "I was thinking that if I could do the trick properly I'd mesmersize old Stickers, and make him stand on his head for a month."

"You are a bad, evil-minded, vicious boy," said Mrs. Jumble as she left the room, "and if I had my mind, you should not remain here another hour. Clear away the rest of the things, and mind you touch nothing."

"That's a nice thing to say to a poor hungry orphan," Slowbob mused when he was alone. "Oh, I ain't to touch nothing, ain't I? What's this? The leg of a chicken— and here's a Gor—gor—gorgeansalem cheese! I'll have a feed."

The page-boy set to work, but he had not taken half-a-dozen bites when he heard the sound of footsteps.

"I'm caught red-hot-handed," Slowbob said. "What shall I do?"

Quick as thought he blew out the candles and dived under the table.

The door opened softly and somebody tripped on tiptoe into the room.

"If it's the ghost, I'm done for," groaned the page-boy under his breath.

It was not the ghost, but Matthew Stickers who had glided into the apartment.

"Mother Jumble is gone to bed, and that demon boy is away," muttered the man-of-all-work, "so I'm safe enough. I wonder if there's anything left about. The smell o' roast fowls always makes me feel like a halligator."

Slowbob grinned and chuckled to himself as the man-of-all-work struck a match and applied it to two of the wax-candles.

"There ain't much to talk of," Stickers said as he glanced at the table, "but it's better than nothink. Here goes, and if there's a row in the morning that imp Slowbob will get the blame."

"Will he?" thought the youth alluded to. "We'll see about that. Stickers, old boy, I'll send you up the stairs quicker than you came down 'em."

The man-of-all-work drew a chair up to the table and sat down.

"They took jolly good care not to leave a drop o' beer about," he said, "but it's just like 'em—all self, and other people may——"

Matthew Stickers put down his knife and fork.

Horror!

One end of the table had risen and fallen, or his eyes had deceived him.

"I ain't quite myself," the man-of-all-work murmured. "I'm hout o' sorts. Stickers, be a man and don't give way to hidle fancies."

Up went the table again, this time with so violent a jerk that one of the candles fell forward and tapped Matthew Stickers on the bridge of the nose.

Slowbob heard a smothered cry: "The ghost!" and then a violent scramble.

"He's off," said the youth, "so I'll finish my supper. Hallo! He's left his handkercher on the floor. I'll keep it and give it to him in the morning."

Slowbob completed his repast and then sought his couch, perfectly satisfied with himself and the world in general.

Let us now follow the footsteps of Alphonse Carleon.

More like a man in a dream than one awake, he took his homeward way.

His eyes were bent upon the ground, his arms swinging loosely, and his mind was so abstracted that he did not see the forms of two men who stood directly in his path.

"How fares it with you, *mon ami?*"

The Frenchman started as he recognised Richard Mornington and his bosom friend Jem Muzzler.

"I have been waiting for you," Richard Mornington said. "Jem, stand on one side for a moment. I have something to say to M. Carleon."

"Anything to obleege a gen'elman," Jem Muzzler returned with a grin. "Talk away and have done with it. I'm tired of hanging about the streets."

"Well, Carleon," said Mornington in a low tone of voice, "how are we progressing?"

"No progress has been made as yet," the Frenchman replied moodily.

"You have not even made a commencement, then?"

"I have not had the opportunity."

"Bah!" said Richard Mornington. "Don't talk such nonsense to me. No opportunity! Listen to me, my amiable friend. You must make a start soon, or——"

"Spare your threats!" interposed Alphonse Carleon, shrugging his shoulders. "Have you no patience?"

"Very little. Come, you must have thought of an idea."

"I have."

"What is it?"

"Your cousin has made an enemy at the Abbey."

"That is good news. Do you think you will be able to make use of this enemy to serve your ends?"

"Your ends," M. Carleon echoed.

"It is all one and the same thing," Richard Mornington said, laughing. "Answer my question!"

"Yes," the Frenchman replied slowly. "I think I can make use of your cousin's enemy, but it will be the work of time."

"How long?"

"Days for certain, and it may be weeks."

"What is the name of my friend, for so I must call Ralph's enemy?"

"John Walbut."

"I like the name," said Richard Mornington. "What kind of a lad is this Walbut?"

"A bully, a coward, and mean-spirited. I hate him!"

"Hate him!" exclaimed the other. "No; you must like him, and make much of him."

"I hate him as I hate myself," Carleon rejoined. "We are well suited in desires and tastes. Let me go now. I will meet you at some other time when and where you will."

"Then let it be at the Miser's Mill to-morrow at midnight," Richard Mornington said. "*Au revoir!* Stay, just one more word."

"I am all attention."

"Have you any money with you?"

"A very little," Carleon replied. "See," he added, opening his purse and displaying the interior, "here are just ten shillings."

"That's unlucky," said Richard Mornington, as he took the half-crown which Carleon handed him. "But I suppose I must be contented with what I can get. How are you paid—monthly or quarterly?"

Alphonse Carleon hurried away without replying to the question, and Richard Mornington's mocking laughter followed him.

"A poor chicken-hearted fool that," said the villain, as Jem Muzzler stepped to his side. "A man wth the soul of a worm."

"A worm turns when trodden on," Jem Muzzler growled. "Don't pinch him too hard, gov'nor; though you know your own business best, of course. Let's go out o' this. I never was in such a place."

"What cause have you to grumble about it?" Richard Mornington demanded.

"Why, coming down the street I tried every door and window I could reach, and all of 'em as close as nutshells."

Richard Mornington turned about, and shook his fist in the ruffian's face.

"Don't attempt such a thing when you are in my company," he said, "or we shall quarrel."

"Better begin at once," Muzzler retorted. "Tell me, my fine young gentleman, who it is that keeps you going now but—— Ah, you wince and shrink, because you don't like to hear the truth. You'd have starved if it hadn't been for my mate, and mind you are civil to him when he takes up his quarters with us."

"Enough!" Richard Mornington said. "Let us go. Jem, here's my hand, and we will say no more about this."

As they went their way a rotund form appeared from the shadow of a doorway, and a moonbeam sparkled upon the buttons of P.C. Worryboy's uniform.

"This is cur'ous," said the constable; "I couldn't hear 'xactly what they said, but I don't like the look of 'em, so I'll make a note, and mark 'em down as suspicious characters. They spoke to M. Carleon; I wonder what he knows about 'em?"

Worryboy tilted his helmet on one side, and scratched his head.

"I'll keep this quiet as far as the Frenchman is concerned," he thought, "for it may be useful to me some day. Hallo! who comes here?"

Worryboy slipped into the doorway again, and, all unconscious of his presence, the pedestrian approached.

"I shall catch it," he was muttering. "Mariar gets wicious if I'm out after nine, and wild as a Hottentot if the clock's gone ten."

"Salem! Salem! you are late," said Worryboy.

The beadle skipped into the roadway, and, holding his sides, gasped for breath.

"What a turn you gave me!" he said as he caught sight of the constable. "I thought as how it was my

Mariar on the rampage. She's the best woman in the world, but a little fiery."

"Yes," assented Worryboy; "I had a specimen of it when you asked me to supper in a weak moment. I've got the mark o' that flat-iron on my back at this very moment."

"Let bygones be bygones," Salem Cockey said mournfully. "Mariar wasn't in one of her hospitable moods that night, but when she is——"

"I don't think I'll try the 'speriment," observed Worryboy, interrupting him. "Salem, old man, drop in at my house to-morrow. Sinkins is coming, and I want to have a chat with you both."

"What about?"

"Money," Worryboy replied in a whisper; "money, old friend. Hush, not a word, now, but come and see me. Go to bed, and dream that you have thousands. P'raps you may wake one morning and find yourself as rich as Water Cresses, and all through me."

"As rich as what?" demanded Cockey.

"Well, I ain't sure that I've got the feller's name right," Worryboy remarked, "but that don't matter. Fare thee well, Salem, and hif for hever fare thee well."

"He's been drinking," Salem Cockey muttered as he hastened up the street. "This is the first time I ever heered him talkin' about money. Where's it to come from? Ah, home at last. Now for it."

"Sa—le—am, you brute!" shrieked a shrill voice; "is that you?"

"Yes, my love."

The banging of a street door startled the silence of the night, and then came a duller sound, as if a human head had been smitten with a rolling-pin.

CHAPTER XIV.

THREE BOLD FISHERMEN—SLOWBOB GOES MAD.

"No ghost last night," our hero remarked the next morning.

"And a good job, too," said Charlie Chadwick. "I slept soundly until the day-bell rang. What a lark it was last night."

"Jolly!" cried Harold Lakeman, looking up from some fishing tackle he was mending. "Here, I say, who's been at my hooks and tied them all up in a bunch?"

"I borrowed one a few weeks ago," Charlie replied, naïvely. "Going fishing?"

"Yes; I saw some fine roach in the old mill dam."

"Then Ralph and I will go with you."

"Willingly," said our hero; "my own rod is packed away in one of my trunks, and I flatter myself I am no mean hand at the gentle craft."

"Can you throw a fly?" Charlie asked.

"I pride myself on the fact that I can."

"Well, then," said Charlie, "you will stand a chance of getting some good trout. There are whoppers in the stream, and they often lie in the shadow of the pollard willows."

It was a half-holiday, and as soon as the boys were at liberty they left the Abbey and made direct for the stream.

It was a bright and beautiful afternoon, and all nature smiled in response to the rays of the glorious sun.

"The fish are on the feed," said Charlie. "See how they rise. My goodness, there goes a five-pounder, at least. Make haste, Ralph, and let us see how long it will take you to fill your basket."

"The more hurry the less speed," Ralph returned as he singled out an artificial fly. "The stream is very narrow, and I can easily cast to the opposite bank."

Suiting the action to the word, our hero gave his whip-like rod a twirl, and away went the line curling to the other side.

"Botheration!" said Ralph; "my hook has caught in something. This comes of trying to be too clever."

"It has caught in those bulrushes," Harold Lakeman observed.

Ralph tugged gently at first, but, losing patience, jerked the rod vigorously.

"I say, you fellows," he said, turning with a puzzled face to his chums, "there's something alive at the end of my line."

"'COME ON, BOTH OF YOU,' SHOUTED MATTHEW STICKERS."—(See page 87.)

"Nonsense!" laughed Charlie Chadwick; "you are joking with us."

"Indeed I am not," our hero replied. "I have caught something, and if it is a fish it is a monster."

In confirmation of Ralph's statement a sudden and violent commotion took place among the rushes, and a human form suddenly arose."

"Herr Halfamann, by all that is wonderful!" Charlie cried.

"Vat is zis?" the German tutor bellowed. "Pad poy dat you are, you haf hooked mine preeches! Is it not bossible dat I cannot take von leetle nap without suffering zee torments?"

"I am sure I am very sorry," said Ralph, who could hardly speak for laughing; "I had not the slightest notion that you were there."

"Zee hook found me out," Herr Halfamann said as he strove in vain to extricate himself. "Ach! it has given me von bainful brick now!"

"Wait a moment, sir," said Ralph, "and I will cross the bridge higher up. You cannot get at the hook very well, but I will——"

"Look out, sir," exclaimed Charlie Chadwick, "there's a white bull coming towards you!"

"A vite pull!" Herr Halfamann shrieked. "Zen I am a lost man. Oh, mine poys! mine good, pad poys! vat shall I do now?"

"Swim across the stream, sir," Harold Lakeman shouted; "it is not very deep."

"Svim!" the German replied; "I should sink to zee pottom, and zee leetle fishes would tickle me too much."

"Do make an attempt to cross the stream," Charlie Chadwick cried; "the bull is very near you."

"I am a dead man!" Herr Halfamann groaned. "Farewell, mine poys, farewell, mine faderland!"

The bull, a young one, full of play, and probably longing to try his horns, made a rush through the reeds.

The German tutor floundered into the stream up to his arm-pits, and raising his hands above his head, uttered such a German howl of anguish that the bull came to a dead stop.

The animal had never heard anything like it before, and, turning tail, went frisking over the meadow, evidently impressed with the idea that browsing among the sweet grass and hollow parsley was better fun than chasing a German.

"I am vet all over. I vill go pack," Herr Halfamann said.

"Don't," Ralph pleaded; "the bull will run after you again. Come along, sir. The water is not anywhere so deep as to go over your head."

"Vell," said Herr Halfamann, who was puffing and blowing like a locomotive getting up steam, "I vill make von try. Dere is as moch mut as vatare."

Gingerly enough the German tutor advanced, and as the water rose his eyes dilated, and his short hair bristled with fright.

"Keep your mouth shut, or you'll get it full of water," cried Harold Lakeman.

The last word had scarcely escaped from the boy's lips when Halfamann slipped, and down he went, but up he bobbed again like a cork.

"Ach, I am full of zee vatare and zee veeds," he spluttered, "and dat hook is not yet out of mine preeches! Oh, it has got hold of me!"

"Keep your feet, sir!" Ralph shouted, as he ran knee-deep into the stream, and stretched out his arm. "Catch hold, sir, and I'll have you out in a moment."

"It is vary vell to say catch hold," Herr Halfamann gurgled. "I can go no furder; mine feet haf stuck in zee mut."

Ralph advanced boldly towards the struggling German, and contrived to remove him from all possible danger by dragging him ashore.

"Mine poys, I vill go home and change my clothes," Halfamann said, "and to-morrow I vill take von pig-stick and teach dat pull vat you call zee manners."

"One moment, sir," said Ralph. "Allow me to remove the hook. You forget you are taking it away with you."

"Oh, no, I will not forget it; it is too bainful. But if you vill make me von bresent of it," Halfamnan said when he was free to depart, "I vill keep it to remind me of zis day."

"Willingly, sir," Ralph replied.

Away went the German tutor, water streaming out of every garment, and squeezing out of his boots, and leaving a long trail behind him.

"I think I will go back to the Abbey and change," Ralph said. "Stay here, Charlie and Harold; I shall not be absent very long."

Our hero thought it would be bad

policy to overtake Herr Fritz Halfamann, and took a different course.

He had not gone far when he
observed in his path a young man,
poorly dressed, but swaggering as
jauntily as if the whole world
belonged to him.

"A strolling player, most likely,"
Ralph thought. "He seems as if he
wishes to speak to me."

Our hero could not help observing
that but for the stranger's poor attire
and unkempt hair, he would have
passed for a handsome young man.

"You are a plucky youngster," he
said as Ralph drew nearer. "I watched
you pull that lump of sour-kraut out
of the water."

"You mean Herr Fritz Halfamann,
I presume?"

"His name is nothing to me. I hate
all foreigners."

The young man shrugged his
shoulders disdainfully, and snapped
his fingers as he spoke.

Ralph made no reply, and would
have passed on his way, but the
stranger barred the path.

"I suppose you are one of the Abbey
boys?" he said.

"Yes."

"A good school that, I should
think," the stranger observed,
musingly. "Do you happen to know
a lad named Ralph Mornington?"

"You are addressing that self-same
individual," our hero replied, opening
his eyes wide with astonishment.
"Do you wish to say anything to me?
If so, you had better do so while we
are walking. You see I am wet
through to the skin."

"No," the stranger returned. "I
have nothing to say. I heard of you
stopping that runaway horse. There
was more pluck in that than saving a
fat German. Good-day, sir."

Ralph nodded his head, and took
himself off towards the Abbey as fast
as his saturated garments would permit.

"My cousin looks well," muttered
Richard Mornington, for he it was.
"What a fine head and open countenance he has! I wonder what he
would think if he knew who I am,
and what—— Bah! cease talking
aloud."

"Quite right," said Jem Muzzler, as
he leaped from a clump of bushes;
"it's a bad practice, guv'nor, and will
get you into trouble one of these days.
So that's your cousin, eh?"

"Yes. What do you make of
him?"

Jem Muzzler rubbed his stubbly
chin, and crunched a wild flower
under his foot.

"You ask me for my opinion," he
said, "and I'll give it frankly. Boy as
he is, I shouldn't care to face him in a
fair stand-up fight. He carries himself like a young giant."

Richard Mornington tried to look
indifferent, but his face fell nevertheless.

The disreputable pair sauntered off,
and presently Ralph came bounding
back.

"Put up your fishing-tackle and
come back to the Abbey," he shouted to
his chums.

"What is the matter?" [they demanded.

"Timothy Slowbob has gone mad."

There was a twinkle in our hero's
eyes as he made this astounding
assertion, but the other lads did not
notice it.

"Gone mad!" cried Charlie Chadwick.

"Madder than a hatter," Ralph
declared. "Poor Slowbob is more
like a tiger let loose than a human
being. He is raging all over the place
after Stickers, with a toasting-fork in
one hand and a frying-pan in the
other."

Away went the boys at full speed,
and on arriving at the Abbey they
heard a terrible commotion.

"Where is Mr. Stormaway?" cried
Charlie Chadwick, aghast at the
uproar.

"Out of the Abbey, and so are the
rest of the masters and Mrs. Jumble,"
Ralph replied. "Come along, lads;
we must stop Slowbob before matters
take too serious a turn."

Opening a door they scampered upstairs.

"Mur—der!" shrieked a voice.
"I'm sufferin' untold hagonies! 'Elp!
'Elp!"

Bang, bang, bang!

"This way!" Ralph shouted. "The
frying-pan is going to work most
viciously."

A little higher they came to the
scene of the dire tragedy.

On the floor lay Matthew Stickers,
with his face to the boards, and his
legs flourishing wildly in the air.

Over him stood Timothy Slowbob,
firing away with the frying-pan, and
occasionally tickling the man-of-all-

work with the toasting-fork by way of variety.

"Hold!" cried Ralph. "Stop, Slowbob!"

"I won't stop," Timothy roared, squinting ferociously. "I'll baste him until he thinks he is a beef-steak, and then I'll toast him."

"I'm a-dyin', young gen'elmen," Stickers moaned. "The young will'in have smitten me in a wital part. I heerd summot bust jus' now."

"A brace-button," said Ralph, as he picked it from the floor. "Come, come, we have had enough of this nonsense. Put down that frying-pan, Slowbob, or I will play a tune with it on your own head."

"My hour of weangeance has come!" Slowbob shrieked. "Stickers has tortured me too long, and now the last camel has broken the straw's back. Let me get at him!"

Ralph caught Timothy round the waist, and dragged him into a corner.

"Away with you, Stickers," he cried. "Take care of him, chums, until I sooth this savage beast."

"I ain't a-goin' to be soothed by nobody nor nothin'!" yelled Timothy as he struggled to get free. "I ain't myself—Stickers has driven me mad! Yaha! Yohoo!"

The terrific howl with which Slowbob finished up accelerated the movements of Matthew Stickers, and, supported by Charlie Chadwick and Harold Lakeman, he fled to the nearest apartment, and that happened to be the German class-room.

CHAPTER XV.

THE MADNESS INCREASES—A SAFE HIDING-PLACE—HERR FRITZ HALFAMANN RECEIVES A SHOCK TO HIS NERVES—MR. MUFFLER IS CONSULTED.

"Now, Slowbob, what is the meaning of all this nonsense?" demanded Ralph.

"I'll tell you if you'll leave off shaking me up like a bottle of physic," Timothy responded with fearfully rolling eyes and chattering teeth.

"Very well," said Ralph, "let me have the whole particulars."

"The fact is," Timothy began, "that Stickers threw a bowl of water over me, so I pretended to go mad, and I want you to help me to keep up the game."

"I am afraid you are incorrigible," Ralph returned. "For my own part I think that poor Stickers has suffered enough already."

"Not half enough, sir," said Slowbob, grinning. "Just stand aside while I indulge in a wild Hijun howl."

Ralph suppressed his laughter as Slowbob yelled with the whole strength of his lungs.

"That will make him shiver and shake," said the page-boy. "Mr. Mornington, would you mind going into the class-room, and let me have a bit of fun."

"I have no objection," Ralph replied, "but mind you don't go too far. The frying-pan must not be used again."

Slowbob retired a few paces as our hero opened the door.

Stickers, pale to the lips, was huddled up on a form, and Charlie and Harold mounted guard over him with rulers in their hands.

"Where is he, sir? He's mad!" Stickers gasped. "Oh, keep him away from me!"

"Hush!" said Ralph. "Slowbob is a little calmer, and I have persuaded him to retire, but there's no telling when the fit may break out again."

"This is a dreadful state of things," groaned the man-of-all-work. "How I wish that Mr. Stormaway would come back!"

He produced a red pocket-handkerchief, large enough to have done duty as a banner at a school-treat, and mopped his face and neck.

"It's hawful to think on," he continued, "and its a wonder that I'm alive to tell the tale. Are you sure that nothink more than a brace-button bu'st?"

"Quite sure," said Ralph. "Halloa! Slowbob is back again."

"Lock and bar the door!" Stickers shrieked. "Pile all the furniture ag'in it. Mercy! I shall go mad myself if he gets near me ag'in."

"Is Matthew Stickers in there?" Slowbob demanded through the key-hole. "If he is, let him prepare to meet his doom. I shall torture him to death."

Ralph ran to the door and feigned to make it fast, while Charlie and Harold pretended to be much alarmed.

"Come forth, Stickers," Timothy cried. "Come forth, I say, or I'll break the door down."

"Go away," said Ralph.

"I won't go away," Slowbob bellowed. "Stickers is in there, and I'll have him out."

The man-of-all-work clasped his hands and turned his affrighted eyes on Ralph.

"What can I do?" he panted. "Is there no place where I can hide?"

"Only the cupboard," Ralph whispered. "But I fear you would be in a worse plight there than here."

"Then I'm a dead 'un," Stickers said, doubling up suddenly. "Oh, rush out upon him and knock him down."

"Couldn't think of such a thing," Ralph interposed. "I ran great risks before, and cannot undertake to do the same again. Slowbob might bite, you know."

"Bite!" echoed the youthful maniac. "Bite! Ha, ha! Bring out Stickers and I'll eat him, boots and all!"

"I wish we had never interfered in this matter," said Charlie Chadwick. "Stickers is quite big enough and strong enough to take his own part. I vote we escape by the window."

"Which is just twenty feet from the ground," Ralph remarked. "I am really at a loss to know what is to be done."

Bang, bang! went Timothy Slow-fists on the panels.

Stickers skipped behind Ralph and uttered a cry of terror.

"Slowbob," the old man whined, "I'll never do it again. My wages will be due next Saturday and I'll give you the lot."

"Wages— rages— razors —swords— pistols!" roared Slowbob. "Come out and meet your fate."

"Stickers," Ralph whispered, "I have an idea which may serve to help you. Creep up the chimney."

"Up the chimney!" Stickers repeated, aghast at the suggestion.

"It is your only hope, and when you are out of sight I will open the door and let Slowbob in."

"Let him in!" the man-of-all-work moaned.

"Yes," said Ralph, "and when he finds that you are not here he may be pacified and go away."

"Just so," Harold Lakeman remarked, striving to keep a serious countenance. "Now then, Stickers, up you go. It is your only chance. The chimney is wide enough to hold two like you."

"It will be the death o' me," Stickers groaned ; "but I had better be up there than be bitten to death by a mad boy."

And up he went, slowly and painfully.

At last his legs were out of sight, and the three boys rolled about in the excess of their mirth.

"Not a word, now," Ralph whispered up the chimney. "Keep silent and all will be well."

"Now, Slowbob," our hero continued, "we are going to open the door to convince you that Stickers is not here. I give you warning that we are all armed with rulers, and down you'll go if you lift a hand against us."

"I have no wenom for anybody but Stickers, and I must kill him and bury him," Slowbob replied.

The moment the door was open he rushed into the room.

He had rumpled his hair all over his head, and smudged the tip of his nose and cheek-bones with red ink.

In a word, Timothy Slowbob presented a terrific appearance.

"What!" he cried as he dived under forms and desks. "Not here! Where is the old vil'un?"

"Not here," said Ralph, solemnly.

"Where has he vanished to?" demanded Slowbob. "Perhap's he's up the chimbley."

"Oh, lor!" gasped a sepulchral voice.

"What's that?" said Slowbob, striking a tragic attitude.

"Only the wind."

"Good," returned Slowbob, calmly ; "I'll wait here for weeks. Pork-chops and mustard ! I'll not be done out of my rewenge !"

At this moment footsteps were heard on the stairs, and our hero, his chums, and Slowbob slipped out of the room, and got away just as Herr Fritz Halfamann appeared.

The German tutor had come to the class-room to correct some exercises, and sitting down at his desk, he went to work at once.

"Mine gootness !" said Halfamann, aloud, after sneezing violently, "vat a cold I have got. I vill nevare go to sleep on zee banks of zee river again."

Stickers heard the German's voice, but it came to his ears dull and indistinct.

"Slowbob's still there," he thought. "I can't stand this much longer. Murder! the soot's fallen! I'm lorst, lorst, lorst!"

Herr Fritz Halfamann dropped the pen he had been using, and stared with all his might at the fireplace.

"Vat a strange t'ing!" he said. "I vas nearly sure that I heard von voice."

"More soot!" said Stickers. "The hend is comin', I can't hold on no longer."

"Who's dat? Vat's dat?" Herr Halfamann shrieked.

"Don't be 'ard on a man hold enough to be your father," Stickers mumbled. "I'm a comin' down."

To Herr Fritz Halfamann's horror a very thin and exceedingly black leg showed itself in the firegrate.

"Ach!" yelled the German, and flung an inkstand at the protruding limb.

"Mur—der!" bellowed a voice.

Up the leg went again, and Herr Fritz Halfamann, distraught with terror, closed the register of the fireplace, and then dashed out of the room.

"It vas a purglar!" he cried, as he went down the stairs three at a time. "T'iefs! Purglars! Mine poys, Mistare Stormaway — everypody! Dere vas t'iefs in zee shimney!"

Across the playground he ran, shouting at the highest pitch of his voice, and in a few moments he was surrounded by a score or more boys.

Mr. Muffler appeared on the scene, and Herr Fritz Halfamann literally flung himself into the usher's arms.

"Mine goot frient Muffler," he cried; "you are von prave man. It s'al be for you to make zis t'ief a brisoner."

"What thief?" demanded Mr. Muffler.

"Dare is von t'ief in the shimney of mine class-room."

"Is there?" stammered Mr. Muffler. "Dear me! I—I think I will go in search of Mr. Stormaway."

"Here he comes," cried a chorus of boys' voices, among which was blended the warbling of the gentle Slowbob.

The page-boy had made himself presentable, and was now enjoying the fun immensely.

Mr. Stormaway was fairly staggered at the news.

"Where is Stickers?" he demanded. "A burglar in the Abbey. Oh, horror! Stickers! Stickers!"

For a very simple reason the man-of-all-work did not answer to his name.

"Slowbob," Mr. Stormaway continued, wildly, "find Worryboy and tell him to come here with all speed. Tell him briefly what is the matter, and impress upon him the necessity of bringing his handcuffs with him."

"He always carry his handycuffs in his pocket, sir," Slowbob said, as he dashed away. "I'll bring him back with me in a quarter-of-an-hour, if I have to carry him."

CHAPTER XVI.

THE BURGLAR IS BROUGHT TO LIGHT, AND MEDICAL ASSISTANCE IS CALLED IN.

MASTERS and boys went in a body to the class-room.

Mr. Stormaway led the way boldly until he reached the door, and then his movements became less lively.

"If the villain makes a rush at me," he said, "I call upon you to aid me."

"We will!" cried all.

"He may creep up ze shimney, but he cannot come down," Herr Halfamann observed. "I vas vary moch frightened, but I had zee bresence of mind to bull down zee register of zee stove and fix him ub."

"I owe you a debt of gratitude," Mr. Stormaway said, warmly, and evidently much relieved. "We had better do nothing until the constable arrives."

At this moment the unhappy prisoner rattled his heels on the register.

"Let me hout!" he cried; "I'm bein' choked up here! Let me hout!"

"Certainly," said Mr. Stormaway, grimly; "you shall come out presently."

A puffing and blowing announced the arrival of Worryboy.

Staff in hand, he ran up the stairs with the delighted Slowbob close on his heels.

"Where is he?" roared the valiant officer. "I ought to be promoted for this 'ere job."

"There," Mr. Stormaway said, pointing to the fireplace. "Your prisoner is there, Worryboy, and you will please arrest him without delay."

"He may have a weppin' with him, such as a rewolver," Worryboy remarked. "I'd better show that we are ready to deal with him. A large fork tied to a broomstick would come in handy."

"I'll fetch 'em," Slowbob cried, delighted.

Away went Timothy in ecstasies, and presently returned with the weapon, the very sight of which turned Mr. Stormaway cold.

"Now for it," said Worryboy. "One of you hoist the register up, and I'll give him just one prod to show him that we don't intend to stand any nonsense."

Matthew Stickers heard voices, but could not get at their meaning.

His own opinion was that Ralph and his chums were engaged in a fearful struggle with Slowbob, but his powers of endurance were limited, and, come what might, he longed to get clear of the chimney.

"It's better to die hout in the hopen hair than in a place like this," he said. "I can't get down, but I may be able to get up."

Pressing his knees and elbows against the sides, he hitched himself up just as the register was raised.

"Come down, will you!" roared Worryboy, applying the fork.

Matthew Stickers did come down, and so suddenly that the constable had not time to dodge the descending feet.

His helmet was bashed over his eyes, and thinking that he had been smitten with a life-preserver, he struck out right and left, flooring Mr. Muffler and Herr Fritz Halfamann.

The scene that ensued beggars description.

Herr Halfamann and Mr. Muffler lay as flat upon the floor as if a cannon-ball had upset them; P.C. Worryboy continued to play a frantic game of blindman's buff in his battered helmet, and Stickers flung himself into the arms of Mr. Storm-away, and completely smothered him with soot.

The boys set up a shout, and Timothy Slowbob, unable to restrain his feelings, leaned against the wall, and gave vent to howls of unearthly mirth.

Mr. Stormaway released himself from Stickers by afflicting him sorely on both sides of the head, and it is probable that as the man-of-all-work fell over a form, he thought that the class-room was performing a waltz.

"This—this is most villainous!" the head-master cried as he cleared his eyes, and gazed at his blackened shirt-front. "Stickers, pack up your boxes and leave the Abbey at once."

"Wait till I get out of this 'ere 'elmet, and I'll run him in!" Worryboy groaned in a muffled tone of voice.

Somebody helped him out of the difficulty, and boiling over with fury, he advanced upon the half-dazed man-of-all-work.

"Get up!" Worryboy thundered. "I mean to have the law of you, so it is no use lyin' there and blinkin' like an howl."

By this time Herr Halfamann and Mr. Muffler had picked themselves up, but such was not the case with Matthew Stickers.

He lay perfectly still, smiling idiotically, and it soon became evident that he had fallen into a maudlin state of mind.

"Cockey!" he said, feebly, "two 'arf-pints don't orter hupset a man in this way. Give me your arm, old friend, and when we gits to the Habbey gates give me a leg-up. I'm late, but Mister Stormaway is hout, so it don't matter."

"Good gracious!" cried the head-master, "this poor fellow is ill. See him to bed, Mr. Muffler. Slowbob, run for Dr. Pillem at once. This is really too much for my nerves."

"It vas too much for zee pack of mine head," chimed in Herr Halfamann. "I vas all plack and plue, and to-morrow I s'al be all pottle creen."

"Pooh — pooh! you are not hurt," said Mr. Stormaway, who was almost beside himself. "Raise Stickers up, Mr. Muffler. Take his arms and I will take his legs."

Still murmuring, the man-of-all-work was carried to his room, and Dr. Pillem was soon in attendance.

"Aha!" said the learned gentleman "The man is perfectly sober; this is a case of sunstroke—a very slight one, but sunstroke, without a doubt."

"Where's Slowbob?" Stickers murmured. "Is he in a loonatic asylum yet?"

"There, there, my good man," Dr. Pillem returned; "you must be quiet. I will soon put you on your feet again."

"Doctor," Mr. Stormaway whispered, in a voice hoarse with emotion, "what can we do for this poor fellow?"

"The treatment I prescribe is very sure. Two mustard-poultices—one on the nape of the neck, and one on the brow."

"They shall be prepared at once," said Mr. Stormaway, and away went Mr. Muffler to the kitchen.

"Where's Slowbob?" Matthew Stickers demanded in a louder key.

"If," resumed Dr. Pillem, "my patient will persist in talking, I shall have to order a dozen leeches in the place of the poultices."

Stickers shot out quite straight, and then turned his eyes upon the head-master.

"I axes you a simple question, sir," the man-of-all-work said. "Where's Slowbob?"

"Downstairs."

"Is he sane now?"

"As sane as he ever was."

"Oh!" Stickers ejaculated, as he drew up his knees with a jerk. "As sane as he ever was? Good! Ha, ha! I've got summat to say on that question to-morrer."

"Quite so," said Mr. Stormaway. "Oh, here is Mr. Muffler."

"I regret to say that there is not an ounce of mustard in the Abbey," said the usher.

"Glad to hear it," Stickers remarked. "I'm goin' to sleep straight orf. Leave me alone. I don't want no mustard, and no leeches, and no boy Slowbob. Mr. Stormaway, I will tell you all about this to-morrer."

"I think we had better retire," said Dr. Pillem. "Sleep is nature's sweet antidote for most maladies."

When Matthew Stickers was left alone, he sat up in bed, and stared round the room.

"It ain't a wision, and it ain't a dream," he said. "Why didn't I hout with it at once? Slowbob is——"

That youth pushed the door a few inches open, and inserting his graceless nose, answered to his own name.

"Don't come near me!" Matthew Stickers cried. "Keep orf, or there's no knowin' what I may do."

"I have something of yours," Slowbob returned, advancing into the room. "It's only a hankercher which you left on the floor when you found that leg of a fowl too tough."

Matthew Stickers groaned, and turned his face to the wall.

"Oh, what a hass I ham to place myself in the power of this himp!" he said.

"Of course you won't say that I hunted you up the chimbley?" Slowbob continued. "Keep my secret, and I'll keep yours."

"This is too hawful!" gasped the man-of-all-work.

"The sunstroke idea is a good one, and you must stick to it," Slowbob resumed. "Here's your handkercher—no, I think I'll keep it a little longer. You'll be better to-morrow, old boy."

Timothy Slowbob departed as quietly as he came, and Matthew Stickers lay for some time like a man in a trance.

"Mustard-poultices and leeches ain't nothink to this," he said at length. "I'm caught in my own trap, and all through that drumstick of a fowl, with a hounce of meat on it. Yes, Slowbob, I'll keep your secret; I'll lock it in my breast, but beware o' me! From this moment Matthew Stickers is your mortial foe!"

<hr>

CHAPTER XVII.

WORRYBOY'S DREAM OF WEALTH—THE OLD MILL AT MIDNIGHT—MISER CARKER'S GHOST.

As evening advanced, peace once more reigned within the walls of Merrytown Abbey.

Consoled with two half-crowns, P.C. Worryboy went about his business.

Stickers was found to be much better, the boys were sent to bed, and

Mr. Stormaway repaired to his study, and proceeded to soothe himself with a glass of good port.

The sun had disappeared, but night was loth to come.

Mr. Stormaway had not as yet sought the aid of artificial light.

He sat pondering and half dreaming of things that had happened in the Abbey during his time, and naturally enough his thoughts reverted to the past.

There were many stories connected with the old building.

Mr. Stormaway knew them all, but one often found a place in his mind, and this was the case just now.

When Bluff King Hal pillaged the monasteries, Merrytown Abbey did not escape the rapacious monarch's notice ; and in the dead of one wintry night, the friars were driven from their home to seek shelter as best they could.

All but one contrived to get away with their lives.

The missing monk was Father Hislem, a devout and beloved man.

He disappeared mysteriously ; none could tell whether he died at the hands of the oppressor, or whether he took to the cells, and made good his escape when the scene of pillage came to an end.

At all events he was never heard of again ; and as time went on, some wiseacre put about a rumour that Father Hislem had died miserably in a cottage hard by the scene of his peaceful life, and that just before his end he declared that his spirit would haunt the Abbey so long as two stones of it held together.

This legend never failed to interest Mr. Stormaway.

He pictured the friar's despair and rage when strange feet echoed through the dim mysterious rooms and corridors ; he saw him driven forth after a sturdy resistance, and heard the bitter cry that burst from his lips as he sank at the feet of the herdsman, who consented, at the peril of his own life, to give him shelter.

The purple shadows fled, and others more sombre took their place.

Thought begets slumber, and Mr. Stormaway, after nodding a few times, began to snore.

He dreamed that Father Hislem appeared, and bade him rise.

They went out into the night, across the darkened meadows, through narrow lanes, until the mournful sound of rushing water mingled with the wind.

The friar pointed to a black shapeless building, and lo ! it suddenly became illuminated with a ruddy light, and an old hump-backed man, appearing at an upper window, cast a sackful of gleaming gold into the air.

Gold it was, but it fell lightly, fluttering here and there, until it floated upon the bosom of the turbulent water.

"Miser Carker's mill and Miser Carker's treasure," said Mr. Stormaway in his dream.

Then he awoke with a start.

The clock was striking eleven.

"Bless me !" said Mr. Stormaway, as he rubbed his eyes and yawned ; "how foolish of me to fall asleep here ! I will go to bed at once."

Without troubling himself to get a light, he crept softly upstairs and reached his room.

"It was a strange dream," he murmured when in bed. "Miser Carker's mill and Miser Carker's treasure. I wonder what could have put such an idea into my head."

Just about this time, Worryboy, Salem Cockey, and Jeremiah Sinkins, the parish clerk, sat in a back room of the police-station.

Their heads were very close together, and they conversed in whispers.

An air of mystery was upon all three, and Salem Cockey, who was as white as the ceiling, paid particular attention to an oil-lamp that manifested a strong desire to go out on the slightest provocation.

"I tell you," said Worryboy, "that there's thousands of pounds hidden in the old mill, or buried near to it. I'm not a greedy man, so I have brought you two here to ask whether you will help me find the money. I have everything ready—pick, mallet, spade, lantern, and matches."

Salem Cockey coughed dubiously behind his hand.

"It's gettin' late," he said, "and my Mariar, the best woman in the world, but a little peppery at times, ain't in one of her best moods."

"Wot's a little bother at home to the chance of making yourself a rich man for life ?" Worryboy rejoined, contemptuously. "If I was a married man, I'd jolly soon find out who was master."

"Would you?" queried Salem. "I wish you would try it. Drat the lamp! It's burnin' blue now."

"Keep on turnin' it up," said Worryboy; "the ile ain't good. Well, Sinkins, wot do you say about goin' to the old mill?"

"I'm with you," Jeremiah Sinkins croaked, passing his hand over his long, wrinkled face. "I can read what is in friend Cockey's mind."

"What is?" demanded the beadle, with a spasmodic kick under the table.

"Old Carker's ghost!"

"No, no," declared Salem.

"Yes, it is," persisted Jeremiah Sinkins. "Ghost! Bah! Follow my calling, and you will soon get that sort of nonsense knocked out of your head. How often have I gone to the church in the dead of night—yes, and down in the vaults, too, and I have never seen anything worse——"

"Than yourself," interposed Worryboy, smiling.

"Worse than a fat, over-fed, over-officious policeman," said Jeremiah Sinkins, firing up.

"Come, come," said Salem Cockey, "don't let the 'armony be spiled by a few hasty words. That's what I often say to my Mariar, one of the best women in the——"

"Oh, bother your Mariar!" Worryboy said. "Sinkins, your 'and. The man as can't stand a joke ain't fit to sit among his fellers. Them's my sentiments, and I sticks to 'em."

Peace being once more restored, the original topic was discussed, and at last it was arranged that a start should be made for the Miser's Mill without delay.

Worryboy furnished the implements for digging, and Sinkins and Cockey concealed them under their cloaks.

"I shall catch it—I shall catch it!" the beadle moaned to himself. "Wisions of Mariar sitting up in a nightcap arise before me. I can see her a comin' downstairs with the rushlight in one 'and and a short brush in the other; but lor! how she will smile if I goes home with my pockets bu'stin' with gold."

It was scarcely likely that the explorers would meet with any interference on the way to Worryboy's Tom Tiddler's Ground, as the presence of the constable would not only disarm suspicion, but put to flight any night-prowlers who might be about.

Through the silent street they went, and into the open country.

The night was as dark as pitch, and not a glimpse of the Miser's Mill did they get until they were within a few yards of it.

"Now for a light," said Worryboy.

He drew the slide from his lantern, and a ghastly glare fell upon the ruinous old place.

"What would my Mariar say if she could see me now?" muttered Salem Cockey, with chattering teeth.

In his fright he dropped the pickaxe, which, falling upon some stones, raised such a clanging that Worryboy recoiled, and trod upon Jeremiah Sinkins's corns, causing that worthy to say things more "frequent and free" than polite.

"Do that ag'in, Cockey, and I'll knock your head off!" Worryboy gasped.

The beadle having apologised, all three crossed the rotten wooden bridge, and entered the mill.

"There's two chambers, and we're in the lower one," said Worryboy as he set the lantern down on the floor. "Carker lived and slept in this. We'll commence by tappin' the walls to see if we can find a holler place."

"Holler!" moaned Cockey. "If I don't holler presently I shall have a fit."

Jeremiah Sinkins undertook the duty suggested by the constable, and, mallet in hand, began to bang the old wooden-cased walls.

"Here's something like a cupboard," he said. "Cast your eyes here, and you'll see where some nails have been puttied and painted over."

"Let me look!" Worryboy cried, excitedly.

He did look, but not for long.

Scarcely had he poised the lantern on high, when it was dashed from his hand, and he received a staggering blow under the chin.

Salem Cockey and Jeremiah Sinkins fared no better.

The former was doubled completely up by something that acted with as great effect as a battering-ram, while the latter was smitten heavily in the ribs, and sent flying on to his back.

There was a sound of hurried footsteps, and then all was still.

"Mariar!" Salem Cockey said, feebly. "Mary—i—ar! What—yes—no. I ain't at home! Worryboy—

Sinkins—don't let me perish. Pertect me from a wiolent end!"

The individuals appealed to had quite enough to do to think of themselves.

Slowly they picked themselves up, and reeled to and fro. Dark as it really was, fanciful lights flitted before their eyes.

"Who put the lantern out?" demanded Worryboy at last. "Cockey, was it you?"

"Was it me?" the beadle almost howled. "Me—I—me as was hit in the weskit by a beam o' timber. The mill's fell on us—that's what's the matter."

"It ain't," said Worryboy as his faculties grew clearer. "O—o—old Car—Car—Carker's sperrit did it. I ain't afraid—n—not a bit, but outside is good enough for me."

Putting his words into practice, he made a dash at the door.

It had been left open when the constable and his friends entered, but now it was closed as far as one rusty hinge would allow it to be so.

Again was Worryboy afflicted. He struck his nose and chin against the obstacle.

With a yell of mingled terror and pain, he kicked the door open, and dashed across the bridge, with Salem Cockey and Jeremiah Sinkins literally treading upon his heels.

Shortness of breath prevented them from uttering cries.

About fifty yards from the bridge they encountered a tall figure stalking towards them.

It was enveloped in snow-white garments, and was fully six feet high.

"Miser Carker's ghost!" Worryboy cried. "Oh, Cockey, we are dead men!"

"I'll speak to it," said Jeremiah Sinkins, who was by far the bravest of the three.

"Don't—don't!" pleaded the constable. "If it speaks its wery breath will injure us."

"I will, I tell you," Sinkins said, "Speak!" he cried, aloud. "Who and what are you? Why do you come in such a form, and what do you seek?"

"My gold—my gold!"

The words sounded hollow and sepulchral.

This was enough.

The three searchers for the hidden treasure fled, each taking a path of his own.

The constable was fat, but he ran like a hare; Sinkins skipped over fences and other obstacles in a manner that would have smitten the heart of a trained athlete with envy; and Salem Cockey, casting aside his official hat and gown, became positively elastic in his endeavour to reach the haven of his domestic bliss.

He did a double knock with his head at the door, and sinking upon the step, uttered the one word that had so often soothed him in the hour of trouble—"Mariar."

"I'll Mariar you," exclaimed a dulcet voice. "Twice this week you have kept me up, and——"

The rest of the words were drowned by a sound as if the amiable lady were preparing a tough steak for the grill, and in less than two minutes the beadle's wife had annexed sufficient of her husband's hair wherewith to make a pin-cushion.

CHAPTER XVIII.

TOMMY TODDLER'S WHITE MICE—A SCENE IN THE SCHOOL-ROOM—THE 'MYSTERIOUS BAGPIPES.

THE Matthew Stickers affair blew over in less than twenty-four hours.

Mr. Stormaway insisted on the man-of-all-work being quiet; Mrs. Jumble, whilst almost kind to him, kept at a respectful distance lest another attack of sunstroke should come on; and Dr. Pillem sent him a bottle of medicine, which if taken would have weakened a horse.

The physic, however, found its way to the dust-hole, and Stickers, free from duty for one day at least, wandered forth, pipe in mouth, to visit a few old cronies.

The boys were putting their books away after the morning lesson, when Tommy Toddler hurried upstairs, and returned with a square box covered with a well-perforated paper.

"Hallo, Toddler, what have you there?" demanded Ralph.

"It's a secret," Tommy replied. "If any fellow wants to see what is in this box he must pay for peeping."

"I declare it is something alive," said Charlie Chadwick, as he and a few other lads gathered round. "Now then, Toddler, take off the paper and let us have a look."

"Guess first."

"Beetles?" said one boy.

"A squirrel?" said another.

"A puppy?" ventured a third.

"All wrong," said Tommy Toddler, grinning.

"I have it," our hero exclaimed; "white mice!"

"Right you are," said Tommy. "White mice they are, and beauties, too. A boy was passing the Abbey gates with them this morning, and I struck a bargain with him for sixpence."

"Where are you going to keep them?" Ralph asked. "White mice are not quite the sort of things for a dormitory."

"I have arranged all that," replied Tommy, his round face expanding with delight. "Slowbob is going to keep them and feed them for a penny a week, and I shall give some of my leisure time to training them."

"What for?" queried Harold Lakeman.

"To make them do all sorts of tricks."

As Tommy Toddler spoke he removed the paper, and revealed three white, fluffy, red-eyed little things peering about a wire cage in search of food.

"Just look here," said Tommy, as he lifted the door of the cage. "They are almost tame now. Oh!"

That mischievous young rascal, Charlie Chadwick, shot his arm under Ralph's, and tilting up the cage released the mice, and away they scampered over the floor.

"I didn't mean to do it, really," said Charlie. "Don't make a fuss about it, Tommy; here is sixpence for you to buy some more."

But Tommy Toddler refused to be comforted. He sat down on a form and took the matter so much to heart that he shed bitter tears.

"Never mind," said Ralph, patting him on the back, "I'll buy you three white rats. They are bigger than mice, you know. Don't make a milksop of yourself."

"I can't help it," Tommy blubbered;

"Char—Charlie is always doing something to me; but I'll be even with him, see if I am not."

"That's right," said Ralph, consolingly; "when you get the white rats train them to bite him."

Tommy took the sixpence and dried his eyes, but continued to threaten Charlie Chadwick with all sorts of dire punishment.

A search was made for the white mice, but not a trace of the little animals could be discovered.

Tommy Toddler sent Slowbob out for six-pennyworth of almond-rock, most of which he devoured before dinner, and not only spoiled his appetite, but suffered such qualms that he forgot all about the loss of his pets before the bell summoned the boys back to their tasks.

Masters and boys were soon in their places, and then commenced that droning sound peculiar to a schoolroom.

There is nothing like it in all the world, and it can only be heard when a number of boys are conning their lessons with the watchful eyes of the schoolmaster upon them.

Herr Fritz Halfamann's desk was in a shady corner of the room. It was furnished with a green silk screen in front, as the German's eyes were none of the best, and it was here that, when his services were not called into requisition, the good-natured Teuton often nodded and dozed peacefully.

The weather was warm, and Herr Fritz Halfamann was sleepy.

He had but one class to examine that afternoon, and as that would not occupy his attention for an hour, he thought that a short nap would be no sin.

Drawing the screen close, he dropped his round head upon his arms and closed his eyes.

But sleep was denied him. Something tickled the back of his neck.

"It vas von pluepottle!" said Halfamann, taking out his handkerchief and whisking it in the air. "Whoosh! Pouf! Fly away, leetle fly, and come again anoder day."

Again did the German call Morpheus to his aid, but with no better result.

No sooner was his head down, and his hands spread upon the desk, than something tickled his knuckles.

"Dese flies haf de spirits of zee

poys," he muttered. "Mine gootness gracious! vhat's dot?"

Two red, fiery little eyes were peering at him from behind the ink-stand, and Halfamann, after remaining petrified with fright for a few moments, snatched up a heavy ruler and flung it at the intruder.

Instantly the red eyes vanished, but the noise made by the ruler, combined by the fact that it flew across the room and shaved the top of Mr. Muffler's head, brought Mr. Stormaway quickly down from his desk.

He expected to find the German seized with a sudden attack of illness, but he only found him looking into the inkstand.

"Are you in your right senses?" demanded the head-master. "In the name of law and order, what do you mean by flinging a ruler about during school-hours?"

"I flings him at zee t'ing mit zee eyes ov fire," Halfamann replied. "He vas all vhite everyvhere else, and him had four lecs, and von tail."

Little dreaming of white mice, Mr. Stormaway stood perfectly still, and actually trembled as he looked into the Teuton's dilated eyes.

"You are labouring under some delusion," he said. "Herr Halfamann, you had better go home at once and to bed. And," he added, a little nervously, "if — if you ever repeat this conduct, we must part. I —I hope to find you in a better frame of mind to-morrow."

"We most bart!" repeated Herr Halfamann. "Mistare Stormaway, I know vat you t'ink, but zee peer dot ve haf here vill not haf zee effect of making mee see zee leedle red eyes. No, no. Dere it is again!"

"Where—where?" cried Mr. Stormaway.

"You vill find him under dose papers," replied Herr Fritz Halfamann, as he skipped from his stool. "There vas two of him."

"This wretched man sees double," Mr. Stormaway groaned. "Was ever a man tortured as I am? Sit down all," he thundered, as the boys began to mount the forms; "I will cane the first boy that I see out of his place."

Mr. Stormaway proceeded to remove the books and papers with which the top of the desk was piled, and he had almost reached the bottom of the heap when out popped two white mice.

One took to the floor, but the other took refuge up the head-master's coat-sleeve.

If Mr. Stormaway had an aversion to anything, it was to mice.

With a cry of horror he started back, tore off his coat, and flung it wildly from him.

The garment, after hovering sportively in the air, descended and enveloped Mr. Muffler's head in its folds, to the dismay of the gentleman so suddenly deprived of sunlight.

But the mouse, wise in its generation, had not remained in the coat-sleeve.

It had sought a safer clime by running down the head-master's back.

Mr. Stormaway felt the crawling and scratching of the little creature, and danced about as if a growth of red-hot nails had suddenly sprouted from the floor.

Almost beside himself as he was, commonsense came to his rescue. He could not undress himself in the school-room, and pale with fright and rage he hastened from it, banging the door in such a way that the diamond-shaped panes of glass in the windows rattled in their leaden settings.

Ere he left the room, Tommy Toddler had fled, and Charlie Chadwick, knowing what the end would be, sat as motionless as a statue.

Some minutes passed before Mr. Stormaway returned. Between his finger and thumb he dangled the now defunct mouse by the tail.

"Who brought this into the Abbey?" he demanded.

Not a voice replied to this question, but the head-master, angry, and placed in a ridiculous position, was not to be denied.

"I ask again, who brought this creature into the Abbey?" he cried in a voice that made many a youth tremble.

Mr. Stormaway very seldom allowed himself to get really angry, but when he did, it meant "Come—prepare," to the offender.

"Oh, sare," said Herr Halfamann, endeavouring to make peace; "zee leedle vhite mice may haf come in by zee vindow."

"Silence!" the head-master shouted. "I will know the truth of this, or punish every boy."

"Bunish every poy!" said the German, lifting his hands. "Vot, for von leedle mice! Let me peg of you, sare——"

Mr. Stormaway turned upon Herr Halfamann in a manner that completely silenced him, and he returned to his desk, shaking his head, and bewailing the fate of "zee poys," of whom he was really fond, and for whom he often smoothed matters over when they promised to take a disagreeable turn.

"Call the roll, Mr. Muffler," said Mr. Stormaway, hoarsely, "and let every boy be questioned. Should there be no confession, the guilty boy will go about with a lie branded on his tongue."

These were strong words; and Mr. Muffler, feeling that it would be a treat to sink through the floor, commenced his distasteful task, while Mr. Stormaway went to his desk, and producing a new cane, bent it to suppleness.

"I—I do not see Thomas Toddler," Mr. Muffler stammered.

"Indeed!" said Mr. Stormaway. "I saw him when I first entered the room. Let him be found at once."

"Charlie," Ralph Mornington whispered across the desk, "put an end to this."

"I will," Chadwick replied, rising. "Mr. Stormaway, I have something to say. The white mice would not have escaped but for me. Toddler is not to blame, though he has run out of the room."

"Who owns the mice?" Mr. Stormaway demanded.

"Toddler, sir; but I knocked the cage over."

"Come this way," said the headmaster. "Mr. Muffler, find Toddler without delay. I will flog him for bringing such vile, evil-smelling things as mice into the Abbey, and Chadwick for his participation in the affair."

"Please let me take the whole of the punishment," Charlie pleaded. "I am perfectly willing to do so, as I am alone to blame."

"Bravo!" cried a voice close to Mr. Stormaway. "That is the sort of boy England should be proud of."

The head-master turned sharply round, but nobody was near him save Alphonse Carleon, whose parted lips and gleaming teeth showed that he had no sympathy with the culprits.

"The voices again," Mr. Stormaway said, pressing his brow. "Is this a house for the demented? Are these delusions catching like a fever?"

At this moment, and just as Mr. Muffler returned with Tommy Toddler, whom he had found shivering on the staircase leading to the dormitories, the wild screech of bag-pipes rang through the school-room.

"Stop that noise at once!" cried Mr. Stormaway. "How dare any itinerant musician pass the Abbey gates without my permission!"

Herr Fritz Halfamann opened the window and put out his head.

"Man mit zee pagbibes, go avay!" he cried.

"I won't go unless you throw me a penny," a voice responded.

"What does he say?" demanded Mr. Stormaway, throwing down the cane and darting across the room.

"He say dot he vill not go unless a benny is t'rown to him!" replied Herr Halfamann.

"I will soon see about that," said Mr. Stormaway. "Stand aside, please, and let me speak to him."

The bagpipes ceased as the headmaster thrust his head and shoulders out of the window.

"You impudent fellow!" he cried; "I will send for the police and have you imprisoned unless you go away immediately. Where are you?"

"On the roof," was the astounding reply.

At this moment the bagpipes struck up afresh, and Mr. Stormaway, staggering back into the school-room, stared in mute bewilderment at Herr Halfamann.

"If zee man mit zee pagbibes is on zee roof, how did him get there?" queried the German.

"That is more than I can tell," Mr. Stormaway rejoined. "The fellow must be a mad Highlander."

On went the fiendish music at a furious rate, and the sound certainly seemed to come from the top of the Abbey.

"Stickers may have left the garden-ladder against the wall," Mr. Muffler suggested. "Perhaps we "—he laid a great emphasis on the "we "—"had better go out and see for ourselves."

"Stickers is a born idiot, and the pest of my life," Mr. Stormaway said in an exasperated tone of voice. "Well, this man shall find out to his cost the penalty of climbing like a cat about my premises. Where is Slowbob?"

"Catching white mice," responded a voice close to his ear.

"That was you!" said Mr. Stormaway, turning to the nearest boy.

"No, sir ! Oh, sir—no, sir ! " cried the youth addressed, with a wary eye upon the head-master's uplifted hand. "I assure you I did not open my lips. The voice seemed to come through the wall."

Mr. Stormaway seized his hair as if he were trying to lift himself off his feet, and then stopped his ears with his fingers, for the shrieking of the bagpipes was truly terrific.

He dashed from the room; Mr. Muffler and Herr Halfamann followed in hot haste after him, but M. Carleon kept his seat and his gaze upon Ralph.

"Let us go too," our hero said. "It is plain to me that there will be no more school to-day ; and, moreover, Mr. Stormaway may require our assistance."

This suggestion was received with acclamation, and Jack Walbut would have joined the rest, but the French master called him back.

"A word with you," Carleon said. "I have taken much notice of you lately, and I desire to ask you a question."

"Yes, monsieur."

Jack Walbut's eyes sought the floor as he spoke, and he seemed to know that some important subject was about to be discussed.

"My question is this," said Alphonse Carleon. "Tell me, is your friendship with Ralph Mornington sincere or only pretended ? "

"It is real," Walbut replied, hesitatingly.

"It is not," the Frenchman said. "Bah ! why do you try to deceive me when I can read your innermost thoughts ? You hate Ralph Mornington—you hate him bitterly, and would do him an injury if it lay in your power."

"Oh, monsieur ! " Walbut exclaimed in accents of alarm, " if you have really the gift of reading my mind, be merciful to me. I——"

He ceased speaking ; but the Frenchman laid his hand on the boy's shoulder, and bade him proceed.

"I must confess that I hate Mornington," continued Walbut, slowly. "On the very day of his arrival he knocked me down, and the boys who used to fear me, now——"

"Laugh at you," said Carleon, filling up the sentence.

"Yes, monsieur ; they laugh at me, and my life is a misery."

Alphonse Carleon smiled, and his eyes glittered with a baneful light.

"You like the game of chess, I understand ? " he said, after a pause.

"Yes, monsieur."

"If you and Ralph Mornington were playing a game, do you think you could check-mate him ? "

"I would try my best to do so."

"Good ! " said Carleon. "I, too, am fond of chess. I will speak to Mr. Stormaway—I will compliment you on the way you do your exercises, and I will ask his permission for you to spend an evening at my lodgings for a game of chess. You understand ? "

"I think I do, monsieur."

"I will try to make you understand," Carleon said. "I do not like Ralph Mornington."

Jack Walbut started and turned pale, but the Frenchman quieted him with a touch of his snaky fingers.

"I do not like him, Walbut," he said, "because I think that you were unjustly used. Mornington is against you in his heart ; the boys are against you, but I am with you. Is that not more than sufficent for you to wish for the game of chess with me ? "

"Yes, monsieur."

"Again," said Carleon, "you have a confederate."

"A confederate, monsieur ? "

Alphonse Carleon laughed aloud.

"Have I not told you that I can read your innermost thoughts ? " he said. "Is it not, then, only feasible that I shoud know your friends ? There is a boy here named Lemon Sleath. He is your friend and confederate. Now go away and say no more on the subject until I refer to it again. That I will do soon—when we play our game of chess."

"WORRYBOY RAN THE BARROW, WITH STICKERS CLINGING TO IT, INTO A CROWD OF PEOPLE.—(See page 95.)

CHAPTER XIX.

THE HIGHLANDER ON THE ROOF—GREAT FALL OF WORRYBOY—CONSTERNATION AND TABLEAU.

OUTSIDE the Abbey a number of faces were directed towards the roof.

No longer the sound of the bagpipes rent the air, but as it was discovered that no ladder had rested against the wall, Mr. Stormaway came to the conclusion that the Highlander must have stolen upstairs and crept through one of the fire-traps—a modern invention which had been added to the building under the head-master's direction.

"Perhaps him creep up zee shimney like Stickares," Herr Halfamann suggested. "A man in vat you call zee kilts vould find it easy vork."

"I cannot accept that theory," Mr. Stormaway observed. "The fellow is either daft, or—well, I don't know what to think. One thing is certain : we must have him down, and as quickly as possible."

"I think I saw something flit past the big stack of chimneys," said Mr. Muffler.

"It was only the shadow of the poplar-tree," said Mr. Stormaway. "Ah ! Here is Slowbob. Has Stickers returned ? "

"No, sir," the page-boy replied, "and I'm much afeared that he will have another fit of sunstroke before night."

"Stay there ! said Mr. Stormaway, paying no attention to Timothy's alarming prophecy ; "I may want you to go to the police-station."

"No need for that, sir," Slowbob remarked. "Here's Worryboy trying to get his head through the gates."

"Let him in," Mr. Stormaway said, adding under his breath : "The man is an ass at his best, but his uniform carries weight."

Worryboy was admitted, and with visions of more half-crowns floating before his eyes, he saluted Mr. Stormaway respectfully, and listened intently to the story of the Highlander.

"I'll believe it when I see it," said the constable, "and not afore."

"But we all heard the bagpipes," Mr. Stormaway rejoined.

"No doubt apout dot," chimed in Herr Halfamann. "Dere is no music so horipple in all zee world as zee pagpibes."

"Except a German band out of tune," said a voice very much like Worryboy's.

"Mine frent zee constable vill do vell to leave zee Sherman pands alone," observed Herr Halfamann, hotly. "Mistare Worrypoy is fond of plowing his own drombet."

"Fond of blowing my own trumpet ! Wot if I am ? " Worryboy cried. "Who's gone and upset you ? "

"Leave zee Sherman pands alone ! " said the Teuton, still ruffled, "and you may plow your own drombet until you purst. Und look here ! " he added, "if you insult mine nation again, I vill smite you in the zee blace vhere you puts your pread and peer."

"He's like the rest on 'em," Worryboy muttered, as he sought shelter behind Mr. Stormaway ; "one 'arf mad, and t'other 'arf don't know a green gooseberry from a helephant."

"Constable," said the head-master, "there is a man—Highlander or no Highlander—on the roof of the Abbey, and he must be secured at once."

"Just so, but who's to do it ? "

"You, of course. Fetch the ladder and ascend to the roof at once."

"Me go up ! " said Worryboy. "Do I look like a man that can crawl about the tiles like a cat ? "

"Mr. Muffler and Herr Fritz Halfamann will render you every assistance," the head-master observed ; "and I—I will stand below to catch the poor fellow if he should happen to fall."

"I am vary moch opliged to Mistare Stormaway," the German remarked, "but I vould rader haf mine feet on zee ground. Mine head goes rount and rount when I look down from von height."

"I experience similar sensations," Mr. Muffler said, hastily. "I don't think I ever climbed a ladder in my life ; and if I did——"

"You vould preak your brecious neck," Halfamann interposed.

In despair Mr. Stormaway slipped half-a-sovereign into Worryboy's hand, and the constable's demeanour changed immediately.

"I'll do it," he said. "Shove the ladder against the wall. I'm speaking to young mulberry there."

"Shove the ladder against the wall

yourself," Slowbob retorted, indignantly.

A compromise was effected by some of the boys volunteering, and Slowbob then consented to lend a hand.

"Couldn't you contrive to give the bobby a poke in the back?" he whispered to Ralph. "It would soothe my feelings to fetch him a bu'ster. Young mulberry, indeed!"

Our hero shook his head and refused to take part in the page-boy's scheme.

The ladder was soon adjusted, and Worryboy prepared to ascend.

"You'll understand," he said, looking round when about half-way up, "if anybody hollers out it will be me, but I'm not afraid."

At this moment the bagpipes commenced again, and then Worryboy went up hand over hand.

"I'll make him sing another tune when I lays hands on him," he growled. "'Arf-a-suvrin ain't bad business to start with. Now then, stop that row and come along o' me."

The last sentence was addressed to the player of Highland music.

Worryboy reached the parapet and climbed on to the roof.

In so doing he loosened a portion of cement with his heel, and Herr Fritz Halfamann received a piece about the size of a dinner-plate on the crown of his head, while Mr. Muffler was stung to madness by a smaller portion alighting on the bridge of his nose.

"It was the boliceman dot fell on me," said Herr Fritz Halfamann, whose faculties were considerably muddled for the moment. "Good gracious! vot vill habben next?"

"Stand clear all!" Mr. Stormaway shouted, as another shower of cement and rubbish came rattling down. "Bless my heart! this is positively blinding! Worryboy! Worryboy!"

"Hallo, there!" the constable shouted back.

"I must ask you to be more careful."

"More careful!" Worryboy gasped. "I'd rather be on the brink of a wolcano than up 'ere! Oh, lor! the tiles are giving way with me."

This was a painful fact. Worryboy was exceedingly corpulent; the tiles were old, and refused to bear his weight.

The cry of a horror-stricken man rent the atmosphere.

A pair of legs, cased in blue, flourished wildly in the air for a moment; and then with a sound like a clap of thunder a portion of the roof gave way, and carried Worryboy with it.

"He's gone," said Herr Fritz Halfamann, calmly; "and py dis time he is on his pack in von of zee pedrooms, and berhabs through zee next floor."

"Wretch!" cried Mr. Stormaway, wildly. "How dare you trifle with a fellow-creature's misfortunes!"

The head-master was in the act of rushing into the Abbey when a shout arose from the spectators.

"'Ere he is," cried Slowbob, joyfully; "and as white as a miller. My heye! ain't he picked up some beautiful cobwebs! Hooroar!"

"I'll—I'll hurrah you!" Mr. Stormaway hissed. "Begone, boy, before I forget myself, and—and positively torture you."

P.C. Worryboy had fallen into the aperture between the roof and ceiling, and beyond being scared out of his senses had sustained no damage.

Covered with bits of plaster and cobwebs, he crawled out, and sat panting on the parapet.

His helmet was gone, and so was the skin from the tip of his nose.

"Take me to a 'orsepital," he moaned. "I've had a ton of tiles on my back, and a beam across my chest. Both my legs are broken, and——"

"Look oot, I'm after you, mon! I'll finish you off this time!" cried a voice in strong Scotch accent.

It was really wonderful to see how Worryboy used his broken legs.

Skipping to his feet, he trotted along the parapet with the agility of a tight-rope dancer, and throwing his legs across the ladder slid down in the style that boys delight in.

Then up rose Mr. Stormaway, no longer to be trifled with, and climbed the ladder.

Ralph, Charlie, and Harold followed, and Mr. Muffler, thinking that he must do something, picked up half-a-pound of cement, and flung it wildly at the stack of chimneys behind which he supposed the Highlander to be hiding.

Mr. Muffler's intentions were good, but his aim was bad.

The lump of cement took Mr. Stormaway in the small of his back, and nearly caused him to relinquish his hold of the ladder.

"Slowpop could haf done petter dan dot," Herr Fritz Halfamann remarked. "Vhen I haf time I vill tell you von story apout a man who did throw a prickpat at mine fader vhen he vas stoobing down to tie his pootlaces."

"Your—your father is a perfect nuisance," retorted Mr. Muffler, who was horror-stricken at what he had done. "Mr. Stormaway, I meant to hit the stack of chimneys and dislodge the fellow."

"The next time you throw at the chimneys, aim at me, and perhaps you will have better success," said Mr. Stormaway, grimly. "Now, boys, we will have the Highlander, bagpipes and all."

But, alas for the head-master's hopes! no Highlander was to be seen.

It would have been some comfort to capture even the bagpipes, but those ear-torturing instruments were also conspicuous by their absence.

"This is the most remarkable thing I have ever experienced," said Mr. Stormaway, as he looked into the hole in the roof made by Worryboy.

"It certainly is very strange," Ralph observed.

"Strange! It is bewildering—maddening!" Mr. Stormaway returned. "What in the name of all that is wonderful can I do to solve these mysteries?"

"Well, sir," said Charlie Chadwick, running his fingers through his hair, "we know that the Abbey is haunted, but who ever heard of a ghost playing bagpipes!"

"It is idle to discuss the matter," Mr. Stormaway replied. "We can do nothing but go down again. The roof must be repaired at once, as yonder cloud promises rain. Dear me! These things will make me ill."

No sooner were they on *terra-firma* again, than Worryboy confronted the head-master.

"You'll come down handsome for this, sir, I s'pose?" he said. "Think o' my suff'rin's. Think o' the time it will take me to clean this noble uniform."

Mr. Stormaway groaned inwardly as he took his purse from his pocket.

"Here is another half-sovereign," he said; "and I ask you as a favour to keep this matter quiet. I have an idea of my own concerning it, but if the people of Merrytown—and they are superstitious, as you know—were to hear the story, they might come in crowds, and disturb such peace as is left in the place."

"Just a word, sir," Worryboy rejoined, stepping aside.

"Well, what is it?"

"There's more than one ghost in Merrytown. Don't you go near the Miser's Mill after dark."

"Why?" demanded the head-master.

"Because," replied Worryboy, in a blood-curdling whisper, "last night as I was on dooty I saw Caleb Carker's speckleter."

"Spectre, you mean! Nonsense!"

"No, sir; it ain't nonsense. Salem Cockey and Jeremiah Sinkins saw it too," Worryboy said. "This is a hawful place, and when my suppleintendent comes round I'll ask him to remove me. Good-day, sir! When the bricklayers are here they can find my 'elmet and send it round. I wouldn't go on that roof ag'in for the Koo-oh-lor daimint!"

Herr Fritz Halfamann and Alphonse Carleon left the Abbey at an early hour; Mr. Stormaway and Mr. Muffler shut themsleves up in their respective studies, and the boys were left to do as they liked.

CHAPTER XX.

STRAWBERRIES-AND-CREAM—A SLIGHT DISTURBANCE—THE LARGEST STRAWBERRY OF THE LOT—A REMARKABLE DISCOVERY.

WHEN the tea-bell had ceased ringing, and Mrs. Jumble took her place at the table, she noticed that several boys were absent.

The housekeeper took down the names of the absentees, who were Ralph Mornington, Charles Chadwick, Harold Lakeman, Thomas Toddler, and Dick Heron.

Those five youths had taken them- selves out of bounds, and instead of regaling themselves with such frugal fare as bread-and-butter and tea, they were siting at their ease at Merrytown fruit-gardens, and enjoying strawberries and cream.

"I call this jolly," said Tom Toddler, stretching out his legs and rubbing his waistcoat. "What stunning strawberries—what lovely cream!"

"Will you take some more, sir?" asked a pretty serving-maid, with cheeks as rosy as the ribbons of her cap.

"Thank you, I will," Toddler replied; "and don't forget the powdered sugar."

"Have a care, Tommy," said our hero, warningly. "That will make your fifth plate."

"A peck of strawberries wouldn't do a fellow harm," said Toddler, with a knowing air. "I should like to come here every day."

Just then four young dandies, employed in a drapery shop, strolled in, and took seats next to the Merrytown boys.

Opposite to them was a fat farmer, and his no less fat wife, with two raw-boned sons and three strapping daughters.

"Four stwawberries-and-cweams," one of the dandies lisped. "Annie, you look perfectly charming to-night. Weally and twooly you do."

The attendant knew her customers, and having served them and taken the money, went her way.

"I thay, Sappy," said the young man who had first spoken, "isn't Annie a pretty girl?"

"Vewy."

"A feller might do worse than marry her, you know."

"Marry a servant!" cried Mr. Sappy. "Oh, horror!"

The farmer threw a glance of scorn at the dandies, who were trifling with their spoons and trying their hardest to look like men of fortune.

"Shut up, you scissors and tape lot, will you!" said a voice like the farmer's. "We came here to enjoy ourselves, and not to be worried by a parcel of apes."

"Chappies, did you hear that?" Mr. Sappy demanded.

The chappies, not being deaf, could not help hearing every word, and they endeavoured to stare the farmer out of countenance, but he went on puffing at his pipe as if he were at peace with all the world.

"I thay, old gentleman," said Mr. Sappy.

"What now?" rejoined the agriculturist in a voice like distant thunder.

"You ought to apologise to us, you know—you ought indeed," said Mr. Sappy in quavering accents. "We are the last fellows in the world to quarrel, but when you call us a scissors and tape lot, it's a little too strong."

The farmer put down his pipe.

"If I said a word I'm a double-barrelled Dutchman," he exclaimed.

"But, my dear chappie——"

"Don't chappie me," growled the farmer.

"Well then, my dear sir."

"That's better."

"We all heard you," Mr. Sappy continued.

"Go away!" said the farmer's wife, bridling up; "and the next time I come to your master's, just see that you give me full measure."

"Ha, ha, ha!" laughed Ralph and his chums in unison.

"Be quiet, you boys," said Mr. Sappy, holding up a walking-cane, "or you will compel me to thrash you!"

Our hero was on his feet in a moment, and Mr. Sappy took a step backwards.

"What will you do?" Ralph demanded. "Come, sir, a joke is a joke all the world over, but you may find that one may be carried too far."

"We decline to be laughed at," said Mr. Sappy, growing pale.

"You should not make yourself ridiculous," Ralph retorted.

"Hear, hear!" cried Tommy Toddler. "I'm short, and don't know how to box much, but I'm game to have a go at one of those mashers. And," added the pugilistic youth, "I'd mash him like strawberries!"

As he spoke, he selected a fine berry, and cast it at Mr. Sappy.

The delicious morsel struck the dandy between the eyes.

Everybody laughed now, except the dandies.

"Weally I must meet this insult with its deserved punishment," said Mr. Sappy, as he rolled up his coat-cuffs slowly—very slowly.

"No, you won't," roared the farmer. "You came here to kick up a bother, and upset everybody's comfort. Joe, Joe!"

"Yes, feyther," responded the elder son.

"You be good enough to tackle him, bean't you?"

"The whole lot, feyther," replied Joe, grinning.

"This is my business," spluttered Tommy Toddler. "Come on, you coward! Do you hear? Come on!"

Tommy danced round the dandy,

flourishing his fists, and kicking up the dust with his heels.

"Be quiet, Toddler," said Ralph; and then, turning to Mr. Sappy: "It strikes me that you have made a mistake. The best thing you can do is to eat up your strawberries, and take yourselves off without delay."

A small crowd had collected by this time, and matters were assuming an ugly complexion, when the proprietor of the gardens, a slim, straight-legged, long-armed man, put in an appearance.

"What's the matter?" he demanded.

Everybody tried to explain at once, but at last he managed to grasp hold of a few of the facts.

"Fight! I'll fight you," bellowed the proprietor, Morbey by name, as he fastened upon Mr. Sappy's ear; "I'll teach you to come here trying to spoil my trade. May I never peg another row of strawberries down if I don't spoil you."

"Ow! ow!" howled Mr. Sappy, "Tinker — Snipp — Nocash! Help! help!"

But Messrs Tinker, Snipp, and Nocash did not rush violently to the rescue of their friend.

They fled in different directions, followed by derisive laughter from the assembly.

Morbey was almost as good as his word. If he did not spoil Mr. Sappy in the literal sense of the term, he afflicted him sorely, finishing up by throwing after him a number eleven boot with a foot in it.

"There," said Morbey, as he swept his hand across his heated brow, "I hope you are content now."

Some people are never satisfied, and Mr. Sappy, with a strawberry-stained visage, and a hat that no old-clothes dealer would have given sixpence for, did not look so.

Gone was his glory, departed for ever his fame. Girls had laughed at him, and he knew that in a few hours the story of his downfall would be all over Merrytown.

"We shall meet again," he said, shaking his fist at Ralph.

"Most likely," our hero replied. "I'll look in at your governor's establishment to-morrow for a packet of thread, and see how you are getting on."

"Enough of this," Morbey interposed. "Lads, you had better take a trot round the gardens, and then strike a line for the Abbey. I strongly suspect that you are here without leave. That is no business of mine, but I don't want Mr. Stormaway here, reading me a lecture."

Ralph and his chums took the hint, and leaving the scene of strife, wandered about the beautiful gardens until the sun sank below the horizon, and the clouds in the west blushed crimson.

"Hallo!" cried Charlie Chadwick, stopping suddenly. "What is that?"

"It sounds like a litter of pigs all fast asleep and snoring," said Ralph. "Surely it cannot be possible for such a noise to come from one nasal organ."

"Boys!" shouted Tommy Toddler, who was a little way in advance. "I have found the largest strawberry we have seen to-day."

"Where is it?" demanded Ralph, running up.

"There!" replied Tommy. "If it isn't a strawberry, it is Stickers's nose."

And Stickers's nose it was.

There, amid the foliage of the delicious fruit, lay the man-of-all-work fast asleep; peacefully, perchance, but creating a prodigious uproar in the way of snoring.

The boys looked at each other and then burst out laughing.

"Upon my word," said Ralph, "this is no joking matter. Stickers has been making the most of his holiday with a vengeance."

"Hi, hi!" shouted Charlie, in Matthew Stickers's ear. "Wake up. Do you know where you are?"

"It's shunstroke, I 'sure you," the man-of-all-work remarked.

He opened his eyes slowly and one at a time.

Then the horrible truth flashed into his brain, and he sprang to his feet.

"Ha, ha!" he said. "So you thought to catch me nappin', did you, but I've caught you instead. You've often had a lark with me, but now the tables is turned."

"It is such a lark that you will do well to take yourself off to the Abbey at once," Ralph returned, sternly. "And mark me, Stickers, if you peach on us, you had better make up your mind to clear out of Merrytown."

"We'll see about that," Stickers muttered, shaking his head obstinately. "We'll see about that. I've leave to be out, but what about you? There'll be a job for me to cut some fresh twigs for birches to-morrow. Ha, Ha !"

With these words he departed, with a singularly erratic gait, as if weakness had taken possession of his knees.

"The old sinner !" said Ralph. "Only let him breathe a word about us being here, and I'll make him skip out of his boots. Chums, we will give him five minutes' start, and then return ourselves."

CHAPTER XXI.

LOCKED OUT—THE CONSEQUENCES OF GOING OUT OF BOUNDS—PRISON DIET—A STARTLING EYE.

IT was nearly dark when the boys came within sight of the Abbey.

Heavy clouds had rolled up from all points of the compass, and raindrops fell on the dry cracked earth.

"I don't like the appearance of things," Charles Chadwick said. "I have a presentiment that something is going to happen."

"The finding of Stickers put that into your head," observed Ralph. "It's a rib of beef to a marrow-bone that he has forgotten all about us. He will have quite enough to do to pass muster and creep to bed."

"I hope he has not fallen across Slowbob," said Harold ; "if he has, there is sure to be a row."

"This is Slowbob's knife-cleaning night," chimed in Tommy Toddler. "I heard him say that the 'workus' was a treat to turning the machine, and thus being helpless to ward off the saucepan-lids which the cook throws at him."

"Poor Slowbob !" laughed Ralph. "He is always in some scrape ; but he has a sound heart. That reminds me of something. During the last few days I have, on more than one occasion, caught him looking at me in a peculiar way."

"Slowbob looks at everybody in a peculiar way," said Charlie.

"Granted," our hero replied ; "but he seems as if he had something to tell me, but does not like to speak out."

"Tackle him on the subject," said Charlie.

"I will think about it."

Ralph's reply brought the boys to the Abbey gates.

Consternation was on every face, and each youth gave a gasp.

The gates were closed and securely locked.

"We've done it now !" groaned Tommy Toddler. "I wish that strawberries-and-cream were never invented.

And—and—I begin to feel so queer about the middle-button of my waist-coat."

"Cheer up !" said our hero. "We all row in one boat ; and after all, we shall get no more than a wigging."

The gates were not only high, but spiked at the top.

There was nothing to do but to ring the bell and face the matter out.

"This is the work of that miscreant Stickers," said Charlie, savagely. "Why didn't we leave him to sleep among the strawberries ?"

"I don't think that we owe this to Stickers," Ralph remarked, as he rang the bell, "for the reason that I don't believe he has returned yet. See, here he comes ! and we'll put him in front to bear the brunt of the fray."

The boys dodged into the shadow of the ivy-covered wall, and presently up came Matthew Stickers.

"Wot a story I've got to tell Mister Stormaway," he mumbled. "I looks a little 'xited, p'raps ; but that I can put down to the boys."

Little did the man-of-all-work think what was in store for him.

Mr. Stormaway was on his way across the playground, with the keys in one hand and a cane in the other, which he concealed behind his back.

Stickers flattened himself against the railings of the gates, so that when they were opened he slid through.

The first thing he experienced was a stinging sensation about the calves of his legs, quickly followed by two open-handed staggerers on each side of the head, and finally the sharp rattling of a somewhat ponderous bunch of keys about his cranium.

"'Ere, I say ! Oh—oh ! Don't ! Do you take me for one of the boys ?" Stickers yelled.

That was exactly the case ; but when Mr. Stormaway discovered his mistake, which was caused by the darkness, his wrath was not appeased.

Seizing Matthew Stickers by the collar, he propped him against the wall.

"You disreputable fellow!" the head-master hectored. "I told you to be home at four, and the clock has chimed half-past eight! Have you seen any of the boys? Bah! what is this vile smell that clings to you?"

"Shunstroke—I mean ginger-beer!" Stickers groaned. "Don't choke a hold man, Mister Stormaway! Respect my grey 'airs. Don't, sir! don't! You're a shakin' hup the ginger-beer!"

"Ginger-beer, indeed!" said the head-master contemptuously. "Beer without the ginger is nearer the mark. Villain! How dare you convert yourself into a walking brewery! I ask you again whether you have seen any of the boys?"

"Yes, sir, he has," said Ralph, stepping forward.

A procession of youthful culprits was at our hero's heels, Tommy Toddler being last of all, and looking as if the five plates of strawberries-and-cream and two bottles of lemonade he had recklessly consumed were quarrelling.

"So!" said Mr. Stormaway, who could scarcely speak for rage. "So! You go beyond bounds without leave, and then have the impudence to tell me so to my face!"

"That is better than trying to sneak out of the matter, sir," Ralph replied. "We own our fault; and if there is anything to be said by way of extenuation, it is that the mysterious Highlander on the roof upset us, and we required a change."

"You shall have a change," Mr. Stormaway remarked. "I have altered my mind. I will not flog you."

"I s'pose I got the lot," interposed Stickers, as he rubbed his legs. "It ain't fair to pitch into a man with the shunstroke."

"You will get some more if you don't hold your tongue," Mr. Stormaway said. "Away with you. Boys, follow me!"

Into the Abbey went the youths, with fast beating hearts.

Never a word more did Mr. Stormaway say as he led the way up the stairs, past the dormitories, and still higher, until nothing but the roof blocked out a view of the cloudy sky.

"I have prepared a chamber for you," the head-master said, grimly, "and here you will remain learning your lessons, sleeping, and taking your meals until I think you have wiped out this offence. Double lessons will be the portion of all, and sound thrashings if they are not well studied. Enter!"

No sooner were the boys in the room than bang went the door behind them.

The huge garret, for the apartment was nothing better, had been fitted with five beds, a desk, and a form, but in all other respects it was comfortless.

Tommy Toddler wept, not so much for the punishment, as in consequence of the sufferings he was enduring.

"I must have been born under an unlucky star!" he gasped. "I feel bad all over, from the roots of my hair to my toes."

"What else can a boy be if he polishes off half-a-crown's worth of fruit in less than an hour?" said Ralph. "Go to bed, and if you have horrible dreams, you will have yourself to thank."

To bed they all went, and were awakened by the sound of a key grating in the lock.

Matthew Stickers, looking wild and haggard, entered, bearing a wicker-basket and a pitcher, with five tin mugs tied to the handle.

"What is the meaning of this?" Ralph demanded.

"It means," replied the man-of-all-work, "that you're to be kept on prison-fare until further notice. 'Ere's five loaves, and 'ere's the water; so now you can make yourselves jolly."

Ralph's face flushed angrily for a moment, but in another he was his old self again.

"As the bed is made so must it be slept upon!" he said. "We brought this upon ourselves, and must put up with the consequences. What's the matter, Stickers? you are positively crying!"

"It ain't for you that I'm a weepin'," replied the man-of-all-work, wiping away a tear. "Mr. Stormaway have given me notice to leave, and where I shall go is more than I can tell."

"A good job, too!" observed Tommy Toddler. "You have never done a kind action unless you have been well paid for its performance."

"It's 'ard for me to 'ear such things from a youth I have loved like a son!" Stickers said, sadly. "It cuts me to the 'art. I'm a hold man, and the world will be an 'owling windymass to me ! "

"Howling wilderness," Ralph corrected.

"It's all one and the same thing," Stickers moaned. "Hif I was hup to book learnin', which I ain't, I'd open a school in hopposition to Mr. Stormaway. I must do somethink, or I shall starve."

"Try the hot-potato line, or the ten-a-penny, all cracked, walnut," Harold Lakeman suggested.

"Taters and walnuts is low," Stickers replied. "Well, well, I must think the matter over. This day week, unless Mr. Stormaway relents, the Abbey will know me never no more."

"We shall not go into mourning for you," cried the irrepressible Toddler. "Now, then, clear out, Stickers. We don't want you standing there gloating over our misery."

"I'm agoin'—agoin' fur away, as the song says," Stickers replied, feebly; "but I shan't be far away. As a cartload o' stone is drawn by the magnet, so I shall hover about the scenes o' my long and faithful servitoode."

Stickers departed, and they heard him groaning deeply as he went down.

"Now, boys," said Ralph, "we must have no snivelling. The best must be made of a bad thing, so let us laugh and make merry as if we were sitting down to a feast of——"

"Strawberries - and - cream," suggested Charlie Chadwick, with a mischievous glance at Toddler.

"Don't!" Tommy pleaded. "If you knew what I went through last night

you would have pity on me. Good gracious, look there ! "

Tommy Toddler's hair was almost on end as he pointed to the door.

There was a hole in one of the panels, and fixed in it was a fearfully-rolling eye.

Such an eye could only belong to Slowbob, and that youth soon made himself heard.

"I knowed you was to be put in here," he said, "so I bored this hole last night. Cheer up, all ! "

"We will," responded Ralph. "Slowbob, don't be caught hanging about here. It would be stupid on your part to get into trouble through us."

"You may leave me to take care of myself," Slowbob replied, as he removed his eye from its airy place of vantage. "Here, catch hold of this piece of string, and pull away until you come to the end."

"What is the idea ?" Ralph asked.

"You hang that string out of the winder to-night, and you'll see," said Slowbob. "There's more than one way to kill a goose, and to eat it, too, as the dorg said when he stole one and took it on the mat. Locks, bolts, and bars may make a prison, but while Timothy lives the wittles sha'n't run short."

"You are a good fellow," said Ralph. "Take some money, and get us whatever you think we shall like."

"Not to-day," Slowbob replied. "The cook is making some pigeon-pies and custards for some o' Mrs. Jumble's friends who are comin' to supper. Precious little pigeon they'll get in them pies. Wait and see."

CHAPTER XXII.

THE GAME OF CHESS.

THE school-room was dreary without Ralph and his chums.

The boys were dull and inclined to be stupid, and so grieved was Herr Fritz Halfamann, that he went about with tears in his eyes.

"Mine poys shut up in von brison," he muttered, casting a reproachful glance at the head-master. "Ach ! They vas vary sorrowful I am sure. Ze leedle strawperry and zee cream haf prought all zis drouble on zem ;

but zey are poys, and poys are poys all zee vorld over."

The culprits were visited several times during the day, and so well did they perform their tasks, perhaps glad enough for something to do, that Mr. Stormaway could find no fault.

The boys were filing out of the school at the conclusion of the afternoon's lessons, when Alphonse Carleon approached the head-master's desk.

"A word with you, sir," he said.

Mr. Stormaway raised his head from the book he was poring over.

"Yes, monsieur," he replied, "I am all attention. Have you any complaints to make to me?"

"On the contrary."

"I am delighted to hear it," said Mr. Stormaway.

"It is of one particular pupil that I wish to speak," Alphonse Carleon responded. "John Walbut is doing remarkably well in his class. His exercises are without fault, and I beg to recommend him to your favourable notice."

The head-master paused ere he spoke again.

He had no great opinion of Jack Walbut, knowing that he had a great deal of the bully in his nature.

"I will make a note of it," he observed," and at the end of the term I may be inclined to give an extra prize."

"I have a favour to ask you, sir," Carleon said.

"Name it."

"I wish to encourage Walbut," the Frenchman returned. "Will you allow him to take tea with me? The boy, it seems, is very fond of the harmless and noble game of chess, and so am I."

"Certainly," said Mr. Stormaway; "you have my unqualified consent. Walbut will, of course, return to the Abbey before nine o'clock?"

"I will bring him back myself, sir," Carleon replied.

The two masters exchanged bows, and M. Carleon, with his head erect and his shoulders thrown back, marched out of the room.

He closed the door behind him, and stood perfectly still.

The echoes of boys' voices floated through the dim mysterious old building, and for a moment the Frenchman's heart was strangely stirred.

"Why was I not left in peace?" he almost sobbed, as he hurried away to the playground. "I was happy—I had almost blotted out the past, and even now—— No, no; Richard Mornington will keep his word of threat, if not his word of honour. It must be done—it *shall* be done!"

He found Jack Walbut with Lemon Sleath, so to speak, under his wing.

"Walbut," Carleon said, curtly, "Mr. Stormaway has granted his permission. He is very glad to hear such a good account of you. Come home with me."

Jack Walbut hesitated and shrank closer to the wall.

"What is the matter?" Alphonse Carleon demanded, with a short, dry laugh. "Are you afraid of me?"

"I am afraid of your eyes," Walbut replied, nervously. "I wish you would not look at me as if——"

"I could read you through and through," interrupted Carleon. "I can do so. Come home with me. Do you hear?"

The tone in which the last three words were uttered caused Jack Walbut to start violently and turn pale.

He followed M. Carleon as submissively as a dog follows its master, but he trembled without knowing exactly why, and would have given everything he possessed to have avoided the engagement.

The Frenchman's lodgings were soon reached, and no sooner was he at home than he threw aside the master and became a genial host.

He laughed and joked with Jack Walbut over the tea-table, sang well, and played both the piano and violin exquisitely, and having thus amused his guest for more than an hour, he suddenly crossed the room and produced a chessboard.

"Now for our game!" he said, as he placed the pieces in their proper positions. "You play well, I believe?"

"Only fairly."

"Then I will give you a knight," Carleon said. "Has it ever struck you how ingeniously the inventor placed the pieces? The castles stand in situations difficult to attack, the knights guard them, and two reverend bishops are in constant attendance upon the king and the queen."

"The pawns represent the men-at-arms," Jack Walbut observed.

"Yes; and as in the days of old, bear the brunt of the battle."

So they chatted as they played.

The game did not last long.

M. Carleon allowed himself to be checkmated, and Jack Walbut was delighted.

"Come—come!" said the Frenchman in a rallying tone of voice, "it was scarcely fair of you to accept a knight from me; you play splendidly."

"Do you really think so?" demanded Walbut.

"I do," Carleon replied. "It is said," he added, musingly, "that a good chess-player must be an excellent strategist. Put the board aside ; time is slipping away, and I have much to say to you."

The chair in which Jack Walbut sat was an antique one, furnished with padded arms, a long, straight back, and strangely carved.

A griffin, in polished black oak, grinned down at the boy as he cowered before the Frenchman's eyes, and drummed his fingers upon two specimens of the carver's skill representing twining serpents.

"You remember what I said to you in the school-room yesterday," Carleon began ; "I spoke of Ralph Mornington, and I will speak of him now. He or I must leave the Abbey."

"Indeed !"

The Frenchman held up his hand, and Jack Walbut remained silent.

"Yes," Carleon said ; "a circumstance has arisen that makes what I have said imperative. It is not I, however, who will leave the Abbey, but Ralph Mornington. I will be plain with you. He must leave the Abbey disgraced, and you must help me to bring about his downfall."

Walbut sat motionless and almost spellbound.

"I am a tower of strength when I choose to become so," Carleon continued ; "and I can also be a very bitter enemy. Walbut, are we to be friends of foes ? "

"Oh, sir," the miserable boy cried ; "I dare not offend you."

"You have taken a sensible view of the situation," the Frenchman returned. "Now listen. Within a few days Mornington will return to his usual place. You must watch him closely, and at the first opportunity take some marked money from my desk and place it in his trunk, and this also."

As Carleon spoke he held up a small key.

"This is a duplicate of the one I use," he said ; "I made it myself, and it fits the lock of my desk perfectly. You understand me, I presume ? "

Jack Walbut's head fell forward, and he grasped the arms of the chair convulsively.

"I am giddy !" he gasped. "Give me a drink of water."

"You shall have wine," the Frenchman said, pouring out a glassful. "There—you are better now."

"Yes ; I am better," Jack Walbut replied, faintly. "Is there no other way—no other scheme you can think of ? "

"None. What, are you faint of heart, or rebellious ? Walbut, beware of offending me ! I have you in my power."

"Tell me how ? " the boy demanded. "What have I done ? What indeed can you accuse me of ? "

"An old saying says that walls have ears," Carleon remarked, smiling, and showing his white teeth. "One morning not long ago there was somebody behind a certain wall, and he heard two voices. One of the voices resembled yours strangely. It told a certain boy, named Lemon Sleath, to steal into Ralph Mornington's room and see what his boxes contained."

"Spare me ! " Walbut moaned.

"I will if you do my bidding ; but if you refuse you know the penalty—expulsion ! " Carleon said. "I read your mind again, my young friend. You think in this way : 'Why should I not reveal this plot to Mr. Stormaway ? ' Bah ! Put this question to yourself. Would he believe you or me ? A word is only needed to make Sleath turn upon you like the cur he is, and how will you stand then ? "

"I consent," Walbut said. "Give me the key."

"Not yet," Carleon replied. "No, no ; wait until the time comes to act. And now we will return to the Abbey."

CHAPTER XXIII.

PIGEON PIES WITHOUT PIGEONS.

JUST about the time that Walbut returned to the Abbey and hurried away to bed, so that the terrified expression of his face might not be seen, Ralph and his fellow-prisoners received Slowbob's signal.

It was a whistle, accompanied by a stone that cracked a pane of glass.

Our hero pushed the window open cautiously and looked out.

"What is it?" he cried.

"All's snug and comfor'ble as wapses in their nest," said Slowbob. "Lower the string. I've got the pigeons in a basket. Send it down to me when it is empty."

Ralph obeyed the page-boy's directions, and in a few moments four plump baked pigeons, with bread, plates, and knives and forks for each, were hauled into the room.

"Good gracious!" said Tommy Toddler, "I can picture Mrs. Jumble's face when she finds out that there is nothing for her friends to eat. She'll go stark staring mad, and—oh lor!—perhaps she may take it into her head to kill Slowbob."

"I anticipate no such tragedy," Ralph returned, laughing. "Slowbob has made his plans safe, you may be sure. What a fellow he is!"

The surreptitious meal was soon over, and Ralph attaching the basket to the string lowered it skilfully.

Slowbob chuckled as he caught it.

"I wish you could see the fun which will foller," he said. "Mrs. Jumble's friends are making themselves hungry by drinkin' orange wine. How they are going it to be sure! Ten o'clock's the time for supper, and I am to wait on 'em. Ha, ha!"

"What have you done with the crust?" demanded Ralph in as loud a voice as he durst.

"You'll hear all about that," replied Slowbob. "I'll come and tell you all the news to-morrow. Good-night, sir."

"Good-night, Timothy."

Chuckling and hugging himself, Slowbob returned, and presented himself dutifully before Mrs. Jumble.

The housekeeper had invited three lady-friends to spend a musical evening.

Cold pigeon pies and custards were to wind up the entertainment, and Mrs. Jumble and her friends were quite ready for them as the hands of the clock approached the hour of ten.

"Rachel, my dear," she said to an old maid whose head was adorned with ringlets, "and all of you, my loves, I hope you will not scold me for giving you so poor a supper."

"Don't name it!" chorused the ladies. "You could give us nothing better."

"Couldn't she?" thought Slowbob, who was balancing himself on one leg in a corner of the room. "The pigeons you'll get will be mighty tough, I'm thinking."

"Boy," said Mrs. Jumble, with as much politeness as if she were addressing a post, "fetch in the supper."

"Yes, marm," Slowbob replied. "But hold hard—wait a moment."

"What have you to say?" demanded Mrs. Jumble, wrathfully.

"I wish to call your attention to the fact that there ain't a drop of orange-wine left," said Slowbob, "so don't you accuse me in the morning of——"

The housekeeper made a dart at the youth in buttons, but failed to reach him.

"That boy will be the death of me, I am sure," she said, fanning herself. "My dears, he is the very bane of my existence."

"What strange eyes he has!" observed Miss Rachel; "they are positively at variance with each other."

"My eyes are as they was put into my head," said Slowbob, as he entered the room carrying a dish upon a tray. "They ain't false like somebody's hair —come now, Madame Corkscrews."

"Oh!" screamed Mrs. Jumble, wringing her hands. "What shall I do with him? Slowbob, you are an audacious, graceless, horrible little villain!"

"Thank'ee, marm," the page-boy returned, calmly. "Compliments don't cost anything, and that's the reason why you can afford to chuck 'em about so freely."

Mrs. Jumble sat down in a chair and panted for breath.

Her friends hovered around her for a moment, and then as if actuated by one impulse bore down upon Slowbob.

"Hold!" he cried. "Touch me— lay one finger on me, and I dashes the wittles on the dirty floor!"

The ladies stood back, and Mrs. Jumble sprang to her feet.

"Let somebody only jog my arm," Slowbob continued, balancing the pie-dish on the tips of his fingers, "and over goes the pigeons, gravy, and crust. If any lady wishes to scratch my face, or pull my ears she is welcome to try it. Come one, come all, I'm ready."

"Pay no heed to the little wretch," Mrs. Jumble said. "Sit down, dears, and when I have served you all I will turn him out of the room."

Timothy Slowbob placed the pie-dish on the table, with a merry twinkle in his odd eyes.

The housekeeper took up a knife and fork, and plunged them through the flakey crust.

"We have a most excellent cook at the Abbey," she observed. "She is positively skilled in pie-making. And yet, dear me, surely the pigeons cannot be sufficiently baked! Tut—tut! How provoking!"

"Shall I fetch a hatchet, marm?" Slowbob asked.

Mrs. Jumble looked as if she could have fetched the page-boy something with anything that came handy.

"Tell the cook to come here instantly," she said, "and remain in the kitchen. Your conduct shall be reported to Mr. Stormaway, I promise you."

"Yes; and so shall your friends," Slowbob replied. "Why did the lady in them ringlets want to insult me for? Can I help it if Nature made me to see round a corner?"

The youth in mulberry-hued attire dug his knuckles into his eyes, and pretended to weep.

"There—there, don't cry," said Mrs. Jumble. "I am sure that nobody meant to hurt your feelings."

"Half-a-crown and the leavin's of the pigeon-pie wouldn't soo—soo—soothe 'em," Slowbob sobbed. "I—I —I——"

What more he would have said is a matter of conjecture.

Mrs. Jumble interrupted him with a terriffic scream.

"See here!" she cried, pointing with the fork into the dish. "Oh, this is monstrous!"

The flakey crust had fallen in, and revealed to the astounded spectators, not four plump-like pigeons, but one of Matthew Stickers's old felt hats, crushed all out of shape, and filled with rags.

"Oh, this is monstrous!" cried Mrs. Jumble.

"Monsterous!" Slowbob said, surveying the dish with a critical and extraordinary glance. "Them's the rummest pigeons that I ever see."

"Let me go!" the housekeeper gasped, pushing him aside. "I will discharge that hussy of a cook. It is plain to me that she has plotted with that wretched old man Stickers to humiliate me."

Mrs. Jumble was in a towering rage.

While she was away Slowbob ate all the crust, and having finished it, cut himself off a piece of bread-and-cheese, to the speechless amazement of the hungry and disappointed guests.

After a lapse of about ten minutes the housekeeper returned, still white with passion, and trembling all over like a jelly.

"I can find neither the cook nor Stickers," she said as she flopped down into a chair. "What shall I do? What can I say? Oh, my dear friends, I could swoon out of pure vexation!"

"Never mind," said Miss Rachel. "We can understand you have been played a malicious trick. I dare say we shall be able to manage with the custards."

"Bring them in," commanded Mrs. Jumble. "Oh, dear, I shall never forget this night as long as I live!"

"Cheer up, marm," observed Slowbob, soothingly, "and never let your spirits go down, as the song says. I pity poor old Stickers—that I do! There's no knowing what a man may do when he's got sunstroke bad!"

Slowbob brought in the custards.

His face was a study as he passed the delicacies round to the guests and moved towards the door.

It was evident by the attitude he assumed that he was ready for flight at any moment.

"What a beautiful colour these custards are!" remarked Miss Rachel, as she toyed with her spoon."

She took a spoonful, and then an extraordinary change came over her face.

Her cheeks grew red, her eyes stood out like hat-pegs, and she began drumming her heels frantically on the floor.

"She is choking!" Mrs. Jumble shrieked. "Pat her back! Slowbob, bring some water!"

But Slowbob answered not. He had glided from the room.

"Mus—mus—mustard!" gasped Miss Rachel with tears streaming down her face. "Mustard, I tell you!"

"Shall I get you some mustard, ma'am?" cried Slowbob, putting his head in the door-way. "How much, old ringlets?"

"What!" cried Mrs. Jumble, starting back, and bumping her head against the nose of the lady behind her. "Mustard, do you say?"

"Ye—es," groaned the victim. "I'm choking. Taste for yourself."

The housekeeper could find no words to give vent to her feelings.

She sat down and shed tears of grief and rage.

"I see it all," she said at last. "There is a conspiracy against me. Leave me. Go at once. I can say nothing and do nothing now, but to-morrow will tell a different tale."

The ladies lost no time in putting on their bonnets and departing from the Abbey, leaving Mrs. Jumble to moan and vow vengeance against the perpetrator of the joke.

CHAPTER XXIV.

RELEASED—RALPH RECEIVES VISITORS—AN EXTRA HALF-HOLIDAY.

EARLY the next morning Slowbob's eye again appeared at the hole he had bored in the door of the prison-chamber.

"I say," said the irrepressible, "there's going to be a row about them pigeons, so I hope you haven't left any bits or crumbs about."

"No," Ralph replied ; "we took good care about that."

"There was custards, too, for supper," giggled Slowbob, "but I had 'em and gave the old gals mustard instead. Only one got a dose, worse luck, but I don't think that Mrs. Jumble will ever give another supper-party."

Slowbob ceased speaking, and, as his eye vanished suddenly, Ralph came to the conclusion that somebody was coming upstairs.

The somebody proved to be Mr. Stormaway, and the boys had just finished dressing when he unlocked the door and entered the room.

Not a word did the head-master speak for nearly a minute.

He peered about the floor, into the cupboards, and, pushing open the window, examined the sill with an amount of cuteness that would have done credit to a trained detective.

"Nothing here," he muttered to himself. "It is plain to me that these boys know nothing about the pigeons, therefore it would be idle to mention the circumstance to them. Poor Mrs. Jumble, how she takes it to heart!"

The head-master having finished his investigation called Ralph to his side.

"Mornington," he said, "and all of you, I hope by this time that you have realised the folly of disobeying the rules I have laid down."

"I think we have, sir," Ralph replied.

"For my part, sir," said Tommy Toddler, "I'll think twice before eating strawberries-and-cream in future. I haven't got over the effects of them yet."

"It was my original intention to keep you here for a week," Mr. Stormaway continued, "but I have relented. I hope this will prove a lesson to you. Go downstairs and take your places at the breakfast-table."

The boys thanked him heartily, and were soon receiving the congratulations of their schoolmates.

Mrs. Jumble was absent from the head of the table, and Halfamann took her place.

"Zee poys must be as hungry as zee vild volves of zee forest," the German tutor said, "and zey sal haf all zey can eat. Slowpop, bass zee tea und pread-und-putter to zee young gentlemens dat vent out of pounds."

Just then the postman arrived and a letter was placed in Ralph's hand.

"I don't know this writing," our hero said as he looked at the address. "Why, I declare it is sealed with a coronet."

"Then it must come from Lord Auburton," said Harold Lakeman.

"Yes, it is from him," Ralph replied as he unfolded a sheet of silky paper. "Oh, I say, he is coming here to-day."

"Never !"

"Yes, he is. I will read you the letter :

"'MY DEAR BOY,—I dare say you wonder you have not heard from me before. My daughter has been unwell and I have been travelling on the Continent with her. I am glad to tell you that she is much better, and will accompany me to Merrytown to-morrow, when we shall have much pleasure in calling on you.—Yours very truly, AUBURTON.'"

"Think of that," cried Harold ; "a real live lord going to call upon you, Ralph. You will go up one in Mr. Stormaway's estimation."

"I have met many lords at my father's house," our hero replied, "and they were for all the world like other men. You don't suppose that they sit down with their coronets on their heads, do you ? "

When Slowbob heard of his lordship's intended visit, he indulged in an extensive wholesale grin.

He was told to array himself in his best suit of livery—the one with but two grease-spots and only four buttons short.

Mr. Stormaway was elated.

The news would spread like wildfire, and perhaps get into the county paper.

The clock was striking eleven when Lord Auburton and his pretty daughter arrived.

They came in a carriage drawn by such a pair of splendid horses that Slowbob was quite affected.

"Your lordship and ladyship will please walk into the drawing-room," he said. "It ain't often used, and was rather damp until Mr. Stormaway told Mary to light a fire."

Lord Auburton smiled, and Ethel was so amused that she could scarcely refrain from laughing outright.

Mr. Stormaway, all smiles and beams, received his distinguished visitors, and after a short chat Ralph Mornington was sent for.

His lordship and his daughter shook hands cordially with our hero, and they were soon chatting away as if they had known each other all their lives.

"You must run down and see us when holiday-time comes," Lord Auburton said; "and if you can persuade two or three of your chums to join you, I will endeavour to make them welcome."

"That will be delightful," Ralph rejoined with sparkling eyes, "and I will most certainly avail myself of your lordship's kind invitation."

"That is right. Mr. Stormaway, I crave a boon. Give the boys an extra half-holiday in honour of this brave lad who saved my daughter's life."

"It is already granted," the headmaster replied. "I am proud to have Mornington here. He is, as you say, a brave lad."

Mr. Stormaway remembered the strawberry-and-cream incident and checked himself.

"Well," he added, "he is everything that one could wish an English boy to be."

"That I am convinced of," said Lord Auburton. "Ralph Mornington, I have a trifle which I beg you will wear for my sake, and I also speak for my daughter. The locket is her gift, and contains her portrait."

A magnificent watch, with chain and locket, were put into our hero's hands, and the lad's face flushed with pleasure and pride.

"I can only thank you," he said; "my heart is too full to allow my tongue to give expression to many words."

"The least said the better," Lord Auburton returned, genially. "And now, Ethel, we will go, as we have a long drive before us, and several calls to make."

The cheering was tremendous when Ralph returned to the school-room and displayed his gift.

"My gootness, vat a peautiful vatch ! " cried Herr Fritz Halfamann, with dilated eyes. "Mine fader had von vatch, and when I vas a leedle poy, I did put in some putter to grease the wheels, and mine fader did not forgive me for von whole day."

The acme of pleasure was reached when Mr. Stormaway announced the half-holiday.

"Isn't this jolly ? " cried Charlie Chadwick, cutting a caper in the playground a little later on. "I say, Ralph, did you notice Jack Walbut's face ? "

"I thought he seemed very pleased at my good fortune."

"So did I at first," said Charlie; "but I happened to glance at him when he thought nobody was looking, and I caught him scowling maliciously."

"You may have imagined it," Ralph observed, good-temperedly. "Well, he has a perfect right to smile or scowl. Now, lads, don't let us mar the fun with dismal forebodings. We have a half-holiday and leave to wander where we like. Where shall we go ? "

"Perhaps," suggested Harold Lakeman, "Tommy Toddler has got over his aversion for strawberries-and-cream, and would like to pay another visit to the fruit gardens."

"No, no," said Tommy. "Let us roam about in search of adventure."

"That is not a bad idea, Tommy," Ralph observed. "I will stand treat, and we will go a gipsying. I wish we could have Slowbob with us; we should not want for fun then."

"BANG! SMASH! CRASH! WENT THE EGGS IN ALL DIRECTIONS."—(See page 103.)

"Here comes the gallant youth," said Charlie Chadwick ; "put the question to him, Ralph."

There was evidently something wrong about the page-boy.

He walked with stiffened legs, and, so to speak, worked himself along by a series of spasmodic jerks.

"What is the matter with you ?" Ralph demanded.

"Everything is the matter," Slowbob replied, wriggling. "Mr. Stormaway pitched into me because I spoke to his lordship about the fire as was lit in the drawin'-room to keep the damp out. He caught me unawares and lor ! didn't he lay it on thick."

"Poor Slowbob !" said our hero ; "you are always in hot water."

"It wasn't hot water," Slowbob remarked, with fearfully rolling eyes ; "it was a new cane bound at the end with a piece of waxed thread. Mr. Stormaway got it up on purpose for me, but I'll teach him to stripe me all over like a mackerel—see if I don't."

"What will you do ?" said Ralph, laughing in spite of himself.

"I haven't made up my mind yet," Slowbob returned ; "but it will be something worth the Queen of England talking about. After he had done with me—and he was a long time about it—he bundled me out of the study, and told me to keep out of his sight for the rest of the day."

"That's lucky," said Ralph.

"What's lucky ?" Slowbob asked, indignantly. "The warming I got ?"

"No, no," our hero responded ; "we are going out this afternoon, and want you to carry some things for us. You will have your share, of course."

"Mr. Mornington," said Slowbob, "I will go. I'm a poor boy without parents, and when I leave here I suppose I shall have to go to some other kind of drudgery, but that doesn't matter to you."

"Yes, it does," Ralph returned, "because you are willing to oblige me."

Timothy Slowbob smote his chest with such violence that two buttons flew from his jacket like peas blown from a shooter.

"I'd go round the world with you," he said, emphatically. "I'd risk anything for your sake. And," he cried, raising his voice, and striking a tragic attitude, "I'd die to save your life or honour !"

Ralph could not help feeling affected at Slowbob's genuine enthusiasm.

"I believe it," he said.

"Thank'ee," Slowbob returned, wiping his eyes with the back of his hand. "One of these days I may have something to tell thee."

"Why not now ?"

"Because I may be wrong."

"Wrong about what ?"

"It's no use, sir," said Slowbob, shaking his head. "I think something, but I had better keep my thoughts to myself for the present. At what time will you requir my services ?"

"At once."

"Then I'm ready. Oh, Lord, there goes another button !" cried Timothy. "I shed 'em like plums in an orchard on a windy day."

CHAPTER XXV.

A LITTLE MISUNDERSTANDING—THE STRANGE OCCURRENCE IN BLUEBELL DALE.

IT was market-day at Merrytown, and Worryboy was of course hovering about, but experience had taught him not to interfere with the boys when walking abroad.

"Chums," said Ralph. "I wish to make a clean breast of something. Like the rest, you have been puzzled by the strange voices heard at the Abbey. It was I who caused them. Yes, I am a ventriloquist !"

"You ? Is it possible ?" cried Charlie Chadwick. "Well, that's jolly, and has taken something off my mind."

"At all events," said Harold, "we know that Ralph is not the ghost, because it appeared before he came."

"That still remains a mystery," our hero observed. "Shall I give you a specimen of my peculiar gift ?"

"Yes—do."

About a dozen old ladies and two or three men were gathered round a butcher's stall.

"What is the price of legs of pork,

to-day ? " Ralph demanded, throwing his voice so as to make it appear that the fattest old lady spoke.

"Sevenpence-ha'penny," responded the butcher. "Buy the best ! Buy the best ! Here is a very willing butcher with a very sharp knife. Buy ! Buy ! Buy ! "

"Cease your clatter ! " the old lady seemed to say. "Weigh that leg, and don't bang your thumb into the scales."

"Don't do what, marm ? " gasped the porkman. "Bang my thumb into the scales ! I'm jiggered if you should have that 'ere leg for a guinea a pound."

The old lady, seeing that she was being spoken to, smiled benignly and put her hand to her ear.

"Would you mind speaking a little louder ? " she said ; "I'm rather hard of hearing."

"Nature has made up for it in your tongue," the butcher shouted. "Move out of the way, twenty stun. You're old enough to know better than to try to ruin a man as is trying to get an honest living."

The old lady understood part of this speech, and she bridled up accordingly.

"How dare you insult me ? " she screamed, growing very red in the face. "I've a good mind to hit you over the head with my umbrella."

"Do it ! " roared the butcher. "Do it ! "

The corpulent lady did. She gave that man of pork such a staggerer on the top of his cranium that he performed a jig on his heels, winding up with a Scotch reel that deposited him on a stall devoted to the sale of whelks and mussels.

A man was enjoying a pennyworth of the first-named luxuries, and so overcome was he by the crash, that he hurled the saucer madly over his shoulder, and put the best part of a half - quarten of vinegar into P.C. Worryboy's face.

Now the constable had been gazing intently at the mussel man, who was sprinkling vinegar and pepper for expectant customers, and the thought naturally struck Worryboy that the vendor of molluscs had purposely assaulted him.

Soured in disposition as well as visage, Worryboy closed with the stall-keeper, and dragging him across the street with his feet rattling over the stones, vowed that he would lock him up forthwith.

"What for ? " the dispenser of shell-fish screeched. "Ain't I been treated badly enough.? What have I done to be bursted into like a showman's drum ? "

"I'll—I'll teach you to serve me like a saucer of mussels," Worryboy gasped. "Come along."

And to the station he certainly would have gone but for the pork-butcher and the old lady, who with uplifted voices threatened each other with summonses, and so explained matters.

"Summon each other, will you ? " said Worryboy. "I'll see to that ! I'll summon the lot of you ! "

"I think we had better be moving," Ralph observed.

"I think so too," Charlie Chadwick assented. "Take me away or I shall explode with laughter."

The boys moved on, Slowbob following in a state of bewilderment.

"If the old lady didn't chaff the butcher I should like to know who did," he muttered.

Ralph overheard the remark, and threw his voice, in imitation of Stickers, behind the page-boy.

"All right, you'll catch it for leaving the Habbey, young swivel-eyes ! "

Timothy Slowbob wheeled round sharply.

Matthew Stickers was nowhere to be seen, and Slowbob rubbed his head.

"This is getting alarming," he said. "Stickers spoke, and yet he ain't here. Mr. Mornington, did you hear anybody call me names ? "

"There must be something peculiar in the atmosphere to-day," Ralph returned. "Everybody is fancying something. Let us get away, or we shall be accused of upsetting somebody."

"Well," said Slowbob, as he glanced over his shoulder, " if that wasn't the woice of Stickers I never heard him speak in my life."

Ralph shrugged his shoulders and passed on with his chums.

Leaving the village, they crossed some fields and halted at a lovely spot called Bluebell Dale.

"Now, Slowbob, open the basket," said Ralph.

The page-boy smacked his lips as he brought forth a number of dainties, and then modestly withdrew to a distance.

The feast had hardly commenced when the sound of voices was heard.

"Hush ! " said Slowbob, dropping upon his hands and knees ; "I know who they are. Keep close, young gentlemen. Don't let them see you."

"Who are they?" Ralph demanded.

Slowbob pointed to an opening in the trees, and to the astonishment of all, Alphonse Carleon and Jack Walbut were seen walking side-by-side, and conversing confidentially.

They passed along, ignorant of the fact that they were observed, and not a word was uttered by Ralph and his chums until they had passed out of hearing and were lost to view.

"I wonder what this means?" Chadwick said, with a troubled face. "We will pack up and get away. There is some plot hatching between them. Why, where is Slowbob? I can see him nowhere."

Timothy had disappeared in the most mysterious manner.

It was very singular.

As the clown, explaining the habits of the lively flea, remarked, "You look at him, and there he is; you look at him again, and there he isn't," so it was with Slowbob.

He was in full sight of everybody one moment, and the next he was gone, no one could say whither.

"This beats everything," Ralph said. "Are we dreaming? Can it be a fact that Timothy came with us at all? We are surrounded by mysteries."

"Let us see if we can find him, at all events," Harold Lakeman remarked, as he ran up the hillock. "Yes, I see his mulberry unspeakables. Why, he is crawling about like a Red Indian on the war-trail. What can it mean?"

"Let him be," said Charlie Chadwick. "We will wait for him here."

"But this is most mysterious," Ralph rejoined. "There must be something wrong indeed for Slowbob to act in this fashion. Oh, here he is at last!"

Yes, there was Timothy, but what a change had come over him.

His face was ghastly pale, he trembled in every limb, and his stubbly hair was literally on end.

"Where have you been?" our hero asked, somewhat sharply.

"I went to catch something and got caught in a bramble bush," Slowbob replied with a sort of gasp.

"Nonsense!" said Ralph; "such a trifle would not account for your appearance. What did you expect to catch?"

"A pair of hawks, but they took to wing."

"You were following M. Carleon and Walbut," Ralph responded, sternly. "Slowbob, it is wrong to play the part of an eavesdropper, no matter under what circumstances, and I am surprised that you should do such a thing."

"Was I following them?" said Slowbob, jerking out the words. "Oh, indeed! Well, I can't help what you may think. I've just got a notion that I ought to go back to the Abbey. Stickers's woice called me, and I'm afraid there's something wrong with the old man."

Timothy turned abruptly on his heel and walked away.

What could be the meaning of his strange behaviour, the chums could not conjecture.

His departure broke up the party.

The sky became cloudy, and a gloom came over all, and although the boys lingered awhile and tried to be merry, their conversation fell flat, and at last they retraced their footsteps in almost absolute silence.

Once Charlie Chadwick broke it.

"Ralph," he said, "I don't want to croak, but we ought to take notice of this sudden outburst of friendship between the Frenchman and Walbut. It means mischief, I tell you."

"To whom?"

"That remains to be seen," Charlie replied. "I for one will keep a watchful eye upon them."

CHAPTER XXVI.

THE GREAT CONJURER AND THE VANISHING MAN-OF-ALL-WORK.

To Ralph's surprise Timothy Slowbob stood at the Abbey gates with his hands deep in his pockets, and whistling a lively air.

"I've been waiting to tell you that all the masters are out," he said, "and that Stickers has a message to say that there will be no lessons to-night."

"That is in honour of you, Ralph," cried Harold Lakeman, patting our hero on the back.

Ralph made some laughing reply, and the lads trooped into the school-room.

It was growing dark, and Matthew Stickers was lighting the lamps and bewailing his hard fate.

Mr. Stormaway had refused to relent, and the man-of-all-work groaned as he thought of how soon he would have to look for some other employment.

"Some people get gold watches, chains, and lockets," he muttered. "It's the way of the world; the young 'uns get all the luck now. I don't s'pose there'll be a subscription got up for me."

At this moment Timothy Slowbob glided into the room, and bestowed a series of harrowing and flesh-creeping winks on the boys, who were passing away the rest of the evening as best they could.

"Matthew," said Slowbob, "I have come to say that I am sorry you are going to leave us."

"You look like it," Stickers growled. "No, no! Wiciousness is your nature, and wicious you will be as long as you live."

"This makes me very sad," said Slowbob, solemnly. "If you can't forget, try to forgive. I came here to tell you that I've found out a wonderful trick, and I want you to help me to do it. Try to be pleasant for once, Matthew. Don't look so much like a crab-apple tree."

"Stickers has a good heart," Ralph remarked; "he could not be angry with anybody long."

"That's true," the man-of-all-work said; "but what I've suffered 'ere have been enough to conwert a man into a walkin' lime-juice factory. I bear no malice, and so, Slowbob, you may put it down that I forgets and forgives."

"Bravo!" chorused the boys. "Now, Timothy, what trick have you found out?"

"The great trick of the vanishing lady," Slowbob replied.

"If you could make Mrs. Jumble vanish from the Abbey instead of me, what a blessin' it would be!" Stickers muttered.

"I don't think she would try the 'speriment," Slowbob returned; "but you will, Stickers. The trick might come in useful to you some day. All I want is a chair, a sheet, and a rope, and after we have 'stonished the young gentlemen, I'll go round with the hat."

"I am sure you will find us liberally disposed," said our hero. "A shilling or two might come in handy to Stickers soon."

"They would," Stickers replied; "but I'm too old a bird to be caught with Slowbob's chaff. I haven't forgot how I was lured hup the chimbley, nor how I was fetched down on a fork, like a bloater."

"This is what he calls forgetting and forgiving," said Timothy Slowbob. "I'm ashamed of him."

"And so am I," Ralph cried; "well, he will be the loser of it."

Matthew Stickers turned the matter slowly over in his mind.

"I want to know something more about this 'ere trick," he said. "Where shall I wanish to?"

Slowbob drew him aside and whispered mysteriously in his ear:

"It's only a lark, and the young gentlemen will laugh at being sold," he said. "When I put the sheet over you and tie you up, I'll turn out the lamps—of course you'll wanish out of sight."

"That I can hunderstand," Stickers responded, nodding his head; "but wot do you want to tie me up for?"

"To make the thing look real," said Timothy. "Don't let a few shillings slip through your fingers."

"I won't; but mind this, Slowbob——"

"Hush! or you will spoil everything," the page-boy interrupted. "Now for the trick."

Timothy descended to the school-laundry, and soon returned with the requisite articles, and Matthew Stickers, with many misgivings, yet longing to extract money from the boys' pockets, sat down.

Slowbob tied him up carefully and securely, and then threw the sheet over him.

"Gentlemen," said the irrepressible, "in a few moments our respected friend will wanish from your gaze."

This was certainly the case, for as Slowbob extinguished the lamps the boys withdrew, leaving the man-of-all-work chuckling.

"Timothy," he said, in a low tone of voice, "just collect them subscriptions at once."

There was no response to this delicate hint.

Slowbob had also withdrawn himself from the room, and the luckless man-of-all-work was not only in the dark, but quite alone.

"Now then," said Matthew, "how long am I to be kept here rolled hup like an 'edge'og?"

He listened for a reply to this all-important question, but it came not.

Suddenly something like the truth dawned upon him.

"It ain't possible that they're a goin' to leave me 'ere all night!" he gasped. "Hoh, hass, hoh, hidiot, that I was to trust one of 'em, for they was all in it!"

Mr. Stickers wriggled, but not only were his ankles tied to the legs of the chair, but his wrists were also encumbered, and the knots held good.

"Marcy!" he gasped. "Wot shall I do? I can hear 'em gigglin' hout-side."

This was a mistake, and only the result of the man-of-all-work's heated imagination; but presently he did actually hear something.

The door opened, and somebody stepped into the room.

"Slowbob's comin' back with them subscriptions," murmured Stickers, smiling under the folds of the sheet. "He ain't sich a bad feller after all."

Alas! it was not Slowbob, but Herr Fritz Halfamann, who, having left his umbrella in a corner of the school-room, had returned to fetch it.

"There vos something always pad apout an umprella," the German said to himself. "You put him down, and somepody vill bick him up, but vhen you puts him up yourself the vind vill plow him inside out, or——"

The little Teuton ceased muttering, and felt his heart thump against his side, for Matthew Stickers had spoken.

"Now then, Slowbob," was his remark, "just you have done with this 'ere nonsense. Hoff with this sheet, and hand hover wot money you've got."

Herr Fritz Halfamann heard the last six words only, and backed slowly towards the door.

"Zee man mit zee pagbibes has come again," he said.

"Are you goin' to let me hout o' this puddin'-cloth, or ain't you?" Stickers yelled. "Boy, with the 'art of a wenomous himp, set me free!"

"It vos dat Stickers, and he has peen taking liperties wit zee peer-parrel again," said Herr Halfamann, as he took a box of vestas from his pocket. "Dot man vill do some mischeef if he is not sent away before zee end of zee week."

The German tutor struck a vesta and held it above his head.

The sight presented by Matthew Stickers fairly staggered him, and the vesta fell from his hand.

"It vas him den dot blayed zee bart of zee ghost," he said, "and it vas von lucky t'ing dat I haf found him out at last. If Mistare Stormaway vas here——"

"I am here," said the voice of the head-master. "What is the matter?"

Herr Fritz Halfamann struck another vesta, and pointed to the victim of the vanishing trick.

"Good gracious! what is it?" Mr. Stormaway gasped.

"You may well ask what is it," Stickers groaned. "Set me free, and I'll tell you all about it."

"I'll set you free!" Mr. Stormaway cried. "Give me a knife—a hatchet—anything that is sharp."

A knife was produced, Stickers's bonds were severed, and Matthew, starting to his feet, threw off the sheet.

Wounded in mind, sore in body, and expecting to be smitten by his irate principal, he threw himself into a pugilistic attitude.

"Come on, both of you," he shouted. "Send for all the boys. Send for Mr. Muffler, Mrs. Jumble, the cook, the housemaids, and Slowbob, and I'll fight the lot. I've got the sack, so I may as well have my fling before I go. Come on! Ha, ha! Bring me a 'orse, bind hup my wounds—Richard is hisself again!"

"This is too dreadful," said Mr. Stormaway, pressing his hand to his brow. "Oh, my friend Halfamann, what are we to do with this man?"

"It vould pe zee pest t'ing in zee vorld to knock him down, und holt him until he vas petter," Herr Halfamann replied.

"Knock me down!" Stickers yelled. "Yahoo! Try it hon, you German sassidge!"

Herr Halfamann was the best-tempered man in the world, but this insult roused all his angry blood.

He went for Matthew Stickers, and closing with him brought him down heavily on his back.

In this recumbent attitude, and with many sighs and moans, the man-of-all-work told the story of his wrongs.

"This is too preposterous — too

outrageous to be endured !" Mr. Stormaway thundered. "Rise, Stickers, and go to your bed; I will see into this at once. I will find Slowbob, and—and—and——"

The head-master could say no more. He rushed from the room, but in vain he searched for the page-boy.

Slowbob had performed the vanishing trick on his own account.

CHAPTER XXVII.

A NOVEL HIDING-PLACE—THE FACES AT THE WINDOW.

As may be imagined, Mr. Stormaway whilst engaged in his search did not forget to peep into the dormitories.

To all appearance the boys were sound asleep, and the head-master argued mentally that to wake them would only add to the commotion.

"To-morrow — to-morrow !" he muttered, with a grim smile on his face, as he returned to his own room. "I will have no more of this. And yet Stickers is most to blame. He must go, even if I have to compensate him for what he has brought on himself. As to Slowbob, of course he is somewhere about the premises. He is my apprentice, alas ! But the law gives me power to deal with him, and that he shall find out to his sorrow."

As Mr. Stormaway banged the door of his room, our hero sat up in bed.

"A narrow escape," he said. "Are you asleep, Charlie ?"

"Not I," Chadwick replied. "We are all as wide-awake as yourself, Ralph. I expect that Mr. Stormaway knows all about Stickers. Poor Slowbob!"

"We must do our best for him," Ralph returned.

"Thank'ee, Mr. Mornington."

"Why, that is Slowbob's voice !" cried our hero in surprise. "Where are you ?"

"Under your bed, sir," replied the cheerful youth. "Mr. Stormaway has been hunting for me everywhere, so I took off my boots and crept up here. Wait a little time and I'll slip back to the cupboard in which I sleep."

Slowbob crawled forth, and sitting upon the floor, nursed his knees and chuckled.

All the boys in the dormitory stared at him as well as they could by the dim light of the rising moon that found its way through the chinks of the blinds.

"Well," said Ralph, after a pause, "this has been an eventful day if you like."

"And the morning isn't here yet," Slowbob returned, significantly.

"You speak in riddles," Charlie Chadwick said. "We are all friends here, so why do you not tell us what you have on your mind ?"

"Mind !" Slowbob echoed. "I never knew I had any worth taking notice of. What do you think I should have on my mind ?"

"Something mysterious, and more than I could fathom," said Ralph.

Slowbob favoured the boys with a hollow laugh, and then took his leave as strangely as he had done earlier in the day.

The room designated as a cupboard by Slowbob, and in which it was his custom to repose, was on the first-floor.

It was furnished with a small window, exactly level with the top of the water-butt, and fitted with an iron bar, so that the page-boy could get his head through with difficulty, and back again with still greater difficulty, as his ears always contrived to be in the way.

Slowbob went to bed, but sleep was denied him.

His eyes persisted in remaining open, and every nerve in his body tingled. It was not the thought of the Abbey ghost—it was not the fear of punishment that kept Timothy Slowbob in this wakeful state. What was it, then ?

He had a vague idea that something was about to happen, and he kept his gaze fixed upon the window.

Suddenly, to his horror, it was filled up with a human face.

What the features were like he could not see, but he thought that he could discern the ends of a pointed moustache.

This face disappeared, and another and a fuller one took its place.

Slowbob lay as in a trance, almost convinced that he was asleep and suffering from nightmare.

His blood ran cold, and colder still

when he saw something pressed against the window.

Then the glass gave way, and something struck the wall with a dull, heavy thud just an inch above Timothy's head.

Gasping with terror he rolled out of bed, and scrambled more dead than alive to the window, just in time to see two dark shadows flit across the kitchen-garden.

Slowbob knew that the object which had struck the wall was nothing more nor less than a bullet from an air-gun.

"Well," said Timothy, whose heart was beating audibly, "if that bullet was meant for me it was a good shot. If old Stickers had been in that bed instead of me it would have shaved his nose off."

All through the night Slowbob sat and watched at the window, but he durst not procure a light for fear that its rays might act as a mark for the dastards who had attempted to take his life, and for all he knew they might be about, waiting for another chance. At last day dawned, and then he searched for the bullet. He found it embedded in the wall.

Poor Slowbob, weak and fatigued, threw himself once more upon the bed and fell sound asleep.

The bells rang. The servants came downstairs and went about their work, the boys scampered to and fro, but Timothy Slowbob slept on.

Mr. Stormaway, full of wrath and determined upon revenge, stole on tiptoe into the page-boy's little room.

"Boy," he cried, "get up and answer to me for your conduct."

Timothy moved uneasily; the muscles of his hand relaxed, and the bullet fell at the head-master's feet.

Mr. Stormaway, picked it up, and gazed at it, and then at the broken window with dilated eyes.

"Slowbob!" he almost shouted, "Slowbob! What is the meaning of this?"

The sleeping boy merely turned over with his face to the wall, murmuring as he did so:

"Mounseer Carleon, you are a villain! I tell you so to your teeth. Shoot away, for I've not much to live for, but if I do live, I'll be even with you yet."

Mr. Stormaway wrote these words in his note-book, and turned away.

Shortly afterwards a loud knock came at Timothy's door.

"Hallo!" he cried, starting up. "Who is there?"

"It vas zee barty dot found Stickares," responded the voice of the German tutor. "I haf prought von cup of tea, and vhen you feel petter, Mistare Stormaway vould like to see you in his study."

"About the wanishing trick, I s'pose," Timothy said, as he stared in amazement at Herr Halfamann. "I don't quite understand. I—I——"

"Mine poy," interrupted the Teuton, placing his hand on the page-boy's shoulder, "not von vord vill pe said apout dat affair. Dere is someting moch more imbortant to discuss. Haf you forgotten zee leedle pullet? Drink dis, den, und see Mistare Stormaway as soon as you can. He vill be all kindness to you."

CHAPTER XXVIII.

THE BREAKFAST BEFORE THE CRICKET-MATCH.

WHAT passed between Mr. Stormaway and Slowbob must be kept a secret for the present.

Timothy was a little more subdued that morning, but he went about his duties in much the same style as usual, and not a word did he say about his adventure.

It need not be told that Mr. Stormaway had confided in Herr Fritz Halfamann, and the German, though mystified and completely bewildered at the occurrence, kept it as close as an oyster.

Stickers was called in, and Mr.

Stormaway, after chaffing him at being so foolish as to allow himself to be made a fool of, dismissed him with five shillings.

"You will keep me hon at the Abbey I hopes now, sir?" Matthew said.

"No," Mr. Stormaway replied; "I will suspend you for a time. You may call on me at the end of a fortnight, and during that period I will think over the matter. Leave the neighbourhood, and perhaps when you return your wits may be clearer."

Stickers departed lamenting, just as

Ralph appeared with an open letter in his hand.

"Come in, Mornington," said Mr. Stormaway. "What have you there ?"

"A challenge from Upton Grammar School Cricket Club, sir," Ralph replied. "They wish to play us on Wednesday next. You will see, sir, that they leave it to us whether we play on our own field or go to Upton."

"They had better come here," said Mr. Stormaway, as he glanced at the letter.

"Very good, sir. Then I may take it that we may play the match."

"Yes."

Away went Ralph in high glee to write to the captain of the Upton Grammar School, and Mr. Stormaway, walking into the playground, met Alphonse Carleon.

"Ah, monsieur !" said the headmaster, cheerfully. "Did you notice the moon last night ? I am told that there was a very fine lunar rainbow."

"No," the Frenchman replied ; "I went to bed early."

Mr. Stormaway looked him full in the face, but Carleon did not flinch or quail.

"I am sorry I missed the sight," the head-master said. "By the way, how is Walbut progressing ?"

"Very well indeed," the Frenchman replied, calmly ; "but he does not seem to be so comfortable as he might be with many of his schoolfellows."

"You must remember," Mr. Stormaway said, "that Walbut did not try to court favour when he first came to the Abbey. He relied upon his size and superior strength, and made himself generally disagreeable."

"That I pointed out to him only yesterday," Carleon remarked.

"Only yesterday ?"

Mr. Stormaway started, and coloured as he repeated the words.

"Perhaps I was wrong to lecture him without your permission," Alphonse Carleon continued ; "but I happened to meet him near Bluebell Dale, and I gave him a good talking to. If it was an error on my part I apologise."

"You did quite right," Mr. Stormaway said, as he turned away with a perplexed look on his face. "Goodmorning, monsieur."

Carleon raised his hat, and bowed with the suave politeness of his race.

"I am all abroad," the head-master murmured, as he walked slowly along. "I must not suspect this man without just cause. Ah me ! What with this inexplicable mystery, the ghost, the strange voices, and—and Slowbob and Stickers, it is a wonder that my mind does not become unhinged."

Saturday came, and with it the departure of Matthew Stickers.

With many sighs and groans that unfortunate being corded his box.

Timothy Slowbob rendered him every assistance, and endeavoured to cheer him up.

"Never mind, old boy," said the irrepressible ; "Mr. Stormaway may take you on again, and if not, you will have a lot of nice things to remember. Think what friends you and I have been. "

"None o' that," Stickers growled. "No more cheek. Just recollect that I'm no longer a servant to Mr. Stormaway. I don't want to create a disturbance, but——"

Timothy was sitting on the trunk while Stickers endeavoured to lock it.

Perhaps it was wrong for Slowbob to slip off at a critical moment, but he did, causing the lid to fly up, and come into contact with Matthew's chin.

Mr. Stickers performed as neat a somersault as was ever accomplished by a trained acrobat, but the performance did not appear to afford him the slightest satisfaction.

"Bravo," cried Slowbob. "That's the best I ever saw you do, Matthew ; where did you learn it ?"

The ex-man-of-all-work looked about for something heavy to hurl at his tormentor, but seeing that Slowbob was preparing to defend himself, he pointed sternly to the door.

"Hout, wampire !" he spluttered. "Hout ! There's p'ison in the wery looks of you !"

"Oh, I'm going," Slowbob said, calmly. "You shouldn't have filled your box so full. Greedy men always get their deserts."

"What do you mean ?" Stickers gasped. "Do you insinewate that I've got anythink 'ere as don't belong to me ?"

"I've heerd say that a guilty conscience needs no accusin'," Slowbob replied.

And then he fled, for Matthew Stickers in his frenzy tore down a row of hat-pegs mounted on a wooden frame, and hurled it wildly through the open door.

It missed Timothy, and crashing through the landing window, astonished the butcher, who was waiting for orders, by alighting on his head.

Indeed, the butcher was so amazed that he sat down and closed his eyes, as if to think the matter out with due deliberation, and then he opened his mouth as if to make a speech on the subject.

There the cook found him, and soothed him with womanly tenderness, but the butcher refused to be comforted.

Naturally enough he wished to know where the row of hat-pegs came from, and having received the information from that gentle peacemaker, Slowbob, he vowed by marrow-bones and cleavers, block and hatchet, that he would wait upon Matthew Stickers in a way that would be far from agreeable to his feelings.

Oil was, however, poured on the troubled waters by Mr. Stormaway, who had again to loosen his purse strings.

"And now," cried that much-tortured gentleman, "if Stickers is not out of the Abbey in five minutes, I will go upstairs and throw him out of the window."

With his box on his shoulder, Matthew Stickers descended to the hall.

Mrs. Jumble bade him farewell in a manner that would have iced a steaming bowl of punch.

"Good-bye," she said; "I wish you well, and I hope you may never come to the workhouse."

"If I does," Stickers retorted, "I hopes that I shall have the pleasure of meetin' you. Let me give you a word of hadwice, marm. Don't gorge yourself with all the good things o' this life, and 'arf starve other people to keep down the 'xpenses."

This hit Mrs. Jumble hard—in point of fact so hard that it took away her breath.

It is impossible to say what would have been said and done, for Slowbob appeared on the scene with an armful of old boots, which he proceeded to hurl at Matthew Stickers.

These messengers of good luck affected their recipient deeply.

He almost shed tears as a somewhat knobby high-low raised a bump on the back of his head, and breathing a parting blessing on Timothy Slowbob, and the inmates of the Abbey generally, he staggered out, and closed the door in a manner that suggested the firing of a cannon.

Matthew Stickers was gone.

Was it a case of "He shall no more return," or would he, like the proverbial shilling, turn up again?

We shall see.

Matters went on pretty smoothly at the Abbey for the next two or three days.

The boys were on their best behaviour, so that nothing might mar the enjoyment of the coming cricket-match.

At last the eventful day dawned.

Ralph Mornington jumped out of bed, and ran to the window.

"Glorious!" he cried. "There is not a cloud in the sky. Hurrah, boys! What a jolly day we shall have!"

The boys cheered so lustily, that Mr. Stormaway sent up a messenger to tap at the door, and say that such things as canes and birches were still in vogue; and if any demonstration of this fact were needed, the boys had only to continue their line of conduct.

This proclamation caused a slight fall in the human barometer, but it went up again, and the lads were soon as jubilant as ever.

How could it be otherwise?

Had not Mr. Stormaway invited the Upton eleven, and their head-master to breakfast?

Was there not to be a brass band in the cricket-field, and were not all sorts of nice people, Lord Auburton and his daughter particularly, to see the match.

Yes, all these things were to be, and it would have been a wonder indeed had there been a frowning face at the Abbey.

At nine o'clock precisely the rattle of wheels and a cheer announced the arrival of the Upton eleven.

In came the Rev. William Hardback, and in came his pupils, with their cricketing attire, and all necessaries for the friendly conflict, in long bags, that persisted in getting in Mr. Stormaway's way as he endeavoured to make a neat speech.

It was somewhat nipped in the bud by his having to rub his shins occasionally; but such a trifle was overlooked, and then, when the boys of the two schools had done shaking hands with each other, all sat down to breakfast.

Mrs. Jumble was arrayed in a new gown; Slowbob, with all his buttons on for once, and with a face polished with yellow soap, was resplendent, and the maid-servants wore blue and amber ribbons in their caps, the colours being those [of the Merrytown Abbey C.C.

"What do you think of my lads?" demanded the Rev. William Hardback, proudly.

These words were addressed to Mr. Stormaway, who, happening to be attending to the requirements of his younger guests, did not hear him.

Ralph took advantage of this, and, imitating the head-master's voice, replied for him.

"Oh, well enough," he said, "but a little too splindly about the legs, and decidedly large-headed."

"Well, I'm blessed!" gasped Slow-bob, who heard the words plainly. "The guv'nor's gone wrong in his head!"

The Rev. William Hardback, whilst waiting for a reply, had taken a mouthful of coffee.

He got rid of it in such a hurry, and looked so dreadful about the eyes, that Herr Fritz Halfamann rushed to his assistance.

"The gentlemans vas choking!" he cried. "Dot coffee vas gone zee vrong vay."

"I am deeply distressed," Mr. Stormaway said. "My dear sir, allow me to pat your back."

But the Rev. William Hardback required no assistance.

He recovered himself, and glared in such an indignant manner at poor Mr. Stormaway, that he felt that something must be wrong.

"What is the matter?" he asked, blandly. "I fear that a fly must have found its way into your coffee."

"Sir," replied the Upton head-master, "there was no fly in my coffee. Will you kindly repeat the remark you made about my pupils?"

"I made no remark about them whatsoever," said Mr. Stormaway in amazement.

"Oh, there's a whopper!" said Slowbob, in an audible whisper.

Mr. Stormaway turned as suddenly as if a wasp had stung him.

"What was that?" he cried.

"A spider, sir," Slowbob returned, "There he goes, sir, near the window."

"Mr. Hardback," said the head-master of Merrytown Abbey, "I assure you as a man of honour, that I made no observation about your pupils. I may as well inform you at once that this house is a mystery. I will explain my meaning fully later on."

"Well, well," responded the Rev. William Hardback, "it would be a pity to spoil the day. I recollect in one of your letters that you mentioned something relative to the Abbey being haunted."

"I almost fear it is," said Mr. Stormaway, sighing, "and I would willingly pay fifty pounds to have the ghost, real or otherwise, laid at rest."

"Perhaps you will allow me to try, and you may save your money."

"With all my heart," said the head-master of the Abbey.

"Very well. We will chat the matter over in the evening."

"Man," said Ralph, in a sepulchral tone, and speaking in the Rev. William Hardback's ear, "I am at your side. Banish me if you can."

"Dear me!" ejaculated the Upton head-master. "Bless my soul! Oh!"

"Zee gentlemans is going to choke again," cried Herr Fritz Halfamann. "It vas a vary trying t'ing to pe alvays choking."

Mr. Stormaway silenced the German tutor with a rebuking glance, and then turned his attention to his portly guest.

"You have heard something more?" he said.

"I have," the Rev. William Hardback replied. "A dreadful voice whispered in my ear. Yes, sir, and if it was not a trick on the part of that page-boy with the astonishing eyes, I shall be inclined to believe that some restless spirit is indeed within these walls."

"The page-boy with the 'stonishing eyes, as you call him, ain't going to have his character taken away for nothing," said Timothy Slowbob. "But put it down to me—pile it up thick. I can bear it, in fact I rather likes it."

Timothy's chest swelled to such an extent with virtuous indignation that one of those fatal buttons flew off, and tapped the Rev. William Hardback on the bridge of his nose.

"Go on, sir," Slowbob continued. "Put everything on my shoulders. I have no friends. Don't spare me a bit, sir."

Off came another button; and this

time it stung the Upton head-master on the upper lip.

"Would you mind turning round if you have any more to say?" requested the sufferer. "Really these random shots are distressing and bewildering."

"Slowbob," said Mr. Stormaway, "there are several hampers to be packed yet. Go and see about them."

"Very good, sir," Timothy replied, dutifully. "But——"

Mr. Stormaway's darkening brow enforced silence on the part of the irrepressible, and he went out, intending to fix the Rev. William Hardback with a wrathful glance; but as it appeared that he was looking at the ceiling, the Upton head-master lost the effect.

CHAPTER XXIX.

GREAT DOINGS IN THE CRICKET-FIELD—AN UNEXPECTED ARRIVAL—P.C. WORRYBOY IS SENT FOR TO EJECT THE UNINVITED GUEST, AND AN EXCITING SCENE ENSUES.

AT eleven o'clock the wickets were pitched, and the Uptonites having won the toss, sent two good and true batsmen to uphold the honour and glory of their school.

Ralph and Charlie Chadwick bowled, and one of the batsmen went out with a duck's-egg, and the other scored no more than three runs.

The field was crowded with spectators, and this excellent bowling brought forth tremendous cheering, for the people of Merrytown were at heart proud of the Abbey boys.

Lord Auburton became a boy again, and applauded as loudly as the rest, and Ethel clapped her daintily-gloved hands, and smiled so sweetly at Ralph that his face grew crimson.

The Upton boys did not repine as they saw their best batsmen surrender to the conqueror, but made up their minds to do their best.

When the clock struck twelve all but three of the Upton eleven were taking a rest, and it was just at that time that a singular and unexpected incident took place.

A side-gate opened, and Matthew Stickers, pushing a barrow before him, entered the cricket-field.

The barrow was neatly laid out with an assortment of tarts, cakes, sweets, and ginger-beer.

Above it waved a banner with "the strange device," cut out in white paper letters, and evidently the work of Stickers himself:

Don't be 'ard on a man as is down
Ginger bere a penny.

Mr. Stormaway was a long-enduring and patient man; but when this announcement, floating proudly on the breeze, met his gaze, his wrath was terrible to behold.

He marched up to Stickers and shook his fist in his face.

"Take that thing down," he said, pointing to the banner, "and take yourself off. How dare you come here without permission?"

"Hoh! hindeed," retorted Matthew Stickers with an exasperating snigger. "Whose permission did I require? Don't frown like that, Mister Stormaway, or you'll get crows' feet hunder your heyes."

The head-master of Merrytown Abbey panted for breath.

"Will you go? Will you go quietly, or do you wish to provoke me to kick you out of the field?" he almost shrieked.

"I begs your parding, but did you make that remark to me?" Stickers rejoined.

"Yes, I did, and I assure you I will carry my threat into execution."

"Mister Stormaway," said Stickers, "why this wrath? Why this sudden bu'stin' up of friendships? Why this sittin' on a hold man as did his best, though kept on short wittles, and wages as have compelled him to go forth inter the cold, cruel world with a barrer of pop, and cakes which are a dead loss if they goes stale."

"Will you go? I ask you again, will you go?" Mr. Stormaway thundered.

"Hopen tarts," Stickers continued, "is hapt to get dusty, and sossidge-rolls don't take well 'cause they are tuppence. Never mind, Mister Stormaway; I bears you no ill will. Will you try a bottle of lemingnade?"

"I can't bear this any longer," the

head-master cried, wildly. "Where is Worryboy?"

"Which I treated him to a bottle," said Stickers, "and he said as how it fizzed down in his chest for a quarter of an hour and squenched his thirst in an hinstant. It takes a lot to squench Worryboy's thirst. I've knowed the time when a four-gallon cask o' beer couldn't have done it. Do try a bottle, sir. Here's one hup, and a strainin' at the cork."

Mr. Stormaway clawed the air with his open hands, and then, turning suddenly, rushed away shouting for Worryboy.

During the brief interval that ensued before the valiant constable was discovered fast asleep behind a tent, Slowbob approached the barrow.

"What, Matthew!" he cried. "Well, this is a treat. How are you getting along?"

Stickers pointed sternly to the barrow.

"I've come 'ere to get my livin', and not to talk to a halligator in buttons," he said. "Do you want anything? If you don't, stand aside for them as does. Lemingnade, ginger-beer, or harmond nuts. Who'll buy a brown hold man for a penny—I mean who'll buy a brown cake of a hold man for a penny?"

"Give me a bottle of ginger-beer," said Slowbob.

"Money fust!" Stickers observed. "If you gets the pop you'll do the wanishing trick with a wengeance."

"Oh, here's the penny," said Timothy, "Now then, don't keep me waiting."

"A Frenchman!" remarked the wary Matthew, glancing at the coin.

"I say it isn't."

"And I say it is."

"Then let me have it back," said Slowbob.

"No," Stickers responded, shaking his head. "I'll keep it for you, or you may get into trouble."

Slowbob had long arms, and shooting one out across the barrow, he annexed Mr. Stickers's nose and held on with such tenacity that his victim squeaked like a pig when interviewed by the relentless butcher.

"Now then," said Timothy; "will you give me my penney back? I'm good enough to hang on here for a week."

"You're killidg be," groaned Matthew Stickers. "Dod't ye see that you are pullidg be dowd amog the oped darts."

"I'll flatten you out on them if you try to cheat me," Timothy cried. "Ah, I thought you would think better of it. Oh, you wicked old sinner!"

The ex-man-of-all-work parted with the penny, but he had not got over the effects of the attack, and his voice was far from clear.

"Owd sidder be blowed," he said. "You got the peddy, but bind I paid it under protest. Oh, my dose! Did man ever suffer such haggody?"

At this moment Mr. Stormaway and Worryboy appeared on the scene.

The constable's helmet was a little on one side, giving him a rakish look; his eyes were bright, and he was smiling to such an extent that there was no appreciable space between the corners of his mouth and ears.

It was evident that Mr. Worryboy had been enjoying himself.

"Ah," said Matthew Stickers, "now we shall get at the rights o' things. Worryboy, I gives Timothy Slowbob in charge for 'sault and battery."

"Pay no attention to him," chimed in Mr. Stormaway. "Constable, remove that man from my premises, and see that the barrow is put outside."

"What!" Stickers cried, "are you in earnest? I thought you was a jokin', and many a joke you and I have had, Mister Stormaway."

"Constable," the head-master said, "I have borne more than enough to provoke a breach of the peace. Do your duty, or I will not be answerable for the consequences."

"Now then," Worryboy began, "you must clear out of this, Stickers. You are a trespassin', which is punishable by the law."

"This comes o' fillin' a man hout with ginger-beer," Matthew said, disdainfully. "Now it so 'appens that I knows the law better than either of you. If I'm wrong it's a case for a summons, so summons away. I won't budge a hinch."

"Won't you?" said Worryboy, suddenly dropping his affable tone. "I'll jolly soon see about that. Lay hold o' them shafts and take the barrer out, or I'll move it for you."

"You daren't," Stickers yelled. "I've been a readin' up the law. By an act made by Charles II., a man may sell vinkles hanywhere and at hany time, 'scept on a Sunday, when, if he was caught, he was hung, drawn, and quartered on the top of Temple Bar. That hact applies to me."

"This man is mad," Mr. Stormaway cried. "Constable, away with him. I will hold you blameless, whatever happens."

"It's rather a dry day for a row, sir," Worryboy remarked.

"When you have ejected this—this monstrosity, you may go to the marquee and order what you please," the head-master replied, hoarsely. "Get rid of him, for mercy's sake, or the enjoyment of the day is over."

"Right you are, sir. Stickers, I calls upon you three time in the name of the law. Will you go? Once."

"No."

"Will you go? Twice."

"I wouldn't go for a harmy of sogers," Stickers replied.

"Three times."

"I wouldn't move for a nurrycane."

"Then I'll move you," said Worry-boy.

Seizing the shafts, he ran the barrow, with Stickers clinging madly to it, into a crowd of people who had not the slightest notion that any dispute was going on.

As ill-luck would have it, the barrow overturned, burying its owner, save his legs, under it, and so working upon the feelings of the ginger-beer and lemonade, that bottle after bottle burst and treated the bystanders to showers of foam.

Mr. Stormaway received a cork between his eyes, and for hours after experienced a sensation as if the smitten spot were being tapped with a red-hot hammer.

Great was the consternation, for not only was the barrow overturned, and Matthew Stickers entombed beneath it, but Worryboy shot clean over the wreck, and lay quivering where he fell.

Then Mr. Stormaway took off his hat, and casting it wildly down, pulled his unoffending hair.

"I am the cause of this," he said, "Why—oh, why did I not let the foolish old man stay? Worryboy, get up, I say! You are not hurt?"

"Ain't I?" moaned the constable. "Every button of my uniform is drove into my body. Marcy! Ain't there a drop o' anything in the field to bring a man round?"

"Yes, yes," said Mr. Stormaway, wildly; "but pray get up and lend a hand with Stickers."

Matthew was still under the barrow, and Worryboy, having consented to rise, which he did, declaring that he would have to put himself on the sick-list for a month, the ginger-beer emporium was raised, and the ex-man-of-all-work dragged by his heels into the light.

Stickers lay quite still, with his eyes closed and his lips compressed.

"The man is dead!" Mr. Storm-away cried, wringing his hands.

"Stand aside, if you please!" cried Dr. Pillem, who was present. "I will soon see into this."

As the medical man spoke, a tremor passed through Matthew Stickers's frame.

The doctor went down on his knees, and put his hand on the fallen hero's heart.

"The fellow is shamming!" Dr. Pillem said. "Will somebody be kind enough to hold my walking-cane while I get at my case of lancets. I always carry them about with me."

"Hif you think you are goin' to bleed me, you're mistaken," Stickers observed in a lively tone of voice.

Up he got, and staring at Mr. Stormaway with lack-lustre eyes, he pointed, like an avenging ghost, at the wreck.

"It ain't my cart—it ain't my ginger-beer and lemingnade, nor is anythink mine!" he said. "I'm honly the hagent, so look hout for a bill as long as your arm, and a writ from my lawyers. Adoo, sir—adoo!"

Mr. Stormaway would have spoken, but Dr. Pillem interfered.

"Let the impostor go!" he said.

"I'll see he does," Worryboy remarked. "Now then, will you——"

"I requires no hassistance from a bloater minion of the law!" Stickers interrupted. "Where can the sense of the Government be to put such a thing as you into a good soot of clothes?"

Worryboy stifled his wrath, and followed Mr. Stormaway to the re-freshment marquee, and when supplied with a liberal quantity of sherry and ham sandwiches, he soon forgot his woes.

Matthew Stickers left the barrow on the field and went out.

"I have him now," he said. "In less than a week I shall be back at the Habbey. Oh, Matthey, you are a knowin' one, and that banner did the trick! I knowed it would!"

CHAPTER XXX.

CONCLUSION OF THE MATCH—A SUDDEN STORM—FLIGHT FROM THE FIELD —WHY THE UPTON BOYS COULD NOT RETURN—A PROCESSION OF GHOSTS.

BARRING this incident, everything went as merrily as a peal of wedding-bells.

The Upton boys went out, and the Abbey boys went in, and beat their opponents by twenty runs; but there were no long faces on the part of the guests.

Everybody was in the best humour, and Mr. Stormaway, having got over his trouble with Stickers, shook hands with the Rev. William Hardback at least twenty times, and took so many glasses of sherry with him that his eyes shone like two miniature harvest-moons.

Up to this time the day had been delightful, but now a copper-coloured hue spread over the sky.

A storm was coming, and it burst with such startling suddenness that all had to scamper for shelter.

The marquee was soon full, as were all the smaller tents.

Down came the rain with a rush and a rattle, and the wind came tearing along as if running a race with the lightning.

Mr. Stormaway got jammed up in a corner just where there was a hole in the tent, and was subjected to the torture of a thin stream of water, that persisted in running down his neck.

Many others fared no better, and poor Slowbob, who was shut out altogether, was drenched to the skin, but was perfectly happy, though the wind had blown his hat clean out of the enclosure, and the rain had wrinkled his mulberry unspeakables like the bellows of a concertina.

Some of the ladies were alarmed at the vivid lightning; but their terror did not last long, for the worst of the storm soon passed away, though it went on raining as if it meant to rain for ever.

There was nothing to be done but to get home somehow.

Those who had come from a distance huddled into their conveyances, and at last Mr. Stormaway gave the order to make for the Abbey.

A regular stampede took place, the boys running with their jackets over their heads, jostling against each other, and thinking it good fun.

Mr. Muffler, who had donned a new silk hat for the occasion, copied this idea; but after he had crashed up against Mr. Stormaway twice, and fallen into a pool of water, he gave it up.

No umbrellas had been taken out, and all were in a pretty pickle when the Abbey was reached.

There was a rush to the dormitories to change clothes, and the Upton boys were fitted out while their own garments were sent down to the laundry to dry.

Then there was more laughing, because it transpired that the waggonette in which the guests had arrived had been left in the open, and that the coachman was replete with something that certainly was not Adam's ale.

There was no chance of the Upton boys going home until the morning, for the rain still came down, and dashed against the Abbey windows as if to say, "Come and try how you like me now."

Extra beds were made up, and a frolic took place, bolster-battles being to the fore.

In Ralph's room there were high jinks indeed, for our hero had secured the captain of the Upton Grammar School Cricket Club and two or three other convivial spirits.

The rival captain's name was Harry Jayson, and he was a youth after our hero's stamp.

"I say," he said, "tell us about this ghost. I think we could make some fun out of it to-night."

Ralph told him as much as he knew, and Jayson burst out laughing.

"I think I have a happy thought," he said. "Why not have a procession of ghosts? We can array ourselves in sheets, you know."

"Good!" said our hero. "I am with you."

While this nice little plot was being hatched, Mr. Stormaway was entertaining the Rev. William Hardback in his study.

They were also discussing the ghost.

"You have never seen the spectre yourself, you say?" said Mr. Stormaway's guest.

"THE UNFORTUNATE GENTLEMAN FELL ON THE PAVEMENT AS IF HE HAD BEEN SHOT.—(See page 115.)

"No; and it has often struck me as strange that it has never paid me a visit."

The Rev. William Hardback leaned his chin upon his hand, and gazed thoughtfully at the wall.

"A trick, sir—a silly practical joke, sir!" he observed.

"So I have often thought," Mr. Stormaway replied; "but how can it be so? The boys, Mrs. Jumble, Mr. Muffler, and many others have seen it. I really do not know what to think."

"How often does it walk?"

"Occasionally. Sometimes the visitations are far apart; at others it is seen nightly for as long as a week at a time."

"If I were here a week," said the Rev. William Hardback, "the ghost would walk no more. I would lay such a trap that escape would be next to impossible."

"Come and stay a week with me during the vacation."

"The ghost would not walk then."

"You think not?"

"I am as certain of it as a man can be certain of anything," the Rev. William Hardback replied. "You have a fearless as well as a troublesome boy here."

"I regret to say I have many," Mr. Stormaway said, with a sigh. "Well, I am more perplexed and worried than I care to own. Dear me, it is eleven o'clock; I had no idea it was so late!"

The Rev. William Hardback took this as a hint that it was time to go to bed. He took his candlestick, and bade his kindly host a courteous goodnight.

"I can find the way to my room," he said, "so pray do not trouble yourself to accompany me, as I am aware that yours lies in a different direction."

They shook hands and parted the best of friends.

If the Rev. William Hardback relished anything more than another, it was to pass a night in the Abbey.

He had paid several visits, and the quaint old place had always afforded him the greatest delight, for he was an antiquary at heart, and belonged to no end of archæological societies.

He lingered a while as he went on his way.

"Ah!" he said, "here are the niches in which the effigies of the saints used to stand. Henry the Eighth," he added, shaking his head gravely, "you were a bad man; and as for you, Oliver Cromwell, you were an ass."

"You're another," said a voice, indignantly. "Don't abuse a man who never did you any harm."

The Rev. William Hardback was a strong-nerved man; but now he trembled in his limbs, and quaked in his heart. He quite expected to see the shade of old Noll start up at his feet.

"Dear me!" he said; "how extraordinary! Pooh! Pooh! I must have been mistaken. I wish I had not taken that last glass of wine."

"There's no mistake about it," the voice rejoined. "You had better take yourself off to bed, before I drop down on you like a cartload of bricks."

"I am sure," observed the learned gentleman, "that Oliver Cromwell was never so vulgar as to talk about cartloads of bricks. I am dreaming."

"You are not," the voice declared; "you were never more wide awake."

"Then," gasped the Rev. William Hardback, "I—I beg you—your pardon."

He was so confused and upset that he made a profound bow, and lost no time in getting to his room.

Having found that there was no lock on the door, he closed it, and sitting down, wiped his brow.

"It is all nonsense," he said. "No more port for me after dinner."

After pacing the room for some minutes, he grew calmer, and went to bed.

"This comes of talking about ghosts," he said. "Absurd—absurd! Go to sleep, man, or you will make yourself ill."

The Rev. William Hardback, however, could not sleep; and for the life of him he could not keep his eyes off the door.

"I wish it had a lock, though I don't exactly know why," he murmured. "Ghosts, I have been told, can go anywhere, and gh—o—o—o——"

He get no farther, for at that moment the door opened, and in stalked several white figures, each of which took a chair in the most graceful and deliberate style.

"It's that port," the Rev. William Hardback groaned. "I must see a doctor to-morrow."

He sat up in bed, and rubbing his eyes hard, stared at the apparitions.

"I'll see what this means though it costs me my life!" he said, as he scrambled out of bed.

"Rash man, beware!" said one of the ghosts, in a sepulchral tone. "It is death to breathe the atmosphere that hovers near us."

The Rev. William Hardback got into bed again most expeditiously.

"Bless my soul and body!" he said; "this is very dreadful! I am afraid that the last glass of port wine has nothing to do with it after all."

"Silence!" cried one of the spectres. "Brethren of the shadowy land, do you behold this poor mortal?"

"We do," replied the rest.

"He has usurped our meeting-place," continued the ghost. "He came here to pry and prowl about the Abbey. Say, then, what shall his punishment be?"

"Let us take him away with us," said one. "He is only a school-master, and nobody will miss him."

"Ha, ha, ha!" laughed the ghosts.

The Rev. William Hardback took an harlequin dive out of the other side of the bed, and crawled under it.

"Poor mortal, let him be!" said the ghost who had first spoken. "Now for our revels, brother spirits!"

They joined hands, and commenced dancing round and round, to Mr. Hardback's horror.

He could not see them, but he could hear them, and he knew what they were about.

Beads of perspiration ran down his face; he turned hot and cold by turns, and it seemed to him that he had a stream of cold water running down his back.

Suddenly, and as if by a preconcerted signal, the ghosts uttered a low long-drawn wail, and glided from the room.

"This is too horrible for human belief," groaned the Rev. William Hardback, as he crawled out of his hiding-place. "I will go at once to Mr. Stormaway. I will beg of him to give me a chair in his room, for I could not pass the night here alone for all the money in the world."

He dressed himself hurriedly with trembling hands and anyhow, for he was in the dark, and he had either mislaid the box of matches or the ghosts had taken a fancy to them.

If they were bad ghosts, of course brimstone and sulphur would be in their way—at least, so argued the Rev.

William Hardback as he struggled vainly to get his legs into the arms of his coat.

At last, however, he was ready to depart, and arming himself with a bootjack, he opened the door and peeped into the passage.

A sharp current of air set his hair on end, and had he been able to see the reflection of his face, it is probable that it would have startled him considerably, for his eyes were twice their usual size, and his mouth was drawn down at the corners.

Plucking up courage, he advanced slowly, swinging the bootjack to and fro, and ready to hurl it at the first moving thing that came in his way.

Now it so happened that Mr. Muffler, fatigued with the pleasures of the day, fell sound asleep in his own study.

When he awoke, he remembered that before going to bed he must make a tour of the dormitories to see that all was well, and slipping off his boots so as to make as little noise as possible, he started off, shading a candle with his hand.

Outside, the rain fell heavily, the wind blew furiously, and a few stray gusts having found their way into the grim old building, went tearing about and bellowing like lost children at a Sunday-school treat.

Out went Mr. Muffler's candle; but as he knew every inch of the Abbey, that trifling misadventure did not trouble his mind much.

His only fear was that the ghost might be walking again, and his heart palpitated violently as he crept along in the dark.

"What should I do if I met it?" he thought, as he turned a corner. "I think I should stand still and shriek for help."

Mr. Muffler did not meet the ghost but he met something else. It was the bootjack wielded by the Rev. William Hardback.

Down it came with a thwack upon the unfortunate usher's head, and down went he with all the colours of the rainbow dancing before his eyes.

The Rev. William Hardback knew that he had smitten something, but he did not know exactly what, and he might have passed on in blissful ignorance of the fact that he had half stunned a harmless fellow-creature, had not a pair of long arms been thrown round his legs.

The learned gentleman's feet flew

up from under him, and he took a seat with startling suddenness on the floor ; but he still held on to the bootjack.

"Monster!" groaned Mr. Muffler. "Wretch, you have slain me! Is this the hideous work of a misguided youth named Slowbob?"

"Dear me, I am very sorry!" gasped the Rev. William Hardback, who recognised the usher's voice at once. "That last glass of wine has much to answer for."

"If you swallowed a butt, that is no reason why you should knock me about," said Mr. Muffler, sitting up and rubbing his cranium. "Sir, you have raised a bump which will necessitate my wearing my hat on one side for a month. How dare you, sir? Shame on you! How dare you take too much to drink, and rush about smiting people in your delirium?"

"Mr. Muffler, I apologise," Hardback replied; "I am not myself. I have seen awful things here. Forgive me. I will make you a handsome present in the morning."

"What have you seen?" the usher demanded.

"Ghosts! Dozens of them," asserted the Rev. William Hardback; "and I have good reason to believe that the shade of Oliver Cromwell was among them, for I beg to assure you that the voice of that once great man rebuked me for calling him an ass."

Mr. Muffler trembled, and skipping to his feet, kept a respectful distance from Mr. Stormaway's guest.

"Nonsense, sir! Go to bed—I will see you to your room," said the usher. "What is that in your hand?"

"A bootjack."

"And you struck me with that murderous weapon!" cried Mr. Muffler. "It is a wonder that I am alive to hear the atrocious statement! Give it to me, sir—give it to me before I fly into a rage and trample you under my feet!"

"Take it," said Hardback. "Don't

be angry with me. I am going to Mr. Stormaway's room."

"You will do nothing of the kind," Mr. Muffler declared, throwing himself into a pugilistic attitude. "Move one inch, and I will ring the alarm-bell."

"But, my dear fellow, think of the ghosts—think of what I am suffering."

"So am I," moaned poor Mr. Muffler. "The bump has grown to a prodigious size—dear me, this pain is agonising—in fact, it will take two pounds of steak to reduce it."

"I am a miserable man," the Rev. William Hardback avowed. "Torture me no more. I will return to my own room ; but mark this, if a drivelling idiot is found in the morning, that drivelling idiot will be me."

Mr. Muffler escorted him back to his room, and refused to leave until he was in bed.

"What are you doing?" demanded the Rev. William Hardback, suddenly.

"I am taking away your clothes," replied Mr. Muffler ; "I will hold myself responsible for the action. You shall not—no, sir, you shall not play madmen's tricks here, and belabour people with bootjacks."

"But, my dear sir——"

Bang went the door, and Mr. Muffler departed in high dudgeon.

"He shall pay for this," he muttered, as he felt the top of his head tenderly. "Bless me, what a bump! Surely it must give me the appearance of being two inches taller."

He did not trouble himself much about the dormitories, but peeped into two or three.

In one, and that was occupied by Ralph, his chums, and some of the guests, Mr. Muffler thought he heard the sound of smothered laughter ; but he put it down to discord produced by nasal organs, and went to his own room, where he soothed his head with cold bandages, and presently fell asleep.

CHAPTER XXXI.

WORRYBOY GETS A CASE AT LAST—TIMOTHY SLOWBOB BEFORE THE MAGISTRATES.

WHEN Timothy Slowbob took up the Rev. William Hardback's shaving-water, he, instead of knocking politely at the door, stood still and stared at it.

"What's this?" cried the irrepressible. "Well, of all the rummy starts! Ha, ha, ha!"

The Rev. William Hardback jumped

out of bed, and opening the door popped out his head.

"How dare you laugh?" he cried.

"It's enough to make a cat die o' larfing," said Slowbob, holding his sides and rolling about as if he were demented.

"What is?" demanded the learned gentleman. "Cease that noise, you little villain, and tell me what you mean. Where is Mr. Muffler? Where are my clothes?"

"I don't know nothing about them," roared Slowbob, spilling the hot water all over the floor. "Ha, ha, ha! Oh, hold me, somebody, or I shall bu'st."

"If I could get at you," gasped Hardback; "if I only had a pair of good thick boots on my feet, or even one, you should find your way downstairs quicker than you came up."

"Look—ha, ha, ha! Look at that!" shrieked Slowbob.

He pointed to a placard pinned on the door, and the Rev. William Hardback turned crimson as he read these words:

"Beware of old crusted eighteen-penny port. Signed: The ghost of Oliver Cromwell."

In his wrath the reverend gentleman made a grab at Slowbob's hair; and missing his aim, plunged wildly against the opposite wall.

"Slowbob! Slowbob!" cried the voice of Mrs. Jumble.

"Yes, mum."

"What is that noise about?"

"This 'ere gentleman is a tryin' to make a hole through the wall with his head," replied Timothy. "Mr. Muffler's taken his clothes, he says, and the ghost of Holiver Cromwell has sent him a post-card."

All this was Dutch to Mrs. Jumble, and she would have sought an explanation, but Slowbob leaned over the landing and stopped her coming upstairs, for a very dreadful thing had happened to the Rev. William Hardback.

As he backed towards his bedroom, the door closed of its own accord, and, securing a considerable portion of his *robe de nuit*, held him in such a position that it was impossible for him to turn round.

He kicked with his heels, and performed double-knocks with the back of his head at the door, but it held fast.

"My boy—my dear boy," he said,

"don't stand there rolling your eyes at me in that fearful manner. Push the door, and it will fly open."

"I'm a dear boy now, but I was a willin a little while ago," Slowbob returned; "but never mind. 'Ere goes."

But Timothy's efforts proved ineffectual. The door was in an obstinate mood, and refused to open.

"Was ever man in such a predicament?" the Rev. William Hardback groaned. "What noise is that?"

"The pupils are a comin' down to breakfast," Slowbob replied.

"Then I shall be held up to ridicule for ever," the head-master of Upton Grammer School cried. "I would not have the boys see me in this position for a thousand pounds."

At this moment Mr. Muffler appeared, carrying the clothes he had taken charge of over his arms.

He took one look at the extraordinary figure struggling and writhing, and then he dropped the garments and fled.

Why Mr. Muffler, who believed that Mr. Hardback was mad, and nothing more or less, should shriek "Fire!" and "Thieves!" at the top of his voice, was best known to himself, but at all events his cries brought Mr. Stormaway from his room.

"Where is the fire—where is the fire?" he demanded.

"Go-o-o upstairs, sir," Mr. Muffler stammered. "My bump—I mean my brain is in a whirl."

Mr. Stormaway waited to hear no more, but bounding up the stairs, reached the landing.

One glance was sufficient for him to take in the situation.

"Stand firm!" he said. "I cannot get at the door where it sticks, so I must strike you."

"Strike me! What have I done?" cried the distinguished guest in dismay. "Oh!"

One thump in the chest—and a vigorous one it was—performed wonders.

It opened the door and sent the Rev. William Hardback through the doorway as if he had been blown out of a cannon; and only just in time, for down came the boys, laughing, romping, joking, and ready for their breakfasts.

"Page-boy," cried the reverend gentleman through the keyhole.

"Yes, sir."

"Tell my coachman to get my waggonette ready without delay."

"Right you are, sir," Slowbob replied, and went downstairs, firing off small explosions of laughter like minute guns at sea.

The Upton boys were loth to leave so early, but there was no help for it.

The head-master required no breakfast, and scarcely allowed his pupils time to finish theirs.

"Good-bye," said Ralph, as he shook hands with Jayson. "We have had a jolly time. I suppose you will often think of Oliver Cromwell's ghost?"

"I shall never forget it," Jayson replied, emphatically. "Who has the card?"

"Mr. Stormaway."

"That's all right. It is in my writing so you will get into no bother."

One loud cheer and they were gone.

Slowly and sadly the Rev. William Hardback turned his head and looked at the Abbey.

"Farewell!" he said. "Little did I dream that I should part thus with your crumbling time-worn walls. Jayson, what are you laughing at?"

"I was thinking what a pleasant time we have had, sir."

"Indeed. Humph! I am glad to hear it," said the Rev. William Hardback. "The next time the Merrytown boys play our club a match they will have to come to Upton."

Mr. Stormaway kept Oliver Cromwell's post card, as Slowbob called it, in his desk, and evinced great interest in the handwriting of his pupils, but he could detect no similarity in style or design in any of the specimens examined by him, and at last thought it better to let the subject drop.

While the duties of the school were proceeding, Mrs. Jumble sent Timothy Slowbob on a double errand.

He was to call on Miss Snip, the milliner, and bring away a new bonnet, and then, on his way back, to purchase five shillings' worth of eggs of Mr. Gammon, the provision merchant.

"And mind that you are careful not to fall down, or loiter on the way," said Mrs. Jumble. "Miss Snip will give you a hand-box, and Mr. Gammon will lend you a basket."

Little dreaming of any coming catastrophe, Timothy started.

He received the bonnet and the eggs, and, on his way back, was passing the Jodson's Will School, when the Blue-bottles came out with a rush, and began to buzz round him.

Benjamin Tite was to the fore, and seeing that both Slowbob's arms were engaged, he took that precious page-boy's nose between his finger and thumb, and tweaked it severely.

"How do you like that, Buttons?" he demanded. "Lor! isn't this a lark?"

"Is it?" cried Slowbob, with tears of anguish running down his cheeks. "If I wasn't lumbered up with this rubbish I'd lark you."

"Let us make him run," shouted a sportive Bluebottle. "Who's got a nice, long, sharp pin?"

"Don't!" Slowbob pleaded. "Act fair if you can. Now then, don't push me about or you'll smash all the eggs."

"Eggs!" repeated Benjamin Tite with a shriek of delight. "That's better and better. Do you think," here he annexed Timothy's nose again, "that I have forgotten what happened a little time ago? Run, run! Do you hear?"

Driven to desperation, Slowbob deposited the box and basket in the roadway and went for Master Tite.

This was a fatal step, for the leader of the Bluebottles bolted, while others attacked the parcels.

One youth thought it capital fun to flop himself down on the bonnet-box, while another kicked over the basket of eggs.

Timothy Slowbob's blood was boiling now. Scattering his cowardly foes right and left, he seized upon the eggs and hurled them about indiscriminately.

The damage was done, and Slowbob thought he might as well suffer for a sheep as for a lamb.

Bang, smash, crash! went the eggs in all directions.

One went through an open window, and saluted a bald-headed old gentleman, while another—alas, for Timothy!—made Worryboy's acquaintance.

It was an ill fate indeed that brought the constable round the corner at so unlucky a moment, and the mischief was scarcely done when Timothy was seized by the strong arm of the law.

"Come on to the lock-up!" Worryboy hectored. "This is the second time within three months that my wision's been effected by a hegg. I'll stand no more of it. The magistrates are a sittin', and if you don't get a month, it will be no fault of mine."

"I didn't mean it for you," was all Timothy said. "I'll go quietly, so don't pull my arms out of joint."

In a few minutes the unfortunate page-boy was under lock and key, but that painful fact had been scarcely accomplished before Mr. Stormaway heard of it by a messenger in the form of a fleet-footed boy who had watched the unequal fight.

"Give me my hat!" cried Mr. Stormaway, excitedly. "Mr. Muffler, Herr Fritz Halfamann, come with me. Slowbob has violently assaulted the police, and brought disgrace upon the Abbey. If ever a boy was born to bring misfortune upon those about him, that boy is Timothy Slowbob."

Merrytown was a small place, and the news that Mr. Stormaway's page-boy was in durance vile spread like wildfire.

Matthew Stickers and Salem Cockey, who were comparing notes at the Swan and Bottle, scampered off in high glee to the justice-room, and managed to reach the door just as Mr. Stormaway and the two under-masters arrived in hot haste.

Matthew Stickers's head was squeezed painfully against the door-post by his late master, and Herr Fritz Halfamann, in the rush, deprived Salem Cockey of his official headgear.

All was hurry, noise, and confusion, and the chairman of the magistrates rose and threatened to commit everybody.

"Sir," said Mr. Stormaway, "I beg the court's pardon, but I have just learned that my page-boy will be charged with assault. May I have a few words with him before he is brought before you?"

"You may not," the chairman replied. "There is no time, and as all the other cases are disposed of, he may as well be brought into court at once."

Timothy was led in by the arm, and placed in the dock.

Mr. Stormaway groaned audibly as he beheld an object that might have been taken for an animated scarecrow instead of a neatly attired page-boy; Mr. Muffler supplied an echo to the groan, and Herr Fritz Halfamann held up his hands.

"Vot a poy dot is!" he said.

"A juvenile demon, you mean," gasped Mr. Stormaway. "Good gracious, what is that?"

It was the wreck of Mrs. Jumble's new bonnet which Worryboy carried into the witness-box, and a titter went round the court.

Slowbob squinted horribly at the magistrates, and made them such a polite bow, that he nearly fell out of the dock.

"Afore that p'liceman starts committin' perjury, I have a few words to say to your washups," he remarked, blandly.

"Silence," said the clerk of the court. "You will have ample opportunity of speaking presently."

"Indeed," said Timothy; "you're wery kind, Mister Tinker."

"My name is Tinkler," shouted the clerk.

"Don't be so pertic'lar about a letter," Slowbob returned, "and don't get red in the face. I asked their washups' permission to ask a question."

"Well, what is it?" demanded the chairman.

"If a man throwed a brick over a wall, and hit a man that he didn't see, could he be charged with assault?"

"Certainly."

"Then I've done," said Slowbob, folding his arms across his chest. "Fire away, Worryboy, but draw it as mild as possible. I s'pose this ain't quite a hanging matter?"

He had the audacity to wink at Mr. Stormaway with one of his wonderfully-constructed eyes, and that gentleman thrust his face into his hat, and groaned again.

"I feel broud of dot poy," said Herr Halfamann in an audible whisper. "He vill pe von match for dot policeman, or I haf no love for zee Faderland of dear old Shermany."

Worryboy gave his evidence, and Slowbob listened with his hand to his ear.

"Now, boy," said the chairman, "have you any questions to ask the constable?"

"Lots of 'em," Timothy replied, cheerfully. "Now, Mister Worryboy, look me straight in the eyes."

"Who can look you straight in the eyes without feelin' queer?" the constable rejoined.

"You must not address the prisoner in that way," said Mr. Tinkler. "Answer his questions."

"Now," said Slowbob, posing himself in a graceful attitude, "afore you received that hegg, did you see any Bluebottles about ? "

"He means Jodson's Willers," Worryboy explained to the bench. "Yes, I did."

"Did you see what they were doing to me ?" the irrepressible demanded.

"No, I didn't, for they was a runnin' like winkin'," Worryboy replied.

"Good," said Timothy. "It's a lovely thing to hear a policeman speak the truth. Now, sir, your on your appledavit, so be careful. Did you see me throw that hegg ? "

"It took me afore I caught sight of you ; but you throwed it."

"Wait a minute," said Slowbob. "This case is likely to go to the House o' Lords, so you had better think twice afore you speak once. I asks you again, did you see me take that hegg in this mortial hand of mine, and throw it at you ? "

"I did not," the constable replied.

"Then there is an end of the case," observed Timothy Slowbob. "Goodday, gentlemen ; and I'm wery much obliged for the trouble you've been to me."

The irrepressible would have walked straight out of the dock, had not the usher of the court detained him.

"What now ?" Timothy demanded.

"Silence !" cried the chairman. "Prisoner, you are doing yourself no good by this show of impudence."

"It's injured innocence, your washup," said Slowbob ; "but go on, sir ; I see that you have made up your mind to do me some injury, as the fox said to the pack of hounds."

"We do not want to hear anything about a fox or a pack of hounds," the chairman observed. "What have you to say in defence ? You are charged with——"

"Don't go over it again, please," Timothy interrupted ; "it's like listening to the band of a penny show, and jars a feller's nerves. May it please your washups, and brother countrymen," here he saluted Mr. Stormaway with a bow, "this morning, in my compacity of a trusted servant to Mr. Stormaway—bless him——"

"I shall go mad," the head-master gurgled. "Like King Henry, I could cry, ' Is there no man who will rid me of this tyrant ? ' "

The next moment he turned pale, for a shout arose from outside the court.

"Three cheers for Slowbob and down with Worryboy ! Hip, hip, hip, hurrah ! "

"It vas zee poys," said Herr Halfamann ; "and dey have come from zee Appey to encourage Slowpop in his grief."

"Your washups hear the woice of the people lifted up against a great wrong," Timothy said, impressively. "It is lifted up against a overfed bobby. It is lifted up for the helpless, which is me. But to resume. Where's my handkercher ? Somethin's ticklin' my nose."

A roar of laughter went through the court, and even the magistrates had to exercise all their self-control to conceal their mirth.

"Now, your washups," continued Slowbob, "I think you will agree with me that this case never ought to have been brought into court. 'Ere's a hegg that hits a p'liceman. He doesn't see where it comes from. There were heggs on the ground, heggs on the walls, and heggs splashed on some o' the winders round about, but do it prove—I asks—do it prove "— Timothy thumped the railing of the dock—"that I threw the identical hegg that smoted Mister Worryboy ? Of course, you are at liberty to say what you like, but I say no. Your washups, I begs to call your attention to the fact that a hoary-headed old man named Matthew Stickers, gingerbeer merchant, and dealer in sassidge-rolls is grinning at me."

"Let that man be removed from the court," said the chairman.

The usher laid violent hands on the ex-man-of-all-work, and before he could utter a word of denial or expostulation, Matthew was shot down three stone steps, and driven into the midst of a crowd of the Abbey boys.

CHAPTER XXXII.

A WITNESS FOR THE DEFENCE—THE END OF THE CASE.

RALPH MORNINGTON contrived to wriggle into court just as Matthew Stickers left it involuntarily, and Slowbob, detecting him in a moment, treated the spectators to an exhibition of his politeness.

Again he bowed, and his face lit up with a triumphant smile.

"I must call a witness for the defence," he said. "Mister Mornington, come forrard."

"What can this youth prove?" demanded the chairman, glancing at our hero.

"There you go," said Slowbob. "You are down on me at once."

"Call your witness," the chairman returned; "but this is surely wasting the time of the court."

Wondering what on earth Timothy could have to say to him, Ralph stepped into the witness-box.

"Mister Mornington," said the youth in trouble, "I have only one question to ask you. Did you ever see me throw a hegg at a policeman?"

"Certainly not," our hero replied.

"There you are, then," said Timothy, smiling. "The case is dismissed of course, and Worryboy will have to pay the costs."

"Nothing of the kind," the chairman observed. "We are of the opinion that the charge is fully proved, and you are fined five shillings."

"Five shillings!" repeated Slowbob. "I've overrun my bankin' account; but I can give you a Hi Ho U."

"I will pay the money for you," Ralph whispered. "Don't say any more, or you'll find yourself out of the frying-pan into the fire."

"My friend and benefactor will pay the fine," Slowbob said. "Good-day, gentlemen all. Worryboy, it grieves my heart to think that hegg wasn't a bad one."

He sailed grandly out of court, treading on Salem Cockey's corns as he went, and leaving Mr. Stormaway in a state of stupefaction.

"Is it possible that I have heard aright?" the head-master gasped. "Can it be that I must endure Slowbob—that I must sit down quietly under my roof while he tortures me for more than six long weary years? Perish the thought! Mr. Muffler— Herr Halfamann, I do not think that I am a bad-hearted man, but hear me swear——"

"I vould not, for it vill pe setting von pad example to zee poys," the German tutor interposed.

"Hear my oath—my vow!" cried Mr. Stormaway. "He shall go! He shall follow in the path of Stickers!"

"Vait von moment," said Herr Halfamann. "You forget von leedle t'ing."

He leaned forward, and whispering something in Mr. Stormaway's ear, caused a great change in that gentleman's manner.

"Quite right," said Mr. Stormaway. "The circumstance had slipped my memory for the moment, but Slowbob shall not sleep at the Abbey."

"Slowpop not sleep at zee Appey!" Herr Halfamann cried. "Vhere, zen, shall he sleep? Oh, Mistare Stormaway, you vill not doom dat poy to sleep in zee oben air?"

"No, no," the head-master replied, hastily. "Sleep in the open air, indeed! Of course not. I will provide him with lodgings. Ah! a good idea strikes me. Mr. Cockey!"

The beadle, who was leaving the court in search of his old friend Stickers, halted, and made Mr. Stormaway the politest of bows.

"You have no children, I believe?" the head-master said.

"There was one," Salem Cockey replied, "but he went afore his time— nipped in the bud, I may say, by death."

"Will you provide a bedroom for my page-boy if I make it worth your while?" demanded Mr. Stormaway.

A dubious expression stole over Salem Cockey's face.

"It's a matter as requires consideration," he said. "I don't know what effect his heyes would have on my Mariar. She's the best woman in the world, but a little peppery at times but I'll name it to her."

"Do," said Mr. Stormaway, "and when you have thought the matter well over, let me know the decision at your earliest convenience."

CHAPTER XXXIII.

THE MEETING AT ALPHONSE CARLEON'S LODGINGS—JEM MUZZLER'S BOSOM FRIEND.

TIMOTHY SLOWBOB was the hero of the hour.

It was acknowledged by all that he had won a moral victory, and he was escorted back to the Abbey in triumph.

"Ain't it wonderful?" observed Matthew Stickers, who followed at a respectful distance. "'Ere's a two-legged mulberry-coloured crorkadile, a monsterosity with swivel heyes, and harms and legs which seem to have been chucked on to his body, a bein' cheered and petted, while a poor hold man like me is left hout in the cold. Oh, my beloved country! wot are you a comin' to?"

Mr. Stickers shed a tear, and smote his battered hat over his eyes—an indiscreet act that caused him to walk plump up against a lamp-post, to the great discomfort of his nose and chin.

"Everythink is ag'in' me," he gasped. "Alars, poor Stickers! your fishing-lines are cast in troubled waters. Ah! 'ere comes Mr. Stormaway."

The head-master approached with his head down, and talking earnestly to Herr Fritz Halfamann, and evidently not at all disposed to catch his late servant's eye.

But the ex-man-of-all-work was not to be denied.

"Sir," he said, planting himself right in Mr. Stormaway's path. "I'd like to know when you mean to settle for the lemingnade and ginger-pop. Two dozen bottles bu'st right off; the tarts was scattered like hautumn leaves, and as for the barrer, it's fit for nothing but firewood."

"Go away!" Mr. Stormaway returned with a threatening flourish of his umbrella. "I will have no more to do with you; you have done your worst to annoy me, and bring disgrace upon my establishment, and if you persist in your present line of conduct, you will find yourself before the magistrates."

"And this is the man that I loved like a bruther!" said Matthew Stickers; "this is him as I never murmured at when wittles was short, and when my wages was over-due. I

wonder how you can sleep o' nights. Why don't you be a man, and say, 'Stickers forgive me; 'ere is my 'and; come back to the Habbey, and do your duty as you did it in the 'appy days of hold.'"

Mr. Stormaway passed on, and parted with Herr Halfamann at the corner of the High Street, for a resumption of school duties that day was quite out of the question.

The head-master, moreover, had not the heart to interview Slowbob on the subject of his arrest.

From inquiries, he gathered that the page-boy had been more sinned against than sinning, and for his own part he was willing to let the matter drop; but it was not so with Mrs. Jumble.

The beauty of her new bonnet was considerably marred by the headgear's having been sat upon by the sportive Bluebottle, and in vain did Slowbob offer to pay for the wrecked headgear by instalments of a penny a week.

She went for the page-boy, and Mr. Stormaway, hearing a bumping sound proceeding from the dining-room, arrived there to behold the astonishing spectacle of a hand-to-hand conflict.

Mrs. Jumble was playing a lively tune on Slowbob's cranium with a carpet-brush, while the afflicted youth retaliated with the dust-pan.

The head-master rushed in between the combatants, and Mrs. Jumble took the opportunity to faint away in his arms.

With visions of Bardell *versus* Pickwick floating before his eyes, Mr. Stormaway deposited the housekeeper on the hearthrug and fled.

"I could tickle her into fits if I liked," Slowbob observed to the servants, who now rushed upon the scene, "but I won't, poor old woman! I say, Mary, just you feel my head. It's like a bunch of onions, all bumps and knobs."

"Serve you right, you little wretch," said Mary. "If I had my mind you should have some more."

Slowbob only grinned as he walked

out of the door, but presently he returned.

"Look after the poor old crittur," he said, " and when she comes round tell her she has my blessing—the blessing of the boy she smote, and I'm sure that will bring her more consolation than all the new bonnets in the world."

The page-boy then took his departure in earnest, and very little was seen of him that day, save at mealtimes, when he was most prompt in attendance, and sat down to the table with a smiling face, and an unimpaired appetite.

About ten o'clock in the evening, Alphonse Carleon was at home.

Dividing the curtains of his sitting-room with his hands, he looked anxiously out into the garden, and now and then glanced over his shoulder at the clock.

The gong struck the hour, and Alphonse Carleon began pacing the room impatiently.

"They promised to be here half-an-hour ago," he muttered. "What can have happened? Is it possible that they have had to flee from the neighbourhood? No! That is Richard Mornington's knock."

As he opened the front door he held up his hand.

"Hush!" he said ; "make as little noise as possible, for the people of the house have gone to bed, and I do not wish to disturb them."

Not only was Jem Muzzler with Richard Mornington, but there was another man—a tall, dark, loose-jointed fellow, with a patch over one eye, and a mark across the bridge of his nose, proclaiming that he had been at loggerheads with somebody at no very distant date.

He nodded at Carleon, and proceeded to make himself at home by selecting the easiest chair in the room.

"This is my old friend, Sam Welcher," said Jem Muzzler ; "and he's come to help us in this little affair. Sam has got a head on his shoulders, he has. He ain't much to look at, but he is as wily as an Old Bailey lawyer, and as artful as a fox."

Alphonse Carleon acknowledged all Mr. Welch's merits by an inclination of the head, and asked him whether he preferred whisky or brandy.

"It don't matter to me," Sam Welcher replied, grinning hideously. "Well, I'll take a pull at the brandy-bottle."

He did, and so earnest was he in the operation, that when he set the bottle down it was half empty.

"I'm rough and ready, you see," he said. "Some people like their liquor in a glass, but give me a bottle."

Carleon glanced at Richard Mornington, who sat, drumming his fingers upon his knees, and anxious to speak.

"Now to business," he said. "Mr. Welcher has promised his assistance in case that we require it. We made a muddle over that page-boy, but there must be no more failures. We will leave him alone until a favourable opportunity presents itself. Now, Carleon, tell me when will this marked money trick be performed?"

"On Saturday," the Frenchman replied ; "when the boys will have a half-holiday, and the Abbey will be deserted by them. It will give Walbut a capital chance to carry out the plan, and on Monday the accusation will be made."

"I hate these arrangements," Sam Welcher observed. "If I had the matter in my hands I'd work it in a different way."

"And so would I," growled Jem Muzzler. "We've been beating about the bush too long already."

"You shall have the satisfaction of dealing with the prying page-boy," said Richard Mornington. "I have told you both that no actual violence must be done to my cousin, and in that I will be obeyed. Brand him as a thief, send him forth as an outcast, and he will die of a broken heart. There must be no mistake about it. He must be so caught in the trap as to be ashamed to look his father in the face."

"Bah!" grunted Sam Welcher. "I wasn't the most dutiful of sons, and yet I was never ashamed of looking my father in the face."

This so tickled Jem Muzzler, that he burst into a roar of laughter.

"Silence!" cried Alphonse Carleon. "If your presence here were known to the people of this house it might ruin everything!"

Jem Muzzler acknowledged his mistake, and having assisted Sam Welcher to finish the brandy, cast longing eyes at the decanter of whisky.

All through the interview Alphonse Carleon was pale and trembling, although he did his best to conceal his agitation.

"This page-boy suspects something," he said. "He follows me about whenever he gets the chance, and Walbut absolutely fears him. Again, Herr Fritz Halfamann has strangely altered of late. He avoids me, and sometimes I think that he more than suspects our plot against Ralph Mornington."

"Oh, let the German fool go!" interrupted Richard Mornington. "Judging from what I have heard of him, he is so simple as to be above suspicion."

"Simple people often think crafty things," Sam Welcher remarked. "To look at me, you'd never imagine that I'm a man of strong notions."

Jem Muzzler very nearly indulged in another explosion of mirth, and to prevent it, he deemed it necessary to throw himself about in his chair, and hold his sides.

"The bird is still in the bush, but it will soon be in the net," Richard Mornington said. "Success must be ours. It is almost impossible that the plot should fail, and if it does, the blame will fall upon Walbut. Carleon, I must see this boy."

"You shall, but not now," the Frenchman replied. "Wait until the work is done, and then he shall meet you here."

"Have you promised him any reward?"

"None at present."

"Then do," said Richard Mornington. "Tell him that at Ralph's death he will have a hundred pounds."

Alphonse Carleon promised to convey this interesting communication to his wretched dupe, and shortly afterwards the meeting broke up.

"The deputation will now withdraw," said Sam Welcher, as he took a glass flask out of his pocket; "but afore we go, I'll take the liberty of filling this up with whisky to keep the cold out."

As they were passing out of the door, Carleon called Richard Mornington back.

"A word with you," he said.

"Be quick, then."

"For mercy's sake, never bring those two men here again!" said Carleon. "They horrify me, and send my blood running cold through my veins."

"I am as much in their power at present as you are in mine," Richard Mornington replied, coolly; "but time will work wonders. I assure you that when the time comes I shall part with them gladly, and the same remark applies to youself, monsieur."

The Frenchman set his teeth.

"Beware!" he said. "Take care, Richard Mornington."

"Beware of what?"

"Of me!"

"Pooh! nonsense!" said the other, disdainfully. "I laugh at your threats. You are like a wounded gladiator in the arena. I am Cæsar, and if I turn down my thumb it will be the signal for your doom."

With these words he passed out of the house, leaving the Frenchman quivering with suppressed fury. But presently Carleon returned to the room.

He unlocked a cabinet and took out the portions of an air-gun, which he fitted together.

"Richard Mornington," he said, "I missed one mark. My hand was unsteady then; but if you were my target, I think I should score. Merciless villain! you have compelled me to part with the little good that was left in me. What have you made of me? A coward, a mean, pitiful wretch, and a lurking assassin!"

He threw himself into a chair, and rocked to and fro, as if his agony were too great to bear; but presently he became calmer, and putting out the lamp, crept upstairs in the dark to his bedroom.

When Richard Mornington and his allies reached the open air, they stood for a moment to deliberate whether it would be safe for all three to pass through the town in company.

They decided not to do so, and Sam Welcher was in the act of walking away in advance, when a sound close at hand attracted his attention.

"There's no wind," he said, "and yet that clump of bushes is moving."

"Fancy, my dear fellow," observed Richard Mornington. "Let us get away."

"I will have just one dig into the bushes," Sam Welcher said, drawing a huge clasp-knife. "I like to satisfy myself in these matters."

Leaving the path, he struck again and again deep into the laurels, and then hustled them about with his hands.

"Nobody there," he said.

"Of course not," Jem Muzzler

returned. "Who did you expect to find ?"

"There's no telling," replied Welcher. "We meet at the old mill, I suppose ?"

"Yes ; it is safe enough there," Richard Mornington said.

They had scarcely vanished into darkness, when a solitary figure occupied the place where they had stood.

It was Timothy Slowbob.

"What a narrow squeak !" he said. "If I hadn't crawled out of them bushes, I shouldn't have done much watching for a long time to come, if ever. It makes me cold to think of it."

Timothy stood perfectly still, as if doubtful whether to return to his former hiding-place or to venture into the road.

"So," he said, "they are at the old mill, are they ? Tim, my boy, you are getting on splendidly. Shall I tell Mr. Stormaway what I have done ? No ; I will keep it bottled up, and one day the cork will come out with such a bang as will startle that Frenchy considerably."

Slowbob waited a little longer, and then ran like a hare, and reached the Abbey wall without being molested, and after groping about the ivy for a minute, he brought a rope to light, and went up it hand over hand.

"I s'pose there would be a row about this if it was known," he said, as he sat on the top of the wall ; "but no matter. I must have a way in and a way out. Ralph Mornington, you may smile at your enemies now ; Timothy Slowbob is down on 'em !"

CHAPTER XXXIV.

THE LOCAL BOARD ELECTION—A NOISY MEETING.

IN the morning, when coming downstairs, Ralph met Walbut, who, to all appearance, was interested in a book he had in his hand.

"Good-morning," said our hero. "Why, I have scarcely set eyes on you since the cricket-match. Wasn't the whole affair jolly ?"

"I didn't think much of it," Walbut returned. "I don't play, you know."

"That is your own fault," said our hero. "You were invited to join the eleven, but you refused."

"Yes, that compliment was paid me ; but my services were not required," Walbut remarked, sneeringly.

"I cannot understand where you get all these strange notions from," Ralph said. "I thought at one time you were going to join us with heart and hand, but I am sorry to say you have fallen into your old ways."

"It is because I wish to be left alone," Walbut rejoined. "See here," he added, tapping the book ; "in a short time I shall be leaving school to commence the real battle of life. I shall have little else than my education to help me along. I am not like you, Mornington ; your bread is already buttered on both sides."

"Well, have it your own way," said Ralph, as Charlie Chadwick came running downstairs. "In time to come you will think of these things with regret."

"If I do I will hold you blameless," Jack Walbut retorted.

Our hero shook his head, and taking Charlie's arm, walked away.

"I wonder you speak to that fellow," Chadwick said. "I have told you over and over again that he means mischief to you. It lurks in his eyes, and it is echoed in his speech. I have sent him to Coventry."

"It is a miserable state of things," Ralph remarked, with a sigh. "It is a mystery to me how he can exist here, shunned, disliked, and suspected."

"It is his nature," returned Charlie.

When they went in to breakfast, Ralph found a letter waiting for him from his father.

"You must tell me all the news," wrote the general. "I look forward to the arrival of every mail, for, my boy. you are all the world to me, and I know that you will live to be a blessing to me in my old age. No true Mornington will ever disgrace himself. and you, Ralph, will never do so. Tell me everything. If you should ever have any difficulties, make a clean breast of them to me. Let me know all about your joys and little troubles, and I will sit me down and reply as becomes your father, your guide, and best of friends."

As soon as the morning lessons were over, he sat down at his desk and wrote so long a reply that he had not finished when the dinner-bell summoned the boys from play-ground and meadow.

It happened to be Wednesday, when the boys were free for the afternoon.

Having finished his letter, Ralph received permission to pay a visit to Merrytown post-office.

It took three boys to post one letter, as Charlie Chadwick and Harold Lakeman insisted upon accompanying our hero.

The first thing that attracted them was a flaring bill affixed to a wall.

It set forth that Mr. Gammon, the provision merchant, was desirous of joining the Merrytown Local Board. Everybody was asked to vote for Gammon, the reformer, the man who would increase trade and decrease the rates.

Gammon was the only man who would do the people of Merrytown justice, and they were invited to the large room of The Swan and Bottle at four o'clock that afternoon to hear what the illustrious candidate had to say.

"Shall we go?" said Ralph. "I think we ought, as some fun can be made out of the affair."

"Of course," Charlie remarked. "But what possessed Gammon to announce a meeting at such a time in the day?"

"The explanation is very easy," said Harold Lakeman. "This is the corn-market day, and as the power of the Local Board extends for some considerable distance, Gammon hopes to find favour in the eyes of some of the small farmers."

"It must be so," Ralph observed. "Come along; let us be in plenty of time, so as to secure good places."

They found their way to the large room of The Swan and Bottle, and for some minutes had it all to themselves.

At last a white-haired rustic, wearing a grey beaver hat, hobbled in and took a seat so near the platform that the boys guessed he was a little deaf.

"Sir," said Ralph, "please to take a seat on the platform. There is plenty of room for influential voters. Mr. Gammon will be delighted to point you out as one of his personal friends."

"Thank'ee—thank'ee," replied the old gentleman. "You're a nice kind lad. I don't mind if I do get a bit nearer"; and on the platform he went.

Suddenly Charlie Chadwick seemed to be seized with a good idea.

He slipped out of the room, and returned in a few minutes with three pea-shooters and an ample stock of ammunition.

Meanwhile, other people had strolled in, all of whom Ralph politely escorted to the platform, and having filled it until there was not a vacant seat, he and his chums retired to a dim window recess, and concealed themselves behind the dark green curtains which had been drawn to keep out the rays of the sun.

The gentlemen occupying the platform were too much engaged in chatting about Mr. Gammon's candidature to notice this manœuvre, and as four o'clock approached the excitement became intense.

Not only was the platform crammed, but the body of the room had a fair sprinkling of local politicians.

At last the great man came. Worry-boy preceded him, Salem Cockey trod on his heels, and Matthew Stickers (hired for the purpose) brought up the rear, bearing in sandwich boards, with "Reform for Merrytown" and "Vote for Gammon" printed thereon.

Mr. Gammon was received with cheers and groans; but he only smiled and bowed, and did not seem to notice anything until he reached the steps leading to the platform.

Then he stopped and stared, for several of his friends who were to address the meeting had by this time entered the room, and were wondering how it was possible for them to obtain seats on the platform.

"What's this?" Mr. Gammon gasped. "Gentlemen, you have taken possession of every chair on the platform. I must ask some of you, at least, to find other seats."

"I won't for one," said Mr. Chopps, the butcher. "A boy put me up here, and here I mean to stick."

"A boy! What boy?"

"I don't know what boy," Mr. Chopps retorted; "all boys are alike. I thought it was your own son."

"No," replied Mr. Gammon; "my lad would never dream of doing such a thing without my authority. Mr. Chopps, though I know that you bear me no good will, yet I ask you civilly to set a proper example and come down."

"I won't," said Chopps, decisively. "You ain't on the Local Board yet, you know."

Mr. Gammon looked pleadingly at Worryboy, but that official was gazing intently at the cracks in the ceiling, and seemed to be lost in thought.

"How can I hold a meeting if there isn't room for me and the other gentlemen who wish to speak on my behalf?" demanded Gammon, raising his voice as his wrath increased.

Mr. Chopps opened his mouth to say something, but the words were never uttered.

He seized his nose, jerked up his feet, and then opened the palm of his hand as if he expected to find the dead body of a wasp in it. Two tears ran down his cheeks, and the expression of his eyes was that of a man who had seen something extremely startling.

"Bless me!" he said, "I've been stung by a hornet or something."

"And so have I!" roared out another man. "There's another! What are they? Where do they come from?"

At this moment P.C. Worryboy rubbed his ears violently; Salem Cockey skipped into the air, and Matthew Stickers shot the sandwich-boards over his head, and forthwith challenged to mortal combat a man who had done nothing worse than thump an antiquated umbrella upon the floor.

Then Mr. Gammon became visibly affected. He rubbed the top of his bald head, scratched his chin, and made a dive with his fingers down his back.

"Peas!" he moaned. "There are boys about."

"There ain't a boy in the room," Worryboy declared—"not the shadder of one."

"Then where do the peas come from?"

"I ain't good at riddles," Worryboy replied. "Merrytown is bu'stin' full o' mysteries."

"And of hiniquities," Matthew Stickers chimed in. "Look at me, a pore hold man, brought down to a sangwitch, and all through a schoolmaster with the 'art of a wiper."

"Get on with the business," bellowed a man. "Chopps, and some of you others, come down, or we will fetch you."

The butcher rolled up the cuffs of his coat, and went into the body of the hall with the intention of soundly thrashing the speaker, but Worryboy interposed.

"Touch that man," he cried—"commit only one piece of the breeches—I mean one breach of the pieces—and you go afore the justices."

"Very well," said Mr. Chopps, sitting down; "I can wait. There'll be another day to-morrow. May I never sell another steak——"

"American beef!" cried Ralph, sending his voice at the back of the butcher's head.

Mr. Chopps turned round and encountered the gaze of a mild linen-draper, who had scarcely the strength to measure out his calico.

"All right," the butcher growled. "There's a plot against me, it seems. I'll settle our little account when we get outside."

"I am not aware that you owe me anything," observed the mild linen-draper.

"You'll find that I do, and that I'm able and willing to pay it," snarled Mr. Chopps.

"Order! Order for Mr. Gammon!" roared a dozen voices.

There was room on the platform now for the candidate and his friends, and the chairman, a tanner by trade, opened the proceedings by getting up and sitting down in such a hurry that the lower part of his anatomy crushed through the cane-bottomed chair.

"No mortal man can bear this," he said. "I got two stingers."

Mr. Gammon turned livid, and Worryboy made a tour round the room, and even peeped behind the green baize window curtains, but it never struck him that the windows were made to open, and that there was a broad parapet beyond them.

"No," he said, "there ain't a boy here. It must be somebody in the room."

"It's Salem Cockey," cried a voice. "I saw him do it. He's got a pea-shooter up his sleeve."

"'And it hover!" said Worryboy. "Cockey, you, a beadle, a hossifer of the peace, to play such tricks! I'm ashamed of you."

"Hand what over?" demanded Cockey.

"The peashooter."

"The what!" the beadle almost shrieked.

"Oh, come now," said the constable, "don't try to look so innercent.

"MRS. COCKEY LAID VIOLENT HANDS ON A TEA-TRAY."—(See page 122.)

You've got it up your sleeve, you know."

"Why, you're mad," Cockey gasped. "The aroma from the bar has got into your head. What does a man of my age want with a peashooter?"

"That's just what I should like to know."

Salem Cockey declared his innocence so vehemently, and at such length, that ten minutes more were wasted.

At last the chairman rose again.

"Gentlemen," he said, "fellow townsmen and electors, we have met here to-day to—to—to—— Oh! I'll have no more of this," he added. "A man who don't mind being stung out of his senses had better take the chair."

"I offer five pounds reward for the capture of this miscreant," Mr. Gammon roared. "Ah, I have it! The peas come through the ventilator on the roof. Mr. Worryboy, you——"

"Not me," interrupted the constable; "I was on the roof of the Habbey not long ago, and that was enough for me."

"Looking after a mad Highlander," cried a shrill voice.

Salem Cockey turned as pale as a ghost.

"Hearts alive!" he gasped. "I didn't know as how my Mariar was here."

A fat man jumped to his feet, and flourished a knobby stick above his head.

"Have we come here to be made fools of?" he roared. "This 'ere's a get up, in fact, it's all gammon, cause Gammon has nothing to say. A nice man he'd make for our Local Board, certainly."

Mr. Gammon swelled visibly with indignation.

"Chunks," he said, "beware how you rile me! I haven't had a fight since I was twelve years of age, but I won't be insulted by a jerry builder. You're afraid that if I am elected I shall be down on you."

Mr. Chunks dashed down his hat, and threw off his coat, but his ardour was cooled and his nose heated by a well-aimed pea.

"There must be boys about," he almost shrieked.

"Perhaps they are on the leads outside," one of the audience suggested.

Ralph and his chums heard these words, and thought it was time to make themselves scarce.

"We must drop into the road," said our hero; "the height is not very great."

"Agreed!" assented Charlie Chadwick; "and here goes for one."

Now it so happened that as Charlie commenced his descent, a gentleman wearing a tall and exceedingly-shiny hat, came out of the bar, which was directly underneath.

Chadwick happened to catch one side of the shiny hat as he dropped, and its unfortunate wearer laid down upon the pavement as if he had been shot.

When he picked himself up, and tore off a few strips of silk and cardboard, he had a dim vision of three boys scampering like rabbits round the corner; but before he could bring his confused mind to bear on the matter, he found himself surrounded by a crowd of men, including, of course, P.C. Worryboy.

"So it was you," said the constable, shaking up the bewildered gentleman like a box of pills. "It was you on the leads with your larks and your peashooter. Why, you're old enough to know better."

"Run him in!" cried Salem Cockey. "What does he mean by forgin' my Mariar's woice, and a throwin' me into a cold perspirashing?"

"If—if," said the gentleman in a tone hoarse with emotion, "you will tell me how the accident occurred I shall be very pleased. I intend to bring an action against the keepers of this inn. Did the parapet fall on me?"

He looked wildly about him, but seeing no *debris*, stared askance at the crowd.

"It's a cur'us thing," said Worryboy, "that somethin' is always happenin' in Merrytown, and nobody does it. Now, sir, who are you?"

"Oh, here is my card," replied the gentleman. "You will observe that my name is Herapath, and that I am a solicitor from London. I looked in at this place to ask my way to the Abbey School, where I have business with one of the pupils. And now I come to think of it," he added, "I fancy I saw three boys running away."

"Of course you did, sir," said Worryboy; "and it was one of 'em as dropped on you. I see it all now. Cockey, how dare you tell me to run the gentleman in? Let me polish your hat up a bit, sir."

"I fear it is wrecked beyond all renovation," Mr. Herapath returned, sadly, "and I must buy another. Dear me! I have had a narrow escape."

"You have, sir," said Worryboy. "Let me take you to a hatter's, and then I will, with your leave, honoured sir, show you the way to the Abbey."

"I want to have a word in this affair," cried Matthew Stickers, pushing his way to the front, "Look 'ere, sir, do you want to be baited like a bull, and drawn like a badger?"

"Of course not," replied Mr. Herapath.

"Then take the hadwice of a pore, sufferin' hold man, and keep clear o' the Habbey," said Stickers. "Haffliction sore long time I bore there with the ghostesses, Slowbob, Missus Jumble, and the whole b'ilin' lot. Keep away from the Habbey, sir, or it's two tuppeny pies to a stale hopen tart that you are a dead man."

"I fear that this man is not quite right in his mind," Mr. Herapath observed. "Lead the way, constable."

"I will, sir," Worryboy replied; and then turning to Mr. Gammon, he said: "You may fire away now. There'll be no more peas and no more interruptions."

"There he goes," said Matthew Stickers, alluding to the solicitor; "yes, there he goes, and I pities him. Hif Mister Stormaway would only remember that he who spoils the rod spares the child, 'ow different things might be!"

CHAPTER XXXV.

TIMOTHY SLOWBOB CHANGES HIS LODGINGS.

MR. HERAPATH purchased a new hat, and having had his clothes brushed, set off to the Abbey with Worryboy, who left him at the principal entrance, and returned with a look of disgust upon his face.

"Only a shillin'," muttered the constable, turning up his nose. "I took him to a place to get a new tile; I brushed him down as gently as if he had been a magistrate instead of a common lawyer; and I led him here like a lamb to the slaughter, and he rounds on me with a shilling—a low mean shilling. I wish that boy had sat flat on his hat—that I do."

Timothy Slowbob admitted Mr. Herapath, and having taken his message to Mr. Stormaway, returned to the drawing-room, and aired his eye at the keyhole so as to take the measure of the London solicitor.

"He's a rum 'un," Timothy murmured; "but he mayn't mean no harm. I'll keep handy in case I'm wanted, and if there's going to be a row I'll be in it."

Slowbob vanished, for at this moment Ralph, having learned from the head-master that Mr. Herapath required his attendance, came running downstairs.

Our hero entered the room, and shook hands with the solicitor, but the lad's face fell when he saw how grave was that of the legal gentleman.

"I hope nothing has happened," Ralph faltered. "I received a letter from my father this morning, and——"

"So did I," interrupted Mr. Herapath, smiling. "All is well with him, so pray do not disturb yourself on that score. He wrote to me by the same mail, but in my letter he mentioned some business which he thought had better come direct from me to yourself."

Wondering what all this could mean, Ralph sat down, and lent an attentive ear to his father's solicitor.

"You are, of course, aware that you have a cousin named Richard Mornington," said Mr. Herapath. "His father died without leaving him a penny, but yours, in his generosity, gave him a thousand pounds with which to make a start in life."

"So I have heard," said Ralph; "and though I know very little about my cousin, I hope that he is doing well."

"He is not doing well," the solicitor returned; "on the contrary, he is doing very badly. Your father has received information in a strange way that leads him to believe that Richard Mornington has not only squandered the money, but is a beggar, the associate of low characters, and, moreover, that he is in this very neighbourhood."

The news almost took Ralph's breath away.

"What could be his object in coming

to such a place as Merrytown?" he said.

"When men are driven to extremes they do peculiar and out-of-the-way things," Mr. Herapath replied. "Let me proceed. The information received by General Mornington was in the form of a letter. I have the envelope and letter here, and I may as well tell you that this extraordinary missive was delayed on account of being insufficiently and oddly addressed. Perhaps you may be able to throw some light on this matter?"

Ralph took the envelope, and in spite of all his anxious curiosity he could not help smiling, as he read, "Toe Gineral Mornington, Indiar."

He then opened the letter, and after some trouble made out the following:

"DERE GINERAL, yore nepher Richyard is at Merrytown, and the riter has strong suchsphons that theer is a plot against yure sun. Cum hoom by the first boot, and beleeve me yures trooly, WATCHDORG."

"I can make nothing out of it," said Ralph. "Nobody writes like this in the Abbey. It must be some silly hoax to frighten my father."

"I do not agree with you there," Mr. Herapath returned. "We men of the law learn to read between the lines of all documents. This is the letter of some ignorant person, who for some reason does not come to you, but thinks it his duty to put the general on his guard."

"Let us take that as granted," said Ralph, "and also that my cousin is here. Why should he attempt to do me harm?"

"Ahem!" the solicitor coughed behind his hand. "Your father has made a communication to me which I think I had better keep to myself, at least for the present. Mr. Mornington, I have engaged the services of an experienced detective, who will arrive by this afternoon's coach. I want you to give me one of your photographs, so that he may know you without calling here."

"This flavours of the dramatic," said Ralph. "Really, I do not comprehend why there should be all this fuss, as I am quite able to take care of myself."

"You may think so," Mr. Herapath remarked; "schoolboys fight with their fists and forget all about it in an hour, but bad men fight with their lying tongues and evil minds. You will let me have your photograph, and should a man touch you on the shoulder and say 'Blackstone,' you will know that he is the detective."

"Very good," Ralph replied; "but I shall be on thorns until my father knows that all is well with me."

"I will telegraph to him at the earliest opportunity," Mr. Herapath said; "and now a word of caution. Say nothing about this business to anybody. If questioned about our interview, you may say, and with truth, that it concerned family affairs."

Ralph fetched a photograph of himself, and Mr. Herapath gathered up his hat and gloves, and prepared to take his leave.

"Good-day," he said, as he took our hero's hand and looked him full in the face; "and—and if you should happen to hear that a boy dropped upon a gentleman's hat this afternoon, present my compliments, and tell him that he considerably upset a part of that mighty machine known as the law."

Ralph Mornington did not return to his school-chums for some time; but paced the room in an agitated state of mind.

"Nonsense!" he ejaculated at last; "what should I fear? The letter is a hoax, and my father has taken it to heart. The idea of being watched over by a detective is too ridiculous."

At this moment he happened to glance into the mirror, and was somewhat startled to see the reflection of Slowbob's head thrust in at the door.

"Come here," said our hero; "what do you mean by watching me in that manner?"

"Me watch you?" Slowbob cried; "no, sir—no. I showed the gentleman out, and I thought that—that—well, I didn't think much, you see, only he gave me half-a-crown, and said he had never seen anything like me in his life. Wasn't it a funny thing for him to say?"

"You are talking nonsense," said Ralph. "You were watching me; don't deny it."

"Well," Timothy stammered, "I thought that the gentleman might have come to kick up a row about somethin', and you might want somebody to help you to pitch into him."

An idea flashed into Ralph Mornington's brain like an electric spark.

"Slowbob," he said, "can you write?"

"Write—what, me write!" cried Timothy, hilarious at the notion. "Ha, ha! A lot o' writin' they taught us at the work'us, surely. I might be able to print my name with a skewer, but that's the furthest I could get."

Ralph said no more, and walked away.

Slowbob made a pretence of going in an opposite direction; but as soon as he was certain that Ralph was well out of the way, he darted back to the drawing-room.

"Tim," he said, staring at himself in the looking-glass, "you're a mean, bad feller—that's what you are. You listen at key-holes, you sneaks out o' nights and lays among bushes under people's winders, and you goes a follerin' folks about as if you was their shadders. But never mind, Tim; if you drags yourself down, you sha'n't see the best young gentleman in all England wictimized by a pack o' willins. No, not if you have to go forth into the world without a blessed button!"

Just then Mr. Stormaway's bell rang, and the irrepressible hastened to answer it. To his surprise he found Salem Cockey, the beadle, fully robed, and to all appearance on excellent terms with the head-master.

"Slowbob," said Mr. Stormaway, "you may sit down, and so may you, Mr. Cockey."

"Thank'ee, sir, I will," the beadle replied.

He smiled so benignly upon Slowbob, that that youth, whose vision may have become dim with conflicting emotions, took the chair selected by Mr. Cockey, and left him to sit upon the floor, which he did with so terrific a crash, that Mr. Stormaway, startled out of his senses, tilted his own backwards, and losing his balance, fell into the fender.

"It's wonderful how some people will knock themselves about," said Slowbob, as he gazed at the soles of Mr. Cockey's boots. "Come, get up. You can't lay about here all day, you know. The guv'nor's on his feet already. Anybody might think that this was a tumblin' match."

"What does this mean?" Mr. Stormaway cried, wildly, as he rubbed the back of his head.

"That there miscreant took the chair from under me," wailed Salem Cockey, scrambling to his feet.

"You mean that you tried to sit down on my chair and missed it." Slowbob said. "This ought to be a lesson to you. Perliteness costs nothing, and will mark you as a gentleman wherever you goes."

Mr. Stormaway turned a basilisk glare on Timothy, who met it unflinchingly.

"This is more than I can bear," the head-master said. "Slowbob, I will not mince matters with you! You get worse and worse every day, and Mr. Cockey is here to take you away from the Abbey."

The irrepressible turned all sorts of colours, and seemed as if he were going to choke.

"I won't go!" he cried. "I tell you I won't go! Wild horses urged on with wire whips couldn't drag me."

"Timothy—Timothy," said Salem Cockey, shaking his head solemnly, "you forget who you are talkin' to."

"Hold your tongue!" Slowbob retorted. "It would take more than all the beadles in the world to frighten me."

"Listen!" Mr. Stormaway continued. "I do not discharge you from my service, I——"

"You can't, sir," interrupted Timothy. "I'm bound to you for seven years, and if you cancels my indenters, you knock all the laws of the country into a cocked hat."

The head-master of Merrytown Abbey seized his hair, as was his custom when his patience was exhausted.

"Will you listen to me?" he roared. "You will take your meals here, and continue to perform the same duties, but you will sleep at Mr. Cockey's house."

"Oh, that's it, is it?" said Slowbob, complacently. "Well, I don't mind. It will be a change. I'm ready; when do I start?"

"At once," Mr. Stormaway replied; "and I trust that you will behave yourself, and try to be good and obedient to Mrs. Cockey, who is a kind and motherly creature."

"One of the best women in the world; only a little peppery at times," the beadle murmured.

"It's rather short notice, sir," Slowbob said; "but my things won't take long to pack up. Cockey, you've got a nice square head, and you can carry my box."

So saying, Timothy slid out of the room, and a few minutes later a heavy bumping proclaimed that he was coming downstairs with all his earthly belongings.

"Here I am," he said, cheerfully. "A few buttons came off on the stairs, and people must be careful how they tread. Now then, Cockey; let me give you a lift up. You've got the finest head I ever saw for a box. Nature made it for carrying heavy weights."

Mr. Stormaway departed in haste, leaving the beadle and the irrepressible to settle the matter between themselves.

"Me carry a load like that!" cried Salem Cockey. "Do you take me for a mule?"

"Not quite, but next door to it," Slowbob returned. "What! are you too proud to lend me a helping hand? Well then, you have lost a lodgeer."

Timothy Slowbob sat down upon his box and folded his arms.

"This is how Napoleon Bonyparty looked ten minutes previous to writing that beautiful song 'Just afore the battle, mother,'" he said.

"I don't care how Bonyparty looked or what he wrote!" Salem Cockey yelled. "Will you get up and carry that box?"

"No, I won't."

"Then I suppose I must," Salem Cockey groaned. "Give me hold of it. Now then, where are you shovin' it to? Hearts alive! don't you see that you are jammin' me against the wall. When my Mariar hears all about this, won't she let you have it!"

"Mind the stairs," said Slowbob; "there's almost forty of 'em, and more than half are loose. Steady! steady! or you will spoil my dress-suit."

Staggering and gasping, Salem Cockey contrived to reach the hall without meeting with any great disaster.

Slowbob opened the door for him, adding at the same time a gentle impetus in the back, and Salem Cockey, plunging wildly forward, shot the box fully twenty feet ahead, and deposited himself at full length upon the ground, with every prospect of a severe attack of the gravel-rash.

The box was slightly corded; the lid flew open, and all sorts of things flew about.

"See what you have done," Slowbob said, sternly. "This is the second time that you have tumbled down to-day without warnin'. What's the matter with your feet? Here, I'll have no more of this; fetch a cab."

"Only wait until I get you home," Mr. Cockey gasped, as he rose. "If copper-sticks can bruise and brush-handles bump, you shall have your full share of 'em."

The box was refilled, and at last Slowbob and his landlord started fairly on their journey, to the great delight of everybody who met them.

CHAPTER XXXVI.

MR. STORMAWAY RECEIVES A DEPUTATION—A SCRIMMAGE AT THE ABBEY.

SALEM COCKEY and Timothy Slowbob had not been out of the Abbey many minutes, when Mrs. Jumble knocked at Mr. Stormaway's study-door, and in response to his voice entered the room.

The housekeeper was pale; she panted for breath, and was altogether so upset that the head-master begged of her to sit down without delay.

"Pray calm yourself, madam," said Mr. Stormaway, "and tell me what has happened. I suppose the boys have——"

"Oh, sir!" Mrs. Jumble interposed, "this is a wretched place. At least fifty men, including many of the town tradesmen, are at the door, and they insist upon seeing you."

"Indeed!" said the head-master. "And pray what do they want? Has some malicious person circulated a report that I am on the verge of bankruptcy?"

"I know nothing, only that they are here, looking very fierce and determined," poor Mrs. Jumble replied. "When I asked them to go away, Mr. Gammon cried out, 'Woman, do your duty!' and a dreadful inebriated man declared that he would not go home till morning."

"I will see them," Mr. Stormaway said, with the air of a martyr. "There is nothing else to be done. I suppose I shall learn something sufficiently horrible to make my hair stand on end."

Downstairs went the head-master, and on opening the door was met with a crowd of faces, that rolled and swayed beneath his gaze like the waves of the ocean.

Messrs. Gammon, Chunks, Chopps, and Puffy were to the fore, while in the rear was a selection of loafers, who were thirsting to learn what the matter was, and ready for a row.

"Gentlemen," said Mr. Stormaway, planting his right hand on his breast, "to what cause may I attribute the honour of this visit?"

"It isn't an honour at all," gasped Mr. Gammon. "A meeting of respectable people of Merrytown has been upset, its dignity disgraced, and its peace disturbed."

"Bless me, you don't say so!" the head-master cried.

"Yes, I do say so," responded Mr. Gammon; "and what is more, I say that you are the cause of it all."

Mr. Stormaway removed his hand from his breast, and smote his manly brow.

"I—I—— Am I dreaming? I the cause of the disturbance!" he stammered. "Why, sir—why, gentlemen, I assure you that I have not left the Abbey since the morning."

"That may be; but some of your boys have," Mr. Gammon retorted. "Why do you let them out to torture us? Why don't you hobble them like —like donkeys in a lane? Why should we put up with being stung to madness with peas, and driven wild by being hallooed at?"

"I am still at a loss to comprehend your meaning," Mr. Stormaway said. "I know no more than the moon what you are talking about."

"Ain't he innercent?" shouted one of the loafers. "Have him down, and pay him out for the lot!"

"Here is Worryboy," continued Mr. Gammon.

The constable stepped to the front.

"Here is our guardian of the peace, paid and kept out of the rates," Gammon continued. "Here he is, I say, and he will tell you that instead of our meeting passing off quietly, it was converted into a nest of hornets."

"Which there was peas, reg'lar stingers, and hollerin', and a gentleman's hat was sot upon and bu'sted," said Worryboy. "I thought as how you would have heard something about it, Mr. Stormaway, for the gentleman came here, and was mean enough to give me a shillin'."

A light suddenly dawned into Mr. Stormaway's mind.

"I think I can place my hands on the culprits," he said. "Please take your leave, gentlemen, and I give you my earnest assurance that I will investigate the matter without delay."

"We will not go away!" cried Mr. Gammon. "We have come here to see the delinquents thrashed, and we refuse to depart until justice has been done."

"'Ear, 'ear!" shouted the amiable voice of Matthew Stickers. "Don't budge a hinch, gents. That there Stormaway is as bad as the wust. He hencourages the himps in their mischief, and is hever ready to be down on pore suff'rin' hold men. Ask him wot he did to my barrer and banner, w'ich took me all night to hornament."

Mr. Stormaway saw that now or never was the time to stand upon his dignity, and stick to his rights as the head of the Abbey.

"My pupils are answerable to me, and to me alone," he said. "You," he added, almost poking his forefinger in Mr. Gammon's eye, "have come here for the evident purpose of creating a disturbance. You, sir, have been to The Swan and Bottle, and therefore I can find some excuse for the thickness of your speech and the unsteadiness of your gait. Go away, and take these fellows with you, or you will compel me to summon assistance."

"Just stand a little back," observed Mr. Gammon, using his elbows pretty freely among the crowd. "Give me room, and none of you interfere. I'm intoxicated, am I?"

"I heerd it," Matthew Stickers chimed in, with a delighted chuckle. "I heerd him say right down flat that you was intoxicated."

Mr. Stormaway turned and fled into the Abbey.

It must not be imagined that he was a coward—far from it; but discretion is the better part of valour, and he saw that a conflict would only bring further disgrace on his establishment.

"I will let them knock, ring, and shout until they are tired," he said, as he sat down upon the umbrella-stand, and wrecked it for ever. "Dear me! how absent-minded I am getting. To-morrow Gammon and Co. shall learn to their cost that they cannot insult me with impunity."

It is probable that the head-master would have kept within the walls of his establishment, but the noise outside was so terrific that the boys could not fail to hear it.

Just as Mr. Gammon was in the act of mounting the steps with the intention of banging at the door with the knocker, an upper window opened, and the contents of a water jug came out.

Every drop went clean over the ham, egg, and pickle man.

It not only cooled him, but sent him staggering back amongst the crowd, scattering them right and left, and, as usual, Matthew Stickers came in for his full share of misfortune.

One of Mr. Gammon's elbows took a fancy to his waistcoat, and the ex-man-of-all-work passed it on to the inebriated gentleman, and the two rolled on the ground in mortal conflict.

Jug of water number one was quickly followed by others, and soon there was a clear path before the door.

Then came the boys themselves.

They swooped down the staircase, and not noticing Mr. Stormaway in the dim dusky light, they fell over him in their hot haste to get into the open air.

The door flew open with a crash, and the lads of Merrytown Abbey, keeping well together, charged the foe.

Many of the deputation were wet through, and unable to make the best use of their legs.

They went down in heaps, rolling and tumbling over each other as if a regiment of cavalry had burst upon them.

Wild cries of entreaty, and still wilder shrieks from the bottom men of the various piles, startled the air of that summer evening, but the boys were merciless.

Led by Ralph, they hit out at every foeman's head until there was not one that did not ache, and sad to say that Herr Fritz Halfamann not only applauded, but played his part in the fray.

The Teuton picked out Matthew Stickers, still suffering from his rough-and-tumble with the inebriated individual, and went for him.

"Marcy!" Stickers cried. "Spare a hold man, whose totterin' limbs have brought him tremblin' to your door. I was dragged into this. I was told that hif I gave hevidence I should get a hextra shillin' for a carryin' of the sangwidge."

"You vas von villain!" said Halfamann as he smote the ex-man-of-all-work on the nose, "and zee poys are well rid of you. Take dat, und dat, und dat, and remember dat a Sherman can fight when his plood vas up."

Stickers had good reason to remember it; indeed, it was not likely he would forget that evening as long as he lived.

His clothes were torn nearly off his back, he was as buttonless as Slowbob, and so swollen of visage that he looked as if he had been too inquisitive with regard to the interior of a bee-hive.

"I shall have to pickle myself with brown paper and vinegar," he moaned as he escaped from the German tutor, and followed the flying crowd. "Lor! 'Ere comes that Ralph Mornington. If he ketches me he'll give me a oner which will top all the others."

But Ralph was too busily engaged with Mr. Chopps to pay attention to the ex-man-of-all-work.

Chopps stood his ground manfully, but he was slow of movement, and after having been thumped about the side of the head until he entertained a vague idea that he was a balloon, he turned and fled with the rest.

The inebriated gentleman had his nose embellished like the tip of a red-hot poker.

At last the Abbey grounds were clear, and such boys as had retained their hats, threw them up and gave three ringing cheers.

"Hoch!—hoch!" bellowed Herr Fritz Halfamann.

He, too, threw up his head-gear. It went down the well never to return, but the German tutor was perfectly satisfied.

At this moment, Mr. Stormaway, with various fragments of the umbrella-stand clinging to him, came staggering out of the Abbey.

"This is more like a hideous dream than a reality," he cried. "Boys—boys, go in, all of you, I beg."

"Certainly, sir," said Ralph. "I hope you do not blame us for acting as we have done."

"No, no," Mr. Stormaway replied; "but these proceedings are disgraceful. I don't think I was ever so upset in my life."

"It vas Mistare Gammons und zee oder shentlemans who vas obset," said Herr Halfamann. "I am broud of zese poys, for zey did save zee Appey. Dot mob vould have purst in, and "gootness only knows vot might have happened."

"That is true," Mr. Stormaway replied, as he locked the playground gates and put the key in his pocket; "but still I regret that the affair took place. I suppose a full account of it will appear in the local papers, unless I pay to keep it out."

"Can a poor hold man have a word with you?" demanded the voice of Matthew Stickers through the railings of the gate.

"Decidedly not," the head-master replied.

"If you've got the 'art of a man, give me a suit of hold clothes," Stickers said. "Look at me—I'm all rags and tatters. There ain't a square hinch o' sound cloth about me."

"I will give you nothing," Mr. Stormaway rejoined, sharply. "Go about your business."

"What bizness have I got to go about?" Stickers whined. "I made a fair start once, but you bu'sted me up. Don't be 'ard on me, sir; I know you wouldn't like to see me starve. I'm a changed man, sir—indeed I am."

Mr. Stormaway reflected for a moment.

"Call to-morrow morning after lessons, and I will talk to you," he said.

Matthew Stickers went his way rejoicing.

"This 'ere fight was a lucky thing for me after all," he chuckled. "Afore another day is over, I shall resoom my dooties at the Abbey."

CHAPTER XXXVII.

SALEM COCKEY'S LODGER—THE VACANT BED—ASTONISHING REAPPEARANCE OF SLOWBOB.

PUFFING and blowing like a locomotive getting up steam, Salem Cockey, with Slowbob at his side, reached the home presided over by the gentle Mariar.

"Are you satisfied now?" Cockey demanded, as he dropped the box rather unceremoniously on the doorstep.

"Quite," Slowbob replied. "What a glorious thing it is to help one another, ain't it?"

The beadle eyed the page-boy viciously.

"Just one word before we go indoors," he said, impressively. "You'll have to eat humble-pie here, my lad."

"What is it made of?" Slowbob asked.

"Humility—obedience to Mariar, or I won't answer for the consequences," Salem Cockey said.

Before Timothy could make any reply the door flew open, and Mrs. Cockey, red of face, and with her eyes glinting appeared.

"Come in, you old fool," said she. "I'd have carried his box for him, certainly. Bah! You call yourself a man to be led by the nose by a boy like that?"

"Hear! hear! Bravo, marm," cried Slowbob, as he walked into the sitting-room. "It strikes me that we shall have a merry time here."

"I wasn't speaking to you, Mister Imperence," said the irate lady.

"I thought you was," Slowbob returned, as he threw himself into the beadle's easy-chair. "What have you got to eat, marm? Something nice, I hope."

"Bread-and-cheese," snapped Mr. Cockey.

Timothy Slowbob sighed, and Salem Cockey, standing near the door, groaned.

"Don't be so peppery, my love," he said.

"So what?" his spouse demanded in a freezing tone of voice.

"So—so warm in your remarks."

"You go upstairs," she said, pointing to a staircase; "and when I want any of your remarks, I'll send for you to make 'em."

"But, my dear——"

Mrs. Cockey laid violent hands on a tea-tray, and her husband took his departure hastily.

"What a wonder you are!" said Slowbob, admiringly. "Mister Cockey seems to be afraid of you; but it's only his fun, I suppose?"

"It isn't his fun; he is afraid of me," replied Mrs. Cockey, emphatically, as she put the bread-and-cheese upon the table.

"He must have been hard to train," Slowbob remarked, helping himself to a quarter of a pound of cheese and the top crust of the loaf. "Lor', how he used to bluster and bully over us poor children! He ain't like the same man."

"Perhaps not," Mrs. Cockey observed; "but what is that to you? Eat your supper and hold your tongue. Your supper, did I say? You are eating enough for six people!"

"Glad to hear you say so," said Slowbob. "Where is the mustard? I likes a little mustard with cheese."

"You'll not get any here," the beadle's wife cried, shrilly.

Timothy Slowbob rose slowly to his feet, and crossed over to a corner of the room in which a cupboard was fixed.

"I s'pose it is in here," he said, musingly. "Well, well, I can wait on myself; I hate to give people trouble."

"Come back!" Mrs. Cockey shrieked. "You little villain! touch anything if you dare!"

Timothy was heedless of this threat. He found the mustard, and returning to the table with it, helped himself plentifully.

Mrs. Cockey looked on aghast.

This was the first time for years that she had been defied in her own house, or even in the locality, for the neighbours gave Mrs. Cockey a wide berth when she was inclined to be peppery.

"Salem!" she cried up the stairs.

"Yes, my dear."

"Bring down the cane you keep for the work'us children."

"Yes, my hangel."

Salem came downstairs dutifully, swinging the cane in his hand.

"Salem," she said, "you must thrash that fellow. He must be taught manners, or we shan't be able to call this house our own."

Slowbob went on munching his bread-and-cheese as if the conversation in no way related to him.

"Do you hear?" cried Mrs. Cockey. "Do you hear me, I say? Take that cane, and thrash him well! You are big enough—old enough—ugly enough to tackle a score like him!"

"My dear," said Salem, meekly, "you don't know what he is. If he was like an ordinary boy I could deal with him; but he ain't. I've heard say that he was a goblin' changeling."

Timothy Slowbob burst out laughing.

"You ain't quite an Apollo, old man," he said. "Cockey, don't you attempt to strike me with that thing, or as sure as you are a beadle I'll double you up."

"What do you think of him?" the beadle gasped.

Mrs. Cockey snatched the cane from her husband's hand, and Timothy Slowbob was on his feet in an instant.

"Marm," he said, "I like a joke. I can give one and take one. If you hit me I can't hit you back again, because you are a woman, in spite of your peppery ways, but I'll smash every window and bit o' crockeryware there is in the place. Now fire away!"

Timothy folded his arms, and stood with his legs wide apart.

Mrs. Cockey dropped the cane, and fell gasping into a chair.

"Oh, Salem, Salem!" she cried, hysterically, "how can you stand still and see me insulted by sich a himp? Oh, to think that I married a man who rejoices to see me laughed to scorn in my own 'ouse! Oh, oh, oh!"

"She's a goin' off," Cockey said; "and it will take hours to bring her round."

"You don't say so," Timothy observed. "You look after her; I'm goin' to bed. This is a nice place for a Christmas party, I should think. Ta, ta, Cockey. Try what a bucket or two of water from the pump will do."

The page-boy marched himself off, and no sooner was he out of sight than Mrs. Cockey arose, and seizing the partner of her joys and sorrows by the arms, she bundled him into a corner, and held him there.

"Salem! Salem!" she shrieked; "would you strike your lawfully married wife? Would you dare to hit me?"

"How can I hit you when you've got my head jammed ag'in' the wall, and are a holdin' my arms?" poor Cockey replied.

"You wretch—you brute!" she screamed. "I've suffered more than mortial woman ever suffered from an idle, good-for-nothin' man. Take that—and that—and that!"

"Don't, Mariar—my love—my only one," Salem Cockey roared; "it does not become a wife to smite her beloved husband. Mur—der!"

"What a time you are having of it down there!" Slowbob called down the staircase. "Keep the pot a b'ilin' ! Let him have it, Mrs. Cockey—he deserves it."

The beadle managed to get free at last, and staggered to the door.

"Mariar," he said, impressively, as he rubbed his ears, "you have struck the man that led you to the halter. That man now bids you adoo. You have driven me to The Swan and Bottle."

"I'll come and fetch you just before closing-time," Mrs. Cockey observed. "Oh !—oh—h—h ! you—you creature to lift your hand against a woman !"

Salem decamped, and only just in time to escape a basin which the amiable Mariar flung at his head.

"The man who wrote 'Lovely, Lovely Woman' was a hass !" Cockey muttered as he went up the street. "The man gets all the smacks, and the woman all the pity."

The beadle did not remain at The Swan and Bottle very long.

He had a wholesome dread that Mariar might arrive with some weapon in the shape of a short brush or a rolling-pin, and forcing a sickly smile on his face, he crept indoors and sat down.

"Mariar," he said, "let bygones be bygones. I know you have had reason to be upset to-night, and so I thought I would bring you a drop o' somethin' to steady your nerves."

Mrs. Cockey eyed a bottle produced by the beadle, and she began to melt visibly.

"Oh, Salem !" she said as she fetched a glass from the cupboard, "why do you try me so ? Why—oh, why do you delight in making me angry ?"

Mr. Cockey coughed behind his hand.

"Perhaps we were both in the wrong," he said; "but let us put it down to Slowbob. Any more trouble with him, Mariar ?"

"No; he has been as quiet as a mouse."

"I feel that I must hit him afore I close my eyes in repoge," the beadle said. "I'll give him just one warm'un, and then lock him in. How I shall enjoy his howls, to be sure !"

"And so shall I," Mrs. Cockey remarked. "Go and do it now."

"I will," said the beadle. "I've got the key of his room, and I'll fix him."

Salem crept up the staircase and listened at Slowbob's door.

"He's an easy sleeper at all events," the beadle said; "I can't hear him breathe."

Softly he turned the handle and peeped into the room.

Then Mr. Cockey turned pale.

The bed was there, but had never been occupied, and Slowbob was conspicuous by his absence.

"I told him where to find his room," Cockey muttered. "Can it be possible that he took the wrong one ? He's wicious enough for anything."

The beadle went into his own sleeping apartment, but Slowbob was not there.

With a frightened face and staring eyes Cockey stole downstairs again.

"Mariar," he said, "you saw, with your own eyes, that boy go upstairs ?"

"Of course I did," she said. "What of it ?"

"He ain't in his room."

"Nonsense !"

"It's a fact," Cockey replied, mildly. "He's nowhere. He's wanished as clean as if a witch on a broomstick has walked off with him."

"And I say again it's nonsense," said Mrs. Cockey, bridling up.

"Very well, my love," Salem returned; "but perhaps you won't mind running upstairs and seeing for yourself."

"Which I will in a few minutes; but there's no hurry. The boy's safe enough, I'll be bound."

She knew that if she left her husband with the quartern bottle there would be precious little in it when she returned.

And so Mrs. Cockey remained in the sitting-room until the last drop was consumed, and then she ascended the stairs.

Slowbob's door was partly open, and the head of the bed was visible in the moonlight.

There was Timothy sleeping as peacefully as if he had a banker's account of ten thousand pounds, and not a care or trouble in the world to disturb his mind.

"That fool of a husband of mine is going wrong in his head !" said Mrs. Cockey. "It's hard when he sees double, but worse when he can see nothing."

When she re-entered the sitting-room her spouse was looking down the neck of the bottle in the vain hope of discovering a few drops.

"Salem !"

"Yes, my love."

"You'd better have a dose of physic —a strong dose—and then take yourself off to bed as quick as possible."

"But why the physic?" demanded Cockey, pleadingly. "There ain't nothin' the matter with me."

"There is," Mariar said, sternly; "you're going silly. That boy is in bed, and as fast asleep as ever he was in his life."

"Well, I never—no, I never!" Salem gasped.

Mariar pointed sternly to the staircase.

"Go," she said. "I've got a lot of clearing-up to do, and I don't want a demented old idiot bothering and worrying about like a dog in a fair."

"Of all the 'strordinary things this is the 'strordinest," Salem said as he rose. "I'll swear he wasn't in bed when——"

Mariar made a clutch at the kettle that was singing on the hob, and Salem departed with the nimbleness of a boy of twelve.

"It's marvellous!" he said, as he took a sly peep at the slumbering Slowbob. "This 'ere boy has got the power of vanishing when he likes. I must be more civil to him, for if he can make himself invisible, what chance has a man—even a parochial beadle—again' him?"

No sooner had Mr. Cockey's footsteps ceased to sound than Slowbob, fully dressed, slipped out of bed, and closing the door, opened the window and slid out on the roof of a chicken-house.

"I was nearly caught," the youth muttered as he reached the ground. "It was lucky that I caught sight of old Cockey. Now for the Miser's Mill. Tim, my boy, if you don't learn something waluable to-night, it will be no fault of yours."

CHAPTER XXXVIII.

"IN TWO DAYS MORE THE DEED WILL BE DONE!"

THE moon was shining too brightly for the irrepressible's liking.

There was not a cloud in the sky, and so light was it, that a man blessed with ordinary eyesight could have perused a newspaper without much difficulty.

Timothy felt a little guilty as he crept along in the shadow of the houses.

"Mr. Stormaway is fond of moonlight walks," he thought. "What would he say if he saw me prowling about like a fox round a fowl-roost?"

But it was late; the street was deserted, and most of the blinds of the houses were drawn, proclaiming that the inhabitants of Merrytown preferred their beds to staring at the moon.

Once Timothy came to a standstill.

He thought he saw Worryboy's shadow, but it turned out to be that of the town pump, and chuckling at the illusion, Slowbob passed out of the street, and wended his way towards the haunted mill.

Just then the clock of Merrytown church struck the hour of eleven, and simultaneously the long dusty road traversed by the page-boy was occupied by the figure of a man.

Timothy recognised Alphonse Carleon, and squeezed himself into a hedge.

It happened to be a prickly holly one, and afflicted Timothy sorely, but not a murmur did he make.

"It's all for Mister Mornington," he said, "and I'd bear it if every leaf turned red-hot."

M. Alphonse Carleon came on, looking furtively on each side of the lane, with the suspicious glances of a guilty man.

He carried a thick and heavy stick in his hand with which he occasionally beat the bank nearest to him, and Timothy narrowly escaped a blow in the ribs, which would have forced a cry of pain to his lips.

Carleon was perfectly ghastly, and muttered to himself as he walked.

"What a pitiful wretch—what a slave I am!" he said. "Is there no courage left in me? Am I so completely under the thumb of this adventurer—so lost to everything that becomes a man, that I must fawn and cringe to him like a beaten cur?"

"He's calling somebody a cur," thought Slowbob, who overheard a part of the words. "There will be a row among the rascals to-night, but

I'll see it out even if it is at the risk of my life."

"Will you ?" growled a voice in his ear.

Slowbob started, but before he could turn fully round, he received a tremendous blow on the back of his head from a bludgeon, and rolled senseless from the hedge into the lane.

"That's settled him," said Sam Welcher, as he stood over the prostrate boy. "What shall I do with him ? Throw him in the river—eh ?"

"No, no," cried Carleon, who, at the sound, had wheeled with the rapidity of lightning. "Oh, horror !—no ! Anything but that. It turns my blood cold to think of the mill-wheel."

"If what Jem Muzzler says is true, you weren't so particular about using the air-gun," Welcher said. "Well, just as you like ; but I had better give him another crack to keep him quiet for some time."

"He has had enough," Carleon returned, stooping and placing his hand on Slowbob's heart. "The boy will trouble us no more—he is dead !"

"What shall I do with his body, then ?" demanded Welcher, brutally. "The river's the place for it, I tell you."

Carleon turned his head away as the ruffian dragged Slowbob's inanimate form towards the river.

"I tell you no," gasped the Frenchman.

"But I say yes," Welcher hissed. "You and I must share this secret ; we needn't mention it to Muzzler or Mornington."

There was a splash. The water, silvered by the moonlight, was agitated for a few moments, and then quieted down over the hapless Slowbob.

"Dead men tell no tales, nor dead boys either," Welcher said. "Now for the mill. Quick ! it is past the time."

But speech and power of limb seemed to have deserted Carleon.

He stood with his hand clasped to his brow, trying to speak, but the utterance was choked and a horrible gurgling came from his throat.

"Come—come," said Welcher ; "be a man. I did it to serve you, you know."

"To serve me ?" Carleon contrived to articulate. "Dog, you lie ! How shall I be served by carrying out this hideous plot ? Ugh ! The blood of that poor boy is on your hands."

Sam Welcher started, and kneeling down dipped his hands in the water.

"It is gone now, at all events," he said.

"No, no !" Carleon cried in terror. "See, it has come again. Nothing can wash it out. Look how the spots return ! They are red—red—red !"

"It's all a mistake, I tell you," Welcher said. "You are in such a mortal fear that you don't know what you are talking about. Come to the mill, or you shall go under it. Hist ! I hear the sound of footsteps. Fool, you will ruin all—come away !"

Carleon braced up his nerves, and, half led, half dragged by Welcher, he reached the entrance to the mill.

"Leave me," he said, as he fell grovelling on his knees. "I am not fit to die, but life is a misery to me. The earth swims—I faint—I die !"

Welcher picked him up as easily as he would have lifted a child, and bore him to the upper chamber.

"Brandy here !" he said ; "the Frenchman is in a fit."

Richard Mornington produced a flask and endeavoured to force a few drops through Carleon's teeth, but they flowed down his neck.

"What has happened ?" he demanded.

"Nothing that I know of," Welcher replied ; "but I fancy he got a scare coming along. He took a tree for a ghost or something. Muzzler, pitch some water over him, and when he comes round leave him to me."

Carleon lay as if life had left him, and, save that his eyelids quivered, he looked for all the world like a dead man.

"This is a nice state of things, I must say," Richard Mornington observed as he stooped and beat the Frenchman's hands together. "Welcher, there is more in this than you care to tell."

"Have it your own way," the ruffian growled. "Steady, my lad. You haven't got your cousin's money yet, and you owe me a trifle."

Richard Mornington made no reply, but he bit his under lip, and his eyes flashed in a manner that boded Sam Welcher no good.

"Carleon is coming round," observed Jem Muzzler. "Lift him up, and loosen his necktie."

The French tutor groaned heavily

as he opened his eyes, and some half-spoken words came from his lips.

In an instant Sam Welcher was at his side.

"Leave him to me, I tell you," he said. "The man has had a fit, and he has come out of it dreaming."

"A curious dream," Richard Mornington observed, suspiciously. "He said something about the page-boy, and murder."

Sam Welcher shook Alphonse Carleon roughly by the shoulder.

"Wake up!" he said. "Wake up, and be a man! It was lucky for you that I was near at hand when you tumbled down all of a heap. If you are subject to that sort of thing you ought not to walk about alone. What is the matter with you?"

"I don't know," Carleon murmured as he sat up and stared vaguely at those around him. "Perhaps the heat of the weather caused the sudden faintness—yes, yes; you may put it down to that."

Richard Mornington handed Carleon the flask, and he drank greedily from it.

"I am better now," he said. "I have come at your bidding. Everything is ready, and in two days more the deed will be done."

"You mean the trump card that is to win the game will be played," said Richard Mornington.

"Why ask the question, when you know what I meant?"

"I like to dwell upon it," Richard Mornington rejoined, rubbing his hands. "It is like music to my ears. And now, Carleon, I and my friends intend to clear out of this place."

"When?"

"To-night—at once," Richard Mornington replied. "I will write to you, and tell you where to find us; but have a care," he added, "there must be no shrinking back—no shuffling."

"There will be nothing of the kind," Carleon replied. "You require me no longer, I suppose?"

"No."

"Look here, Frenchy," said Sam Welcher; "you had better go back across the fields. If I am not mistaken, I heard a third party about just as I met you. Before you are home, we shall be out of this place."

CHAPTER XXXIX.

MR. JOSHUA BLACKSTONE—A SWIM IN THE MOONLIGHT.

SAM WELCHER had made no mistake.

He had heard the sound of footsteps in the stillness of the night, but they were not on the same side of the river as Carleon and himself.

A tall stalwart man, with keen searching eyes, was strolling through an avenue of willows, whose drooping branches hid the opposite bank from view.

Suddenly he stopped, for a loud splash, as if a tree had succumbed to age and fallen into the river, came to his ears; but Mr. Joshua Blackstone, the experienced private detective, was not the man to let such an incident pass without satisfying himself as to the cause.

The path on which he was walking was full of holes and ruts, and the moonlight, as it danced through the branches swaying in the breeze, played such vagaries that it behoved him to proceed with great caution.

"It must have been a tree or something of the sort," Joshua Blackstone said to himself as he reached the river bank. "I heard no cry, and even if some poor wretch, tired of his life, had taken a header, I don't think he would have made such a splash as I heard."

He ran his piercing eyes along the surface of the now calm and passive stream.

He was in the act of turning away when he saw what at first he took to be a log of wood rise to the surface; but this notion was banished from his mind as the moon shone upon a white upturned face.

In a moment Joshua Blackstone's coat and waistcoat were thrown aside, as were also his boots, which he kicked off with commendable alacrity.

Splash!

Joshua Blackstone was an excellent swimmer.

He struck out for the floating figure, and as he stretched out his hand to grasp it, it disappeared; but, nothing daunted, Joshua Blackstone dived, and presently reappeared with Timothy Slowbob.

To drag him ashore was the work of scarcely a minute, and then the detective proceeded to examine his prize in a calm business-like way.

"There has been foul play here," he said. "This boy never got into the water by his own free will. I had better run with him to the police-station without delay. I hope the poor little chap is not dead."

Timothy put an end to all argument on that question by suddenly opening his eyes—those wonderful eyes—and glaring at his rescuer in a strange meaningless way.

Joshua Blackstone did not even stop for the portions of his attire he had thrown aside, but bore Slowbob as rapidly as he could to P. C. Worryboy's residence, which also included the lock-up.

The valiant constable had just returned from a beat and was considerably startled at the appearance of Joshua Blackstone and his burden, both of whom were naturally dripping with water.

"Wot's this?" he demanded. "Has Slowbob committed susancide. If Cockey and his wife druv him to it they'll have to answer for the consequences."

"You know this poor boy, it appears," said Blackstone.

"Know him!" cried Worryboy. "Of course I do! Is there anybody in Merrytown who don't? You're a stranger or you wouldn't ask me if I knew him."

"I am a stranger, but not quite such an idiot as you seem to be," Joshua Blackstone said. "Unless you are blind, you must see that the lad is more dead than alive, and yet you stand staring at him like a moonstruck fool."

"Like a wot?" exclaimed Worryboy. "I'll have you know——"

"Pooh! pooh! I know all about it," said Blackstone, interrupting him as he laid Timothy Slowbob at full length upon a bench. "Of course you are constable, inspector, superintendent, and all the force rolled into one. It's the way you country policemen have. Run for a doctor, and be sharp about it, or your chief constable shall hear of your conduct."

Worryboy was not only taken aback, but thoroughly cowed.

"I was a goin'," he said, "and you needn't have come down upon a man like a bunderholt—I mean thunder bolt."

The constable thumped his helmet viciously on his head, and made a great show of being in a violent hurry; but he fell into his usual waddle before he had gone a hundred yards, and reached Dr. Pillem's house perfectly cool and breathing freely.

Worryboy blew up the pipe placed in the wall for the convenience of late callers, and presently Dr. Pillem responded:

"Who is there?"

"Constable Worryboy."

"What do you want?"

"Mr. Stormaway's page-boy——"

"Oh, I can't bother my head about Mr. Stormaway's page-boy," Dr. Pillem interposed. "Go away! How dare you call me out of bed for such a trivial matter?"

"It ain't a trivial matter," Worryboy replied. "Slowbob's been picked out o' the river, and it seems to me that there will be a hinquest held on his buttons."

"An inquest held on what?" Dr. Pillem gurgled down the pipe.

"I'm so confoosed with runnin' that I hardly know what I am talking about," Worryboy said. "What I mean to say is that I'm afeared there'll be a hinquest held on his body."

"I'll be down in a minute," the doctor replied. "Where is the boy?"

"At the station."

"Did you pick him out of the river?"

"Not quite," Worryboy responded; "but since I have had him in my charge I've been a father to him."

"Very well," said Dr. Pillem. "Run back to the station, and I will be there almost as soon as yourself."

P.C. Worryboy did use his legs to some purpose on this occasion.

He ran so fast that he did not see the figures of three men, who were, from the fact that they separated and took different directions, evidently desirous of escaping observation.

In hot haste the constable arrived at the station-house. He tripped over the doorstep, and shot himself in like a rocket, much to the wrath of Mr. Joshua Blackstone, who was doing all he could for poor Timothy Slowbob.

"The doctor's a comin'," Worryboy said as he picked himself up. "I blowed up the night-pipe, and told him to make haste in the name of the law."

"IT IS SLOWBOB BEING BROUGHT BACK TO THE ABBEY," JACK WALBUT SAID.—(See page 133.)

No. 9.

"You must be an important personage here," Joshua Blackstone observed. "Excuse me wearing my hat in your presence."

"Certainly," said Worryboy, affably, as he took out his pocket-book. "Now I'll make a few notes of this case."

"You had better let the doctor do that," Blackstone suggested.

Dr. Pillem, with a number of bandages streaming over one arm, and a box of instruments under the other, came bustling in.

"Why, this boy is positively wet," he said.

"So would you be if you came from the same place as he did," Joshua Blackstone returned. "The poor little fellow has not only had a dip in the river, but he has been badly beaten about the head. If he dies, somebody will have to answer for his murder."

Dr. Pillem's face was very grave as he examined and proceeded to dress Slowbob's head.

"It is not the wound I am afraid of," he said, "but the shock to the system. May I ask who you are, sir?"

"Humph, I think we had better leave explanations for the present," the detective replied. "Do what you can for the boy, and we can have a chat in the morning, when I will call upon you."

"He must be put into hot blankets, and carried to bed at once," Dr. Pillem said.

"I've got a good 'art for one in affliction, and I'll carry him to the Abbey," Worryboy remarked.

"You will do nothing of the kind," Dr. Pillem said; "he must not be removed—I forbid it."

"The cells are a trifle cold," Worryboy returned, coughing behind his hand; "and you see, sir——"

"Cells!" cried Joshua Blackstone, interrupting him. "Man, you talk about your heart! Where is it? You are a fool—an ass. If the occasion were not such a solemn one I would punch your stupid head."

"I'll make a note of that," Worryboy gasped.

"And add that I would also kick you out of the station-house," said Joshua Blackstone, calmly; "and having got you into the road, drop you into the first horse-pond I could drag you to."

"Why, this is aimin' a blow at the Crown and Skepter," cried Worryboy, holding up his hands.

"Perhaps that's the name of your favourite public-house," said Blackstone, as he raised Timothy Slowbob in his arms. "Have the goodness to lead the way to your own bed-room."

"Of course—why, yes—it's funny that I never thought of it before," the constable remarked.

"Very," replied Joshua Blackstone, dryly.

In a few minutes Timothy was tucked up snugly in bed, and the doctor and Joshua Blackstone remained with him far into the night; while Worryboy sallied forth to arrest any suspicious characters that might come in his way.

The valiant constable returned empty-handed just as Dr. Pillem was putting on his hat and gloves.

"Will the boy live?" Joshua Blackstone demanded.

"I think so," the doctor replied, "but it seems to me that he will have a long illness. His pulse is high, and there is every symptom of fever."

"Not brain-fever," Worryboy ventured with a giggle. "It ain't possible that Timothy Slowbob could have that."

Joshua Blackstone pushed the constable out of the room.

"The next time you make such a remark as that," he said, "you will require the assistance of an undertaker."

"I made the joke 'cause I was glad that Slowbob wouldn't die," said the astonished policeman.

"I don't believe it," Joshua Blackstone replied. "I have learned to read a man's thoughts, and I know you hate the poor lad."

He turned away, leaving the constable in a state of bewilderment.

"The world's gone mad," he panted. "Me a hass—a fool! Worryboy, your power is on the wane. You must spry up, old man, and sit on this interferin' feller, or you'll be the laughin'-stock of Merrytown. And all this 'ere's through a low menial boy with a bump on his head. May I be b'iled if I don't write to the Home Seckertary."

CHAPTER XL.

MR. STORMAWAY GIVES VENT TO HIS FEELINGS—AN INTERVIEW BETWEEN
JACK WALBUT AND ALPHONSE CARLEON—THE INTERESTING INVALID.

LONG before Salem Cockey and Maria —the best woman in the world, only a little peppery—had discovered the loss of their lodger, Dr. Pillem was on his way to the Abbey.

As soon as he thought that the servants would be about, he presented himself at the gates, and having been admitted, requested to see Mr. Stormaway.

"I come on urgent business, and must be admitted to his bedroom," he said.

"Very good, sir," the servant replied. "Follow me, if you please. Mr. Stormaway is an early riser, and it is just possible that he is up and dressed."

But for once the head-master of Merrytown Abbey was in a lazy mood, and, though wide awake, was in no wise inclined to leave his bed.

He sat bolt upright as the doctor entered, and opened his eyes wide with surprise.

"Why, doctor," he said, "what brings you here at such a time? Really, this unexpected appearance has taken my breath away."

"You must be calm," Dr. Pillem replied. "Let me feel your pulse."

"I see how it is," said Mr. Stormaway, laughing. "You have been made the victim of a hoax. Those dreadful boys again, I suppose. I was never better in my life."

"My friend," the doctor returned, "I'm the victim of no hoax, but I ask you to be calm, cool, and collected, because I am the bearer of extraordinary news."

"Good or bad?"

"Bad."

Mr. Stormaway took up his nightcap, and fanned his face with it.

"Let me hear it," he said, faintly. "I suppose it concerns the boys in some way?"

"It concerns a boy connected with your establishment, but not a pupil."

"Slowbob, of course," said Mr. Stormaway, with a groan.

"Yes, and he has been brutally assaulted; and if he escapes with his life, I shall mark it down in my book as a good case."

"Good gracious!" Mr. Stormaway exclaimed. "Don't tell me that Cockey has done this; I have always known him to be a pompous, overbearing fellow, but——"

"The beadle has no more to do with this affair than yourself," Dr. Pillem interposed. "Listen, and I will tell you all I know of the matter."

He did so, and Mr. Stormaway heard him with bated breath, but without interrupting. When the doleful story was told to the end, Mr. Stormaway fished his handkerchief from under a pillow and wiped his eyes.

"Doctor," he said, "I am truly sorry to hear this. That Slowbob has acted disobediently in leaving Salem Cockey's house cannot be disputed, but that he has fallen into the hands of some dastard must be deeply deplored. Of course it was the work of some tramp or vagabond?"

"That remains to be seen," Dr. Pillem replied. "It will be weeks, and may be months, before he will be able to give a coherent account of what has happened. He is lying in a state of coma, and nothing but careful nursing will accomplish his recovery."

Genuine tears rolled down the headmaster's cheeks, which had grown paler and paler until they were nearly white.

"He must be brought here," he said. "But I forget myself. Doctor, will it be safe to remove him?"

"Yes, if done at once. I will send an ambulance for him, and make arrangements with a nurse without delay."

"Do," said Mr. Stormaway. "Pillem, I never liked your physic, but you are one of the best fellows in the world. Think nothing of expense. Poor Slowbob—poor Slowbob! He has tormented me almost out of my life, but I would not lose him for all I possess. I believe that he is really attached to me, and besides, he is a curiosity."

"There never was a boy like him," Dr. Pillem remarked.

"And never will be another," Mr. Stormaway said, mournfully.

The news of Timothy Slowbob's misfortune flew through the Abbey with lightning-like rapidity.

There was sorrowing and commiseration throughout the house, and a gloom fell upon everybody and everything.

Salem Cockey came to the Abbey about eight o'clock, and when he was enlightened as to what had taken place, he shook his head.

"Ah!" he said, "me and my Mariar would have been a father and mother to him, and——"

Mary the housemaid banged the door in his face with such force and suddenness that the knocker rebounded with the shock, and caught Mr. Cockey on the nose.

The beadle staggered down the steps, tripped over the scraper, and sat down, all clad as he was in his official robes.

"That young woman and my Mariar are about a match," he gasped. "It's a cur'us thing, and a painful fact, that the femingnine gender have no respect for the law. Here's me—beadle, stuck on the proboskis by a brass knocker. Worryboy is right; a revolution is a brewin'!"

Mr. Salem Cockey departed just as Jack Walbut, with his head down and his hands clasped before him, slouched into the playground.

Breakfast had been put off for an hour pending the arrival of Slowbob, for whom every comfort was being prepared.

Walbut was alone in the playground, and from there he strolled into a part of the adjoining meadow where a belt of trees hid him from observation.

Here he stopped and looked nervously about him.

"I don't like this," he said, in an audible whisper. "It seems to me that Carleon must have had a hand in this affair."

"Do you think so?"

The French tutor was at the boy's side, and his hand upon his shoulder.

"Don't touch me," Walbut said, shudderingly, as he shook him off. "You frighten me. You come and go at will as if you were possessed of powers unknown to mortals."

"What! rebellious?" Carleon exclaimed.

"No; I'm terrified," Walbut replied. "Last night my sleep was haunted with horrible dreams, and this morning's news has added to my horror. I wish I was dead," he wailed —"indeed I do—I wish I was dead."

Alphonse Carleon tightened his grip upon Walbut's shoulder, and pointed with his disengaged hand to the Abbey.

"If I hear another word from you," he said, "I will go straight to Mr. Stormaway, and acquaint him with a few facts that will surely cause your downfall here. I will do more than that, I will follow you up through life and work your ruin. Be sensible, Walbut. What is this page-boy to you? Perform the task I have set you, and all will be well. Go now, and let me have no more of this nonsense."

Jack Walbut walked a few paces, and then turned back again.

"Monsieur," he said, "permit me to have just one more word with you."

"Speak out," returned the Frenchman, "and that quickly. Under the present circumstances it would not do for us to be seen together."

"They tell me that Slowbob may be ill for months."

"So much the better," Carleon responded. "He has suspected that something was between us, but now his mouth will be closed until all trouble is over."

"When—when am I to receive the hundred pounds?" Walbut asked.

"As soon as Ralph Mornington is on the other side of the Abbey gates."

"I put the question because I cannot stay here after he has gone," Walbut said. "I should go mad and blurt out the whole truth. As soon as I get the money I will run away—I will do anything and go anywhere, but remain here I cannot."

"You shall do exactly as you please," Alphonse Carleon replied, smiling in a peculiar way. "*Au revoir.* I hear the sound of many footsteps. We must part."

"It is Slowbob being brought back to the Abbey," Jack Walbut said.

He walked quickly away, for he durst not face the mournful procession that was on its way to the house.

"I wish I was dead," he only said, wringing his hands. "Life, that might be so happy, is a burden to me."

The airiest room, the best bed, the softest pillows, were got ready for Timothy Slowbob, but he knew nothing of all these kind attentions.

It seemed as if the irrepressible had gone mad in reality.

He laughed, raved, sang, and cried all in a breath.

The nurse looked anxious, Dr. Pillem shook his head, and Mr. Stormaway was in such a state of nervousness that he could not remain in one place more than one minute at a time.

"Oh, sir," said Ralph, meeting the distracted head-master, "may I see poor Slowbob? I have an idea that he would know me."

Dr. Pillem was consulted; he saw no objection to the arrangement, providing that Ralph gave his solemn promise not to speak to the patient; and in a few minutes our hero was standing at the foot of the bed.

The effect was magical.

Timothy Slowbob, who had been rolling his head on the pillow, now lay perfectly still. Suddenly he made an effort to rise, but was, of course, restrained from doing so by the nurse.

"I must get up—I tell you I must get up!" he said. "Haven't I got to go to the Miser's Mill? They want to kill him—they have killed him! Look! don't you see? There is his ghost."

"You had better retire," the doctor whispered to Ralph.

Our hero did so, and Dr. Pillem bent over Slowbob and smoothed his brow.

"My boy," he said, "do you know me?"

"Yes," Timothy replied; "you are old Cockey's grandmother."

This startling reply staggered Doctor Pillem considerably, and the nurse turned her head aside so that he might not see the involuntary smile that was forced to her lips.

"No, no," said the medical man. "I am the doctor—Doctor Pillem. Ha, ha! You know me now, Slowbob, eh?"

"If you're the doctor, why do you come here like the man who sells winkles?" Slowbob required. "Give us a penn'orth."

"It is no use talking to him," Dr. Pillem said. "My fears are established. The fever has flown to his brain. Nurse, I will leave him in your charge now. Send for me at any time you think necessary, and I will come immediately."

The nurse was a practical woman, and, after a little trouble, contrived to get half-a-glass of medicine down Timothy Slowbob's throat.

Then she sat down, and, taking up some needlework, began to sew.

"It's near upon eleven o'clock, and I must go," said Timothy Slowbob. "The Miser's Mill is more than a mile off, and I shall be late."

The nurse dropped her work, and listened intently.

"Watchdog—Watchdog!" Timothy continued in his ravings. "Ha, ha! They shall find that I can bite as well as bark. Bow-wow! Look out for my teeth. Hullo, Mrs. Jumble!"

"Yes," said the nurse, thinking to get some sensible remark from the invalid.

"The next time you make a pigeon-pie, don't put an old hat in it."

The nurse went on with her sewing again.

"There's the mill," continued Timothy, "and here they come. One—two—three—four. Oh, what beauties they are! Let me see. I must be careful. Yes, there they are; and now—now—now—hold me—I'm sinking—catch hold of me! I'm goin' down—down—down!"

The nurse took Timothy's hand in her own, and patted it assuringly.

"I'm in a pit!" Slowbob cried—"in a pit as dark as night. Drag me out. Hi—hi! Mister Mornington, where are you? I see you—that's right—you're the best friend I have in the world. I've got hold of the rope; pull away, but look out; they are all behind you. One—two—three—four."

"This is a bad case," the nurse thought. "The doctor may say what he likes, but I don't believe that the boy will recover."

CHAPTER XLI.

MATTHEW STICKERS REJOICES, BUT IS LAID LOW IN THE HOUR OF HIS TRIUMPH.

LATER on, Slowbob fell asleep, and Dr. Pillem, who called again before noon, stated that there were some signs of improvement.

The page-boy had been placed in a wing of the Abbey where no noise could reach him, and Mr. Stormaway, with a somewhat lightened heart, resumed his duties, and the boys their lessons.

"Don't pe down-hearted," Herr Halfamann said to Ralph; "Slowpop vill regover. Vot is a crack on zee head to a poy like dat? It vill make him a leedle queer, but he vill get up again, and return dat crack to zee man dat gave it."

"What is your opinion about the affair, professor?" Ralph asked when school was over.

Herr Halfamann pushed up his spectacles and ran his fingers through his hair, as if the question puzzled him sorely.

"I do not know vat to t'ink," he said. "It s'al not pe highway roppery, for vot had boor Slowpop to pe ropped of put his puttons, and there vas many of dem gone? No, no; it vas not roppery dat brompted zee act."

"What then?"

"Mine poy," said the German tutor, "I vould like to find an answer mineself. Here vas Mistare Muffler, and berhaps he can thow some light on zee matter."

"From the bottom of my heart I wish I could," the usher returned. "I am not a muscular man, but if I should ever meet the scoundrel who dealt that blow to Slowbob, I will hurl myself upon him, and hold him until the officers of justice arrest him."

"Pravo! pravo!" cried Herr Fritz Halfamann, clapping his hands. "Dat vas a vary goot sbeech indeed. Mine fader vonce got von crack on his head mit a stick. Did I ever tell you dat story, mine friend Muffler?"

"No," the usher replied; "and, excuse me, I am in no mood to listen to anything mirth-provoking."

"Mirt-brovoking," cried the Teuton in astonishment. "Vot is dere mirt-brovoking in mine fader getting von crack on his head?"

Before any reply could be made, Mr. Stormaway, with a gentleman at his side, passed through the school-room.

"Blackstone," said the stranger quietly in Ralph's ear, as he tapped him lightly on the shoulder.

Our hero looked up sharply, but the gentleman took not the slightest notice of him, but went on talking to Mr. Stormaway.

"That's the man Mr. Herapath spoke of," Ralph thought. "I shall never forget him. When he looked at me his eyes seemed to pierce me through and through."

Joshua Blackstone had merely called to know how Slowbob was progressing.

The head-master made much of him as the rescuer of the boy, and invited him to dinner; but the detective excused himself on the plea that he had important business on hand, and presently took his leave.

Mr. Stormaway escorted him to the door, and there found himself confronted by Matthew Stickers.

The head-master gazed at him in silence, and reflected. One thing was quite certain—he must have a male servant in the house; and now that Slowbob was *hors de combat*, he thought that he could not do better than re-engage Stickers, at least for a time.

"Come in," he said. "I will give you one more trial; it will be your last, so understand that if I catch you tripping you will walk out of this door never to re-enter it."

"Hoh, sir," cried Matthew, "this is the most j'iful moment of my life. My 'art is a swellin' with hemotion. Hoh, Mister Stormaway, I've heerd about pore, pore Slowbob. Let me nuss him—let me sit hup with him hall through the long nights. He was a little playful at times, but I luved him like a brother."

"Oh, yes, I daresay you did," remarked the head-master, sarcastically. "You know your way to the kitchen, but you had better report yourself to Mrs. Jumble, and tell her that I have consented to take you back again."

Matthew Stickers required no second bidding.

He frisked up the staircase in a lamb-like fashion, and chuckled with glee as he knocked at the door of the housekeeper's sitting-room.

"Come in," said Mrs. Jumble.

Matthew Stickers stalked into the apartment like the ghost of Hamlet's father.

"What! is it you?" cried the housekeeper. "Who has dared admit you into the Abbey?"

"Your master and mine," Matthew replied, boldly. "I wants my Sunday soot of liv'ry. for I'm hengaged again."

"More's the pity," remarked Mrs. Jumble, closing her teeth with a snap.

"I hexpected summat o' that sort from you," Matthew Stickers said. "Ah, Missus Jumble, don't be so wicious. You may come to a barrer with sassige rolls and ginger-beer yet, or heven a tater-can. Then, marm, you will feel wot a stony world this is."

"I come to a potato-can!" exclaimed Mrs. Jumble. "How dare you?"

"I knowed a woman who came down to fly-catchers in the summer and 'ot chesternuts in the winter," Matthew continued. "She did well until she married, and then all her hearnings went in payin' fines for her 'usband."

"Go away," said the housekeeper. "I will see about your livery presently. I cannot understand what Mr. Stormaway can be thinking of. There are thousands of deserving men out of work."

"W'ich remark might also be applied to a female party I knows of," Matthew Stickers retorted. "She ain't more than a mile away, and is given to make uncalled-for remarks about them as is her superior in hevery sense of the word."

With this, Matthew departed haughtily, and, bent on making his presence known with all possible expedition, he walked into the schoolroom, thinking to find a few of the boys there.

He was disappointed. There were no boys, and Herr Fritz Halfamann had full possession of the room. He sat at his desk with his head resting on his hand, and evidently in a deep train of thought.

"He smote me on the nose," Stickers muttered, savagely. "I never thought it was in him, but it must have been the himpulse of a moment. I'll strike while the hiron is 'ot, and ask him to 'pologise."

Marching up to the day-dreaming German tutor, he tapped him on the shoulder.

Herr Fritz Halfamann swung slowly round, but, not believing his eyes, he took off their artificial assistants, and rubbed them clean with a silk handkerchief.

"Yes," he said; "it vas Stickares. Vell, vat you vant vith me?"

"I begs your pardin'," Matthew rejoined; "but perhaps you have forgotten that you——?"

"No, no," Halfamann interrupted; "I haf not forgotten dat I did bunch your head. Haf you come for anoder?"

Matthew Stickers did not relish the tone in which the last five words were spoken, and he retreated a few paces.

"It comes to this," he said; "I'm on my hold footin' again, and I wishes to be friends with everybody. You're a husher, and I'm a futman. There ain't much diff'rence between us, so take this 'and—though it's 'ard to give the 'and where the 'art can never be, as the song ses—and let us be as we was afore."

"Jost so," responded Herr Halfamann, skipping off his stool. "Mistare Stickares, I vill drouble you to valk out of dat door at vonce."

Matthew Stickers smiled feebly, and extended a trembling hand.

"Don't let your German blood rile," he said. "Hact like a man and a brother. I always respected your nation. You beat the Frenchies, and if there was a kick-up between you and that 'ere Carleon, you'd knock him into fits. I've said it over and over again."

"You vas von low fellow," Halfamann returned, puffing out his cheeks. "Vill you leave the room? or s'al I take you py your preeches and zee collar of your coat, and valk you down zee stairs tree at von time?"

It was Matthew Stickers's turn now to bridle up.

"Hif it comes to that," he said, "there would have to be a consenting party, and that's me."

"Vary well," Herr Halfamann rejoined; "if you get von proken head, don't plame anypody but yourself."

The Teuton took off his coat, and folded it up very carefully.

He then rolled up his shirt-sleeves, doubled his fists, and advanced upon Matthew Stickers in such a determined way that the man-of-all-work shrank back until he came in contact with a sharp angle of the wall, against which he bumped himself with such force that he was jerked forward, and literally fell upon Herr Halfamann.

The German tutor, thinking that Stickers intended to assault him, struck out wildly, but effectively, and down went Matthew all of a heap.

"Oh!" shrieked Stickers; "I'm done for. There'll be two hinwalids in this 'ouse instead of one."

Herr Fritz Halfamann performed a frantic dance round his prostrate foe.

"Get up," he said. "Get up and go away. Anypody vould t'ink dat you vas hurt."

"I'm hit in a wital part," Stickers groaned. "There was a penknife in my veskit pocket, and you've druv it into me."

As the man-of-all-work refused to

rise, Herr Fritz Halfamann picked him up, and more than carried out his threat, for Matthew Stickers went down the stairs with such velocity that his heels rattled as if they were drumsticks.

Matthew made a clutch at the balustrade railings, and brought them down with a run; but perhaps the mischief would have ended there, had not Mr. Stormaway, who heard the noise, and wondered what it was all about, rushed out of his study.

He saw something coming down—a something that looked like a Fifth of November guy with an armful of dummy rockets; and, little dreaming what it really was, he stretched out his arms to catch it.

To say that he caught the figure would be to convey the situation poorly.

Matthew Stickers went plump into his arms, and before Mr. Stormaway had time to make out what had happened, he was sitting on the mat in the hall, and gazing idiotically at an inverted view of his re-engaged man-servant.

Stickers did not speak. He crawled away on his hands and knees, and the head-master of Merrytown Abbey let him go; for, in point of fact, he was in such a confused state of mind that he was not quite sure of the identity of the individual who had bowled him over so neatly.

The hall was dark, and when Herr Fritz Halfamann appeared on the scene he took Mr. Stormaway for Matthew Stickers.

"Vell, mine friend," said the professor, laughing, "have you had enough?"

"Have I had enough!" returned Mr. Stormaway, passing his hand across his brow. "Was ever such a ridiculous question asked a man?"

Herr Fritz Halfamann discovered his mistake in a moment.

He assisted the head-master to rise to his feet, and dusted him down gently.

"Vhere vas dat Stickares?" the German asked. "It is not bossible dat he has gone through zee floor?"

"Stickers—oh, yes, of course, Stickers," said Mr. Stormaway, vaguely. "Dear me, of course it was he who fell on me. I saw him, but one cannot recognise a man by his legs. Herr Halfamann, would you mind rubbing the small of my back gently?"

"You did make von mistake vhen you took dat man pack in your embloy," Halfamann observed, as he performed the operation. "He come into zee schoolroom, and vas so imbertinent dat I put him out."

"You must have put him out all at once," Mr. Stormaway said.

"I did, and if you vill give me leave I vill put him out of zee front door," the Teuton returned.

"No, no," said Mr. Stormaway, hastily. "I see through it all now, but do not wish for any more violence. We must remember that poor Slowbob is lying here ill—though out of hearing of any commotion, I am glad to say."

"It was zee thought of Slowpop as moch as anyding dat made me go for Stickares," Halfamann remarked. "He vas vary unkind to dat peautiful poy, and vhen Slowpop gets better he s'al haf his revenge."

"Will there never be a moment's peace in the house?" the head-master cried. "Halfamann, I beg of you to help me to keep order. Come with me to my study; I have a few things I wish to talk to you about."

"I vas at your disbosal, sare," said the professor, bowing.

CHAPTER XLII.

THE EVENTFUL DAY.

SATURDAY came. The day opened close and sultry, but about noon a thunder shower cleared the air, and the boys were able to enjoy their half-holiday.

Their play lacked some of its mirth, for the thought of Timothy Slowbob lying at the Abbey, stricken down with fever, and raving about the strangest things imaginable, caused them to hush their voices.

The dim mysterious old house was almost deserted.

The masters were out; the servants went quietly about their work; and Matthew Stickers, feeling secure from the fact that the boys were in the cricket-field, dozed and nodded in a shady corner of the playground.

Suddenly a clattering of feet awoke him with a start.

He saw a boy, holding a handkerchief before his face, rush out of the Abbey and make for the gates, as if a mad bull were after him.

Matthew Stickers paid little attention to this incident.

To see a boy running was no matter for surprise, and he returned to his slumbers and dreamed that he had opened a school on his own account, and was doing fearful execution amongst his pupils with a cane as thick as a broomstick.

He did not wake again until nearly tea-time.

The boys were coming in flushed with healthful exercise, and as hungry as young Nimrods.

Ralph Mornington looked the picture of youth and happiness.

With his arm linked in Charlie Chadwick's, he was chatting about the approaching holidays, and Charlie was beaming with joy, for in his pocket was a letter from his father, inviting our hero to stay through the vacation down at the old hall in Leicestershire.

"What fun we will have!" said Charlie. "I have a pony, and we will get you one too, Ralph, and won't we gallop across the meadows!"

"It makes me happy to think of it," Ralph replied. "And then there is the visit we are to make at Lord Auburton's. Heigho! The time will slip away quickly enough. Here comes Walbut. Just look at him, Charlie!"

Charlie turned, and was struck with Jack Walbut's singular appearance.

He was pale, and looked as if he had been crying; his eyes were red, and in his cheeks were lines that made him look ten years older than he really was.

"Poor fellow! perhaps he has had some bad news," said Ralph. "Shall we ask him what is the matter?"

"No," Charlie replied. "Ralph, I hope you don't think I am boorish and unkind, but I have made up my mind to let Walbut go entirely his own way. He has never sought our sympathy, and why should we worry ourselves about his troubles?"

"I don't like to see him thus," our hero remarked. "He leads a lonely, wretched life; but that is an old story.

Here comes M. Carleon; it is not often he takes tea at the Abbey on Saturday afternoons."

"Only on the last Saturday in the month, as this happens to be," Charlie replied; "he balances up the marks we have made, you know."

"Right," said Ralph, "I had forgotten that. I wonder how you stand for a prize, Charlie?"

Chadwick laughed and shook his head.

"I am out of the hunt, I fear," he responded. "I am so thoroughly English that my tongue refuses to pronounce any other language."

At that moment M. Alphonse Carleon overtook the boys.

He was striding along, swinging his arms and humming a merry tune; but as he saw Ralph he stopped and placed his hand lightly on the boy's shoulder.

"Mornington," he said, "this will be an eventful day for you. I am going to make up my balance-sheet this evening, and I have more than a notion that you are at the top of the list."

Before Ralph could reply, the Frenchman passed on, and the boys went on chatting.

"He has taken to you lately," Charlie Chadwick said. "What stunning news you will have to write to the general, if you should take the first French prize!"

Our hero's eyes sparkled, for in his mind's eye he saw his good father's delight as he read the news of his son's triumph.

Tea was soon over, and the boys returned to the meadow, as there were no night lessons to be learned on Saturday evening, and they resumed their play with light hearts, for Mr. Stormaway had announced that Timothy Slowbob was improving slowly, though it might be some time before he would be about again.

It was growing dusk when M. Alphonse Carleon sat down at his desk.

He examined the lock before he raised the lid, and when he did so a half-sad yet sinister smile played on his lips.

"Walbut has done his work well," he said. "Now let me think. Shall I give the alarm now or wait? To-morrow is Sunday. It is always a quiet day here, and it would be best that Mornington should leave without creating too much attention. The news of his downfall will not pass the gates until Monday, and then—ah well! what matters it to me whither he goes or what he does?"

M. Alphonse Carleon rose and rang the bell.

It was the duty of Matthew Stickers to answer it, and he did so, thinking that the French master required the lamps to be lighted.

"It are a bit misty to-night, ain't it, moosoo?" Stickers remarked. "How many lamps shall I light, sir?"

"I will attend to the lamps myself," Carleon replied. "Please to tell Mr. Stormaway that I desire to see him at once, either here or in his study."

The Frenchman spoke so seriously, and in such a constrained tone, that Matthew Stickers felt certain that something very much out of the usual course had transpired.

He hastened to the head-master without delay, and Mr. Stormaway sent his compliments back, and begged of M. Carleon to wait on him in his study.

In a few minutes Carleon, very pale and agitated, entered the room.

"Mr. Stormaway," he said, "I regret to inform you that a very dreadful thing has happened. I have been robbed."

The head-master of Merrytown Abbey started, and turned quite as pale as the French master.

"Robbed!" he exclaimed. "Robbed—here in this Abbey? Surely there must be some mistake!"

"I wish I could think so, sir," Carleon returned; "I will explain all as briefly as possible."

Mr. Stormaway inclined his head, and though he endeavoured to keep calm, his lips quivered, and his limbs trembled.

"This is not the first time I have been robbed," Carleon said, speaking slowly and deliberately; "I have been in the habit of placing certain moneys in my desk under lock and key, and from time to time I have missed small sums."

Mr. Stormaway leaned his head upon his hand, and groaned in the bitterness of his heart.

"I could have borne anything but this," he said. "A thief here—a mean, despicable thief! Oh, horror! But pray proceed, monsieur, and pardon me for interrupting you."

"At first I was not quite sure," Carleon resumed. "I thought the mistake was mine; but, alas! my suspicions have been more than confirmed this evening. Yesterday I marked four half-crowns, and placed them under some papers in my desk. The half-crowns are no longer there, and from the fact that the lock does not seem to have been forced or tampered with, I conclude that somebody has a duplicate key."

Mr. Stormaway rose from his chair, and paced the room with unsteady steps.

Grief and anger were written upon his face, and every now and then there came an expression of doubt, as if he deemed it impossible that such a thing could have happened under the roof of his hitherto honourable house.

"Monsieur," he said, "this is a matter calling for investigation without delay. I could not rest in my bed with such a thing pressing upon my mind. May I ask you to go downstairs and summon all the boys and the servants to the schoolroom?"

"Certainly, sir," Carleon replied. "The duty to be performed is a painful one, but it must be done."

"If I discover the culprit," said Mr. Stormaway, bringing his hand down heavily on the table, "he or she shall leave these doors never to darken them again!"

Alphonse Carleon was leaving the study, when the head-master called him back.

"One thing is quite certain," he said, "we cannot connect Slowbob with this affair in any way. Whoever committed the last robbery was guilty of the others."

"I am of your opinion," Carleon returned. "I have never for a moment suspected the page-boy."

"You have had suspicions?"

"Yes."

"Of whom?"

Alphonse Carleon shrugged his shoulders.

"I would rather keep that to myself," he said. "If I am wrong, I shall be sorry in secret. I do not wish to give expression to my thoughts, for if I did, and I were wrong, it would behove me to apologise humbly."

"Well," Mr. Stormaway returned, "you may be right. Silence is golden in some instances. Go now, monsieur, and in a quarter of an hour I will be in the schoolroom."

The greatest consternation prevailed

when Carleon delivered Mr. Stormaway's message.

A hundred questions were put to him, but he replied to none, and was just as brusque to Mr. Muffler and to Herr Fritz Halfamann as to the rest.

Mrs. Jumble and the female dependents naturally took umbrage at being ordered to appear in the schoolroom without knowing why their presence was required; but at last all were there, and when the buzz of excitement and anticipation had strengthened into a perfect Babel of tongues, Mr. Stormaway entered, and went straight to his desk.

He drank a glass of water before speaking, and then seemed to experience some difficulty in articulating with his usual clearness.

He repeated what Alphonse Carleon had told him, and then cast his eyes round the room.

Boys and servants stood in mute astonishment at the news, and Matthew Stickers was so overcome that he trod upon Mrs. Jumble's most painful bunion, and brought down that lady's wrath upon its benighted head.

"It has been a miserable thing for me to stand here and make such a statement," Mr. Stormaway continued. "My duty is clear. I see no other way to put an end to such a scandal but to stamp it out at once. If the guilty party is present let him or her confess to save all further trouble."

"'Her' indeed!" cried Mary the housemaid, bridling up, and glowing as red as the bow of ribbon in her cap. "I wish you to know, sir, that I have a character to lose."

"Hand so 'ave hi," cried Stickers; "though I went forth into the stony world with a barrer w'ich was bu'st hup, I'd scorn to take a pin as wasn't mine!"

"Silence," exclaimed Mr. Stormaway, sternly. "Nobody is accused, but all must feel with me that now—this night—this very hour—the guilty must be discovered. In order that this may be done, I command that Mrs. Jumble and M. Carleon accompany me to search every trunk and place where the stolen money may be hidden."

"Search our trunks!" cried Ralph. "Oh, this is monstrous!"

"Mornington objects," Alphonse Carleon observed with a peculiar smile.

"I do object," our hero said; "not because I fear the result for myself or for any of the pupils. My objection is that we are to be treated like suspected felons."

"Mornington objects," said Carleon again.

"That is only natural," Mr. Stormaway remarked, kindly. "But I feel convinced that Mornington is as anxious as I am that this matter should be cleared up. I have tried to think of some other way, but in vain. All will remain here until Mrs. Jumble, monsieur, and myself return; and then, if no discovery has been made, I shall even go so far as to ask—and Heaven knows it pains me to utter the words—that all pockets may be turned out."

"'Ere's a pretty state o' things," cried Stickers, when the three searchers had departed on their mission. "'Ere's a 'splosion in the Habbey! 'Ere's a smash up of confidence!"

His fellow-servants acknowledged it with sighs and groans.

"Ah," he continued, "it ain't them as is poor as is always thieves. A party as wore a white choker, and with a face like a cherub, once took me in with a meersham pipe, which he said he wished for to part with on account of seein' the herror of smoking. I paid four-and-six for that pipe in coins of the currant realm, and it turned out a duffer. The fust time I smoked it, I was that bad that Salem Cockey had to 'arf carry me home. The effluvium of that pipe was like a parryfine lamp."

This memory of a painful past excited but little attention, and Matthew Stickers, discovering that nobody cared to listen to his sweet discourse, went upon a new tack.

"I ain't afraid to turn hout *my* pockets," he said, suiting the action to the word. "'Ere's a thre'penny bit with a hole in it, w'ich was given me in my yooth for good conduct. 'Ere's a penknife—a sooveneer from my grandfather as met with his hend by trippin' over a trolley and shootin' down a cellar, w'ich the man below thought he was a sack o' coals. 'Ere's the French penny w'ich Slowbob deceived me with when he called for ginger-beer and hung on to my nose like a wampire——"

"You vill blease not pring Slowpop into zee question," Herr Fritz Halfamann interposed, indignantly. "I did shoot you vonce down zee stairs, and if you say von vord about dat boor poy I vill put you out of zee vindow."

"Hoh, hindeed!" Stickers retorted. "It seems to me that Hengland is inwaded by furriners. Wot with horgangrinders, and them German fellers as blows hagony out o' trombones in the street, and them as come 'ere to take the bread hout o' the mouths of the British workin'-man, this 'ere country is a dwindlin' down from beef-steaks to bread-and-cheese."

A row was imminent, but before it could take place Mr. Stormaway walked into the room.

The head-master's face was literally ghastly, and a dead silence reigned among the assembly as he crossed the floor.

"Where is Mornington?" he demanded in a voice hoarse with emotion. "I do not see him."

"I am here, sir," said our hero, rising from a box on which he had been sitting.

Mr. Stormaway looked the lad steadily in the face for a few moments without speaking, and then, taking him gently but firmly by the arm, led him out of the room.

"What may this mean, sir?" asked Ralph when they were outside.

The head-master made no reply, but conducted him to the dormitory.

Mrs. Jumble and M. Alphonse Carleon stood before an open trunk, and our hero started violently as he saw it was his own.

Mr. Stormaway felt the lad start, and then extending one arm towards the trunk, said:

"Mornington, I regret to say that the missing money has been found hidden under some clothing in your box. What have you to say to the discovery?"

At first Ralph Mornington could not speak.

His heart leaped and bounded, his eyes grew dim, and the floor seemed to heave beneath his feet.

"Marked money found in my trunk!" he gasped at last. "Oh, sir, you cannot believe that I am guilty. I know no more about this than yourself. I have been made the victim of some dastardly conspiracy."

"What has M. Carleon to say to that?" demanded Mr. Stormaway, turning suddenly to the French master.

"I say that I have been robbed, and that Ralph Mornington is the thief," Carleon replied.

"It is false—false!" cried Ralph, "and you know it. I steal—I turn thief! I say again that I am the victim of a conspiracy!"

"That you must prove before the magistrates," Carleon returned, coolly. "Mr. Stormaway, will you kindly send a servant for a police-officer?"

"Oh, no, no," the head-master said, imploringly. "Monsieur, you will not prosecute? I beg of you not to go so far as that."

"Why not?" Carleon rejoined. "My salary is not so great that I can afford to be robbed with impunity. I have missed money over and over again, and now I will say to Mornington before his face that I have always suspected him of being the thief."

Ralph twisted himself from Mr. Stormaway's grasp, and would have rushed upon the Frenchman, but the head-master caught him again and held him fast.

"This is madness," Mr. Stormaway said. "Mrs. Jumble, I beg that you will retire. This scene is not fit for a lady to witness."

"Mrs. Jumble will remember that she found the money, and I the duplicate key," Carleon said, as the housekeeper, crying bitterly, approached the door.

"Duplicate key!" Ralph repeated. "What key?"

"The key you have opened my desk with many a time," Carleon replied. "I discovered it in the pocket of one of your waistcoats."

Our hero burst into a torrent of passionate tears, and sinking on a chair, he sobbed as if his heart would break.

"False! false!" he moaned. "I have never done a mean or discreditable action in my life. Is it likely that I should commit a theft when I am well supplied with money? If I were starving I would not do so. Oh, this will kill me—this will kill me!"

"Monsieur," said Mr. Stormaway, "there may be some mistake. The real thief may have taken fright, and to shield himself put the money in Mornington's trunk."

"That will be a question for the jury to decide," Alphonse Carleon returned.

"Then you have made up your mind to carry this matter out to the end?"

"What other course would you have me pursue?" the Frenchman demanded. "By the laws of your country it is a punishable offence to compound a felony."

"Yes, yes, I know that," Mr. Stormaway said, hastily and angrily; "but I say again there may be some mistake. Give the lad time to prove his innocence—give him one short week. I ask it not only for his sake, but for mine."

"I am sorry I cannot take the same view of the matter as yourself," Carleon replied. "We have two distinct facts. I have been robbed, and the proceeds of the robbery have been found in Mornington's trunk. What other proof would you have? I demand his deliverance to the law. If you, sir, will not send for the policeman, I will go for him myself."

Mr. Stormaway went to Ralph's side.

The lad was calmer now, though his breast still heaved convulsively with the storm of emotion that had swept through it.

"Mornington," said the head-master, "I can do nothing now. You see that M. Carleon is merciless."

"I expected no mercy from him," Ralph replied. "A light begins to dawn on me; but what I think I will keep to myself. There is no necessity to send for a policeman, sir; I will go quietly with you to the station."

Mr. Stormaway cast an appealing glance at Carleon; but the Frenchman's brows were knit with a heavy frown, and his lips compressed as if they were of iron.

"Stay!" he said, as Ralph rose. "I have thought the matter over. On one condition I will refrain from prosecuting."

"Name your condition?" Mr. Stormaway said.

"That Ralph Mornington leaves the Abbey within four-and-twenty hours."

"You hear?" said Mr. Stormaway, touching Ralph on the shoulder.

"Yes, I hear," Ralph replied, dreamily. "But why should I go branded with a felon's name when I am innocent?"

"That may be," the head-master whispered in his ear, "and you have my word that I believe in your innocence. I will procure lodgings for you in a village near here until the next ship returns to India. You must go back to your father."

"Go back to my father!" Ralph echoed. "Go back to him with this stigma clinging to me. You do not know me, or you would not make such a proposition. Do you think that I could look him in the face and take his hand? No—a thousand times no! I would rather that he blotted his son out of his memory."

"Hush!" Mr. Stormaway interposed. "You will think better of this to-morrow."

"Does Mornington consent?" Carleon asked.

"I will answer for him," the head-master said. "Yes, he does consent."

"Then there is the end of the matter so far as I am concerned," the Frenchman returned, with a sigh of relief, as if a great weight had been removed from his mind. "I have only a few more words to say. Mornington must not be here on Monday morning, or I may repent of what I have said."

He gave our hero one sharp look, and then turning upon his heel left the room.

"Mornington," Mr. Stormaway said, after a pause, "it will be better that you occupy a room by yourself to-night. This bad news will travel quite fast enough, and I do not wish you to have communication with your old schoolmates."

"I have one favour to ask, and I hope you will not refuse it," said Ralph.

"Name it."

"Before I go I should like to speak to Charlie Chadwick and Harold Lakeman," Ralph said, as tears welled into his eyes again. "They have been my friends, and they will scorn the notion of my guilt. May I see them, sir, only for one short half-hour?"

"Yes," Mr. Stormaway replied; "I will arrange that the interview takes place in the morning before we go to church. Oh, Mornington! you were a youth of promise, and I had great hopes of seeing you go forth from here with an honoured name."

"My name is untarnished as it ever was," Ralph said, almost fiercely. "Is this the way you believe in my innocence?"

"But the proofs are against you," Mr. Stormaway returned. "Be patient; the truth will come out one day."

CHAPTER XLIII.

WHAT HERR FRITZ HALFAMANN THOUGHT—CHARLIE CHADWICK AND JACK WALBUT ALMOST COME TO BLOWS.

IT would be idle to attempt to describe the effect caused on the inmates of Merrytown Abbey by Ralph Mornington's downfall.

At first the majority declined to believe in the report; but when the facts became known beyond contradiction, the whole place was in an uproar.

Herr Fritz Halfamann sat down at his desk and watered his spectacles with his tears.

"Mine poy Mornington a t'ief—dat prave poy steal anyting! Ach! it is not bossible," he said. "I vill not pelieve it. Dere has been more villainy aproad, and it is von bity dat Slowpop is pad."

As for Charlie Chadwick and Harold Lakeman, they were nearly wild with grief and excitement; but Walbut and Lemon Sleath stood apart, and maintained a moody silence.

"You are a precious pair!" cried Charlie, advancing upon them. "Have you no word of pity for the best and bravest lad that ever walked under this roof?"

"Don't put yourself in a temper," said Walbut, sneeringly. "It is not my fault if your chum has been found out. You cannot accuse me of being his companion, and I am heartily glad that I never shared in his generosity."

Charlie raised his arm, but he dropped it, and fixed a look of scorn on the bully and his toady.

"Walbut," he said, "and you too, Lemon Sleath—this matter is not yet ended. Ralph may be suffering now, but he will triumph, and I have a strong fancy that one or two people I could mention will be glad to give him a wide berth."

"Why don't you speak out and give the people their proper names?" Jack Walbut rejoined.

"Because I do not choose to do so."

"You throw out hints without being able to bring proofs forward," Walbut said. "Mind that tongue of yours does not get you into trouble, Chadwick."

"Your head will get into trouble before my tongue," Charlie retorted, as he moved away. "I wish you would give me some provocation."

"Why?"

"Because it would give me the greatest delight in the world to thrash you."

"Many thanks," said Walbut. "You are very kind; but I decline the favour."

"You are a coward," Charlie cried, hotly.

"I care nothing for your opinion."

"You are a bully."

"Again I am obliged to you," Walbut said. "Have you no other pleasant names to hurl at my head?"

"Yes," Charlie said. "I believe you to be capable of anything that is mean and despicable. I believe you to be a villain in the guise of a gentleman."

Walbut's face flushed crimson, and he advanced a step.

Charlie Chadwick stood like a rock to meet him, and the bully halted.

"You shall have reason to repent of this," he hissed. "I never wished to quarrel with you, but you have forced it upon me. Have a care, Chadwick, or you will find that our account will be an unpleasant one to settle."

"You used similar words when Ralph Mornington knocked you down," Charlie retorted. "Ralph has fallen, and you are glad of it; I read it in your face, and in the saffron-hued face of your sneak and toady, Lemon Sleath. If I have provoked you why not fight it out?"

"All in good time," Jack Walbut returned, nodding his head. "There is no hurry."

"Bah!" cried Charlie. "You are a cad, and there is no shoeblack in the whole country but would be ashamed of your society if he knew you as I do."

Jack Walbut's face turned an ashy hue, and the veins of his forehead stood out like whipcord.

Lemon Sleath's teeth chattered, and his hair bristled with fright.

He expected to see Jack Walbut fly at Charlie Chadwick, but nothing of the kind happened.

Walbut, after clutching at his throat as if he were choking, recovered his self-control, and spoke calmly.

"I will not allow you to provoke

me," he said. "I know it would give you the greatest pleasure to see me lose my temper, but I will disappoint you, and bide my time."

Charlie Chadwick snapped his fingers contemptuously, and turning upon his heel, ran full butt against Matthew Stickers.

"'Ere's a go!" Stickers cried. "'Ere's a go! Honly fancy that Ralph Mornington, him as I would have trusted with millions, should go for and do such a thing!"

Harold Lakeman swung the man-of-all-work round by the collar, and pinioned him against the wall.

"Do you believe that Ralph is guilty?" Harold demanded.

"What ham I to believe?" Stickers rejoined. "The money was found in his box, you know. I could weep when I thinks of it! Hoh, what a fallin' orf is 'ere, as the Hirish labourer said when he slipped off a ladder."

Further discussion became impossible, for Mr. Stormaway entered the room and ordered the boys to bed.

CHAPTER XLIV.

THE GHOST WALKS FOR THE LAST TIME.

WHEN the house was quiet, Mr. Stormaway went to his study and sat down to think the matter out; indeed, he had so many things to reflect upon, that his brain was in a whirl with conflicting emotions.

In the first place there was Slowbob babbling away—on the slow road to recovery truly, but still insisting that Dr. Pillem was Salem Cockey's grandmother.

Who had struck the boy down, and how came that shot through the window on a previous occasion?

Timothy told Mr. Stormaway that he was all but certain that he had seen Alphonse Carleon's face at the window a moment before the bullet struck the wall, but there was neither direct proof nor a tangible clue to act upon.

To add to the pain and misery of the thing, came Ralph Mornington's downfall.

Sick at heart, and brainweary, the head-master sought surcease from his troubled mind in the first book that came to hand.

It happened to contain the story of Father Hislem, the monk who was driven forth from Merrytown Abbey in the time of Henry VIII., and though Mr. Stormaway knew the narrative by heart, he read it again, and in doing so dropped off to sleep.

*   *   *   *

Herr Fritz Halfamann had not left the Abbey for his own lodgings.

A bed was made up for him at his urgent request in a room next to that occupied by Mr. Muffler.

The Teuton seemed loth to leave the house out of which our hero must soon pass; but what good he thought he could do by remaining was best known to himself.

"Mine poy—mine goot poy!" Halfamann almost sobbed, as he placed his head on the pillow. "It is von dreadful t'ing to contemblate! Vot vill he do? Oh, dat I could tell him—dat I could act zee bart of his friend! Fritz, you have peen a boor man all your life and never grumbled, but now you vish dat you vas rich for zee sake of Ralph Mornington, zee pest, zee pravest, and zee most peautiful poy in zee Appey!"

It was a long time before Herr Fritz Halfamann could close his eyes with any probability of going to sleep, but at last he began to snore and wandered safely, if not pleasantly, in the land of dreams.

He had not slumbered many minutes when the door of the room opened noiselessly, and the ghost of Merrytown Abbey glided in.

Grim, weird, and ghastly was the figure as it stalked across the floor. It halted by the window, and stretching out a nude arm from under its white flowing garb, pulled the curtains back, and raising the sash, seemed to gaze down into the garden below.

The noise awoke Herr Fritz Halfamann.

The little German rubbed his eyes, but he could see nothing in the gloom without his spectacles.

He skipped out of bed to fetch them, and skipped back again in double-quick time when he had put them on.

"It vas zee ghost!" he gasped.

"DOWN WENT MATTHEW ALL OF A HEAP."—(*See page* 136.)

"*Ach*! Dis vas very horriple. Vat s'all I do? If I call for help I s'all be called a coward, but if I lie here I s'all die of zee frights."

Herr Fritz Halfamann took another look at the ghost.

There it stood motionless, grim and gruesome as before.

"Berhabs it vas one leedle trick after all," the German tutor thought. "I rememper dat Stickares did give me zee frights in the school-room, and it may be dot he t'inks of giving me more frights. Fritz, you s'all lay zee ghost, if it costs you your abbointment at zee Appey."

Halfamann did not make the attack at once.

He lay still a few moments, but as the ghost did not move, he glided out of bed again—it must be owned that he trembled—and stepped gingerly over the floor.

Herr Fritz Halfamann was about to challenge the unwelcome guest when the figure turned and bumped itself rather violently against a chair.

"Confound it!" said the ghost.

"Pless my heart!" the German cried, "dis vas more vonderful still. Vhere vas zee matches? Ah! I have them now."

But before he could strike a light there was a thud, followed by a loud cry. The ghost had came into contact with the chest-of-drawers, and was now sprawling on the floor.

"Help!" cried the apparition. "Where am I? Help!"

Herr Fritz Halfamann recognised Mr. Stormaway's voice, and cried, "Oh! dis is wonderful. Zee ghost is zee master, walking in his sleep!"

He assisted the head-master to rise, and holding the candle close to his face, looked him in the eyes as if he deemed him mad.

Mr. Stormaway was partly dressed, and the sheet in which he had been enveloped bore evidence to the fact that it was he, and he alone, who had given Herr Fritz Halfamann "zee frights."

"Vhat vas zee meaning of dis, sare?" the German demanded.

"I don't know," Mr. Stormaway said, vaguely. "Where am I?"

"You vas in mine pedroom," Halfamann replied. "Oh, sare, I did not think that you vould blay von leedle lark mit me!"

"A lark!" repeated Mr. Stormaway. "My dear professor, let me assure you that I never dreamed of such a thing. I must have been walking in my sleep."

"Vhat!" cried Halfamann. "Dis is vot I thought."

"There is no doubt about it," the head-master continued. "An idea strikes me. Is it possible that I have been walking in my sleep, and that I am the ghost of Merrytown Abbey?"

"I could laugh if boor Mornington was not in such trouple," Herr Halfamann said. "Yes, sare, it vas you all zee vhile, a walking ghost in your sleeb."

"It must be so," responded Mr. Stormaway, aghast at the discovery. "There is one thing quite certain: the ghost never paid me a visit. Really this is very distressing, and I must seek medical advice at once. I have often wondered why I was troubled with so many colds."

Herr Fritz Halfamann sat down and surveyed his principal from head to foot.

"Sare," he said, "it is a great vonder dat you did not fall down zee stairs and preak your neck. You must pe tied in ped every night, or berhaps you may find your vay to zee roof and jumb into zee school-grounds."

"It is a horrible thought, yet it is possible," Mr. Stormaway replied. "I have had bad dreams, which have in some mysterious way connected me with Father Hislem."

"Dere it is, den," cried Herr Halfamann, smiting the palms of his hands together. "You have hit zee right nail on zee head. If it bleases you, I vill come ub every night ven you are in ped and tie your pig toe to zee ped-bost."

"No," said Mr. Stormaway, smiling in spite of himself. "I thank you very kindly for the offer. I have had such a shock to my feelings that I don't think I shall ever walk in my sleep again. At all events I shall act wisely by consulting Dr. Pillem."

Gathering up the sheet and shivering with cold, he bade the German professor good-night and walked towards the door.

"Professor," he said, stopping.

"Yes, sare."

"You will say nothing about this affair until——"

"I know vhat you vould say," Halfamann interposed, sadly. "Not von vord s'all bass my libs until Monday; and not den unless you vish it."

"I think the statement ought to come from me," Mr. Stormaway said. "We have solved one mystery, and I am heartily glad of it. Poor Mr. Swately!—poor Mr. Muffler! what will they say when they know that it was I who upset them so badly?"

The head-master closed the door and went softly to his own room.

"I shudder at the thought of the risks I have run!" he murmured. "Ugh! This comes of poring over old legends late at night. No more suppers. No more reading of ghostly legends before going to rest."

The morning found Ralph Mornington pale and haggard, yet calm and self-possessed.

He sat at the window listening to the church bells chiming.

The sweet air laden with fragrance from meadow and woodland filled the room, and the sun shone in all its splendour upon the earth,

Ralph's heart sank lower.

Although he loved the abbey and its grounds, he had never thought them so beautiful as they appeared now.

And he must leave the dear old place, and his chums, disgraced and fallen.

Mr. Stormaway had mercifully refrained from making an actual prisoner of Ralph, and had the boy chosen he could have walked out of the house unchallenged.

But he was innocent, and too proud to turn his back upon the Abbey in such a way.

The church bells had scarcely ceased chiming when there came a tap at the door.

"Come in!" Ralph said.

His face flushed, as he expected to see Charlie Chadwick and Harold Lakeman, but to his astonishment Joshua Blackstone glided in, with his hat in his hand, and a calm business-like expression on his face.

"Good-morning, sir," he said. "I obtained permission to see you. If it had been refused me, I—ahem!—think it very possible that I should have turned burglar, and come through the window."

"You know all?" Ralph said.

"Yes, I know all," the detective replied, taking out a note-book, and nibbling the end of a metallic pencil. "And it is a bad thing for you, Mr. Mornington."

"Bad!" Ralph echoed. "Bad, do you say? It means shame—ruin—

utter degradation—unless I can discover the miscreant who has brought me to this."

"Steady, my lad," Joshua Blackstone said. "Remember that Rome was not built in a day. The object of my visit is to ask you whether I shall write at once to Mr. Herapath, and acquaint him with all the facts, or whether I shall wait a few days?"

"It matters little what you do," Ralph replied, sadly. "What *I* am to do is the question that perplexes me most sorely."

"I will tell you," the detective returned, advancing and placing his hand on the lad's shoulder. "Show a bold face to the world, and fight out the battle bravely. You have a secret enemy, and I will help you to discover him. You are young, strong, and healthy, and it would be a pity if you were to sink under so cowardly a blow."

"You believe me innocent?" said Ralph, as a flash of the old bright light filled his eyes.

"If I believed you guilty I should not be here," Joshua Blackstone replied.

"I thank you for that," said Ralph, as he shook hands with the detective. "But what can I do?"

"Work," Blackstone responded. "Write to your father, and conceal nothing from him. Tell him that, as Heaven is your witness, you are guiltless of the crime, and he will believe you. Tell him also that when you have proved your innocence you will return to him, but not before."

"It is all very well to tell me to work," Ralph observed, "but who will give me employment without a character?"

Joshua Blackstone pursed up his lips, and threw his head a little on one side as he looked at our hero.

"Have you a retentive memory?" he asked.

"Yes," Ralph replied; "I never forget anything I have seen or read—indeed, I can commit a poem to memory after perusing it a few times."

"That's lucky," Blackstone said. "Ahem! You have a good figure. How would you like to be an actor?"

Ralph Mornington started. The suggestion struck forcibly into his mind, for he had often thought he would like to follow the profession, if only for amusement.

"I should like it very much indeed,"

he said; "but I have no influence, and no practical knowledge of the stage; and where is the manager who would engage me without one or the other?"

"I think I know of one," Joshua Blackstone observed, closing his left eye, and taking a mental shot at Ralph. "You have some money, I suppose?"

"More than sufficient for my present wants."

"Five pounds?"

"Nearer ten."

"That is a small fortune if you are careful with it," said Blackstone. "See, here is a card with a name and address on it. I place it in an envelope, and you must promise me not to open it until you are ten miles from Merrytown. When you part with me, for with me you will leave the Abbey, turn your face to the east, and keep on until you have accomplished the distance, and then you may consult the card. I will forward your luggage on after you."

"This is rather mysterious," Ralph remarked.

"It is mysterious because it is safe," Blackstone replied. "I have seen Mr. Stormaway, and he thinks you are going to London with me. Do not undeceive him, or mention this to your chums. When you are at—ahem! —where the card tells you to go, you may write to anyone you can trust, for it will have to remain a secret until you are cleared of this accusation."

"How can I thank you?" demanded Ralph.

"By doing exactly as I tell you," Blackstone said. "I have arranged to call here for you at ten precisely, and you will go as far as the station with me. I must go now, for I hear footsteps approaching."

"Ralph—dear Ralph!" cried Charlie Chadwick, as he burst into the room and threw his arms round our hero. "Oh, what can I say to you? How can I find words to tell you how my heart aches for you?"

Harold Lakeman tried to speak; but he broke down and only sobbed his sympathy.

Joshua Blackstone became suddenly afflicted with a troublesome cough, and as he turned away and walked slowly downstairs, he wiped his eyes several times.

"Charlie—Harold," Ralph said, "I know and feel what you would say to me. Help me to be brave. Smile as you used to smile, talk as you used to talk, and say nothing about parting until the last moment comes. Then we will shake hands and hope for better days. It does me good to see you."

But how could the boys think or talk of anything but the matter uppermost in their minds?

"Look here!" said Charlie, smiting his thigh with his open hand; "now that we are here, we can talk freely. It is my firm belief that both Jack Walbut and Lemon Sleath know more about this most villainous affair than they care to tell."

"I think so, too," remarked Harold Lakeman, drying his eyes, and trying to speak calmly. "Ralph, you may depend that we shall keep sharp eyes on them until you come back."

"Surely you don't think I shall return?" Ralph said. "No, my dear chums; my career at Merrytown Abbey is drawing to a close."

"But supposing your innocence is proved in a day or two?" Charlie urged. "I reckon that we would have you back in triumph, then, even if it were against your will."

"We will talk about that when it happens," Ralph observed. "And now, my chums, I will ask you one or two favours. Think of me sometimes, as I have always thought of you, and my heart will tell me that I am held in your remembrance."

He almost broke down, but checked the tears that welled into his eyes, and went on speaking calmly.

"You will hear from me by-and-by," he continued; "and you must let me know how poor Timothy Slowbob progresses. I have a notion that if anybody within these walls can shed a light on this mystery it is Slowbob."

"That has never occurred to me," Charlie said, brightening up; "but now I come to think of it he seemed to take a great interest in Walbut's actions."

"And in Carleon's too," chimed in Harold Lakeman. "I am dying to know who struck Timothy down."

"We may know that and more when he recovers," Ralph said. "I don't think I have anything else to ask, and now——"

He held out his hands, and his tears came at last.

"Oh, Ralph, Ralph, I cannot bear it!" Charlie cried, as a wild paroxysm of grief swept like a storm through his breast. "My heart is breaking. Don't let us part—I will not part with you! If you must face the world, I will go with you."

"Charlie, do not talk like this," Ralph said. "I thought to have passed through this ordeal without a tear. I promised myself that I would do so, but my heart has overflowed. Go, I beg of you—yet stay one moment. Charlie, keep my cricket-bat, and you, Harold, my fishing-rod, as souvenirs. When the days are long and fine as they are now, the trifles will call me to mind."

Sobbing audibly, Charlie pressed a locket upon Ralph, and Harold a silver ring which he had sometimes sported when safe from the observation of Mr. Stormaway's eyes.

These gifts had scarcely changed hands, when the head-master entered the room with Matthew Stickers, who carried a tray containing Ralph's breakfast.

Mr. Stormaway led the two sorrowing lads out of the room, and during his temporary absence, Stickers approached Ralph on tip-toe.

"Well," said our hero, indignantly, "why are you staring at me in that impudent manner?"

"W'ich it are a thought as comed into my mind just now," Matthew replied. "If you didn't do the deed, who did? Ah, there's the question!"

"If you speak to me again I will remove you from the room," Ralph said. "My sufferings are more than sufficient without the addition of your taunts."

"There you goes like a bottle of lemingnade in the sun," Stickers returned. "I was a comin' to my hidea. W'at if it were Slowbob as prigged the money?"

"How dare you suggest such a thing?" Ralph said. "If it were not Sunday I would carry out my threat."

"Jest so," Stickers rejoined with the air of a martyr. "I say supposin' that Slowbob——"

"You scoundrel!" Ralph cried. "Poor Slowbob met with his misfortune before the money was placed in my box."

Matthew Stickers ran his fingers through his hair and meditated.

What he would have said cannot even be conjectured, as Mr. Stormaway returned and ordered him out of the room.

The head-master and our hero, no longer the pupil, sat talking until a trap arrived at the door, and Matthew Stickers staggered out with Ralph's luggage, and arranged it after a few stormy skirmishes with the driver.

"Pupils don't generally leave on the Sunday, do they?" the latter asked.

"Mind your hown biziness!" Stickers retorted. "You'll find quite enough to do to keep that bag o' bones on his legs."

This libel on the horse invoked the driver's wrath.

"I wish you had been born a 'orse!" he said.

"Why?" demanded Matthew Stickers, thrown off his guard.

"Because I should like to have had the drivin' of you, that's all!" the man replied. "But lor, what am I thinkin' about? Donkeys is more in your line."

Matthew Stickers scowled as he thrust the last portmanteau into a corner, and as he stepped back to survey the arrangements he had made, Mr. Joshua Blackstone came up.

"All ready?" he asked.

"Yes, sir," Matthew replied, pulling a tuft of hair that rose from his head like a tassel. "'Ot weather, ain't it, sir?"

Joshua Blackstone refused to take the hint.

He kept his eye on the staircase, down which he knew that Ralph must come.

And he came, bidding a silent but fond farewell to the dear old familiar place.

Before our hero was the playground; then the meadow, with its wooden paling on one side, and it seemed impossible that the green sward would know the tread of his feet no more.

The very porch, with its huge carved figures of monks with bowed heads on each side, had special interest in his eyes, and his hand trembled in Mr. Stormaway's.

The head-master's eyes were moist, and his lips quivered as Joshua Blackstone held the door of the waggonette open, and beckoned to Ralph.

"And so we must part, Mornington," Mr. Stormaway said; "but I hope not for ever. My boy—my boy, may Heaven bless and guide you!"

The good, noble-hearted man turned his head away, and tears coursed down his cheeks.

Ralph uttered a few half-incoherent words, in which he expressed his thanks for the sympathy shown him, and then leaped into the trap, saying, "Remember, sir, I am innocent."

One glance, and only one he took at the upper windows.

There was not a face visible, for the blinds had been drawn by Mr. Stormaway's order, but Ralph knew that friendly eyes were peeping at him through the chinks.

A crack of the whip, the wheels began to revolve, and in a few minutes our hero had turned his back upon Merrytown Abbey.

CHAPTER XLV.

THE JOURNEY ON FOOT, AND WHAT HAPPENED AT THE SEVEN STARS INN.

JOSHUA BLACKSTONE was the first to speak.

"I begin to breathe more freely, now," he said. "Courage, lad—courage. Take a lesson out of Nature's book. She weeps in April and smiles in May. Look up, and be thankful that you are young."

"I cannot help feeling sad."

"Certainly not, but I ask you to hope," said Joshua Blackstone.

"I will," Ralph replied, glancing upwards; "I will trust in Providence to bring me out of this trouble."

"That is the way I like to hear you speak," Blackstone replied, encouragingly. "It is well to look on the bright side of a picture. There is nothing but canvas and cobwebs on the reverse."

The waggonette pulled up at the station, the driver was dismissed, and Joshua Blackstone was saying a few words to Ralph before parting with him, when they saw the figure of a man waving a huge red handkerchief, flying down the road.

"It is Matthew Stickers," said Ralph.

"Confound him!" Joshua Blackstone returned. "He must be got rid of without delay, for Mr. Stormaway supposes that you are going to London with me."

"Hoy! hoy!" cried Stickers. "Mr. Mornington! Mis—ter Morn—ing—ton!"

He came up very red in the face, and out of breath.

"What is the matter?" Blackstone demanded. "Anybody might think that you were engaged in a bull-fight."

"I've left the Habbey unbeknown to hanybody," Stickers panted. "Dr. Pillem's just been, and told Mr. Stormaway that Slowbob has come round to his reason."

"I am heartily glad to hear it," Ralph said.

He placed his hand in his pocket, but Joshua Blackstone, guessing his motive, checked him.

"No," he said; "you will want all the money you possess. Stickers, here is half-a-crown for you, and now——"

He pointed up the road with an imperative forefinger, and Matthew Stickers's face fell.

"I thought I should like to see the last o' Mr. Mornington," he said, meekly. "The train is comin' in, and——"

"Matthew Stickers," Joshua Blackstone interposed, "I have generally had my own way in most things, more especially in the selection of my boots. You will observe they are stoutly made, with nails, and constructed for heavy walking. If you are not out of sight, and on your way back to the Abbey before I count twenty, one of those self-same boots will help you materially."

Stickers took the hint and himself off as fast as his legs could carry him.

"And now," said Blackstone, grasping both of Ralph's hands, "good-bye, and Heaven bless you! I will say but a few more words. Yonder lies your road, and I earnestly trust that it will lead to fame and fortune. That your good name will be returned to you one day I have no more doubt than that I am a sinner."

As he uttered the last word he turned abruptly aside and sprang into the train, which just then pulled up with a jerk into the station.

Ralph made a movement as if he would have spoken to the detective again, but the guard's shrill whistle rang out, the engine shrieked a defiant response, and our hero was left alone on the platform.

One last look he took at the train

winding its way like a huge serpent on the iron road, and then with a prayer for strength quivering on his lips, he turned his footsteps to the east.

On he went past stately mansion, cosy farmhouse, and peasant's cottage.

He counted the mile-stones, and at last came to the tenth one.

Just opposite to the silent director stood an old-fashioned inn bearing the sign of The Seven Stars.

The jolly-looking landlord and his no less jolly-looking wife, standing chatting at the door, matched well with the house.

They smiled and nodded as Ralph hesitated, wondering whether it would be policy on his part to enter the house and there make himself acquainted with the contents of the letter which he carried in his pocket.

He was tired and needed rest, and he decided to enter the inn.

The host and hostess made room for him to pass and enquired his pleasure.

"Only to sit down until dinner is ready," Ralph replied, smiling. "Perhaps I ought to have asked whether I can be supplied with dinner here."

"If a cut out of a leg of mutton, and an apple tart to follow, will suit you," the landlord replied, "we shall be happy to serve you."

"You could not give me anything better," Ralph replied.

"Out for a long walk?" queried the landlord with a glance at our hero's dusty boots.

"Yes."

"Going farther on, sir?"

"I am not certain yet," Ralph replied. "At all events, I think I have walked far enough until the evening."

The landlord would have asked more questions, but Ralph picked up a country newspaper and began to read.

When he put the paper down, he discovered, much to his relief, that the landlord had quitted the parlour.

"He thinks I have run away," he said to himself; "and I wonder if he will try to make out where I came from."

Our hero's conjecture was right.

The landlord went back to his wife, and they put their heads together.

"He's bolted from somewhere, Jane," said the host.

"I'm sure he is every inch a gentleman, Bob," Jane replied. "Perhaps he is a younger brother and has been badly treated. Well, well, it is no business of ours."

"I ain't sure about that," said Bob, properly named Robert Buttle. "S'pose we let him go, and to-morrow up comes a carriage with a nobleman inside, making enquiries for his son. A nice pair of fools we should look, certainly, if the young gent was gone."

"But how are you to keep him if he makes up his mind to go?" Jane demanded.

"I'll think over it," observed Bob Buttle, tapping his forehead sagely. "Let him have everything of the best. Tell him there's something better for supper than he had for dinner, and perhaps that will keep him here. Boys like two things—mischief and good living."

Neither Bob Buttle nor his wife needed to have troubled on Ralph's account, as will be presently seen when the contents of Joshua Blackstone's letter are made known to the reader.

With strange emotions filling his heart and brain, and with trembling fingers, Ralph broke the seal and opened the envelope.

It contained a sheet of paper, of which one side was barely filled.

The instructions were as follows:

"If you have passed The Seven Stars Inn before you read this, go back, and stay there until Monday morning. A carrier's cart will call at ten o'clock in the morning, and take you as far as Ipswich. Book then by train to Norwich, and on arriving there ask your way to the Shakespeare Tavern, Theatre-street, and enquire for Mr. Orlando Ravington. Show him this, and all will be well. There is no need for me to sign this, as Ravington knows my writing as well as his own. I have dispensed with my signature as you might lose this. If so, wire to Nemo, Queen's Hotel, Aldersgate-street."

Ralph replaced the precious document in his breast-pocket, and buttoned his jacket.

"I have not much fear of losing it," he said. "Oh, here is that inquisitive landlord again. I suppose I shall be pestered with no end of questions. I shall be truly thankful when to-morrow morning comes, and I shall set out to begin my fight against the world, and, it may be, win my way to fame and fortune!"

CHAPTER XLVI.

SLOWBOB WAKES UP.

ALTHOUGH Slowbob's reason became sufficiently clear on the morning of Ralph's departure to recognise Dr. Pillem, his mind was still confused.

He lay moaning at intervals, and talking as the nurse thought, at random; but as the day advanced he fell into a calm refreshing sleep, and when he awoke, the colour of returning health was on his cheeks.

Suddenly he opened his eyes wide.

The right one seemed to be making an observation of a cupboard in the corner of the room, whilst the left appeared to be looking out of the window; but in reality both Timothy's optics were focussed upon the nurse.

"Hallo!" he said. "Who are you?"

The nurse explained, bidding her patient to be quiet until he had taken his medicine.

"Medicine!" Timothy cried. "What do I want medicine for? Oh, lor!" he added as he tried to sit up and failed. "I'm awfully weak, and nothin' but skin and bone. Come here and tell me all about it. Have I been ill long?"

"For some days," the nurse said, sitting down in her usual place; "and you have had a marvellous recovery. We all thought you would have died."

"Who's 'we'?" demanded Slowbob, looking round the room. "Didn't I—didn't I go to lodge at Salem Cockey's house?"

"You did, but you are not there now."

"Where am I, then?"

"At the Abbey."

Timothy Slowbob breathed hard as he gazed at the ceiling.

Slowly, very slowly his memory was returning.

"Didn't I have a fall or somethin'?" he asked.

"Yes, something of that kind," the nurse replied, "and a gentleman pulled you out of the river. But you must not talk now. Are you thirsty?"

Slowbob smacked his lips, and stretched out his thin hand for an orange.

He lay perfectly still for about a quarter of an hour, and then became restless again.

"It's no use," he said; "I must talk. Wasn't I hit over the head? I remember leaving Cockey's house, but the rest is confused. I seem to be looking at something through a veil."

"I don't know much about it," the nurse replied; "you had better ask the doctor."

"Let me think," Slowbob mused. "I went down the road. Then I saw the Frenchman coming, and I crept into a hedge, and then—and then—I don't remember any more."

The nurse let him talk on, making mental notes of what he said.

"You saw a Frenchman coming," she said, after a little while. "What Frenchman?"

"Why, that chap Alphonse Carleon, of course," Slowbob replied. "He was going to the Miser's Mill to meet the other three."

"The other three!" returned the nurse, quickly. "I'm afraid you have been dreaming all this."

"No, I haven't," Timothy Slowbob replied. "One of them was Richard Mornington, cousin to Ralph Mornington, who is here, you know. I don't know the names of the other two. Ah me, I feel tired again, and I think I'll go to sleep."

"Do," said the nurse; "but before you settle down, drink this."

Timothy Slowbob, patient and obedient, drank the medicine, and in less than a minute his calm, measured breathing announced that he was once more partaking freely of Nature's sweet restorer.

The nurse, after satisfying herself that Timothy Slowbob would not wake for at least an hour, slipped quietly out of the room, and having demanded an audience with Mr. Stormaway, acquainted him with what she had heard from Slowbob's lips.

The head-master of Merrytown Abbey rubbed his distracted head until he almost blistered it.

"I don't know what to make of all this," he said. "Sometimes I think I must be dreaming myself. Do you think I may question Slowbob?"

"Yes, sir, when he wakes again," the nurse replied; "but you must not overtax him. The moment you see him growing excited, you must cease talking and leave the room."

"He shall find me at his side when he wakes," Mr. Stormaway said. "I will go to him now. Mr. Muffler can take the boys to church. Ah me, they will miss one from his old place !"

The nurse had not been made aware of what had taken place, but she guessed that there was something wrong at the Abbey.

She led the way to the sick-room, and both sat watching Timothy Slowbob, who at intervals talked in his sleep.

"This poor boy talks of nothing but Richard Mornington, M. Carleon, and the Miser's Mill," Mr. Stormaway said. "There is a mystery here, and the sooner it is solved the better it will be for my peace of mind. I think," he added under his breath, "I have been hasty in allowing Ralph Mornington to leave the Abbey. I do not think that Carleon would have carried out his threat, after all."

Slowbob slept on, and as the clock was striking twelve, Dr. Pillem called again.

"I forbid anyone to question my patient," he said, after listening to Mr. Stormaway. "The fever has abated, but may return at any moment. Mr. Stormaway, do not compel me to ask you to leave the room ; but act as your common-sense dictates. And as for you, nurse, please do not refer to the cause of the boy's illness. If you cannot stop him, let him talk on, until he is tired."

"Yes, doctor," the nurse replied, meekly. "He seemed so much better, that I thought——"

"You will please not to think again until you have consulted me !" Dr. Pillem interposed. "Give your patient the cooling-draughts at regular intervals, and perhaps we shall see a great improvement to-morrow."

At that moment Timothy Slowbob woke up with a start.

"Where are my clothes ?" he cried. "I must go to the Miser's Mill. Don't stop me ! They are trying to kill him. Look ! here comes the Frenchman and the rest. Run, Mr. Mornington—run ! or they'll overtake you !"

"See what you have done," the doctor said, looking sternly at the nurse.

Timothy tried to scramble out of bed, but Mr. Stormaway caught him in his arms and pressed him gently back.

"Slowbob," he said, softly, "don't you know me, poor boy ?"

The paroxysm passed away, and Timothy Slowbob became himself again.

"Yes, I know you, sir," he said. "Ah, here's the doctor again ; more physic for me, I s'pose ? I've had a nasty dream, that's all. Lor', how weak I am ! Please may I see Mr. Ralph Mornington ? I am sure the sight of him would do me lots of good."

Mr. Stormaway did not know how to answer this request ; but Dr. Pillem came to the rescue.

"You must not see anybody until I say yes," he answered ; "and I say no, now."

"But I want to tell him something that I ought to have told him before," Timothy urged. "Oh, do let me see him, please. I may have made a mistake, of course ; but——"

"I will have no more talking," said Dr. Pillem, interrupting him. "Mr. Stormaway, leave the room. Slowbob," he added, shaking his finger playfully, yet meaningly, at the patient, "if you say another word, I'll mix you up a bottle of extra nasty physic."

"I don't care for your physic," Timothy cried. "I want to see Mr. Mornington. I must see him, and I will see him."

The effort cost poor Slowbob too much. He sank back, and fell into a kind of stupor.

"If all I have done is not undone, it will be a wonder," Dr. Pillem said, gravely. "It is natural that he should rave in this way. There is nothing new in it, I can assure you."

"But there are circumstances, I am certain——" began Mr. Stormaway.

"And I assure you," interposed Dr. Pillem, "that if you allow the boy to excite himself by your presence again, you will kill him."

"Heaven forbid !" the head-master ejaculated.

"I beg of you to leave the room," the doctor said.

Mr. Stormaway did so, and brooded all day long in his study, and the boys wandered disconsolately about the Abbey as if they had lost something, as indeed they had.

CHAPTER XLVII.

ALPHONSE CARLEON GETS DISSATISFIED WITH HIS SITUATION.

MONDAY came, and with it the time for paying the masters their quarterly stipend.

Mr. Muffler went into the study first with a very thin purse, and came out with a fairly corpulent one.

Herr Fritz Halfamann took the next turn, and, last of all, M. Alphonse Carleon presented himself before Mr. Stormaway.

The Frenchman's money was ready, and the head-master, without saying a word, handed it to him.

Carleon picked up the coins, and, without counting them, dropped them into his pocket.

"Mr. Stormaway," he said, "a word with you."

"I am at your service," the head-master replied.

"After what has occurred here," said Carleon, "I do not think I feel justified in remaining."

Mr. Stormaway pushed up his spectacles and elevated his eyebrows.

"This is rather sudden, monsieur," he said. "Do I understand that you wish to give me a quarter's notice?"

Alphonse Carleon shrugged his shoulders and clenched his hands.

"I hope you will not demand such a notice of me," he said. "Mr. Stormaway, I will be plain with you. You never liked me, and like me less now that I have proved one of your pet pupils to be a thief."

The head-master rose and leaned one hand on the table, as if about to make a speech.

"Indeed!" he said, "and pray how long have you made this astonishing discovery?"

"You need not ask me what you know already," Carleon replied, sullenly. "I have spoken my mind."

"And I will speak mine!" said Mr. Stormaway, whose wrath was rising rapidly. "I know of no likes or dislikes. I have an equal interest in my pupils, and I endeavour to discharge my duty to all. How dare you insult me at such a time as this, when my mind is filled with trouble, and my heart overflowing with sorrow?"

"I speak but the truth," the Frenchman muttered, quailing before Mr. Stormaway's gaze. "I wish to go because I think it will be better for both of us. I have been offered a situation in my own country, and I have decided to embrace the opportunity."

"In that case," said Mr. Stormaway, "you will require a reference. Have a care, monsieur; I am an easy-tempered man, but you may try me too far."

"That, for your reference and your threat!" Carleon cried, snapping his fingers. "I am unhappy—miserable here. One of your pupils robs me, the rest disobey me. And, sir, I will be plainer. You wink at their disobedience and smile at my unhappiness, because I am a poor underpaid Frenchman. Well, indeed, my countrymen exclaim, 'Perfidious Albion!'"

Mr. Stormaway held his hand to his ear as if he could not credit what he heard.

"You shall go, but not until I know your destination," he said.

"How does that concern you?" Carleon demanded.

"In more ways than one," the head-master replied. "I may want you to help to clear up the mystery that hangs over Ralph Mornington."

"The mystery ended with the discovery of the marked money."

"I do not think so," said Mr. Stormaway. "You arrogate to yourself the virtue of plain-speaking. Speak out now. When did you make the acquaintance of Ralph Mornington's cousin Richard, and what were you doing on the road near the Miser's Mill on the night that Slowbob was murderously assaulted?"

The head-master of Merrytown Abbey expected to see the Frenchman flinch and cringe under these burning questions, but he was disappointed.

Carleon laughed scornfully, and changed his stiff attitude for an easy one.

"With respect to Richard Mornington I will satisfy you at once," he said. "He came into this town a vagabond, begging, and for all I know stealing. I met him by chance; he told me who he was, and I assisted him out of my own purse rather than he should annoy his—his honourable cousin!"

Mr. Stormaway was taken aback, for the explanation, if not feasible, was just possible.

"I will also enlighten you as to my journey to the Miser's Mill," Carleon continued. "Richard Mornington told me that he had taken up his abode there with two or three vagrants he had picked up with on the road. You follow me, I suppose, Mr. Stormaway?"

"Yes," the head-master replied, "I am listening to you very attentively."

"I put myself to the trouble of going to the Miser's Mill to warn—to beg Richard Mornington not to come near the Abbey for his cousin's sake," Carleon pursued. "Nay, I even gave him a small amount of money to quit the place. And what is my reward, sir? I am suspected groundlessly, but suspected of what? Answer!"

Mr. Stormaway was silenced.

It struck him very forcibly that he had found a mare's nest, and for the life of him he did not know what to say.

"I am perfectly aware that I have been spied upon and followed about by your page-boy," went on Alphonse Carleon, "and judging by what you have just said, I can come to no other conclusion than that he did so with your consent."

"No," said Mr. Stormaway, emphatically. "No."

"Well," returned Carleon, "be that as it may, the Abbey is no longer a place for me. I have borne all this and much more with patience. I have kept down my angry feelings when they have risen with just cause within my breast, and——"

"I am very sorry, monsieur," Mr. Stormaway said. "If you have suffered innocently——"

"Innocently!" cried the Frenchman, whose brow grew dark and lowering. "What do you accuse me of?"

"Nothing, only I thought it strange that you should be in communication with this man and his vile associates."

"You have listened to idle prattle," Carleon said, sternly. "You have watched me closely—you have thought me guilty of some plot. Mr. Stormaway, the laws of your country protect poor and rich alike. Take care, or I may call heavily on your purse for slander."

The head-master groaned, and rubbed his perspiring brow.

"I am very sorry that this has occurred," he murmured.

"Sorry!" Carleon echoed. "Who in the world can be more sorry than myself? But let it pass. We must part, Mr. Stormaway, and at once."

"At once!" repeated the head-master. "Surely you will remain here a little time, at least!"

"No," Carleon replied. "I have reason to hate the place and its associations, and I shall be better away."

Mr. Stormaway opened his mouth to speak, but the words were never uttered.

The door flew open with a crash.

Rushing into the study came Slowbob, clad in his unspeakables, and like the youth in the nursery rhyme, with "one shoe off and one shoe on."

Clinging to his braces was Matthew Stickers, and Herr Fritz Halfamann brought up the rear, clinging in his turn to the tails of the man-of-all-work's coat.

Alphonse Carleon turned deathly pale, and Mr. Stormaway, starting to his feet, recoiled in horror towards the fire-grate.

It is probable that he would have fallen into it, but the fender checked his progress, and he brought himself up with a jerk.

"How did that unfortunate lad contrive to escape from his bed?" the head-master gasped.

"The nuss left the room for a moment," Matthew Stickers said, "and Slowbob took advantage of it."

"It vas a vonderful t'ing!" observed Halfamann. "I met dem coming down zee stairs, and t'ink dat I had petter hold on to Stickares."

Slowbob laughed a hollow, sepulchral laugh, and pointed at Alphonse Carleon, who seemed to cower before him.

"There he is!" Timothy cried. "Stop him—don't let him go! Bring Mr. Mornington here, and let him hear what I have to say. I'm all right now, I tell you!"

"This boy is mad!" Carleon said, trying to speak calmly.

"If I'm mad, I ain't a murderer!" Slowbob almost shrieked. "I'll have my say out, if I die!"

"Mr. Stormaway," said Carleon, "matters have taken a new turn. I'm perfectly willing to listen to this poor lad, if you think it worth the while."

"No, no," Mr. Stormaway replied. "Stickers—Herr Halfamann, I beg that you will take Slowbob back to his bed."

"But I won't go," Timothy yelled. "I'm weak and faint of body, but my heart is strong. I can bear it no longer. Where is Mr. Mornington? Why don't you send for him?"

Slowbob wailed out the last words and would have fallen, but Mr. Stormaway rushed forward and caught him in his arms.

"Dis is too horriple!" Herr Fritz Halfamann said, holding up his hands. "Oh, monsieur, vat haf you done to make poor Slowpop look at you in such a vay?"

"Can I find a reason for all the madness in Bedlam?" the Frenchman retorted. "The boy ought to be put under restraint and without delay."

"There vas no doubt about dat," the German tutor said, as Mr. Stormaway bore Slowbob, struggling and shrieking, out of the room. "I did never see anyt'ing like dis in all my life. Slowpop vill die now—dere is no hobe for him."

CHAPTER XLVIII.

THE STRANGER AT THE SEVEN STARS INN.

"ENJOYED your dinner, sir?" asked Bob Buttle, putting his head in at the parlour door.

"Yes, thank you," Ralph replied; "I never enjoyed anything better in my life."

"I'm glad to hear you say that," the landlord remarked, gliding into the room and sitting down.

Ralph picked up the county paper, but Bob Buttle was not to be denied this time.

"You're very much like Lord Wolverton's eldest son," he said.

"Am I? You don't mean that for a compliment, I hope."

"Not a bit, sir," Buttle said. "You've got the same coloured hair and eyes, and——"

"And yet I am not Lord Wolverton's son," Ralph interposed.

"Well, the likeness is wonderful," Bob Buttle said, in a disappointed tone of voice.

"If it will be any satisfaction to you, I will tell you what I am," Ralph said.

"I should feel honoured to know, sir."

"I am your customer," Ralph replied; "and, as such, I am quite able to pay you for the accommodation I receive."

Bob Buttle's face fell considerably as he received this sharp rap over the knuckles.

"I never doubted it, sir," he said, humbly. "I hope you are not angry with me, sir."

"Not a bit," Ralph responded; "but I hate to be bothered about matters that only concern myself."

As the landlord, crestfallen, and looking extremely sheepish, rose to leave the room, the door communicating with the road flew open, and a young man entered.

It was Richard Mornington.

His appearance had altered since the night that he parted with Alphonse Carleon at the Miser's Mill.

He wore a cheap, ready-made suit, a pot-hat stuck jauntily on one side of his head, and in his mouth was a long, rank, evil-smelling cigar.

"What!" he cried, striking the floor with his stick, "all asleep here! Hi! landlord—landlady—somebody!"

Bob Buttle confronted Richard Mornington and looked him up and down.

"We don't hold fairs inside this house," he said, "and upon my word you make as much noise as the proprietor of a peep-show. Perhaps you are in the line?"

"No, I am a gentleman," Richard Mornington returned, laughing lightly.

"Then behave yourself like one," Bob Buttle said. "What do you require?"

"First of all, a room in which I can sit down, and, secondly, a bottle of wine."

Bob Buttle looked a little more civil, and pointed to the parlour door.

"Anybody in there?" demanded Richard Mornington.

"Only a young gentleman," said Buttle, with an emphasis on the last word.

Richard Mornington walked into the room, and glanced at Ralph.

He started, but recovering himself instantly sat down.

"Fine day, isn't it?" said Richard Mornington.

"Very," Ralph replied, curtly.

Our hero did not recognise in the flashly-dressed fellow, the ragged vagabond he had met near the Miser's Mill some time ago.

"You don't smoke, I suppose?" Richard Mornington said.

"No."

"Then I shall save a cigar."

Richard Mornington laughed as he spoke, and, rising, went to the window.

Ralph watched him with growing dislike.

"I am a stranger in this part of the country," Richard Mornington said. "Do you happen to know such a place as Merrytown?"

It was Ralph's turn to start now, but he did so without knowing why.

"Merrytown is ten miles distant," he said. "Follow the road that runs due west, and you cannot miss it."

"I thank you," Richard Mornington replied. "Are you acquainted with the place?"

"I have been there."

"I have been told," said Richard Mornington after a pause, "that it is a quaint old village, and that there are some things worth seeing—an Abbey, for instance."

"Indeed!" Ralph returned. "Very likely you are right."

Richard Mornington walked to the table, and drawing a chair up to it, sat down.

"You seem dull, my lad," he said. "Come, we are fellow travellers, and may as well be chatty."

"There is nothing to talk about," Ralph replied. "Excuse me; I am much occupied with my thoughts. I hope you will not think me rude in not wishing to converse."

"Have it your own way," Richard Mornington remarked, carelessly, as he threw the end of his burnt-out cigar into the grate, and lighted another. "You look too young and healthy to have a fit of the blues. Come, let me give you a glass of wine."

"I do not take strong drink," Ralph said; "I thank you all the same."

He rose, and leaving the room, walked into the garden that sloped down from the rear of the house to a pretty little stream that babbled and laughed its way to the broad and shining river.

"So," Richard Mornington soliloquised, throwing himself back in the chair, "Carleon has kept his word, and my honest cousin is on his way to ruin. Ha, ha! how nicely I have tricked the Frenchman! He will seek me and my comrades at the address given him in London, but I think it would puzzle the Postmaster-General to find it."

He laughed again as he held up his glass to the light.

"Not bad for such a house as this," he said. "Richard, my boy, I drink to your health. I should not like to part company with this youngster without knowing where he is going to. It is scarcely possible that he has said anything to the landlord, but I will pump him."

He rang the bell, and Bob Buttle appeared in so short a time that he must have been in close proximity to the door when summoned.

"Landlord," Richard Mornington said, "I am a convivial animal, and cannot drink alone. Will you help me to finish the bottle?"

"I don't mind wishing you prosperity over a glass of wine," Buttle replied. "Thank you, sir; you are very good."

"That is a strange youngster you have here," Richard Mornington said.

"I can make nothing of him; he is a mystery to me."

Richard Mornington leaned forward and stared the landlord full in the face.

"I don't wish to make remarks about your customers," he said, "but that boy has been up to some trick that he has reason to be ashamed of."

"I don't believe it," Bob Buttle rejoined, bluntly; "I have said before that he is a gentleman, and I think so still."

"That is because you are good-natured, and loth to believe that a lad with a fair open face can be guilty of evil things," Richard Mornington said. "Supposing that I know who he is, where he has come from, and the reason he had to leave?"

"You do!" Buttle exclaimed, starting.

"Hush!" whispered Richard Mornington, tapping the landlord on the arm. "Can you keep a secret? If I tell you something, will you give me your solemn promise not to mention it even to your wife?"

"I will," said Bob Buttle, running his fingers through his hair, which had bristled to an alarming extent.

"Then," Richard Mornington replied, "I am a London detective, and I have been sent down here to watch that boy with the wonderful open countenance. He is nothing more or less than a young swindler and a thief. If you allow him to sleep here, don't be surprised if you miss him in the morning and some of your property."

This statement took Bob Buttle's breath away.

He could do nothing but sit still and gasp.

"He a swindler and a thief?" he contrived to articulate at last. "Is it possible?"

"It is true," Richard Mornington observed, nodding his head. "He is one of a clever band, and though I cannot find sufficient cause to put the handcuffs on him, I have the best of reasons to believe that he has committed at least a dozen robberies, and contrived to forward the proceeds to his associates."

"Then out of my house he goes," cried Bob Buttle.

He would have jumped up there and then, and ordered Ralph off his premises, but Richard Mornington restrained him.

"Steady," he said; "no good ever comes of being impatient. Tell him quietly you have discovered that he cannot sleep here. If he murmurs, then you can point the way to the door."

"I'll do that sharp enough," said the deluded landlord. "A thief in my house, and on Sunday, too! Bless me! I feel quite ill."

"Not a word to your wife or anybody," said Richard Mornington, warningly. "The boy is coming back, and it will not do to let him see you and I conversing."

"You may trust me, sir; and I thank you for the information," Buttle replied.

He passed out of the room as Ralph re-entered it.

"I shall require tea, but no supper," our hero said. "I am very tired and should like to go to bed at sundown."

Bob Buttle twined his fingers together, and looked a little confused.

"Well, it's like this, you see," he stammered. "I hope you will take it kindly, but you can't have a bed here."

"Why not?" Ralph demanded, looking at Richard Mornington, though he scarcely knew why.

"Why not?" Buttle repeated, bridling up. "I suppose a man is master of his own house."

"Just so," Ralph replied; "but I shall take it as a great favour if——"

"It can't be done at any price," Buttle interposed in a tone of voice that admitted of no further argument. "When I say you can't have a bed, you can't, so there is an end of the matter."

"In that case," our hero observed, "I had better start at once, for I must find a resting-place."

Bob Buttle was much relieved.

He brought his bill, and looked carefully at every coin tendered in payment by our hero, and marched stiffly behind him to the door.

"Thank goodness, he is gone!" he said. "Phew! I have had a narrow escape. I shall never believe in a good-looking face again as long as I live."

Poor Ralph stood in the dusty road, wondering at the change in the landlord's demeanour.

"I am sure the stranger had something to do with this," he said. "I wonder who he is?"

A sudden thought flashed into Ralph's mind, but he banished it as quickly.

"No," he murmured; "he cannot be my cousin. There is no likeness, and nothing to proclaim that the blood of the Morningtons runs in his veins. Heigho! I suppose I had better start; but stay, such a course would not be following the directions of the letter."

He halted and stood pondering as to what he should do.

"I will try to get a lodging at some cottage," he said. "How glad I shall be when to-morrow comes, for then I shall be well on my journey!"

CHAPTER XLIX.

ALPHONSE CARLEON'S FLIGHT—JACK WALBUT FOLLOWS SUIT—THE BEST
WOMAN IN THE WORLD UPSETS THE DIGNITY OF THE LAW.

WHEN Alphonse Carleon walked out of the Abbey, he did so never to return.

He went straight to his lodgings, and hastily packing up his luggage had it conveyed to the station, and thither he turned his footsteps.

Carleon had more than an hour to spare, but he preferred the dreary, deserted platform to the open street.

He had a horror of meeting with anybody who might question him.

Pacing up and down he tried to read the advertisements.

A newspaper contents'-bill caught his eye, and he stopped, fascinated by a line printed in large type : " The Biter Bitten."

He read it again and again until the black letters swam before his eyes, but suddenly he turned, with a mocking laugh on his lips.

"I am a poor creature to take notice of such a trifle," he said. " How the time drags ! Will the train that is to bear me from this hateful place never start ? "

The empty carriages were waiting for the engine to be attached to them, and presently an official unlocked and opened them.

There were now two or three people on the platform.

A sleepy-looking clerk woke up and dispensed tickets with a surly grace, and a still sleepier bookstall attendant took down the shutters of his emporium of literature, but for lack of custom leaned his back against a row of volumes reduced in price, and circumstances as far as appearances went, and blinked lazily at the sun.

Alphonse Carleon procured his ticket as soon as possible, and was about to enter the train when he felt a tap on the shoulder.

The guilty need no accusing.

The Frenchman uttered a suppressed cry, and became livid as he turned and found himself confronted by P.C. Worryboy.

The guard, porters, and the few travellers heard the cry, and brought their eyes to bear upon Carleon, who looked for all the world as if he had been just arrested.

"Beg pardon, mounseer," said Worryboy. "I met Stickers just now, and he told me as how you was a goin' to leave us."

"Yes," Carleon replied ; "I am going now. You startled me, constable."

"So it seems," Worryboy said. " Well, Merrytown ain't a lively place 'cept for boys. Good-bye, mounseer. So you are goin' back to Parry, I hear ? If I had money enough and could do the parley-woo, I would go to Parry ; I hear it is a wonderful place."

"Yes," Carleon replied, impatiently ; " it is one of the most beautiful cities in the world. Good-bye, Worryboy, and I hope you will soon earn promotion."

"Just a few more words, mounseer," said Worryboy. " I have often wished to ask you a question, but did not like to take the liberty."

"Well ? "

"One night, some time ago," Worryboy continued, " I was a-doin' of my dooty in the High-street, when I saw you in the company of two strange men. Would you mind tellin' me who they were ? "

A greenish hue spread over Alphonse Carleon's face.

"They were two beggars, most likely," he said.

"If they was, you seemed to know 'em pretty well," Worryboy remarked, little guessing the confusion and terror he was creating in the Frenchman's mind.

"I really do not understand you," Carleon said, trembling in spite of all the control he exercised. "Let me think. Ah, yes. I remember being stopped by two men who thought they knew me. They discovered their mistake, and after a short chat we parted."

"Oh," mused Worryboy, "they thought they knew you ! It was funny that you promised to meet them again."

For once Worryboy was doing a sensible thing.

To a certain extent he was keeping his own counsel, while he made Carleon feel wretchedly uncomfortable.

"MR. MUFFLER SENT LEMON SLEATH THROUGH THE LID OF AN EMPTY BOX."—(See page 169.)

Just then a local train came rumbling and bumping over the points into the station.

A strangely-attired man, wearing a green patch over one eye, and a heavy moustache completely covering his mouth, stepped out, and changed into the London train.

"Right away," shouted the guard, and the train began to move.

Carleon was already in his seat, and he tossed half-a-crown to Worryboy, who caught it as it shimmered and whirled in mid-air.

"I ain't satisfied," Worryboy said, as he stood alone on the platform. "Why did the Frenchy start and tremble like an ash-pan when I touched him on the shoulder? There is something' rotten in the state of Denmark, as 'Amlet said."

Worryboy continued to shake his head, until the booking-clerk banged down the wicket and issued forth to bask in the sun.

"No, I ain't satisfied," Worryboy said, as he waddled out of the station. "There's somethin' as wants to be cleared up, and that somethin's connected with the Abbey, I'm sure."

Strolling along and blessing the man who invented a tight-fitting uniform, he encountered Salem Cockey and Matthew Stickers, who were walking hurriedly along looking right and left.

"Hallo!" said Worryboy; "what is up now?"

"What is up now?" Stickers rejoined. "You may well ask the question. You know young Walbut?"

"Oh yes; I know him," Worryboy replied.

"Well, he's cut and run—leastways, he can't be found," Matthew Stickers replied. "I'm off to the station to see if he's in the London train."

"You want longer legs than yours to catch it," Worryboy observed. "I was on the platform when it started ten minutes ago."

"Then Walbut wasn't there?"

"No," the constable replied; "he was not. There weren't more than half-a-dozen passengers, and they were all grown up."

"That is sassidgefactory, at all events," Stickers said. "Mr. Stormaway is in a dreadful state of mind; but p'raps the boy is skulking somewheres. He's just the sort o' one to skulk—it comes nat'ral to him."

"The mounseer was in the train,"

Worryboy remarked; "and we had a few pleasant words together before he started. Cockey, this is your wages-day, so——"

"My Mariar drawed the wages," the beadle interrupted with a sigh. "I haven't got a brass farden."

"Why do you put up with it?" said Worryboy.

"That's what I says," Stickers chimed in. "Cockey, it's never too late to start on a new footin'. I'd have my 'ard-hearned money, and do what I liked with it."

"I will!" the beadle cried, tilting his hat over his eyes. "I'll tell my Mariar so when I see her."

"If I ain't mistaken, I see her a coming down the road," said Worryboy.

"I think I had better retire," Salem remarked, meekly. "She's the best woman in the world, only a little peppery, you know."

"She's all pepper," said Worryboy.

"Cayenne," Matthew Stickers remarked. "When she's on the rampage after you, Salem, the wery sight o' her is enough to make a feller's heyes water."

Salem Cockey did not hear these last remarks.

He turned and fled just as the best woman in the world came up.

"So," she said, "you have lured my 'usband out agin, have you?"

"Lured him hout!" Stickers said, with a gasp. "Missus Cockey, did you redress yourself to me?"

"I speak to both of you—idle, good-for-nothin' fellers that you are!" Mariar cried, shrilly. "Oh, the wicious ways of men! Here's my 'usband drawn half his wages in advance, and spent the money at The Swan and Bottle, no doubt."

"That's a painful thing to copper-plate," Matthew Stickers said, solemnly.

"Of course it is," screamed the beadle's wife, placing her arms akimbo; "but I daresay you and this—this thing in blue helped him to spend it."

"Here, I say, you just moderate your langwidge," said Worryboy.

But Mrs. Cockey had the power to moderate neither her remarks nor her temper.

Suddenly, and without a word of warning, she went for the constable, and in less than ten seconds his helmet was rolling in the kennel, and one side of his face was much redder than the other.

"You mustn't knock the law about," he cried, skipping behind Matthew Stickers, who by no means relished his prominent position; "for if you do, the law will run you in."

"The law, indeed!" Mariar sneered. "If you're a representative of it, the country is in a pretty state, certainly."

"My dear Mrs. Cockey," said Matthew Stickers, "let me pour a little troubled water on the hoil. Why so winagry, why so——"

"I'll 'my dear' you!" shrieked the beadle's wife. "Oh! oh! Where's my 'usband? Salem! Salem! Air you above the earth and can rest when your lawful wife is called 'my dear?'"

"I'm off," Worryboy whispered to Stickers, as he recovered his helmet. "There's more mischief in that there woman than in a nest of wampires."

"I'm off too," said Stickers. "Don't keep on dodgin' behind me. Bolt, and I'll foller you."

Worryboy suddenly took to his heels, and Matthew Stickers went after him as hard as he could pelt.

"She's arter us," he panted. "I can 'ear her a comin'. Run, Worryboy; if you falls down, or if she catches you, she'll do you a mortial hinjury."

"You look after yourself," Worryboy shouted back.

"She's a comin' nearer and nearer, I tell you," Matthew groaned. "I'm a goin' to climb the first lamp I come to."

As he made this novel resolution he dashed round a corner and ran full butt against Mr. Muffler and Herr Fritz Halfamann, who, arm-in-arm, were taking a stroll.

"Pless me!" said the Teuton, as he rolled heavily on his back; "vas it von runaway horse?"

"No," said Mr. Muffler, who had also occasion to pick himself up; "it is Matthew Stickers."

"It are me, a fleein' from the wrath of a wild and fiery woman," Stickers replied. "There she goes after Worryboy now, and she'll catch him afore he reaches the station."

"It vas von curious t'ing," said Herr Halfamann, "but vhere dere is von corner, Stickares vas sure to dash round it. He vas porn to knock peoples down."

"Which I asks pardon," Stickers replied. "Look at me, drenched with persperashing. Ah, she's got him!"

A wild yell proclaimed the fact that the best woman in the world had overtaken P.C. Worryboy.

Again did his helmet roll sportively on the ground, and yet again was he smitten by that peppery hand.

"Mariar! oh, my Mariar!" said Salem Cockey, appearing on the scene. "You don't know what you are a doing of. You'll get a month without the hoption of a fine, and I shall be disrobed."

"Only wait till I get you home," Mariar gurgled, as Worryboy crawled down three steps into a greengrocer's shop; "I'll teach you to draw your money in advance."

"Take her away," said Worryboy, looking over the top of a pile of cabbages. "Cockey, I respects you, and for that reason I'll look over this; but take her away afore I forgets that she belongs to the feminine ginger."

The order of things was, however, reversed.

It was Maria who led Salem away, which she did by annexing one of his ears.

"He's a dead 'un," said Matthew Stickers. "It's hall hover with 'im. Farewell to the best beadle as the world ever saw."

"You had better return to the Abbey at once," Mr. Muffler said. "Really, these disturbances are most distressing. For a second time this summer my hat has been severely damaged. My dear Halfamann, we will continue our walk."

"Vait until I find mine sbectacles," the German tutor replied. "They did seem to pe plown off from the pridge of mine nose, and I have von fear dat when I find dem dey sal pe proken. Och, Stickares, vhen you take your valks abroad, keep in von street vhere dere are no corners!"

CHAPTER L.

SLOWBOB HIMSELF AGAIN—HIS ANGUISH AT HEARING OF RALPH'S MIS-
FORTUNES, AND HIS RESOLVE.

THOUGH ill and feeble when he burst so suddenly into Mr. Stormaway's study, Timothy Slowbob was in full possession of his senses.

He tried to make the head-master and the nurse understand that such was the case, but they only tried to soothe him, and failing to do so, Dr. Pillem's arrival was looked forward to with anxiety.

When he called, Carleon and Walbut had already left the Abbey.

"This is a remarkable case, and a still more remarkable boy," said the doctor. "The fever has almost gone. Slowbob is on the high-road to recovery."

"I'm all right," observed the irrepressible; "but I want to see Mister Mornington. Why do you keep him away from me?"

"May I tell him?" Mr. Stormaway whispered to Dr. Pillem.

"Yes," the doctor replied.

As if he were dreaming, Slowbob listened to the story of our hero's woes.

"Why didn't you let me speak when I came down to your study?" cried Timothy, actually shaking his fist at Mr. Stormaway. "I knew how it would be all along—I tell you I knew it!"

"You knew what?" said the head-master.

"That he would be accused of something," Slowbob responded. "Didn't I hide under the Frenchman's window and hear him plotting and planning? Didn't I hear Richard Mornington ask when it was to be done?"

"My poor boy," said Mr. Stormaway, taken aback at the words, "it seems that you have told me only half a story. Why did you not tell me of this before?"

"Because I was a fool," Slowbob owned, with refreshing frankness. "I thought I would keep the best to myself and then drop down all of a sudden on the guilty parties. I wrote to Gen'ral Mornington, and signed myself 'Watchdog.' I told him to come here at once, and I meant to confoose the willains."

"This is an extraordinary statement," Mr. Stormaway said, looking at the doctor.

"It is," returned the medical man. "Dear me! I am afraid that some morbid matter is still left in Slowbob's system."

"Morbid what?" Timothy cried. "Where are my clothes? Why have you taken them away?"

"To prevent you going abroad," said Mr. Stormaway.

"Of course," Slowbob observed; "and while I'm lyin' here the greatest rascal under the sun is free, and poor Mister Mornington is a sufferin' through no fault of his own. Where is that Walbut?"

"I regret to say that he has left the Abbey in the most mysterieus way," Mr. Stormaway said.

Slowbob laughed scornfully.

"Just what I thought!" he said. "Look 'ere, believe it or believe it not, it was him as put the money in Mister Mornington's box."

"What proof can you bring forward in support of that statement?" demanded Mr. Stormaway.

"Well," said Slowbob, "he and the Frenchman were often together; and this I know—that Walbut used to cry and wring his hands whenever they parted. He was in it, I tell you."

"It looks suspicious," Dr. Pillem observed.

"So it does," Mr. Stormaway assented; "but that goes for nothing."

"If Walbut isn't here, I s'pose that there Lemon Sleath is?" said Slowbob. "He was Walbut's toady and spy, and——"

"We will have no more accusations," Mr. Stormaway interposed. "I will fetch Lemon Sleath in one moment."

For a man of his years and weight, the head-master skipped downstairs in a wonderful style.

He opened the schoolroom door, and beheld the object of his search in a strange and uncomfortable attitude.

Lemon Sleath was standing upon his head, and Charlie Chadwick was keeping him in that position by occasionally digging him in the waistcoat with a ruler, and a number of youths were standing round admiring the performance.

Mr. Stormaway coughed.

Charlie Chadwick dropped the ruler, Lemon Sleath came down with a crash, and the audience became intensely interested in the ink-stained maps suspended from the walls.

"This is not a circus," Mr. Stormaway observed.

He had something else to think of than to be angry, and he sought refuge in sarcasm.

"Oh, if you please, sir," Lemon Sleath whined, "they made me do it, and they kept me up there until my head feels as big as a balloon.

"Your head does not need an increase in size," Mr. Stormaway said. "Come with me, Sleath; I have something to say to you."

Wondering what could be required of him, Lemon Sleath followed the head-master.

Mr. Stormaway led the way to Slowbob's room.

"Go in," he said, pushing the door open.

Lemon Sleath sneaked into the room, and he was confronted by Slowbob, who was now sitting upright in bed.

The irrepressible squinted at Sleath in such a hideous fashion that Lemon felt sick and giddy.

"Sleath," Mr. Stormaway said, as he closed the door and turned the key noiselessly, "you were Walbut's friend, I believe?"

"I was," Lemon said.

"Do you know why he has run away from the Abbey?"

"I do not, sir," Lemon Sleath replied, applying his knuckles to his eyes and beginning to weep.

"He's a-cryin' because he knows that he is guilty," Slowbob remarked.

"Hush, hush!" said Mr. Stormaway; "let me question him, please. Sleath——"

"Yes, sir—oh, if you please, sir, yes!"

"If you were Walbut's confidant, you must know something about his thoughts and actions," the head-master said. "Do you happen to know whether he shared any secret with M. Carleon?"

Lemon Sleath went down on his knees, and grovelled at Mr. Stormaway's feet.

"I only know that they were friends," he sobbed. "What else should I know?"

"But why this exhibition of grief?" demanded Mr. Stormaway.

"Because, sir—oh, because I thought you were going to ask me something about the marked money!"

Mr. Stormaway started, Dr. Pillem ejaculated "Ah!" and Slowbob squinted more hideously than ever.

"Why should you think so?" the head-master asked, sternly.

"Because everybody is talking about it," Lemon Sleath replied. "It is so dinned into my ears that I cannot get it out of my head. I shall soon begin to think that I put the money in Ralph Mornington's trunk myself."

"Perhaps you did," said Slowbob.

Mr. Stormaway held up his hand, and was about to speak when a knock came at the door.

"Come in," said the head-master, unlocking the door.

Matthew Stickers entered with a telegram in his hand.

"The boy is a-waitin' for a harnser, sir," he said; "and he likewise said as 'ow tuppence would come in 'andy to buy a bottle o' lemingnade this 'ot weather."

"Ah—hum! From Walbut's father, I suppose," he said. "Yes, I thought so," then reading:

"I have heard nothing of my son. You must find him, or I shall hold you responsible."

"This is a nice state of things," gasped the head-master. "I really think I will retire from scholastic life without delay. You may go, Stickers; I will send the reply presently."

"What about the tuppence, sir?"

"Certainly not," said Mr. Stormaway; "the boy is paid for doing his duty."

"Better pay it, sir," Matthew Stickers urged. "I know these boys—give 'em nothin' and they take longer than the post, but tip 'em occasionally, and they become young hexpress hengines."

The head-master parted with the money, which Stickers promptly dropped into his waistcoat pocket as soon as he was out of sight, and then went downstairs with a message to the effect that Mr. Stormaway would reserve his benevolence until Christmas-time.

Meanwhile the head-master was trying to get out of Lemon Sleath all he knew, but the toady held to one story.

He knew nothing — positively nothing.

"But why do you think Walbut has run away?" asked the headmaster.

"Because he was so disliked," Sleath replied. "I have often heard him say that he would leave suddenly, but I put it down as a joke, and never troubled my mind about it."

At last Mr. Stormaway was compelled to let him go, but Timothy Slowbob was not satisfied.

"Only let me get up," he said, "and I'll be on their track in a jiffey."

Dr. Pillem shook his head.

"To-morrow I may consent that you take an airing," he said. "Slowbob, don't be silly; if you kill yourself you destroy the very thing you wish to live for."

"That's true, sir," Timothy replied; "I never thought of that. But oh! it is agony stopping 'ere when Mister Mornington is in misery. Where is he?"

"In London, I presume," said Mr. Stormaway. "Mr. Blackstone, his friend, promised to send me Mornington's address as soon as he was settled in town."

Slowbob uttering a groan sank back.

"Settled in town!" he said, dismally. "And is that all you know about him?"

"Yes, indeed," Mr. Stormaway replied. "That is the extent of my information at present."

"Thank you, sir," Slowbob returned after a pause. "I am very much obliged to you."

Timothy's face was a study as he uttered these words.

He feigned weariness and closed his eyes.

Seeing this, Dr. Pillem and Mr. Stormaway left the invalid to his repose, and glided silently out of the room.

When the next day dawned, Timothy was so lively that he was allowed to rise, and walk on the sunny side of the playground.

There was something in the irrepressible's mind which he kept to himself, and when certain that he was not observed, he gave vent to strange mutterings, and occasionally shook his fist at some visionary foe.

"I'll do it," he said, apparently addressing a flight of rooks which were passing over his head. "Wait till I'm a bit stronger, and I'll do it."

We will now return for a few moments to Ralph, who felt himself friendless and alone indeed.

He was at a loss to know what course to pursue, unless he, as he meditated, sought shelter in a cottage.

"That is my only plan," he said. "Here comes a man, and perhaps he can put me in the way of a night's lodging."

The man, a rustic, with a sun-tanned face, approached, and listened politely to Ralph's request.

"Yes," he said; "you can sleep at my house. I relieve the carrier at this place, and take the cart on to Ipswich."

"Nothing could be better," Ralph replied. "I am going to Ipswich myself in the morning, so we shall be company."

Delighted at finding a resting-place, our hero followed his guide, and after partaking of a frugal meal, went to bed, and in spite of all his troubles was soon asleep.

Early in the morning he was well on the way towards his destination, and we must leave him for the present, and peep once more through the Abbey windows and see how things are going on there.

CHAPTER LI.

SLOWBOB PERFORMS THE VANISHING-TRICK WITH A VENGEANCE—MR. STORMAWAY'S RESOLUTION, AND THE SENSATION IT CAUSES — A GENERAL BREAK-UP.

"COME in," said Mr. Stormaway, in answer to a knock at his study-door.

Mrs. Jumble staggered into the room.

She was followed by the nurse and Matthew Stickers, in whose eyes there was a wild expression.

"Dear me!" said Mr. Stormaway; "what has happened?"

"That boy—oh, that boy!" Mrs. Jumble gasped.

"Yes, indeed, sir—that boy!" cried the nurse. "I assure you, it is not my fault."

Mr. Stormaway had recourse to his old expedient, and laid violent hold of his scanty stock of hair.

"What boy? Of whom are you speaking?" he demanded.

"W'ich sir, it is Slowbob they are reluding to," said Matthew Stickers.

"Ah—h—h!" said Mr. Stormaway, drawing a deep breath; "what has he been doing? Making hinself worse again, I suppose?"

"He's cut and runned away with the holdest soot of mulberries—them with only three buttings on the jacket," Stickers explained.

"What!" Mr. Stormaway exclaimed. "Slowbob gone, ill as he is! Pooh, pooh! Nonsense! he is somewhere about the premises."

"Indeed, sir, he is not," said the nurse, endangering her eyesight with a corner of her apron. "Read this, sir."

She placed a piece of paper in the astonished head-master's hands, and he read the following missive :

"SIR,—This comes, hopping that you are better than I are, though stronger on my leggs. I have gone in search of Mr. Mornington; I mean to find him if he is above the earth or under the see. Forgive me, sir, for leeving you, and council my inbentures, but when I have found Mr. Mornington I will come back and work my time out.—Youres obbedently,   TIMOTHY SLOWBOB."

"This is almost beyond belief," Mr. Stormaway said. "Where was this found?"

"On the dressing-table of his room, when I went in with his breakfast," the nurse replied. "The bed was empty, and evidently had not been slept in for several hours."

"He must have left at daybreak," Mrs. Jumble observed. "Mary reports that she found one of the kitchen windows unfastened, and, of course, I can come to no other conclusion than that Slowbob left the Abbey in that way, as all the doors were fastened as usual."

"This is most distressing," Mr. Stormaway said with a groan. "Slowbob must be pursued and brought back without delay, or we shall hear something dreadful about him. I will see to it myself. Stickers, come with me."

"Yes, sir," said Matthew, tripping over the mat and shooting out of the room as if he had been kicked. "Shall I fetch your stick, sir?"

"You may," replied the headmaster, who was nearly started out of his senses by the man-of-all-work's acrobatic feat; "and you had better mind how you behave yourself when I get hold of it."

To say that Slowbob was to be pursued was one thing; but to catch him was quite another matter.

Turn whichever way he liked, Mr. Stormaway could get no information of the fugitive.

Worryboy was interviewed, and he wisely insinuated that the letter was a ruse, and that Slowbob had run away to enlist in the army.

"That be blowed for a tale!" said Matthew Stickers, who was not called upon to speak. "Do you think they would henlist a boy with heyes like his in the harmy? He'd haim at the henemy and shoot his s'perior hossifer."

Mr. Stormaway glared at his manservant as if he could have swallowed him without the addition of a pinch of salt.

"If I have another word from you," he said, clutching his walking-stick, "I will—well, you will sorely tempt me to commit a breach of the peace."

"Wery good, sir," Matthew returned. "Of course it ain't my place to hinterfere. I'm only a poor hold man, and——"

"Will you hold your tongue?" Mr. Stormaway almost shrieked.

"W'ich, sir, it's my place to do so," Matthew observed; "but there are times when heven a poor hold man's 'art may be full to bu'stin'. And, sir"—here he produced the red handkerchief—"when I thinks of poor Slowbob 'arf crazy a wanderin' about the fields, or p'r'aps 'ead down'ards in a pond with his legs stickin' hup, I—Oh!"

Mr. Stormaway could stand it no longer.

He took two steps backwards, one forward, and smacked Matthew Stickers's head with his open hand.

"There," said the head-master, "I hope you are satisfied. You have something to talk about now."

Matthew Stickers was more than satisfied, and, not being a greedy man in all things, he bestowed a similar favour on the constable by shooting out his fist and catching him on the tip of the nose, thus producing a sensation that a wasp might have been proud of having caused.

As usual, the head-master of Merrytown Abbey had to put matters right by the production of half-a-crown, and then he once more sallied forth on his hopeless errand.

Hopeless indeed ; for after many hours of trotting backwards and forwards, he and Matthew Stickers returned to the Abbey, thoroughly worn out and dispirited.

Slowbob had fled.

The news spread like wildfire through the quaint old building.

It was whispered in the schoolroom and shouted in the playground by the boys, two of whom, however, were not so very much surprised or upset.

"Slowbob knows what he is doing," Charlie Chadwick said.

"No doubt about that," acquiesced Harold Lakeman. "I only wish he was a little stronger, and then I should have no fear of him. He will keep his word, and find Ralph."

Lemon Sleath felt much relieved at Slowbob's departure.

In a few days more the term would come to an end, and Sleath made up his mind never to return to Merrytown Abbey if he could help it.

He was saved all trouble on that score by a speech made the next morning by the head-master.

After a sleepless night, Mr. Stormaway mounted his desk, and told the boys to put away their books and listen to him.

They almost guessed what he was going to say before he began. Mr. Stormaway had resolved to retire.

He dwelt on the matter with much feeling, and tears were in his eyes when he spoke of parting with the pupils.

These tears were not only copied, but magnified into sobs by Herr Fritz Halfamann, who, thrusting his head into his desk, made a most alarming noise, and almost convinced those who heard it that he was choking.

The little Teuton banished all anxiety by thrusting his head over the green baize curtains and favouring the assembly with a view of his hair rumpled all over his head, a pair of streaming eyes, and a nose rendered crimson from having been dipped in a pot of red ink.

Mr. Muffler gazed at this apparition with some alarm, and felt quite relieved when Herr Halfamann, stepping down from his stool, put his hair right, and looked something like a reasonable being.

The German professor walked straight up to Mr. Stormaway, and seized his hands.

"Poys," he cried in a husky voice, "mine poys, I call for t'ree cheers for zee pest man dot ever kept von school ! I vill lead you, mine boys. Hib, hib, hib—hurrah ! "

The boys took up the shout, and repeated it again and again until the old oak ceiling rang with the sound.

Then up rose Mr. Muffler with a snowy white handkerchief before his eyes.

He had thought of a nice little speech which he commenced to deliver as he crossed the floor, but not being able to see, he fell over Lemon Sleath, and sent that youth crashing through the lid of an empty box.

Master Sleath was wedged, knees and chin together, in the receptacle, and a roar of delight went up at his discomfiture.

Even Mr. Stormaway smiled as Herr Fritz Halfamann laid hold of suffering Lemon, and endeavoured vainly to drag him out.

"He vas fixed vary much," said the German professor, "and zee voodvork must be cut away."

"I am being suffocated," Sleath groaned. "Surely you will not leave me here to die."

"Nonsense ! " said Mr. Stormaway. "Stand aside, Herr Halfamann, and I will have the boy out in a twinkling."

The head-master was a strong man, and as he laid hold of Lemon Sleath, there was a sound like a prodigious cork being drawn. But alas ! the rescued one left a portion of his attire clinging to the box, and was promptly banished from the scene for repairs.

"And now," said Mr. Stormaway, turning to the boys, "go to the playground. Lessons are over for good. With regard to prizes, I will give each and every one of you a volume to remind you of the days you spent at Merrytown Abbey."

The Abbey looked grim and gloomy as the lads wandered about in groups.

There was little mirth, although most of them looked forward with pleasure to going home.

"If Ralph were only here," said Charlie Chadwick, "it would break my heart to part with the old place !"

"If Ralph had remained," Harold Lakeman observed, "it is my firm opinion that Mr. Stormaway would never have dreamed of retiring."

"I think so too," said Tommy Toddler. "I wonder what he will do with himself ? He is too fond of work to become a lazy man."

"Do you know," remarked Dick Heron, who was one of the party, "I rather fancy that he will travel in search of evidence to prove Ralph's innocence ?"

"That never struck me," said Charlie Chadwick. "Perhaps you are right, Dick."

"What strange things have happened in a short time !" Tommy Toddler said. "Poor Ralph digraced, Slowbob and Walbut are away, and——"

"It's the way of the world," Harold Lakeman interposed, philosophically. "In two days more the Abbey will know us no longer. I wonder if we shall meet again ?"

"The world is wide, but it is a small one after all," said Charlie Chadwick. "Here comes Matthew Stickers, blubbering like a bull-calf !"

"Once more a houtcast on the wide, wide world," groaned the man-of-all-work as he came up. "Sacked, when I'd made hup my mind for a life of hease and comfort. Ah, hif I had honly stuck to the binger-geer and the topen harts—I mean hopen tarts—I'd never come to this."

"Don't cry, Stickers," said Harold Lakeman. "You look like the boy who discovered that he was born before his mother, and never smiled again."

"Gen'elmen !" Stickers wailed, "it's all very well for you. You're a goin' 'ome to waller in the lap o' luxury, but what will pore, pore me do ? Must I go forth to be pushed from piller to post ? Must I go forth to eat grass like the rhinochios of the jungle ?"

"Oh, shut up—do," cried Charlie Chadwick. "I know what all this means. You want us to get up a subscription for you."

"W'ich," said Matthew Stickers, "I've got a little dockyment here ready for signin'. Mister Chadwick, you've got a wonderful reception of what is right."

"Give me hold of the paper," Charlie observed, "and we will see what we can do for you."

Matthew Stickers chuckled, but his face fell considerably when the document was returned to him.

"What's this ?" he gasped. "'Two slate-pencils, Charles Chadwick ; 'arf a happle, 'Arold Lakeman ; three chipped marbles, Thomas Toddler ; a pair of hold boots, Dick Heron.' Hoh, this is 'ard, 'ard—'arder than the bone chucked to the surly dog !"

Matthew commenced weeping afresh, and went his way bewailing his hard fate.

"Farewell—a long farewell to hall my greatness, as Cardinal Wooly said," he moaned. "'Twas hever thus from child'ood's 'our. Alas, alas ! Matthew Stickers, you went hup like a rocket, and now you've come down like a stick. The light o' your triumph was a 'a' penny dip, and it's gone hout with a fizzle."

The day for departure came.

At the best it was a sad one, and Mr. Stormaway's eyes were dim and moist as he shook hands with the boys, and wished them every blessing that this world can give.

The head-master had determined to part with everbody save Mr. Muffler—re-engaged for a month—Mrs. Jumble, and two servants.

The Abbey was already advertised in the local paper, and numbers of replies had been received, and among the applicants was Lord Auburton, who promised to see Mr. Stormaway in a few days with a view to settling the matter.

The critical moment arrived. All kinds of vehicles drew up at the door.

There was a tremendous amount of jostling as the luggage was packed away. A half-sorrowful cheer, a waving of hats and handkerchiefs, and Mr. Stormaway stood listening to the rumbling of wheels dying away in the distance.

"They are gone, and I am alone—quite alone !" he said, wearily. "There is a vacant place in my heart which may never be filled."

He started violently as he saw Mrs. Jumble, who had crept stealthily to his side.

"Oh, sir," she said, "it makes me unhappy to see you sorrowful. Cannot I help you to bear your trouble—is there nothing I can do ?"

"Yes, madame," replied Mr. Stormaway, sharply ; "perhaps you can tell me why Matthew Stickers has absented himself this morning when he was most needed."

"Not having seen him I can give no information," Mrs. Jumble said, tartly.

And then she sighed so deeply that Mr. Stormaway trotted down the steps, and stood bareheaded in the open air.

To his great relief he saw Mr. Muffler approaching.

"All gone?" queried Mr. Stormaway.

"Yes, sir," Mr. Muffler replied. "They just caught the train, and rushed into it like an invaded host."

"Boy-like—boy-like," Mr. Stormaway said, with glistening eyes. "Yes, they are all gone—all gone!"

Mrs. Jumble sighed again, but finding that no notice whatever was taken of the zephyr-like productions from her sympathising heart, she sniffed the air scornfully and retired.

"Perfidious creature!" she said. "He thinks of those rude boys, but has not a word for me. Never mind, I can fall back upon Mr. Muffler, when he gets another situation."

It would have been highly detrimental to Mr. Muffler's comfort if the housekeeper had fallen back upon him in a literal sense, and he would have been of that opinion had he heard the remark; but he loved Mrs. Jumble, not only for her ample charms, but because it was well known that she had a good banking account.

"Leave me now," said Mr. Stormaway. "I have a fancy for wandering about the old place alone. It will be the last time that I shall do so."

Mr. Muffler made no reply, but walked into the Abbey, and went to his own room.

Mr. Stormaway walked slowly upstairs with light footsteps, as if fearful of awaking the echoes, and he entered the schoolroom.

His heart was moved as he gazed at the ink-splashed floor, the forms, and desks, all useless now.

Herr Fritz Halfamann sat at his desk, making out his quarterly account, or rather gazing vaguely at the sheet of paper before him.

Mr. Stormaway did not disturb the professor, but continued his ascent to the now lonely dormitories.

He wandered through them; but passed by the one that Ralph Mornington and his chums had occupied, for he had not the courage to go there.

At last he stood in the room in which Jack Walbut's trunks were piled in a corner ready to be sent away.

The good old man's face darkened, and he seemed to be undergoing a mental struggle with himself.

"I don't think I ever did a mean action in my life," he said, musingly; "but if this unhappy lad has run away through complicity in Ralph Mornington's affair, will it be mean on my part to look for some clue? No; I will do it."

He drew a bunch of keys from his pocket, and tried several, and at last he found one that fitted the largest trunk.

It contained clothing, odds and ends, a box of colours, and a pocket-book with a faded cover.

This last article lay on the top of all, and had been evidently thrown there in a hurry; and Mr. Stormaway came to the conclusion that its removal had been intended.

He opened the pocket-book, and turned the pages over carefully.

Some of the leaves were blank, but here and there one was filled with close writing. At last he came to some memoranda that made him stare.

"Mem.—To keep my eye upon Ralph Mornington; to hate him for the blow he struck me, and to have revenge, whether here or in years to come!"

"A nice youth this!" Mr. Stormaway said.

He continued reading.

"Mem.—To go to Carleon's place and play a game of chess. I know the sort of game he wants me to play. I am afraid of the man. His eyes haunt me everywhere. Awake, they follow me about, and in my dreams they glare at me."

"This is getting interesting," Mr. Stormaway observed, gravely. "If I read on I shall come to something yet more startling."

"Mem.—I knew as much. Carleon wants me to do his dirty work. Why could he not have selected Lemon Sleath who is more fitted for it? I am more afraid than ever of Carleon. If I do not obey him he will kill me."

Mr. Stormaway breathed harder, and the pocket-book trembled in his hands.

He had come to the end of one page of writing, and turned over another, only to find to his disappointment that it was a blank.

A little farther on he came to some disjointed notes, which ran as follows:

"Saturday—two o'clock. Make Carleon keep his promise—one hundred pounds without delay. America if possible."

Then followed the address: "Moor-street, Seven Dials, Greek-street end, corner, left-hand side."

"This is a marvellous discovery," Mr. Stormaway said, as he put the note-book in his pocket; "but still there is no tangible clue to what I hoped to find. That Carleon and this unhappy lad have shared some secret is evident. The mystery increases instead of lessening."

Mr. Stormaway paced up and down the room, rubbing his chin and the top of his head by turns.

"Saturday—two o'clock. Make Carleon keep his promise!" he said, repeating what he had read. "Moor-street, Greek-street end, corner, left-hand side. Hah! As soon as I have settled with Lord Auburton I will make a journey to London."

He took a few more turns up and down the room, and then stopped.

"I cannot imagine why Blackstone has not written as he promised to do," he murmured. "Where is Morning-ton? where is Slowbob? and, good gracious! where is Stickers? Has he run away from me before his time has expired? No, no; I know Stickers too well for that. He will return for his money, if for nothing else."

Mr. Stormaway was not out of his reckoning when he made this observation concerning the man-of-all-work.

He had scarcely spoken when there was a stumbling sound on the stairs, and he heard Matthew Stickers's voice trying to sing, "I cannot mind my wheel, mother," which he converted into "I cannot grind my meal, mother."

The head-master's hair bristled, and he stood aghast as the man-of-all work entered the room.

Matthew Stickers seemed to have changed eyes with Slowbob, and he stood with his hands upon his hips, and his knees together as if about to say, "Here we are again!" like a clown when he bounds on in the transformation-scene.

"Mr. S'tm'way," he said, "now that the young 'uns have gone, you and me will step round to the Swab and Tottle —the Bon and Swattle—you know what I mean ter say—and spend a convivial hour for old Land Sign."

Mr. Stormaway knocked Matthew Stickers down and shouted for help.

Herr Fritz Halfamann appeared on the scene.

"I vill put him in zee dustpin until he vas soper," said the professor, as he took Stickers by the heels and bumped him downstairs. "Oh, sare, it vas no vonder dat you vas tired of zee Appey. If dere vas two Stickers in von blace, life vould pe von misery!"

"I agree with you," said Mr. Storm-away.

CHAPTER LII.

A VISIT TO THE MISER'S MILL.

At the very time that Mr. Stormaway and Matthew Stickers were hunting high and low for Timothy Slowbob, that irrepressible youth was making himself as comfortable as possible within the ruined mill.

The interesting invalid, now on the fair road to recovery, having paid a visit to a shop situated at the far end of the village, purchased some pro-visions, and reached the mill by traversing unfrequented paths.

"I'll stay the night here," Timothy said, "and start at dawn. Nobody will dream of coming here to look for me, but if I venture out now I shall be seen, and taken back to the Abbey."

Slowbob sighed as he unpacked his store of provisions and gazed dubiously at them.

"I wonder if a cold pork-chop and ginger-beer are good for me," he mused. "Dr. Pillem would have a fit if he saw such things afore me. Any-how, I'm awfully hungry, so here goes."

Strange to say Timothy Slowbob seemed all the better for his repast, and after a short nap he arose like a giant refreshed.

"Now to have a look round the place," he said. "I may find some-thing that will lead to a clue."

If Timothy's eyes were peculiar they

were remarkably keen, and it was not long before he got on the right scent.

In one corner he discovered some scraps of paper covered with writing, which he put in his pocket, and continuing his search he found a kid glove.

Slowbob smiled as he recognised it as one of a pair he had seen Alphonse Carleon wear.

"I'm getting on," said the irrepressible. "Now then to put the bits of paper together like a puzzle, and see what I can make of them."

He spread them out carefully on the floor, and after much trouble he completed his task satisfactorily.

It was a letter which had been written by Richard Mornington, but destroyed, as if the person it was intended for had arrived and made its despatch unnecessary.

"You must see me oftener," the letter was worded. "No harm will come to you even in this ghastly old place. These delays are fretting me; and the trick must be done soon, or you and I will fall out. Let there be no mistake made on your part as to my meaning. You swindled me out of the best part of a thousand pounds, and though I intend to act fairly in the event of success, I also intend to make use of you. Come at once. My two friends are getting as impatient as myself."

The note bore no names, but Timothy Slowbob had not the slightest doubt that Carleon was the person alluded to, and that the writing was the work of Richard Mornington's hand.

"This is rather confusing, as the man remarked when he slipped down the cellar stairs head first into an empty barrel," Slowbob said. "If the letter was only signed, the clue would be a good one indeed. But that fellow Richard Mornington is as cunning as a fox, but he will find that 'watchdog' will run him to earth."

Timothy felt hungry again, and so reduced his stock of provisions that it seemed doubtful whether he would leave anything for breakfast.

He then took another turn round the mill, but finding nothing more, made such arrangements as he could for the night.

A few pieces of old sacking did duty for a bed, and Timothy lay down, and, though not without thinking that Miser Carker's ghost might pay him a visit, fell asleep.

The rosy dawn of a fine morning was rolling back the curtain of night when he awoke from a dream in which he and Carleon were engaged in a mortal struggle, and Timothy, running down to the river, laved his face and hands in the cool clear water, and felt ready for his journey.

He made a hasty breakfast and then set out.

One glance he took at Merrytown.

The rising sun was gilding the roofs of the quaint old houses, the birds were singing their morning songs, and Timothy's heart sank.

Tears stood in his eyes, but he brushed them away, and his face resumed a resolute expression as he turned his back upon the scene of so much happines and misery.

"I've got to find Mr. Mornington," he said, "and I'll do it if my life is spared. But which way shall I go? I'll trust to chance. I'll go the way the wind blows."

Timothy walked on sturdily until he came to a church, and glancing up he saw that the vane pointed to the east.

"East is it, and east I goes," Slowbob said. "If I'm wrong, I can only turn back again. Lor'! the world isn't so big after all. I've read of men who have been round it half-a-dozen times, and ready to do the same again. Keep up your pecker, Mr. Mornington, and look out, you precious band of conspirators. Watchdog is on your track."

Timothy gave no thought to himself, nor did he heed the fact that his supply of money amounted to but one shilling and a few halfpence.

How he was going to live on the road never occurred to him, and if it had, it would have caused him no uneasiness.

By noontide Timothy was not only covered with dust and leg-weary, but hungry.

"Sixpence for my dinner," he said, counting his money; "tuppence for my tea. I can hold out two days, and p'raps somethin' will fall in my way before then. But where am I going to sleep?"

At that moment a carrier's cart came jolting along, and Timothy took the liberty of hanging on behind, and in such manner he rode until the vehicle pulled up at the door of The Seven Stars Inn.

"I don't know why I should think so," said Slowbob, "but I have an idea that Mr. Mornington may have stopped here. I'll ask."

He interviewed Bob Buttle, and having described our hero, was overcome with amazement at the sudden change that came over the landlord.

Buttle took Timothy by the ear, and having led him into the middle of the road, stared him full in the face.

"So," he said, "you are one of the gang."

"What gang?" Timothy gasped.

"Oh, I know all about you!" Buttle replied, chuckling. "I've been put on my guard, so if you don't want to be locked up, take yourself off."

"I don't know what you mean!" Slowbob yelled. "Has the young gent I described been here?"

"Gent—thief, you mean," said Bob Buttle. "He came from Merrytown; but I was warned against him."

The awful truth dawned into Slowbob's mind, and sitting down on a bank, he sobbed bitterly.

"So," he moaned, "they won't leave him alone even now. They are on his track. What shall I do—what shall I do?"

Timothy now began to realise how lonely and helpless he was; but he did not despair. He wiped away his tears, and as the carrier's cart moved away, he hailed the driver.

"How far will you take me for a shilling?" Timothy demanded. "It's nearly all the money I have in the world."

"To Ipswich," the man replied.

"Right you are," said Timothy.

And in another moment he was seated in the same vehicle, talking to the same driver, and journeying along the same road as Ralph Mornington had done only two days before.